The girl I was BEFORE

~ Book 3 in the Falling Series ~

A Novel By Ginger Scott

For those of us who love fairy tales.

Prologue:

Paige

One photo.

It took a fraction of a second to take it.

The light was low, but I can still see what needs to be seen. I can see faces—one face. The only face that matters in this picture.

This single image; it could change everything.

The picture on my phone screen is condemning. Chandra Campbell always holds the power—in everything she does. She rules the college's Greek system, thus ruling McConnell's social circles. She says who gets into a party, who gets elected to Greek council. If you want to date certain men, she has to approve. It's all part of her name—the daughter of Texas oil, ruling the school her father graduated from and has since pumped dollars into at the same speed his company sucks oil from the ground.

She sits on this pedestal—one we've all put her on, me included—and she rules from it. The problem with pedestals is the taller they are, the harder the fall from the top. Maybe that's not a problem. Maybe in Chandra's case, that's a good thing. And I'm probably evil for thinking that, but I've been evil before. I've been selfish, heartless, calculated—*cold.* I'm starting to think the problem is that it's taken me this long to find the line between the good side and the bad, and right now, I'm straddling.

With one press of my finger on my phone, I can send Chandra to the ground. I'm holding her power hostage, afraid of the responsibility that comes along with gambling with it. No, that's not the truth. I'm not afraid of the responsibility at all. What scare me are the consequences.

I can't explain what compelled me to climb the steps in the Delta House tonight. I walked past the bodies of my drunken, passed out sorority sisters, ignoring the frat boys still roaring with laughter on the sofa in front of the TV in our common area downstairs while they watched some female fighter beat the shit out of another girl in a cage.

There were several shots coursing through me, the last one something the guys called a fireball. The feel of the alcohol left my skin numb, but my mind was somehow still sharp. I sensed things were off, so I followed my instincts up the stairs, to Chandra's room.

I don't go in there much. She's the house president, and while I've quickly moved into her inner circle, she still didn't trust me enough to let me into her personal space often. My other sisters had their theories about her need for privacy. I'd heard the rumors; we all had. Many of the girls didn't believe them—naïve to how well someone can hide a secret.

But I wasn't.

While secrets can be buried, they always leave a trail. The trick is talking those who uncover your secrets into staying quiet about them. I'm not so great at keeping my lips sealed. I've burned a lot of bridges by sharing people's secrets—people I love—like my sister, Cass. My mouth has caused a lot of pain, but I've also learned from those mistakes. I've learned how to read people, how to read *liars*.

Chandra...is a liar.

I knew Chandra had a drug problem. Her mother has one too, though I hear hers is of the prescription variety. Chandra's talked to me about her mom before, and there was always something in the way she emphasized her hurt and disappointment over her mother's overdoses or failed trips to rehab. I'm not saying she wasn't affected by her mom's choices,

2

but rather, she was terrified over what it meant for her own habits. There was always a story behind her eyes, like a whisper begging me not to see her own problems.

Chandra's recreational habits are more damning; hers are the ugly kind that people like to gossip about—white powder, but never needles. Needles leave marks, and marks are evidence. I had heard that sometimes she smoked her addiction, always counting on her wealth and family name to keep questions away.

But tonight there was *a lot* of powder. Tonight, Chandra was careless. It's hard to hide photographs. No matter how wealthy you are, when things go viral on the Internet, they can no longer be contained by dollar signs.

When I stepped into her quiet bedroom upstairs, I had no business being in there, no real reason to enter the room at all. Something else urged me forward, drew me in. The mirror was flat in the center of the bed, and Chandra and a guy I didn't recognize were half clothed, comatose, in a drug-induced slumber that would carry them through the entire next day. I don't remember actually taking the photo. I'm not sure if anyone was awake as I passed back through the halls to the patio at the back of the house—to this small bench pushed close to the brick fire pit outside. The fire inside is old, its embers dying.

But I'm here. I've been here, staring at the proof on my phone screen for almost an hour, my finger too timid to finish the deed and my heart too afraid of losing everything I know. I'm a Delta sister; at Chandra's side, I would take over the reigns when she graduated. That attention, the power—it feels. So. Good.

It also feels dirty.

I played that way to get here, to be Chandra's favorite freshman. During rush week, I was almost pushed out. I'd overheard the board talking, heard my name mentioned among a list of girls who *I knew* were not going to make it. And I panicked. My parents weren't legacies, and while my father was a lawyer, we weren't exactly riding an upper-class wave. There would be no last-minute donations of impressive amounts in Paige Owens's name. My options were limited, and I was desperate.

Desperate. Perhaps that's just the excuse I've told myself.

Chandra was on her phone, walking into the common room, mere hours before the selection meeting, and I heard her complaining about a new girl on the soccer team—a superstar that was going to take away her starting position. She wanted her father to do something about it, but his hands were tied.

I knew who this threat was—my twin sister, Cass.

Cass is the reason I'm at this school. I never really wanted to come here, but my sister suffers from multiple sclerosis, and my parents were too worried to let her attend school thousands of miles from home. So I changed my path, bending it to coincide with hers. A part of me resented Cass for it too. Maybe that's why I did what I did? Or maybe that's just next in the long line of excuses I've given myself.

Whatever the justification, somehow, I found myself by Chandra's side the moment her phone call ended. I gave her details about my sister's multiple sclerosis, filling her in on my parents' disapproval of Cass playing competitive sports and exerting herself. I told myself it was all in Cass's best interest anyway. What I was doing, it served two purposes—one that I just happened to gain from.

While my insight piqued Chandra's interest, I could tell I wasn't giving her enough. She was walking away, her back to me, my window of opportunity closing fast. That's when I crossed the line.

I told her about Cass's past, not completely spelling it out, but saying just the right things to have her believe my sister had an affair with a teacher in high school, letting her draw her own false conclusions from other girls she knew who had given her gossip, not worrying about what it meant for Cass.

I didn't worry because Chandra's arm was looped through mine. I gave her more as we waited for the other girls to arrive, and she sat me close to her on the sofa. Soon, she whispered something to her vice president. I tilted my head enough to see the list on the clipboard; I saw my name with a line drawn through it. An hour later, when it wasn't called among the dozen other girls formally dismissed from our pledge class, I felt a rush.

Cass's secrets had bought me access—and for a while, I got away with it.

I didn't feel guilt—not at first. My indiscretion hadn't caused Cass any real pain. She'd still made the team. She was happy. I was happy. Her secrets...they seemed to die right there on that sofa where I'd spilled them.

It was harmless; so I thought.

For the last three nights I've replayed the look on Cass's face—the pain in her eyes as she told me Chandra had used my words against her, had tormented her secretly with the things I'd confided in this woman who I thought was my friend. My sister was assaulted by someone Chandra knew. While Chandra acted appalled in front of me, she was nothing but cruel to Cass, quick to lay blame at my sister's feet. She even fed the rumor that Cass had acted inappropriately, just like she had in the past—sleeping her way through school and into a spot on the team.

There was no way around feeling the punch in my gut that came along with knowing this was all my fault—I'd given Chandra the impression treating my sister that way was allowed. I haven't been alone with Chandra since coming back from break. I'm afraid of the words that will no doubt fly freely from my mouth. While she deserves them, I'm not sure I'm ready for the consequences waiting for me if I let go of my tongue.

Chandra—she holds the power. My new life, it only exists because of her. I know I'm a bitch for thinking of myself, but this existence—the parties, the boyfriend, the popularity and status—it's all I've ever wanted. It sounds shallow, but is it really so different from wanting to be the lead in a play or the star athlete? I wanted to be looked up to, admired and envied, and Chandra was my ticket.

"I don't know what I'm supposed to do," I whisper to myself, the last vestige of the fire burning out before me.

A small piece of ash—the final evidence of warmth—floats down from the sky, its silvery reflection lit by the faint light shining through the window behind me. My eyes watch its path, the tears wrestling loose and sliding down my cheek, racing it to the earth until both the ash and my sorrow land at my feet.

The vision of my feet against the cold cement drifts in and out of focus. I concentrate on my black slipper shoes and the perfect line against the paleness of my ankle. Then I notice the haphazard swirls of beads interrupting everything.

Cass made me this ankle bracelet, using the beads from our mother's store to thank me for coming here. She gave it to me the day we packed up our belongings and drove with our parents across the country to McConnell. She handed it to me in the back seat, a small note wrapped around it expressing her thanks. She didn't want my mother seeing, because it wasn't about getting credit for the gesture. It was about her love for me—despite my flaws.

With one thumb rubbing the largest bead, I pull my phone forward to rest in my other hand, my legs now folded up in front of me.

By morning, everyone will see Chandra for who she is. The story will spread slowly to start, but near the end, it will be rapid. Her coach will know. The athletic director will know. The college president will know.

Everyone. Will. Know.

I hit SEND.

These friends that I've made—the ones passed out in the house behind me, the same people who love me because Chandra told them to—they'll know I'm the one who did it.

And my life will shift.

This will change everything.

Chapter 1

Paige

I'm only half listening to Chandra bark orders over the phone.

"We're going to need more food. The homecoming parties are always crowded. Sigma is coming, and they'll easily push us over five hundred. And get more shrimp. You didn't get enough shrimp..."

Somewhere along the way, she hung up. I must have said *goodbye*. I'm sure I said goodbye.

I hate her.

I hate her for what she did to my sister. I hate her for this invisible power she has over me because she's the president of our sorority. I hate her because her boyfriend is friends with my boyfriend.

I hate her because part of me wants to be like her, and I hate her because the weaker part of me doesn't.

And I hate the person I am when I'm around her. When I sent that photo, I hadn't counted on the weekend. My wits were with me enough to do the right thing—for once in my goddamned life—but not with me enough to think about *timing*. The anxiety of everything unraveling is killing me, and every time Chandra calls, I expect it to be about that—about the photo.

The one *I* sent.

"Seventeen!" My number is called. Great...it's the same guy working the deli counter today. He was the one who took my order for the party last week. Carson was with me. He was drunk...and an asshole. This guy, he knew Carson was drunk—and he judged me for it. Or at least, it felt like he did.

"I'm seventeen," I say, stepping up to the glass case and handing over my number.

"I don't really need the number," he smirks. Maybe he doesn't remember me. "Adding to your order?"

Shit. He remembers me.

"Yeah. Party just got a little bigger," I say, smiling. I can't help but smile at him—he has one of those faces. It's like a forced reflection, and I want to mimic whatever he does.

"Okay, hang on. I'll get the file from the back," he says, patting the counter once and winking.

Houston.

I noticed his nametag the last time, too. I like the name. That's why I noticed—not because he's tall, broad shouldered, with dark hair that flops over the top of his visor and green eyes practically glowing under the shadow.

I like the name. That's it.

"Okay, let's see...Paige. Right...I've got you here," he says, pulling the pen from behind his ear and clicking it to take more notes. "What are you adding?"

"You better not have ordered yet!" Carson's voice bellows from behind me. "Did she order yet? Get mine in on this ticket. I don't have a lot of time."

"I haven't gotten lunch yet. This was just the party order, relax," I say, turning to face him, dreading turning back around to Houston, the guy with the cute name. I turn anyway because I have no choice, and Houston is wearing that same look—the judgmental one.

"Order that crap second. I've got practice, so I only have a few minutes. Hey, yeah...get me one of those burrito things," Carson says, leaning over the counter and pointing down as if Houston wouldn't know what he was talking about. When he leans back on his heels, he lays his heavy arm over my shoulder and pulls me into him tightly.

"I guess I'll have one of those too," I say, my eyes on Houston's nametag instead of his eyes. I don't want to see the look in his eyes. I don't even like burritos.

"We only have one left," he says. Of course they do.

"Oh," I suck in my top lip and look into the case of food for an alternative. I'm not hungry anymore. "I'll just take a sandwich then. Tuna."

"Right...okay," he says, reaching to the side for a bag. He pauses, though, before picking out one of the pre-made sandwiches for me. "Or...maybe *this guy* could pick something else and let *you* have the burrito."

"Fuck that, bro! I ordered first. Give me the burrito. She's fine with a sandwich," Carson says, his voice actually echoing. He's so...loud. His phone rings, so he steps to the side and answers the call. "Yo, what up, man?"

I can still hear his entire conversation even though he's twenty feet away. Everyone can hear him.

Houston is standing still, his arms propped on top of the counter and his brow bunched while he stares at my boyfriend. Carson is pacing and talking so loudly, he's starting to interrupt others eating lunch at the small tables in the corner of the market.

I used to like his big personality. His confidence was what turned me on when we first met at the Sigma-Delta mixer. He's a starter on the McConnell team, a fullback, and year older than I am—I liked that too.

Houston is moving again, wrapping the burrito and dropping it in a plastic bag. He lets the burrito hit the counter with a thud, and he watches Carson pace the entire time. When he sees his burrito is ready, he reaches across my body and grabs the bag, holding his phone to his chest and kissing me with nothing but forceful indifference. "I gotta run. You got this?" he asks...sort of.

I nod, only because he's already gone before I could answer.

"That guy's your boyfriend?" Houston asks, finally packing up my sandwich. Normally, I'd respond with something snarky, a confident quip would put him and that damned disapproving look in its place. I can't seem to find that fire today.

"I still need to place the party orders," I say, opting to ignore his question completely.

"Right," he says, his lips pushed into a tight, flat line.

I add two more trays of shrimp and up the number of platters of meat and cheese. Houston notes it all on the order sheet. I wait at the register while he walks to the office and tucks my ticket away again. When he comes back, he slides a bottle of tea toward me—the same sweet tea I drank the last time I came.

He remembered. It makes me smile.

Propping my purse on the counter, I pull out my wallet and unsnap the clasp so I can pay for my lunch, but Houston stops me. The warmth of his hand is surprising against mine. I don't jerk or flinch; I only freeze. It takes me a second or two to look up at him—to register he's stopping me from paying for my lunch. I don't like that. I don't like being beholden to someone. Favors—they're like making a trade sometimes. The last favors I gave away cost me too much.

"It's on me," he says, and I refuse quickly, shaking my head *no*. His hand squeezes mine tighter. "I won't take your money. Not for your lunch...or *his*. It's on me."

"I can buy my own lunch, thank you," I say, resenting being pushed around. I shake his grip from my hand and hold out my card. He takes it and swipes it hard along the register, shaking his head and mumbling under his breath.

"Damn, you mean that asshole can tell you to do something, and you just obey, but me—an actual *nice* guy—I can't buy you lunch without getting your foot up my ass?"

"I'd like my receipt," I say, ignoring him again. He rips it off and crumples it in his hand and throws it along with my card on the counter. "Thank you," I say, stuffing it in my purse and clutching my sandwich bag in my other hand.

I can feel the force of his eyes on me as I turn to leave; my heart is kicking the insides of my chest in anticipation of his voice. The closer I get to the door, the stronger the sensation. I almost make it outside when I feel his hand on my shoulder. I spin around, ready to lay into him—my fire flickering.

"You can do better," he says before I can open my lips to speak. His gaze is direct, and it halts me, if only for this moment. "That's all I want to say. I just thought you should know. You. Can do. Better."

His face is serious. There's a part of me that wonders if he's flirting. But it doesn't feel like a pick-up line. Houston—his being here today, his words—*this* feels more like a rescue.

I smile, perhaps a little indignantly, and turn and step through the exit. When I round the building, I tuck my purse higher on my arm, and I clutch my sandwich and tea to my chest, running my hand along the cool spot on my skin where Houston touched me seconds ago.

Save your heroics for someone else. I have a plan. I'm sticking to it. And I don't need rescuing.

No, I don't need rescuing.

I used to think that I lucked out having a room of my own at the Delta House. So many of the other girls shared, but I had a room all to my self—a big corner one with two windows and a desk with a huge credenza nestled into the corner. But lately, I feel like I'm alone because nobody here really *wants* to room with me.

I never thought about it before; I was distracted by this fantasy I dreamt about for so long. I've always been dazzled by things. This desk—it dazzled me. I've been staring at it, at the various pictures I have stuck to the corkboard in the back, and those propped up on the shelves at the top. Most of the photos are of Chandra and me, sometimes together with our boyfriends.

Chandra—she hypnotized me too.

The house is empty. It's a weekend, and everyone has something to do. Chandra is at the stadium, watching her boyfriend practice. I guess she's watching mine practice too. We have one football game left—it's homecoming, and we're going to lose. I don't really see the point in practicing, but I'm also glad that's where Carson is.

I feel like I'm waiting for a rocket to launch through my window, for an earthquake to happen. I really shouldn't assume things will unravel that way. Maybe there's a chance the photo won't get picked up. I sent it to the student media, and to a few of the social sites that post about the campus *who's who*. Maybe they aren't interested? *Of course they're interested.*

The longer I toss around in my brain what I've done, the more I start to regret sending the photo in the first place. Then, I feel guilty for regretting it. This cycle—it's stupid.

I grab my backpack, stuffing it with every single book I own. I'm a design major, and my finals aren't really something I need to worry about. But I'll be damned if I'm going to sit around this empty house waiting for the sun to fall. Hell, I might just study right on through Saturday night. I'm sure the party will be at our house again, and drinking seems to turn my subconscious into a superhero—out to save the world and correct all the bad shit Paige Owens does when she's sober. It's pretty sad when the good version of yourself is the drunk one.

"Ugh, finals," I huff, rolling my eyes as I pass two of the upper-class Deltas sitting in the common area downstairs. They nod and smile, but don't say anything while I open and close the door behind me. Why didn't they say anything? Do they already know? Have they seen the picture? Are they talking about what to do with me—the traitor? They've never really talked to me before, so why would they now?

I need to get to the library before I die from paranoia.

Houston

Six shifts wasn't enough. It wasn't even close to enough. Chuck was good to me when he could be; I knew it—I hated to be that guy who begged. I hate begging. It feels like I do it a lot, though.

I keep checking my watch while I pace outside his office in the front of the grocery store. The glass is reflective; it's security glass and Chuck's seeing me pace.

I'm about to sit down on the small wooden bench by the ice and chopped wood bundles when Chuck steps out of his office. He pulls his ill-fitting jeans up over his round belly and tucks the pencil behind his ear with his other hand. The small tuft of hair he has left on his head almost makes it look like a quill.

"Best I can do is add on some produce and cart time. That should bump you up ten more hours though. That do?" It will help, and I don't want to make him feel bad; I nod and smile, shaking his hand and folding my apron up to tuck under my arm.

"Thanks, Chuck. I'll be here bright and early to open." I pull my keys from my pocket. An old, bent stick of gum falls to the ground, so I pick it up and toss it in the trash.

"Houston, here—" Sheila calls after me, pivoting around the butcher counter. It's a family-run grocery store, and she and Chuck have kept me employed for three years, through every up and down. "You have enough time to stop by the house?"

"I do," I smile, taking the large bundle of steak she's wrapped for me. "Thanks, Sheila."

I don't really have time, but I learned you don't turn down Sheila's kindness—especially when it comes in the form of ten-ounce porterhouses. Thankfully, Mom's home when I pull into the driveway. I don't even bother turning the car off. She must have just sent the neighbor home from watching Leah.

"Mmmmm, smells good. Whatcha cooking?" I ask, kissing Leah on the head while she slurps alphabet noodles from her bowl. My mom is standing over a large pot my nose recognizes to be her chili. Leaning over, I kiss my mom on the cheek and flash the handful of steak in front of her.

"That from Sheila?"

"Who else?" I say, tossing it into the freezer and grabbing a spoon from the drawer next to my mom. I dip into her pot, and she smacks my hand playfully. When she rolls her eyes, I go in farther, pulling out a spoonful of steaming, red awesomeness. "Oh man. I love it when you make this."

"Well good, because I'm making enough to freeze for the week," she says, going back to stirring and adding dashes of whatever bottles she has before her on the counter. My mom cooks everything by instinct; it's what makes her food so damned good.

"Well, I'm gonna need a lot of frozen meals this week. I've got thirty hours at the store, and finals," I say. I can feel her lecture boiling under the surface as she sets the spoon down on the counter, rolling her hands into the dishtowel and leaning on her hip, turning to look at me. "I know. I know. But this semester's almost done. I promise; no more than two classes at a time from now on."

"You do too much," she says, her lips pursed and her eyes worried. Funny, I feel like I don't do enough.

"I need to pay my way," I say, tearing off a corner of the bread and dipping it in the pot for one last bite.

"I've got money, Houston. I pay the bills. And I can pay your tuition, too—" I interrupt her before I have a chance to agree with her.

"Yeah, but I'd feel a lot better if you didn't have to," I say, distracted by the bubbles Leah is blowing in her milk. She looks up at me with a giggle and wipes away the white mustache above her lip. The smoke alarm starts blaring. Before I can get to the garage door to pull out the ladder, my mom is standing on top of the kitchen chair, poking at the screaming siren with the end of a spatula, while waving the dishtowel in her other hand to clear the smoke from the bit of sauce that spilled on one of the stove burners.

I should stay and help.

"Don't do that. I see that look on your face. I'm fine, Houston. Now get to class; you're paying for it," she says, her mouth in that sideways smile that matches mine.

"Okay, I'll be quiet when I get home," I say, propping the garage door open to air out the kitchen while I leave. I rush to my idling car with a can of soda and a few crackers—it will have to tide me over until I get home tonight.

Thank god my mom lives only a mile away from campus. That's half the reason I stay there. Everything in my life is orchestrated down to the second, because, well...yeah, I do too much. But not doing this much would just feel lazy. Thankfully, the single stoplight between home and campus cooperates today. I pull into the library parking lot and guzzle the rest of my soda, tossing the can in the trash by the door.

The email said the group would be studying by the reference desk, but no one is there yet. I suck at Spanish. I tried to petition the school to let me count HTML as my language credit, but that petition got about as far as the shredder. I only need a year of a language for my computer science degree. Two semesters. But I was about to fail the first one. Not a good start.

My backpack falls on the table, and I sink into one of the well-worn chairs, my body descending deep into the cushions. I run my hands along the wooden arms and the pencil-grooved marks—attempts to carve initials. I wonder how many people have touched this chair and tried to own it with their initials? What a stupid thing to claim as your kingdom.

There's no way I'm early. I was running late when I dipped the spoon in my mom's chili, so unless time stopped—and rewound—this tutoring session wasn't gonna happen. I *need* this tutoring session to happen.

Leaning forward, I pull my Spanish book from my bag and prop it on my lap, the pencil still wedged in the middle, where I got lost while studying last night. My brain isn't made for conjugating verbs, or knowing when to use feminine and masculine articles.

"Fuuuuuuuuuuuuuuuuck," I breathe, pulling the pencil out and tossing it on top of my bag on the ground.

I spend about ten minutes reading through the various words, saying them in my head. Then I close my eyes and try to quiz myself. I even fail this way—when all I have to do is crack an eyelid to cheat.

I'm tempted to quit, but I've blocked out two hours for studying. I need to study before I meet up with Casey. I'm pretty sure his hard drive is fried, but I didn't have the heart to tell him over the phone. Either way, I have a feeling I'll be at his house for the rest of the night trying to save a semester's worth of my best friend's economics assignments.

Shutting my eyes, I go in for one more try at the self-quiz, when I hear the sound of metal crashing onto tile.

"Mother-fucking-piece-of-shit..." She thinks she's talking quietly, gritting the swear words through her teeth. She kicks at the giant trash can snared in her purse strap, dragging it around her in a circle near the library entrance. I should probably get up and help, but I'm so caught up in the scene she's making—by trying not to make a scene—I somehow forget to stand. When her gaze lands right on mine, I feel like a dick. But then she sneers at me and kicks the can one more time, tearing it from her purse and dropping her backpack and other things in a pile on the floor. It makes me chuckle.

I toss my book to the side, because I'm not learning anything from it anyhow, and jog over to her at the entrance.

"Good thing it's a Saturday and the library's empty," I say, reaching to help her set the can back in its place. She swats at me at first.

"Stop it! Just go back...over there. You know, to watch me for a while and do nothing." There's a well-deserved bite to her tone. *Yeah, I feel like a dick.*

"I'm sorry. You sort of stunned me—what with all the kicking and clanging and sailor-mouthing," I say through a soft laugh. She's different right now. It's still the same girl who orders sandwiches and party trays from me at the deli, but there's also something different. "I'm Houston, by the way," I say, brushing my hand off along my pants and reaching it forward to her. She looks at it for a few seconds, like she's making sure it isn't dirty. I'm almost offended, but I've sort of learned that Paige is just *offensive.* It's her thing. She finally shakes my hand, but doesn't hide the fact that she wipes her palm along her jeans afterward, which makes me chuckle.

"I know your name," she says. Bothered. Indignant. "You wear it on your shirt."

I look down and realize she's right; I do still have my nametag on.

"Oh, shit!" I say, pulling the pin off and stuffing it in my front pocket.

"Who's the sailor now?" she asks, her lip twisting up, her eyes almost giving me a wink. She tugs her bag back over her shoulder and picks her keys up from the floor before waving goodbye with her fingers. I watch her for a few seconds, noting the way her ass sways in the opposite direction of her hair. She's like this perfect blonde bombshell, but damn can she be mean.

I was going to apologize for what I said earlier—not the words so much as the way I said it. I could tell it offended her, and I could tell she was embarrassed that her boyfriend is such a prick. But I wasn't judging her. She *can* do better; I meant it. I spoke up because I can't stand watching assholes bully women. My grandpa used to bully my grandmother, always putting her down and making her feel stupid and small in front of people. He never hit her, and I guess that's why he thought it was okay.

She never looks back over her shoulder as she walks to the study lounge on the other side of the room. I give up and turn to get back to the miserable reason I came here in the first place.

For the next thirty minutes, I write down every word I need to know, with my own version of how I *think* it's supposed to be pronounced. The help desk is closed—*I mean who studies on a Saturday night?* After a good five minutes of peering over the desk for scissors, I eventually give up and tear my small quarter-pieces of paper into flashcards.

Only three or four of the tears come out straight, the rest veering offline, leaving me with shreds of notebook-paper triangles with my scribble on both sides. I can't even get this part of studying right. I'm pushing my sad little study cards together into a pile when I sense her legs step closer to my table.

"Have you ever been in a library before?" The way she asks the question, it sounds so sincere, almost...sweet. She must be looking for something, like the vending machines or computers.

"I'm here a lot. Whatcha need?" I ask, pressing my stack of words together between my thumb and forefinger, already overwhelmed by the thickness of the stack I have to memorize.

"I don't need anything. I just figured you must not ever have been in a library before. I mean, why *else* would you come in here and think you could throw a noisy craft party that's so loud I can hear it through the glass walls of the study lab?" Her hip juts out to the side as she points at me with her pen, clicking it open and closed while she waits for my response.

She's pissed about earlier.

"Do you know Spanish?" I ask, figuring really...what do I have to lose?

"Fuck off," she spits back, kind of quickly, and I wonder if she actually heard me because her reaction seems like it was prepared for something else. She's walking away when I keep talking.

"Because that's why I made these flashcards. I'm studying for my Spanish final. And I suck at this language, and the study group never showed," I mumble, spreading the word papers out in front of me like a dealer in Vegas. I pull one out, and read the back, holding it up for her to see. "*Caw-meeee-day.*"

I'm not even close; I know that much. I'm exaggerating my poor pronunciation, though not by much. Her shoulders hunch up when I speak, and she flips around, taking quick steps back to me, and ripping the small paper from my fingers.

I watch her lips as she reads my writing, pronouncing the Spanish word for *food*, and I'm pretty sure she's getting the full picture of how pathetic I am.

"Let me see these," she says, not really waiting for me, grabbing them all in her hands and flipping through a few, letting others fall loosely to the ground. I reach to pick them up, but give up quickly. Who am I kidding?

"When's your test?" she asks with a sigh.

"Monday. Early," I say, holding her gaze. Goddamn does she have nice eyes. They're blue. Ocean blue. I notice them every time she comes into the store.

After a few long seconds, she wads my papers up in her hands and marches to the trashcan a few feet away, tossing my *craft project* away. She drags an extra chair over to the opposite side of the coffee table from me, then pauses, looking at me again while she chews at the inside of her lip. I can actually see her tongue pushing on the inside of her mouth like she's working really hard to avoid calling me something. Her eyes flutter in this annoyed blink-like movement, and to most people, it's probably irritating, but it makes me smirk. Her mannerisms are familiar somehow.

She holds up a finger before walking quickly back to the study room she was sitting in. When she comes back, she's carrying all of her belongings—her bag not fully zipped, like she probably just tossed everything in quickly. She drops everything next to the chair, then sits in it and slides forward until her knees touch the table. She folds her legs up in her chair, then leans forward to grab my book, flipping it around so she can look at it. Her shirt is navy blue—I know that much—but I can't tell you if it has a pattern on it, a scoop-neck or whatever else comes on a chick's shirt. I can tell you that it's loose enough to drape forward when she leans down, and I can tell you that I now love pink bras.

I'm too slow to pull my eyes back, and she catches me staring. Even though her eyes look angry, her mouth curls the tiniest bit on one side, and I know she's not angry at all that she caught me looking. If she were angry, she'd have pulled her shirt up and quit leaning over; Paige did neither.

"Is it a verbal or a written exam?" she asks, and I shake my head to pay attention just like Bugs Bunny does when Lola Bunny shows up and makes him all jelly-brained.

"Both," I say, and catch her wince a little. She's heard my verbal.

"How long do you have tonight?" she asks.

"How long do you need?" I'm already prepping myself for the text I'm about to send Casey that I'm not coming. This isn't about the pink bra. Well, okay, maybe it's *a little* about the pink bra. But honestly, if Paige can help me pass my Spanish final, I'll forgo eating and sleeping for twenty-four hours if I have to.

"Judging from the way you just butchered *comida*? I'd say we're going to be here for a while." I get caught up in her lips for a few seconds when the word literally falls from them, sounding like I'm sure it's supposed to. It's both the hottest and most amazing thing I've witnessed in a while—that, or I'm desperate—for tutoring *and* a woman.

"Give me a second," I say, pulling my phone out and firing off the text to Casey that I won't be able to make it.

He types back.

CASEY: *You're a dick. What am I supposed to do now?*

ME: *Sorry. Try the computer commons. They have lots of geeks there.*

CASEY: *They're not as geeky as you.*

ME: *You can't sweet-talk me. I'm sorry. Something important came up.*

CASEY: *You owe me beer.*

ME: *When don't I?*

Casey sends me one final text, an icon of a middle finger. I toss my phone down to my backpack, smirking, and lean forward, my elbows on my knees, ready for Paige to work a miracle.

"I'm all yours," I say, and she looks at me the same way she did when I stared at her boobs—eyes hazed, but mouth curled. This girl is an enigma.

I feel a little guilty. I've checked Paige out; I even look forward to her coming in to pick up orders, pulling the tickets before Sheila has a chance to go through them, just to make sure hers are in my pile. I do it because I think she's cute. But—and I'm an asshole for assuming—I never thought she was *smart*. I've been sitting on the floor for the last two hours, my legs stretched out under the coffee table while she grills me on Spanish vocabulary, forcing the words into my head, and somehow pulling them from my mouth correctly. I'm going to pass my Spanish final, and Paige is a genius.

I can tell she's sleepy. She keeps standing and stretching, yawning with her arms over her head. We've got a few empty energy drink cans on the table between us, and I feel wired enough to run home. I kind of don't think Paige would make it past the fountain out in front of the library before curling up and dreaming.

"You're tired. I think I've got this now. Let's call it a night," I say, moving to close the book and gather my notes.

"No, it's okay. I'm not that tired, and we still need to go over your verbs again." She's shuffling through papers in front of me, searching for the one she wrote the verbs on. I list off the verbs in order, my pronunciation as close to perfect as *I'm* going to get.

"See, I think I'm good," I say. Paige lets out a big breath, her eyes grazing over the pile of papers in front of her before flicking them up to meet mine. There's the blue.

"You're...sure?" She twists one corner of her lip up, scrunching her right eye.

"Honestly, if I would have been here alone all night, no...I wouldn't have been sure. But you are like a Jedi master," I say, and she rolls her eyes, standing to pack her things, pulling a thick sweatshirt out from her bag.

"Boys and *Star Wars*. I don't get it," she says.

"Ohhhhh, do not bag on *Star Wars*. The force is not to be reckoned with. It's strong with you," I say, feeling the twitch in my lips as I try not to laugh at the way she's looking at me.

"Wow. You just went all convention there on me, didn't ya?" she says, waving her hand from side to side.

"I did," I laugh, zipping up the last of my things and pulling my bag over my shoulders. She walks next to me all the way to the door, and I can't help but think how much nicer she is when that asshat she's dating isn't around. I'm about to bring him up, when she speaks, stopping me.

"You don't have figurines, do you? Please tell me you don't have figurines," she says, and I keep my eyes forward. I *may* have one...or three or four. I don't remember. They're in a box in

Mom's closet. But only because I asked her to hang onto them for safekeeping, and...

"Ohhhh my god! You have dolls! Like, figurines! You should meet my sister's boyfriend. You two would so get along. He has a thing for teddy bears," she's talking fast, and there's this smile on her face that I've never seen on her before. "What?" she asks, pausing in the middle of her *make-fun-of-Houston-fest*.

"Nothing, I just noticed..." I start, but then rethink where I'm going with this. Ah, what the hell. "I just noticed you have a nice smile. You don't show that one a lot. You should; it's...." I stop before the word pretty slips out, but that's what I'm thinking. Paige's smile is pretty.

"What do you know?" she says back, the smile gone and her defensive tone right back where I've grown used to it. I nod and make a mental note to add another second to my *think-before-talking* rule. "It's not like you've seen me a lot, or even know me very well. You work at the deli counter. Whatever."

I've never had my employment thrown back in my face quite like that, and I know I should be offended, but her backlash only makes me laugh.

"What?" she asks, still letting her anger rule her demeanor.

"You," I say, and she furrows her brow, her eyes zeroing in on me as we near the parking lot. "That's all I've got. Just...you. You're...I don't know. You."

I click twice to unlock my car, then scan the parking lot looking for hers, but soon realize she didn't drive here. She walked. And it's dark outside, the sidewalks empty.

"You want a ride home?" I ask.

"I have a boyfriend!" She almost yells it at me, and I work hard, pushing my lips together with every bit of control I have as I try not to laugh.

"Wow," I mouth. I can see her start to feel embarrassed. "I'm sorry. That's...I know. I've met him, remember?"

She nods, rolling her eyes a little. She's covering, and I'm going to let her.

"I just meant...it's late. I don't like the idea of you walking anywhere far—alone," I say, pushing the passenger door a little wider.

"It's not far," she says, her face looking off to the side, her lips hanging open, her breath held along with her thoughts. "But...a ride would be nice. I'm just at the Delta House, on Main."

"Easy enough. I'll drop you off," I say, pushing the door all the way open now. She slides in, her bag and purse on her lap. My car has one of those automatic seatbelts; it's old, and I'm pretty sure it's been recalled. Paige lets it fold over her before unraveling it from her purse and bag. Watching her through the closed door makes me smile. She catches me looking and shrugs her shoulders; I jog over to my side, toss my bag in the back, and start the engine.

"Your seatbelts are stupid," she says, her lame insult catching that nerve in my mouth, making me smile again. It's funny that those words come out of the same mouth that speaks perfect Spanish.

"So, why do you know Spanish so well?" I ask, doing my best to make small talk during the short ride.

"My dad speaks it. He's a lawyer, and he's done a lot of foreign contracts. He was learning the language when my sister and I were kids. So, for a year, he made our house completely bilingual. It made Spanish in high school a piece of cake. I tested out for full credit here," she says.

"That's so cool. I would give anything to have that luxury. I think the only thing I could test out of would be wrestling. And that's not going to happen," I say. Her eyes widen when I mention wrestling, and I answer the question before she asks. "I'm not on the team or anything. I had a chance...to wrestle in college. But, it just wasn't the right fit. I want to focus on computer science and programming, and sports take up too much time."

Her enthusiasm wilts so fast, I'd swear she punched me if I didn't know there was no way she could get her arm out from that pile of stuff in her lap.

"You have a sister?" I ask. She was already looking out her window when I spoke, but something makes her focus away from me even more.

"I do," she says, her voice softer. "We're twins."

"Wow. Twins. Did you do that thing in grade school where you switch places with each other and trick your teachers?" I ask, and she pulls her things in close to her body, bracing her hand on the door.

"It's right there. You can just drop me out front," she says, looking at the brightly-lit brick house, the bushes out front cut in perfect squares, outlining a long, green lawn. I slow as we approach the front walkway. She smiles with a closed mouth as she turns to face me. "Cass and I are fraternal. That wouldn't work, we're too...different."

She reaches for the handle, pushing the door open and stepping out quickly. She turns on her heels at the curb, her hand stretched out, but barely touching the door.

"Thanks for the crash course," I say, realizing the knots in my stomach from the anxiety over my test are gone—totally gone.

"Thanks for all the sandwiches," she says, flinging my door closed and walking away. I indulge in watching the sway of her ass, and even though she was doing her best to insult me just then, she lifted the back of her shirt just now, and she knows exactly what my eyes are looking.

After a few seconds of being a perv, I push the car into drive and head home, flipping the lights off before I hit the driveway so I don't wake up the house. I tiptoe inside, turn the locks, and climb the stairs—smiling at the small light I still see spilling from underneath my mother's door. All these years, and she still has to wait up for me to make sure I made it home safely.

I'd love to shower, get the smell of salami out from my hair and fingernails, but I'm too tired. It's almost midnight, on a Saturday. I haven't been out this late for anything other than work in months. And I can't say it was for a party or a date. No, it was for studying. Maybe I *am* one of those convention dorks. I rub my eyes and pull my pants and shirt off, tossing them by my door in the pile that I secretly love my mother picks up for me every day. I crawl on my hands and knees to the pillow, letting my face collapse into the coolness, and fall asleep with Paige's voice rolling *R's* in my head.

Chapter 2

Paige

When nothing happened Sunday, I chalked it up to the weekend. But then Monday came and went. And Tuesday, too. The anticipation of confrontation was almost worse than shit actually hitting the fan.

I'm so consumed with finding Chandra's name on the campus news website's gossip page, I almost miss it—*almost.*

ASSOCIATE FACULTY MEMBER FILES LAWSUIT AGAINST
SCHOOL FOR WRONGFUL TERMINATION

The headline couldn't be more wrong, and the story is total bullshit. The home page of the news site is dedicated to my sister's attacker. I scan it quickly, my heart racing that Cass's name might be in there.

It's not.

Paul Cotterman is my sister's physics professor. He got a little touchy-feely during a tutoring session a few weeks ago, so Cass kneed him in the nuts and punched him in the temple.

Paul Cotterman is also Chandra's ex—of course he is. Two gross people dating; what's more perfect than that? I can't believe they broke up.

I read the story all the way through, laughing out loud by the end over how innocent the quotes make him sound.

"Oh my god, did you read that? Isn't that guy the one Chandra dated? I feel so bad for him," says Ashley, a freshman who joined Delta when I did. Keeping my back to her, I let her glance over my shoulder at my laptop. I know if I turn around, I'm going to tell her to get the fuck out of my room, but I'm going to need allies when Chandra's story comes out.

"Yeah, that's the guy. But...I don't know. I get a real sleazy vibe from him," I say, my eyes penetrating his name on my screen.

"Huh," Ashley says. "Not me. I think he's super hot."

I twist in my chair, but Ashley's back is to me as she's walking out the door—probably a good thing, because my rebuttal was perched on my lips, and it wasn't nice.

She pauses at the door, and leans into my room with her hand gripping the frame; her head tilts so she's looking at me upside down, like she's about to start a back bend. "Delta meeting in ten minutes, by the way," she smiles, then flips upright and rounds the corner.

My breath comes in slow and hard. It could just be an end-of-the-year thing. There are academic requirements to stay in the house—maybe it's a grade check or announcement for study sessions through finals.

I close my laptop and slip it into my backpack, along with a few of my books. My classes are all done, and tomorrow is campus study-day. The only thing left is finals. I'm starting to think spending the rest of this semester at the library wouldn't be a bad idea.

A month ago, I never wanted to leave my room. Now, it feels like a trap. It's disguised as a place I should love. Looking at it now, I'm starting to think it's all part of the plan, to lull me into a false sense of comfort until I break.

My room is purple, the furniture white with fancy trim. We all have special doorknobs—that's sort of a thing they do for the girls who get selected to move in. Every Delta gets to pick a doorknob from the *Restoration Hardware* catalog. The girls who have roommates have to agree. But I'm alone, so I got to pick my own door décor. My knob is glass, with purple and silver swirls inside, cut like crystal. There's a matching coat hanger—which I paid for on my own—mounted in the center near the top; I used half a month's spending allowance.

Cass probably spent her money on granola bars and Gatorade, with lots of change to spare. I bought a hundred-dollar coat hanger. Now, I can't help but fixate on it, noticing how small it is. The mount is made of iron, but the ball at the end is plastic. I chuckle quietly the more I think of how much it cost.

"Meeting starting," someone yells from downstairs.

My small fit of laughter fades, and my frown feels heavy. I grab my bag, making sure I have my essentials inside—books, music player, phone, keys, purse, gum...yeah, I think that's it.

The common room is pretty full by the time I get downstairs, so I plop my bag at the base of the steps and take my seat on the bottom stair, another girl standing next to me, leaning on the rail.

Chandra is sitting on the main sofa. That's her seat—right in the middle cushion. Her jet-black hair shines against the purple velvet of the couch. It's kind of pretty. Ashley is next to her...in the seat I usually take. A week ago, I think Chandra would have told Ashley to move. Chandra's best friend, Talia, the vice president of our sorority, is on the other side. I wait for several seconds, just to be sure my instincts are right. In that time, I notice neither of them look up for me. They purposely avoid turning in my direction at all.

This isn't going to be a meeting; it's a public hanging. I need to decide if I want to slip my neck into the noose.

"Thank you for coming, ladies. I know we're all very busy right now," Chandra starts, and the room quiets faster than it does in any of my survey classes. I'm internally amused; Chandra commands more respect than a professor who won a laureate for helping guide the country through an economic crisis.

"Just a quick meeting; I promise," she says, gazing over the room, never fully looking in my direction. I'm across from her, nobody in our path. And I can feel the rope slipping over my head.

"Tutoring hours have been posted in the kitchen. Please check to make sure you are taking advantage of any and all help the Delta House provides you. Remember, part of our dues goes toward ensuring academic success. And your success in the Deltas rests partly on your academic performance," she says, her eyes crossing the room again in a sweep. I wait for her to stop short of me, like she did the last few times. But she doesn't.

Chandra's eyes stop right on mine; her lip raises the slightest bit, revealing her inner thrill of catching me. She knows. And I'm having a hard time breathing.

"Also..." she says, her eyes scanning to her left and right, but coming back to me. She's pretending this speech is for everyone else, but it's not. "I wanted you all to hear this unfortunate news from me first. There are some...well...*vicious* rumors making the rounds about me, along with some photos that are absolutely false."

I'm careful here, my energy focused on keeping my lips in a flat line, my eyes on hers, my blinking normal. Nothing about my outside can show the absolute chaos happening within.

"What's worse? These rumors...they started with one of our own," she says, sparing a few glances to either side, coming back to rest on me. "Someone fabricated some pretty terrible things."

Talia is nodding next to her, eating up every word, aiding Chandra's performance. Ashley is chewing her nails; she looks like she's about to cry, concerned for her leader. I want to vomit.

"This is painful for me to even ask," she says, feigning concern. *She's so fake! How did I not see this before? I had to have seen it. Maybe I just didn't care.*

"We're going to begin our own interviews into this matter. I'm afraid we're going to need to see everyone's social media and the photos on your phones." I pull my knees in and leverage myself so I can stand, lifting my bag over my shoulder—ready for whatever is about to come at me.

"Chandra?" I speak up, somehow finding my confidence. I need to keep this shit together; remember who I am. "You might need to get someone involved, like...legally. I'm pretty sure you can't just ask to see someone's personal information like that."

When I'm done, I purposefully bend down and unzip my purse and reach for my mirror and lipstick, giving my hands something to do. Disinterested—I need to keep up the appearance as long as I can that I'm clueless to what this is about.

"If they want to remain a Delta sister, I can," she says back fast. I notice my eyes grow a hint wider in my reflection. The entire room is aware of her tone; a few more heads have turned to look at me. She's right. We all signed contracts when we joined, contracts that gave the executive board—a.k.a. Chandra—the right to examine things like our phones and social media to make sure we were representing the Delta House in the best light.

"Okay, well...I just wouldn't want you to get *sued*," I say, snapping my mirror shut and touching my finger to the corners of my mouth before pulling my lips into a tight smile. Chandra is looking back at me with the exact same expression.

While the rest of the sisters start their rounds of gossip about which one of us is the cause of all of this, I pull both straps of my backpack over my shoulders and move to the door. I'm almost to the porch when Ashley catches up to me.

"Oh my gosh, you don't think they're really going to look at *everything*...do you?" she asks, her eyes wide, the blueness framed by the spider legs of her eyelashes. If I'm still here next week, I should really pull her aside and do her makeup.

"I think Chandra is going to do whatever she wants to do. But I wouldn't sweat it. Unless you have something on your phone you don't want them to see," I say, letting my eyes linger on hers for a few seconds, just enough to catch the gulp in her throat and the small glint of panic. I know I'm the only person being targeted for snapping a druggie pic of Chandra. I can't help but smirk knowing Ashley has something on her phone too.

"They're starting the interviews now. They can't tell if I delete something...can they?" she asks.

I shrug. How the hell do I know what they know how to do? Maybe she has nude photos. I don't know. I can guarantee that's not what they're interested in uncovering. I could tell her that right now—allay her fears—but I don't, because as much as I think Ashley's a nice girl, I know she'd sell me out in a heartbeat just to get into that inner circle. I know, because I did a lot of selling out to get there too.

Ashley is clutching her phone at her side, her thumb rubbing nervously over the edge. I open my mouth to almost erase her anxiety...*almost.* Instead, I curve it into a smile before turning and stepping down the porch to the front walkway.

"Where are you going?" she asks. "Chandra's going to wonder where you are."

"I just have an errand to run. They won't even know I left," I say over my shoulder, my cool face quickly growing hotter, more worried with every step I take toward the road. When I glance back, Ashley's gone inside.

I pick up my pace until I hit campus, turning down one of the more-narrow paths behind the literature building, and ducking around a corner where a few picnic tables are lined up. My nose is running from the chill outside, and the corners of my eyes are watering. I'm not crying, but I'm so shell-shocked my eyes can't seem to find the power to blink.

What the fuck have I done?

These are the kinds of things sisters go to each other for—but I don't have that luxury. My real sister wouldn't answer my call, and my sorority sisters aren't really interested in helping me. Honestly, at this point, I'd be willing to call my sister's friend and roommate, Rowe. We aren't very close, but she's surprisingly a really good listener. She left campus, though—something about a family emergency.

"I am actually, really, totally, and completely—alone," I whisper aloud, my chest constricting with a single laugh over the fact that I could have screamed those same words, and nobody would have heard me.

There's a text on my phone—I see the small icon of red lips and know it's Chandra. I swipe her message open.

You're going to have to deal with this eventually.

Yeah, I probably am. But I'm not in the mood for it right now. I pick up my things and push off the bench, dusting the dirt from the back of my pants. I walk through the empty walkways of campus. Today was the final day of classes, and a lot of them were cancelled in lieu of studying time for finals. I notice a few people sitting along the edge of the main fountain, which is really more of a statue now that they've turned the water off in preparation for winter. Sometimes, it snows here.

I let my feet take over, shuffling slowly along the walk to the library door, and I welcome the rush of heat on my face when I step inside. The library is empty too. Spectacular.

My legs keep going until I reach the grouping of chairs and couches to the left. Dropping my bag at my feet, I let myself fall into one of the lounge chairs. It's not the same one Houston sat in, but it's close. Of all places, I came *here*. I pull my biology book out and flip through a few of the pages, not really needing to study anything at all. Most of my classes feel like repeats of my senior year of high school, and if I don't have the parts of the cell memorized after two straight years of charts and diagrams, then I don't deserve to get a diploma.

I toss the book on the table in front of me, and shut my eyes, bringing my fingertips to my temple and rubbing.

"No book throwing in the library, ma'am," a voice says, startling me. I blink my lids open, and when I realize Houston is standing in front of me, I feel a strange sense of relief.

"What are you doing here?" I sound bitchy. I immediately regret how that came out, and I regret it more when I see him jump back and grimace at me. "Sorry. I've had...am *about* to have...a really bad day."

"It seems to me if you can predict it's coming, then you can probably prevent it," he says, taking the seat across from me, kicking his feet up on the block table in front of us, and resting his backpack on top of his knees.

"Not this one, I can't," I retort, laying my head to rest on the hard wood of the chair. I stare at the ceiling, waiting for another response from Houston. There isn't one, and the longer we sit in silence, the more I wonder why the hell he's still here in the first place.

"Do you need something?" I ask as I flip my head forward, my eyes on him wondering why he's looking at me. Has he been staring at me this entire time? God, I hope my chin doesn't look fat. Is that what he was looking at? And why do I care what he thinks about my chin? He's...he's deli guy. I mean, he's *hot* deli guy, but he's still the stupid deli guy.

"No, uh...no," he says, pulling his feet back to the ground in front of him and moving his bag along his shoulder as he stands. He runs his hand forward through his hair, into his eyes, pinching the bridge of his nose. "I just saw you and wanted to thank you. You know, for studying? Then you looked kind of sad..."

"I'm not sad," I fire back. Am I sad? I'm worried, and I set off a chain reaction that is bound to ruin my social life, but...fuck. I'm sad.

"Oh, well I guess that's good," he says, and his eyes fall to his feet. He doesn't believe me, and it's irritating me. I don't care if I am sad; I don't need the guy who makes my sandwiches coming in and making things better.

Before I can open my mouth, my phone buzzes at my side. I pull it out to check who's calling—it's Carson. I let my phone rest on my leg long enough for Houston to notice. I can tell he does by the way his right cheek lifts with his slight smirk, just before he gestures for me to go ahead. I answer in front of him, smiling tightly and raising eyebrows so he'll get the hint: we're done here, and I'm not sad as far as he's concerned.

"Hey, baby," I say, laying it on a little thick. Houston holds up a hand and nods before turning and heading out the main door. I'm left to talk to Carson in privacy, and now that I'm alone, I wish I could hang up.

"Hey! Get the fuck off of my bike!" Carson yells at someone in the background. "Sorry, babe. Douchebags don't know how to leave my shit alone."

He rides a motorcycle, some Ninja something or another. It was sexy the first time he took me out on it. Now, it's just one more thing he obsesses over.

"Right, so...you called me," I say after a few long seconds of silence. He's probably still death-staring someone for touching his bike.

"Oh, yeah, yeah, yeah." He says this a lot. Three *yeahs*. It's so goddamned annoying. I bite my tongue and wait for him to find his rhythm again, remember his point. "Party, tonight at Smokey's. Sigmas are buying, and I know how much you like their fruity drinks."

"I do," I smile, remembering the first time Carson took me to the cowboy bar at the edge of town. It's this huge indoor-outdoor barn-looking thing, and there's an enormous dance floor. I was glued to it for three hours, my body drenched with sweat by the time Carson took me home. He spent that entire night watching me, and I loved his attention. We'd only been seeing each other for a few days at that point, and everything was new and sexy. Maybe a trip to Smokey's was all I needed.

"Cool, so I'll pick you up at the house. Be ready at nine," he says, before holding the phone away from his mouth and screaming more obscenities at whoever was still touching his bike. "I gotta go."

He hangs up without another word, and I'm left right back where I started—alone in the library, brushed off by my boyfriend who makes me feel embarrassed sometimes, and regretful others. I might be pathetic.

My phone buzzes again; this time, with a text from Ashley.

You were right. They looked at my phone and Facebook page, but only for a few seconds. I think Chandra's looking for you. Where'd you go?

I begin typing, but then delete quickly, turning my phone off, and zipping it away in the bottom of my purse. There's no sense in putting this off any longer; I'm going to have to confront Chandra eventually. For a while, I thought I might lie. But she'd see right through that. I don't want her thinking I'm afraid. I'm not. I feel sick about everything I know I'll have to give up, but losing Chandra isn't something I'll regret. I'd regret lying more.

My pace back to the house is nearly as fast as it was when I ran away. As a kid, I used to hate getting shots or pulling off Band-Aids. My mom would make me count backward from ten, and after I got to seven, she'd always rip the bandage away or tell the nurse to proceed with the needle. My pain was always over quickly that way. I love my mom for giving me the false expectation that something painful would take longer than it really did. I'm thinking of this now—my steps coming quicker. By the time I count down to zero in my head, I'm at the front door of the Delta House, my hand rested on the ornate iron handle, and the only sound I hear is the blood rushing over my eardrums as my heart rate climbs.

When I step inside, Chandra is sitting right where I left her—waiting for me. She's alone, not because she wants to give me privacy; this has nothing to do with her respect for me. This is about her, and wanting to make sure I don't spread the poison. I won't. It will spread on its own; it's just a matter of time.

"Have second thoughts about running away, Paige?" she asks, her legs folded up in front of her, a pillow on her lap, her hands resting neatly on top. She's anxious. I've learned some of her tells over the few months we've been friends, and when she's sure of herself, she stands, lets her arms and hands be free—so she can make gestures and move with her speech. She's compact right now, hiding under the chenille butterfly pillow. No matter what happens, I've won this round, because I intend on standing.

"I was gone for thirty minutes. I'd hardly call that running away," I say, turning my back to her and taking my time to pull my bag from my arms, then removing the sweatshirt from over my head. I want her to think I'm making her wait, that I'm not nervous, but really…I'm just buying myself time until I can think of exactly what I'm going to say. I think it depends on what she asks.

"You'll need to be out by tonight," she says, speaking the second I'm done pulling the cloth over my head, trying to catch me off guard. And she has.

That is not what I thought she would lead with. Seems we're not going to go through the pretense of checking my phone and social media. Just as I thought, that was all part of the performance. I'm sure she'll tell everyone they did a *thorough* investigation, and everyone will believe it, because she's checked everyone's phone—but mine.

"Pretty sure you don't have the right to kick me out," I say. Benefit of being a lawyer's daughter is a shallow understanding of the law. I know more than Chandra does, and that's all that matters. Sticking to my promise to myself, I don't move from my spot about twenty feet away from her. I stand there, in the open foyer, where my voice echoes. And I revel in how it makes her uncomfortable.

"How did you think this was going to go?" she asks, never fully admitting to anything—never really laying out what *this* is all about.

"Not sure what you mean?" I say, resisting the urge to fold my arms. I won't close my body off to her. These might seem like tiny wins in the chess game of interpersonal communication, but I need every tiny win I can get.

Chandra looks down at the pillow, running her hands along it, pulling at the corners to make it even and straight. She lifts it from her lap and sets it to the side, then untangles her legs, walking over to me slowly. I hold my ground.

"You will be out by tonight, or I will make your life so fucking miserable, you will literally run home to California," she says, each word coming out amid her steps, until her elbows are brushing my body and her breath is choking me she's so close.

I don't blink. Not once. Inside, I'm crumbling, because I didn't expect Chandra to fight so hard. That picture; it will ruin her. But she's acting as if she has it completely contained. I know how rumors spread. I've helped pass them along. I've watched my dad spend millions trying to stop them. And when there's something as sexy as a photo of the campus *it* girl with a shitload of drugs—it's only a matter of time.

"Do your worst," I say, waiting for her to flinch. She doesn't, and the only thing I have left is my sister. I think of my sister, and the shitty things I started, and the cruel things this girl standing across from me has done. I know I'm right, and good has to win. I'm not naïve enough to think it always wins, but this time, it has to. And I'm willing to be a relentless bitch just to get my way.

Chandra doesn't respond. She let's the half smile on her overly-red lips linger, and waits for me to back away, which I finally do, retreating to my purple room. I pull the small screwdriver from my desk drawer as soon as I step inside and take down the overpriced coat hanger I bought with my own money. I place it in the side pocket of my duffle bag.

One way or another, I'll be out of this house soon. And I'll be damned if I'm donating my good decorating taste to this place.

Chapter 3

Houston

"Remind me how much they're paying you for this...and how much you're giving me for being here?" I ask Casey while I lie under a table shielded by a black tablecloth. There are at least a dozen cords in my hands, and I'm trying to find a way to weave them through a one-inch space in the plywood, makeshift-stage we're propped up on.

"Two K," he says, "and I said I'd give you half. Of course, that was when I thought you would fix my shit, not lend me yours."

"Way I see it, the fact that I'm spending the night here with you is worth way more," I say, peering up at him with my back flat on the floor.

"Wow, is that your best pickup line? No wonder you haven't been laid in...what, two years?" he says, feeding one more cord down to me from the back of his speakers.

"If you're going to be a dickhead all night, I can leave..." I start to get up.

"You're not leaving. I know how much a thousand bucks means to you," he says quickly, holding the end of the cord out for me. I take it, because he's right. That's at least a week and a half of shifts and tips at the grocery store.

"And I'll fix your hard drive. Let me take it home with me tonight. It's easier for me to get things done at home," I say, going back to work connecting the power.

Casey is an engineering student, but he's sort of made a name for himself deejaying for some of the hotter bars around the college. His parents aren't real hip over the idea of him moving into sound engineering, but it's hard to argue with two thousand dollars for a night's worth of work.

"What'd you say this event was again?" I ask, pulling myself out from under the table, moving to my laptop, which I've loaded all of Casey's programs onto.

"Some frat house is having an end-of the-year party," he says, his fingers practically twitching while he waits for me to get out of his way. I step to the side when I get everything pulled up, and he starts testing mixes and sound.

"This school has a lot of parties," I say.

"Yeah, like you'd know," he laughs.

"Har dee har," I say. Casey twists his head in my direction, pulling his sunglasses down to look at me—sunglasses he doesn't need, because we're inside, in a very dimly lit bar. "What?"

"Har dee har? You sound like an old fart," he snorts, pushing his glasses up and moving through a few more screens on the computer.

"Yeah, well you look like a tweaker in those sunglasses, so fuck off," I say. He raises his right hand and flips me off, never taking his eyes away from his work. Of course, maybe he did look at me. I can't tell, because the douchebag is wearing sunglasses inside.

Casey spends the next thirty minutes pre-loading a series of songs, mixing them into each other, overlapping and coming up with a pretty cool vibe. What he does is really damn impressive, especially to a guy like me who can't even sing along with the car stereo. I wish his parents saw it that way. Casey's parents are both mechanical engineers at a big oil and fuel company in Oklahoma City. Casey has been bred to follow their footsteps, and while that's what his degree is for, his heart is for something else. His father cut him off last year, dropped his tuition payments, and told him he couldn't live at home. That's when he started taking the deejaying seriously, and so far, he's been able to pay his bills. He's finishing out his degree because he's only two semesters away.

"You want something to drink, man? I'm buying," he says, pausing in front of the stage, a twenty in his hand.

"Just a Coke," I say, and he rolls his eyes.

"One day, I'm going to get you drunk, just like the old days," he says over his shoulder as he walks to the bar.

"Yeah, well I was sixteen in the old days," I say to his back. He doesn't hear me, but I flash to those simpler days for a few seconds. High school was so much better than being twenty-one. I had no idea how much five years would change my family's life.

Besides, Casey's gotten me drunk since then—a few times over the last year. That usually ends with me waking up somewhere I don't belong with a bellyache made of guilt and remorse. I think I'm capped out on regret for the year.

The bar isn't very crowded, and there's an old country song on the jukebox in the corner. It's funny how the bars near McConnell shift throughout the day, catering to the old-timers until the late-night crowd of college kids starts to stream in. I can tell we're on the cusp when a Taylor Swift song plays next.

There are a few old men shooting a game of pool in the back room. I look at my watch and kick away from the stage, picking up my Coke from Casey on my way.

"I'm gonna get a game or two in. What time do things start?" I ask.

"They start paying me at ten," he says. I nod and head over to the pool table, introducing myself to the guys and calling the next game. They're playing for money, but when they ask me if I want in on the action, I turn it down. I'm rusty, but I would probably still kick their asses at nine-ball. Something doesn't quite feel right about taking twenty bucks from sixty-year-old men, though—even if I could use it.

"Make sure you have the good shit on tap. We're not paying for that piss you usually serve!" I'm fairly confident I recognize

40

the voice without turning around, so I don't bother. I wait for him to say something else, because if it's that guy who Paige is seeing—*Carson, I think?*—I know he won't be able to shut up. My suspicions are confirmed when, after a short-lived five seconds without having to hear his voice, he begins singing loudly with the country song finishing on the jukebox.

"Dude, get this shit off! You—isn't it time for you to start playing the real music?" I turn around to see him snapping his fingers at Casey, who only glances up for a second, looks down at his watch, then returns to Carson's attention shaking his head *no.* Casey comes from a large Italian family, and I've seen his dad work him into a corner, screaming at him and threatening to hit him. He never did, but Casey's four older sisters would take over, smacking him until his skin was practically pink all over. Carson may be large, but the worst thing he could do is punch Casey and knock him out—and in Casey's world, a nap isn't so bad.

"What the fuck. You're fired!" Carson's moving closer, and as funny as it is to watch my small friend sit there, finishing his sandwich—as if the Neanderthal yelling at him were invisible—it's also almost ten at night in the middle of the week. If I'm out right now, I need to be getting paid for it, which won't happen if Casey gets fired from this job.

"Hey, chill out. He gets time for dinner. That's sort of a law, and we're not technically on the clock yet. He's got you covered," I say, totally making up that bit about the law. It sounded good, and I get the feeling Carson isn't the sharpest tool in the shed, so I took a gamble saying it.

"Hey...I know you!" *Great.* I glance down at Casey, who looks up at me with a full mouth and chuckles, his shoulders shaking. I let my eyes roll up and wait for it. "You're that grocery-store dude. Yeah...hey, you make, like, the best fuckin' sandwiches, yo!"

"WOW," I mouth to Casey, my back still to Carson. I'm not sure how you respond to this. Are people really friends with this asshole? Does Paige actually kiss him? Not that I really care who Paige kisses, but she's pretty, and he's so...

"Yep, *sandwich dude*. In the flesh." I shake his hand and regret every second of this conversation. I regret it more when I see Paige walk in behind him, her eyes zeroing in on our hands. I'm shaking this asshole's hand—the guy I told her she was better than. I look like such a jerk.

I pull my hand away and look back to Casey. "I'll get everything ready to go; you about done?"

Casey's being obstinate on purpose, chewing slower, taking his time, adding things like salt and pepper to the last few bites of his dinner. He's doing it mostly because Carson was trying to bully him. But now he's taking it out on me. I kick his foot out, and his sandwich falls from his lap. He catches it, but barely before it hits the floor.

"What the fuck?" he yells, breadcrumbs spilling from his stuffed mouth.

"Sorry, man. Not in the mood for a scene tonight. I want to get this going and get home," I say. I don't do late nights, because I do early mornings. We're not getting out of here until two in the morning, and I've been toying with the idea of just staying up all night. My shift begins at seven.

Casey wads up his food wrapper and tosses it in an empty box near the stage. "All right, let's get this shit started then," he says, pulling the headphones from his console and moving a few of his settings until that devilish smile spreads over his face slowly. He's always loved music, but when he started collecting things for mixing—making his own tracks—he got really obsessed with it. I actually love watching him work. I help sometimes, when he needs to borrow my computer. He doesn't really need me, but I think he feels bad using my stuff without paying me for it. I really don't do much, but I need the money, so I take it.

His blend of pop and techno starts to take over the joint, and eventually, my pool buddies are the last of the afternoon and early evening crowd to leave, the rest of the bar filled with college kids looking to hook up and let off steam before finals week kicks in.

Sometimes it gets to me that I miss out on this stuff. But I can't leave my mom with everything; that wouldn't be right. And really, what am I *truly* missing out on? I think this just as two girls start to grind with one another—practically making out while they dance in the center of the floor, the spotlights helping to accent the right see-through places on their shirts. Yeah...this is what I'm missing out on.

"Every job has its perks," Casey says, slinging his arm over my shoulder, his headphones resting around his neck.

"So, is this your thing?" Her voice does something to my chest, kind of like a sucker punch. I feel like I've been caught, but I'm not sure what I've been caught doing. No, that's a lie—I've been caught ogling two chicks touch each other in a way that I didn't think was real until right this moment. I'm not sure why I feel all sweaty and panicked over it.

"Hmmmm?" I ask, pretending I didn't hear Paige behind me. I keep my eyes on the prize, Casey still looking at the scene with me. But all I'm doing is blinking, wondering why she came to talk to me, wondering why I care...and maybe wondering a little bit if her fuck-hole boyfriend is watching, waiting to start crap again.

"You crash parties to get your fill of girl-on-girl action. That's your...thing?" she says, leaving her eyes on me, her lips tight. I don't even have to look down to know she's crossing her arms.

"Well, I didn't crash. I'm working," I say, nodding to Casey next to me, who offers a small wave with his fingers before turning his attention back to the girls on the floor. "But to be honest with you, yes. This is very much my thing."

I'm so satisfied with my response, and I kind of love the fact that I've left her speechless. She's siting next to me, maybe a full body-width from me, but I can feel her looking at me. I want to see her reaction, but I also don't like the fact that I care about her reaction. She may have helped me get a *B* on my Spanish exam, but every time I try to be nice to this girl, to help her, she steps all over me. I'm kind of sick of it.

43

"Typical," she says, after I spend several long seconds under her heated stare. She pushes off, and when I know it's safe, I turn to look at her walk away, and well...shit. She's wearing this red dress that hugs her body so well, I regret wasting all of my ogling energy on the two girls on the floor. Now all I want to know is what the front of that dress looks like—and if her body moves in the front the same way it does from behind.

"Who was that chick?" Casey asks, elbow at my rib.

"Paige Owens. She's this pain-in-the-ass customer of mine," I say, chewing at my lip wondering what else to say about her.

"She's hot, dude," he says, climbing back to his feet, to set up the next set at his table.

"Yeah...she is," I say, my voice low enough I know he didn't hear. I said it out loud, though, so it counts. I'm not too chicken to admit it. Paige Owens is hot. But she's still a pain in the ass.

Casey lets me set up a series of mixes after the first hour, and after his touch, they don't sound too bad. I work on some of the connections for him, making my computer jive with his equipment, then head to the restrooms in the back while we have a small break.

I'm in the back hallway thinking about what an easy gig this is for a thousand bucks when a mountain of a fist smashes into my jaw. My head flails to the right, bumping into the wall with enough force that I'm pretty sure I'm going to have a cartoon-type goose egg on my head in the morning.

"What the fu—" I'm about to protest when a second punch comes at me. I'm more prepared for this one, so I block most of its force, wobbling on my feet and getting my bearings back. My eyes finally focus on a very drunk, very big Carson standing in front of me. It might just be the effects of his punch, but I swear he looks like Popeye. His blond hair and barely-there beard frame his round face, and his body looks like it could crush me—and I'm not small.

"You see that girl right there?" I look around, and there are at least thirty people jammed into this tight space, all looking at us. I know who he means, but I'm not going to make this easy for him—not after he blindsided me with his knuckles!

"There are...lots of girls here?" I say, rubbing my jaw, but keeping my guard up. If he hits me again, I'll be ready. And I have a feeling I might surprise him.

"Dude, don't play that shit with me!" He comes at me, and I step back, raising my fist. He quickly moves his hand to my shoulder, turning me to face the back corner, where Paige and another girl are leaning, both of their mouths open, a little shocked at this ridiculous scene. "That. One! Right there! Red dress. Big tits."

Okay, I'm done with whatever *Twilight Zone* episode this is I've walked into. "I'm sorry...which one do you mean?" I ask, just to be a dick. My eyes fall on Paige's for a brief second, and she sneers at me. Seriously? I'm the one out of place here?

I feel his shove come from behind, and I falter a few steps in her direction, catching my balance with my arms stretched out on both walls. She sighs heavily, handing her drink to her friend.

"Carson, knock it off! What are you doing?" she says, looking around me. Her hands are on her hips while she confronts her unleashed boyfriend.

"I'm telling sandwich boy here to keep his hands off of what's mine!" he yells. Out of everything he says, *sandwich boy* is actually what pisses me off the most. I spin around quickly, catching him by complete surprise, and punch him squarely in the nose. The blood comes fast. I shake my hand at my side, and flex my fingers. That felt both good and really fucking terrible at the same time.

"She is not your property, asshole! And you're way out of line. I've barely talked to her tonight...in fact, *ever*! So if you could just get the hell out of my way, I'd like to go take a piss now," I say, pointing to the men's room door behind him. There's blood on my shirt, and that ticks me off, too. I have, like, four really nice shirts, and this is one of them. I hate this guy!

"Then why am I getting texts all night from people telling me you and her have a thing going? This one had these pictures, of you and her meeting up at the library." He's holding the phone out, like I can actually make out a postage-stamp sized photo from six feet away...after taking a few punches.

"Let me see your phone," Paige says, brushing past me. Carson pulls it away at first, but she grabs his wrist and jerks the phone from him. He doesn't fight her, but he looks at her with such contempt, I almost want to punch him again for no reason. Or maybe she is my reason. Why am I so involved in this?

"Who sent you this?" she asks, and Carson bunches his brow, pulling his eyes in and shaking his head.

"I don't know, but I've gotten six or seven of them, just in the last half hour," he says, grabbing the phone back from her to slide to another photo. He hands it back and she taps on his screen, her lips moving as she says the number. She takes over, tapping on his phone more, and holding her hand up when he reaches in to stop her. Putting the phone on her ear, she cups the other side so she can hear clearly. After a few seconds, her eyes close. She shuts the phone, and hands it back to him, shoving it at his chest, then turns to walk away. Her eyes catch me as she passes. For a split second, I think she's telepathically apologizing for all of this.

"Hey!" Carson yells. I don't turn to him, instead keeping my eyes on her. She downs the rest of her drink and hands her glass back to the girl standing next to her, then adjusts the strap of her purse on her shoulder, never acknowledging the shouts coming from the guy who thinks he owns her.

"I said *hey!*" he shouts again, and I can tell by the tone in his voice that he's embarrassed that she's ignoring him. Paige is incredibly calm, smoothing out the back of her dress, pulling it lower on her legs, careful to make sure she's still covered. She may be hot, but she's also a lady. I think that's what I notice most. She whispers something to the girl standing by her, then takes a few steps toward the bar, toward the exit. "Hey, you stupid bitch!"

That one gets her. It gets me too, and I flex my raw fingers, testing the burn of my knuckles, readying my arm to let this guy feel something that will stick with him well into tomorrow. I don't take my eyes away from Paige though. She stops on her heels and turns slowly, brushing her long, blond curls from her shoulders and raising one brow at him in question as she meets his eyes.

"Who the hell was that? Who did you call? And where the hell do you think you're going?" His intoxication is picking up steam, his words linking together to form new words. Paige leaves her eyes on him for several long seconds, and the hallway around us grows quiet, waiting for whatever she could possibly say to this insensitive asswipe. I'm pretty sure we're all rooting for her to make him look like a fool.

"That—" she lowers her eyes to his phone, still clutched in his hands, "is my problem, and has *nothing* to do with you. And as for where I'm going, I'm going home."

"You can't just...what...leave? Fuck that, you owe me some answers. Who the fuck is this guy? And what the hell's going on between you two?" Carson asks, still trying to show his control, as if he ever had it.

Paige starts laughing before he even finishes speaking, and by the time he's done, she's laughing out loud, her shoulders rising and falling, her arms once again crossed in front of her body—everything about her is calm.

"This guy?" She points at me with her thumb, barely unfolding her arms. "He's the one who told me I could do better," she says, and my eyebrows raise a little, feeling the spotlight of, well, everyone. "And ya know what? He's right."

She turns around fast. She's moving through the hallway quickly, people stepping out of her way, drunk faces stunned and impressed. She doesn't even pause when she passes the high-back chair she was sitting at, snagging the jacket from the chair back, and pulling it around her body while she takes these long, powerful steps. I'm so damned impressed, my feet don't work, and even though I want to run after her to give her a high five, maybe throw her up on my shoulder and parade her around the room, rubbing more salt in Carson's wound, I don't—because I'm stunned.

When I finally wake up from my trance, I don't move after her because Carson has now knocked my ass to the floor. I'm able to get with it quickly enough to anticipate his foot coming at me. I grab and twist it, sending him into the wall, a small chunk of drywall chipping away with the impact his shoulder has against it.

He doesn't bother with words, instead using his last pieces of sobriety to claw and swing at me wildly, grabbing at the collar of my shirt and doing his best to land a punch. But I'm filled with adrenaline now—and while he's been drinking pints, I've had nothing but caffeine. I get to my feet quickly, and after four swings, I have him stumbling on his knees.

"If I were you, I wouldn't order any more sandwiches from me," I say, pushing him back so he's flat on the floor. I step over him, into the men's room, and when I come out, a few of his friends have him balanced on a stool near the corner of the bar.

My face looks like shit, and my mom is going to freak out, but I have one more hour to help Casey, and I'm not leaving here without that grand. I've earned it.

"What the hell, man? You look—" I hold up my hand to stop Casey midsentence.

"I don't want to talk about it, dude. Weird fuckin' shit went down, and I'm not quite sure what the hell it was all about. Let's just finish this up, and I promise I'll catch you up tomorrow."

He stares at me, doing that slow-blink thing he's always done when he's baffled by me, then he pulls his headphones back up and turns his eyes back to my computer screen. A few windows have popped up, so I reach over him and click them closed, ignoring the update warnings.

And just because he could, my best friend makes a mix out of Kanye's "Stronger" and "Eye of the Tiger"—a serenade for Sandwich Guy, the superhero.

48

Chapter 4

Paige

I may have underestimated my enemies. I didn't expect Ashley to jump ship and join my cause necessarily. But I also didn't expect her to sell me out so fast.

But that's foolish. I would have done the same thing—probably still would, if I found something that worked in my favor. Ashley wants to be in with Chandra, to rise to the top at Delta. Sinking me—that's the new shortcut.

Being here, in this house—it's miserable. I came home from the party and the house was quiet. Most of the girls were in the tutoring lab or in their rooms studying, or at least that's what I told myself. The quiet is there again this morning, and I can't seem to tell myself the same lies. I'm being ignored.

Chandra knows she would have to beat me to the ground to get her hands on my phone. I don't care what I signed; she doesn't have a right to see some things. So she's squeezing me out in other ways. What I can't figure is who followed me to the library—who saw me talking to Houston?

"Whatever," I say to no one. That's me, two thousand miles from home and living with no one.

I pick up my phone and take a deep breath...time to perform.

"Paige?" My dad answers fast. "Is something wrong? Is your sister okay?"

It's always my sister. Cass has always been daddy's girl.

"She's fine," I say, packing my bag for the day, readying myself to study for my two easy tests—biology and ancient history. I turned in my English paper already, so nothing left to do but study—for the next twenty-four hours. I flop on the bed knowing I don't have enough to fill my time to keep me out of here until my plane leaves next week.

"Good, I was worried. The case, the assault charges...it looks like everything's going to be closed. This should all go away," my father says, and I barely hear him. He has no idea how far from *going away* things are for me. In one spontaneous decision to avenge my sister, I swapped places with her, and just as her nightmares are fading, mine are beginning.

I pinch the bridge of my nose and shut my eyes. I should have called my mom. But my dad's the one who handles plane reservations. My parents don't really know that I moved out to live in the sorority house. They know I joined, but they didn't want me to leave Cass—that's why I'm here, after all: to *watch her*. Funny how I wish I hadn't moved out now, though. I'd give anything to be back in that dorm room with her and her other roommate, Rowe.

"Can I come home early?" I blurt out, hoping to catch him off guard. Of the two of us—my sister and me—I'm *the emotional one*. I used to cry to get my way, but I've found the tears come easier since this divide with my sister has grown. I let the threat of a cry show in my voice—I use it. I'm not fully pretending, because if I let myself, I could cry right now. But I use this awful feeling to my advantage, because I deserve to get something from feeling this way.

"Uh...sure, I...I guess. Are you done early? Can your sister come, too?" he asks.

No, she can't. That's the point—I need to get out of here, to get away, to come home and be on my own. This has to be about *me*, for *me*—just this one time!

"She has tests on Monday. But I'll be done tomorrow. My semester was just really hard, and with everything that's happened, with Cass and the assault...it's taken a toll," I say, my voice losing ground the longer I talk. I'm not lying—not completely, anyhow. My classes are easy, but this semester has been painful. And I know...Cass bore the brunt. She was assaulted, and it was awful. What happened—*awful!* And I'm angry about it. I want to hurt people for her. I'm also tired, and now I feel like I don't belong...anywhere.

My dad was there for the argument between Cass and me at Thanksgiving; he's not naïve to what's going on. He just doesn't want to be in the middle of it, and that's precisely what I'm counting on.

"All right, Paige. I understand, sweetheart. Let me see what I can do. I'll text you when my secretary finds out about switching your flight, okay?" That's what I needed. I'm breathing. I'm hoping, and I'm thankful.

"Thanks, Daddy," I say, ending our call.

I look at my belongings all piled up on my desk. My bag is heavy, still stuffed with the things I care about. I'm not leaving anything alone in this room. A door creaks down the hallway, and I hear feet scuffling along the wood floors. There's a short pause near my door, and I watch as Ashley scurries by quickly, a teacup in her hand, the bag's string dangling over the edge. She practically races to the stairs to get into the kitchen—*away from me.*

"Weakling," I whisper to myself. Maybe I'm calling myself that. I pick up my bag and close my door, walking through the deserted hallway, down the stairs and into the common room. Two girls are studying on the sofa, and one looks up at me, but quickly averts her gaze.

That's right; I'm invisible. Mustn't let the boss see you *seeing* me. This whole thing is stupid. I let the door slam to a close behind me when I leave.

My original intent was to go to the library again, but honestly, if I study the books in my bag for one more minute, I think I may tilt the scales to crazy. I have things memorized, and I already know my tests are going to be multiple-choice. At this point, I'm shooting for the fastest time in the testing room.

I walk past the library and through the rows of brick buildings, letting my finger run along the slick windows of the architecture college. It's my favorite building; it's everyone's favorite. Made from what was once the main hall on campus, the structure has gone through several renovations over the years until now it is a cool collaboration of the old styles and the new. I love the lines and the colors, but more than that—I love the design wing on the inside.

I've only looked through the floor-to-ceiling windows, but next year, I get to sit in those classrooms—to make those rooms look as I think they should. McConnell puts students in design apprenticeships as sophomores, and it is the *one* perk I have left in coming here.

My mind goes numb for the rest of my walk, and somehow I find myself at the market just off campus. Even this parking lot is empty now that half of the town's population has gone elsewhere for the holidays. That's what stops me. Amidst the emptiness, Houston is jogging, hopping over the white lines where cars are supposed to sit, his green apron dangling around his neck, the knot loose behind his back. It's nine in the morning, and he's practically skipping. I swear he's even whistling. The sight of it makes me laugh. I don't know how he's functioning, let alone looking so carefree. He was out later than I was—I know, because I left sometime after watching him get his ass kicked by Carson, who I'm pretty sure isn't my boyfriend anymore.

He grabs for the last cart in the lot and begins pushing them toward the door in one long line, his eyes down at the wheels. I take this opportunity to move to the door with my back to him. I don't need him to know I was watching...that I was...*noticing* him.

"That door's locked," he yells. I turn quickly, and his eyes are still fixed at the wheels of the carts.

"Why?" I ask. That's a stupid response.

He smirks, and his lip makes that small quirk it does when he looks at me from the other side of the counter—the dimple in his cheek the only sign he's laughing at me. He's still far enough away that I could just turn to leave, and he wouldn't be able to catch up to me—unless he ran. He wouldn't run after me, would he?

I busy myself with these thoughts for a few seconds and lose my window. I'm kind of glad about that, though, because Houston might be my only friend.

"It's just me and Sheila right now. When she's in there alone, I keep one side locked. I don't like her being alone, even if it is during the day," he says, squinting a little from the sun shining on his face. I can tell from the cut on his lip and the bruising under his right eye that Carson took some good swings at him. I know it's not my fault, but I still sort of feel like it is. And now that he said that chivalrous crap about not wanting to leave Sheila-whoever inside alone, I feel worse.

"Does it hurt?" I nod at him, knowing after last night, I could probably point to anything on his body and find a bruise. He takes a quick breath in, inhaling a short laugh.

"It hurts like hell," he chuckles, pushing the carts through the door with a small grunt of force.

Houston is not like Carson at all. I haven't seen Carson, and I probably won't, but I can almost guarantee he's not admitting to any pain for the marks Houston left behind. I notice the bruising on his knuckles as his hands wrap around the carts. I also notice the flexing of his forearms, and the way the blue-and-red plaid shirt he's wearing is rolled up to his elbows, the bottom untucked. Now that I'm looking at the bottom of his shirt, I can't help but also take in his faded jeans that hug his hips but slouch just enough so I see the top of his boxers when he turns and pulls, his muscles working and his body hard to ignore.

When he stops moving, I look up. He's smiling at me, his lips pushed together tightly and his eyebrows raised.

"Did you need something?" he asks.

"Oh...no. I was just out walking, was going to study, but didn't feel like the library. I sort of ended up here," I say, my mouth jumbling the words because I'm literally thinking of them milliseconds before they come out. I sound pathetic.

Houston keeps his eyes on me for a few seconds, his smile still sweet. His face has stubble on it, probably because he didn't have much time to shave this morning. He's wearing a hat. He looks good in hats.

"You want a breakfast burrito? I make a killer burrito. Come on," he says, urging me over to the deli counter. He jogs around a swinging door to the other side, leaping over a few crates on the floor. *Still skipping.*

"Aren't those super bad for you?" I ask.

"Uh, well...I guess that depends," he says, pulling out two tortillas and reaching into a warming drawer for a bin of something that I think is eggs.

"Are those...eggs?" I can't help but twist my face looking at a bin that's filled with yellow, buttery...ugh, I don't know.

Houston lets out a short laugh and shakes his head. "Eggs are full of protein, and I just made these, maybe ten minutes ago. They're still fresh. Just do me a favor," he leaves his sentence there, his eyes coming up to meet mine while his hands work on the counter, scooping peppers and onions and some sort of meat-something into the tortilla.

"What favor?" I ask, and I know that I'm still making the face. Whatever he's making—it looks awful.

"Don't overthink my food. Just eat it," he says, pulling the tortilla tight, wrapping the bottom in wax paper, and handing it to me over the counter. His hand covers mine during the exchange, and I notice. It's not like fireworks or magic or heat...well, maybe some heat. But...I notice.

"I don't know," I say, looking at the most fattening thing I've eaten in probably two years.

"It has less calories than that pink drink you were sipping on last night," he says, and I look up at him, getting a good look at the deep purple around his eye.

"Fine," I breathe, opening my mouth and taking a small bite of egg, cheese, and tortilla. I reach to hand it back to him immediately, but he pushes my hands back to me. He touches me again. I notice.

"That was the most pathetic bite I've ever seen. Take a real bite. *Be a man!*" he says so loudly, Sheila chuckles from far behind him. I can feel my cheeks fire up. I don't like being

54

embarrassed, but there's something about the way he's teasing me right now. It's...nice.

I look at the concoction in my hand, working the wrapper to get a better grip, and I peer up at him once more. His eyes make the smallest movement to my lips before coming back to meet mine, but I notice. "You can't watch if I'm going to take a bite out of this," I say, pausing with my lips right at the tortilla.

"You are strange. Shut up and eat my awesome breakfast burrito," he says.

"I'm serious," I say, pointing with my right hand, twirling my finger. "Turn around or something."

"Oh my god, fine," he huffs, turning to lean his back against the counter. I allow myself a huge bite the second he does, but he turns quickly, catching me with cheese and onion hanging from my lips.

"Stawp it, tune awound," I mumble, my mouth way too full. His chest rises with a short laugh, and he shakes his head.

"No. It's too late. I've already seen you with egg on your face," he laughs harder, handing me a paper towel.

"Haw haw, vewy funny," I say, chewing behind the napkin. This is quite possibly the best thing I've ever eaten, but I can't tell him that. I press the napkin to my lips, finishing my bite, before I swallow and hand the burrito back to him.

"Well?" he asks, his eyebrows raised expectantly.

"Meh," I say. Liar.

His tongue pushes at the inside of his cheek, and he squints one eye, looking at me hard for a few seconds. This is his bullshit meter.

"All right, it's good. Whatever," I say, shrugging. I hate him. No, I don't.

He laughs and hands the plate back to me.

"Finish it then. I'm not eating a half-eaten burrito. Especially when there's lipstick on the tortilla," he smirks. I blush a little because he's right; I left a pink mark on the end.

"Thanks," I say, softer now, and take a seat at a nearby table, dropping my heavy bag into a chair next to me. I glance over to the magazine rack by the door, and the classified listing catches my eye, so I walk over and pick a copy up. I notice a corkboard by the stand, too, with lots of cards posting and looking for roommates; I pause and read a few of them.

THREE GIRLS LOOKING FOR 4th ROOMMATE – TWO BEDROOM

Yeah, I'm not sharing a bedroom; at least not something in an apartment with that many people. I look over a few more cards, one looking for a smoker, one looking for someone who likes cats and another that only wants a guy, unless you're "hot," according to the ad. I'll pass.

"You moving? Trouble at the Delta House?" He's joking with me. I remind myself of that before I let my natural instincts say something bitchy. He's being conversational, and he fed me breakfast. And he's nice. Nice is...refreshing.

"Something like that," I say. I move back to the table and flip through the classified listing, my pen poised to circle the dozens of options I'm sure to have. But after thirty minutes of looking, I'm no better off than I was before, the only listings looking for guys, people who are willing to live way off campus— or in places that, well, I wouldn't live.

This whole thing; it's complicated. I could stay where I am. Part of me wants to, because I don't like the idea of Chandra winning—*anything!* But, I also don't like worrying over what they're doing to my room, what they're doing to my things, about what they're all *saying* behind my back—or worse, to my face. My first campus-housing fee was transferred to cover my room and board this semester. My parents were going to have to give me a separate check to cover this semester anyhow. I was going to have to come clean about not living with Cass. But not living on campus at all—this was going to be a nightmare of a conversation. I'm not sure what side of my coin is more daunting—the one where I live with evil, plotting bitches who want to bug my room with cameras and post the footage to YouTube, or the one where my parents find out I totally abandoned my sister and broke my promise to them.

56

I'm tapping my pen on the table when suddenly a Styrofoam cup slides under its path, and the steam from coffee hits my nose. I do like coffee.

"Thanks," I say, smiling up at Houston. He pulls out a chair across from me and slides in comfortably. I watch him over the top of my cup while I blow on the liquid, sending a trail of steam toward him.

He looks at me in this certain way at least once every time we interact. It's like he's looking for my secret, trying to solve my puzzle. I'm not very puzzling, but I don't want to tell him that. If I'm being honest with myself, I like it when he looks at me. He pulls his green apron off, folding it haphazardly into a crumpled mess on the table. He has a gray thermal shirt on under his plaid button-down. I can see it through the open buttons on the front of his shirt. He's slouching, one of his long legs stretching underneath the table, the other bent so he can lean to one side. He's a big guy, his body taking up most of the space around us. There's some scruff on his face, and he's chewing at a toothpick. The guy looks like a lumberjack, and for some reason, that thought amuses me, so I giggle quietly.

"What's funny?" he asks, leaning forward now, propping his elbows on the table, leaving the small splinter of wood between his lips. He flips it around with his tongue once, before finally pulling it out and smirking, two perfect dimples like quotation marks around his lips.

"You look like the woodsman," I say, holding my lips together tightly, trying not to giggle anymore.

"Woodsman..." he breathes, thinking about it as he leans back again in his chair. "Yeah...that's better than *sandwich guy.* I'll take *woodsman.*"

I can't help but laugh. I look down at his apron and pull it closer to me along the table, tapping my finger a few times on the plastic nametag.

"What's up with your name?" I ask.

He smirks again.

"I was born in Texas. And I was *not* planned. My mom wasn't supposed to be able to have kids. My dad was in the Coast

Guard, stationed in Houston, and they had one *wild night*—or so I've been told." His face animates as he tells me this story, and I watch every movement of his mouth and eyes. "My mom says Houston is lucky, so..."

"Wow, that's like a cheesy pickup line," I say, taking a big sip of my finally cool-enough coffee. Houston holds my gaze for a few seconds, watching me sip, his head cocked slightly to the side. "I was kidding," I finally say. "That was sweet."

His mouth falls into a more relaxed smile, and he looks down at his hands, rapping them a few times on the table, his fingers playing out various beats. I finish my coffee, and flip open the ad in front of me for one more pass. I notice Houston reading from upside down, and he keeps fidgeting, looking behind him and then leaning to look out the door.

"Are you a spy?" I finally ask.

"Uh...I'm sorry?" he says.

"A spy. You know. Like that Bond guy. Or, maybe a bad guy? Or...I don't know. You're really jumpy, and you keep looking out for someone, and I'm starting to think maybe someone has a hit out on me...or maybe it's you? You're freaking me out a little."

He squeezes his eyes closed tightly and laughs. It's that breathy laugh he does, deep and sincere.

"I'm sorry. I was just thinking..." he stops, his finger pulling down at the edge of my newspaper, his eyes staring at the black print, his breath held. "We have a room. At my house. Well, it's my mom's house, really. And we rent it. But we didn't this semester, because we couldn't get our post up in time, and we've just been too busy to post yet, and it's a nice room. You'd have your own bathroom. Well, you'd have to share with me, but I'm easy. It's close to campus, so..."

All I can do is blink at him. I'm not sure how to react. There's a weird part of me that jumped excitedly when he started talking, and I'm not sure what that part of me is or what it's doing. Then there was this wave of relief. But there's also this strange nervous feeling, like I should just say *no* and end this conversation. I should probably say *no* because I don't like getting help or handouts or whatever this is, but I also need

58

somewhere to go, unless I'm staying at the Delta House, and I just don't know what the right thing to do is.

Houston's eyes haven't left the paper in front of me, and his lips are glued shut. He's frozen. The poor guy is actually frozen.

"Oh, Houston, that's…that's really nice of you. I'm just not sure…" I start, but I can see his eyes wince. He's regretting offering, and that makes me feel bad. "I mean, I'm not sure if I'm ready to move out or not. I have some things to think through. I might just be overreacting."

"There he is!" I hear an older woman proclaim through the main grocery store entrance. The woman is striking—tall, like Houston, and her dark hair cut short, to rest at her shoulders. This is definitely his mom. I'm so surprised by her—I don't notice the tiny girl, with hair just as dark as his mother's, darting toward Houston. He stands to meet her sprint, and she locks onto his leg fast, burying her face into the side of his jeans. Her hair is pulled to both sides in adorable pigtails.

"Sorry," Houston mouths through a smile.

"It's okay," I say, softly, rethinking the idea of living with his family. This scene right here in front of me—it's very appealing. "Your family, I'm guessing?"

"Yeah," he chuckles, reaching down to pick up the bouncing girl, tucking her so naturally in his arm. She finds her place quickly at his neck, her head resting comfortably on his shoulder. "This is my mom, Joyce. And this is Leah…my daughter."

My face just went seven shades paler. I felt it. Normally, I can lie through my teeth, give off the cool and calm vibe. But my heart just started beating in my stomach with such force, I can feel it in my belly button. Houston is staring at me, our eyes having a silent conversation. His saying *sorry* for the surprise, and mine doing their damnedest to pretend I'm not shocked or surprised or disappointed or any of those things that I feel right now.

"Daddy, I'm sooooooooo hungry. I waited for your eggs. Can I have some? Pweeeeeeeeeeeeese?" Leah's legs are swinging around Houston, and his arm is clutching her body, his muscles flexing in their protection. He turns his face to this small girl, who looks like she's maybe four, and pushes his nose to hers. They are almost exact duplicates.

"Yes," he smiles, and she raises her hands in victory.

"I got it for her, Houston. You finish up talking with your friend and your mom," Sheila calls from the back. Leah goes running behind the counter, hugging Sheila's leg next and climbing up a tall stool at the back table. It's her stool—there for her. She probably comes to visit him all the time, in the morning, when I'm never around.

"So..." he starts, stopping though, because there's really nothing he needs to say or explain. There it is. Houston is a father, with a room, that he'd like me to move into.

His mom looks between both of us and her eyes haze slightly before she turns to face her son.

"I'm going to pick up a few things. I'll be done by the time Leah's ready. I'll get her to pre-school," she says, kissing her son on the cheek and glancing at me once over her shoulder before moving down a nearby aisle.

"You're...married," I say, my insides twisting the second I say the *M* word, wondering why in the hell that's the first thing I asked.

"Not exactly," he says, his thumbs hooked in his pockets, and his eyes peering down at his feet. He takes a long deep breath, and I take the opportunity to do the same.

"You're...separated?" I ask, pretty sure that's not much better. This situation is feeling stranger the longer we talk. I'm pretty sure living like a paranoid-crazy woman in the Delta House is winning the mental address war happening in my head.

"I'm..." he says, stopping for one more heavy breath before pulling his eyes up to meet mine. "I'm widowed."

Houston

Well, that's not how I saw this going. But how else could it really have gone? I can't invite a girl to move into our house just because I think she's cute and quirky and she makes me feel like the twenty-one-year-old I really am. I lost that privilege the

60

moment I heard Leah's first cry. And I lost it again when Bethany died.

Paige is looking rapidly from her bag, which is still slung over the chair she was sitting in, then back to me, then to Leah, who is humming while she eats at the counter just behind me. She always hums when she eats. It's the greatest sound in the world.

"Oh, I'm...sorry," Paige says, her voice unsure. Nobody ever knows quite what to say. It's not a conversation a guy my age usually has to have.

"It's okay. It's been almost four years," I say, pulling the bottom corner of my lip into my mouth, keeping myself from *over* sharing. I can see Paige doing the math in her head. Yes, I'm a young dad.

"Seventeen," I say. Let's just get this out of the way.

She looks at me, her eyes pinched. She's pretending not to understand.

"That's how old I was when we had Leah. You were wondering...I...I could tell. I've seen that look before," I say.

"Oh, no that's not what I was...oh...fine. Okay, that's what I was trying to figure out. So, you had her in high school then, huh?" Paige asks.

"That's kind of what seventeen means," I say. I can see her eyes flinch, and I feel badly. I didn't mean to be snarky or hurt her feelings. "I was being funny."

"You're not very funny," she says back fast. She's always fast. I know she's trying to put up a front now, but her comebacks are cute. I can't help it, and I chuckle.

"So, that thing we were talking about..." I say. I should probably talk to my mom about it, but we had a discussion about the room just last weekend. I know she wants to rent it again. And we could use the cash.

"Oh, don't worry. I know you were just trying to be nice," Paige says.

"No, no. That's not what I meant. I was going to say think about it? Maybe just think about it. I know *all this*," I say, pointing behind me to my daughter, who is now singing songs to

Sheila. "I know that seems overwhelming, but it's not. You'd have total privacy. And Leah's a great kid. I work so much, you'd probably see my mom more than anyone else."

"I don't know..." she says, her lips in a hard line. Her shoulders are hunched up, and I can actually see the tension in her neck, arms, and face.

"Paige. I'm asking you to sign a lease. I'm not asking you out on a date," I say.

That flinch in her eyes from before—it's back. I know that sounded mean, but I don't want her getting the wrong idea either. Yeah, I think she's cute, and flirting feels good. It's been a while. I like our banter, and having a live-in Spanish tutor isn't a bad thing either. But she's, what, eighteen? Maybe nineteen? And I'm a dad. I'm on the seven-year college plan. Paige strikes me as someone who's driven. I'm a speed bump. And I'm not sure I could ever really be whole for someone else.

"Here," I say, reaching forward and tearing off a piece of the newspaper. I grab the pen she was using to circle ads, and make note of the fact she's only circled one—an ad she's also crossed out.

"Here's my number," I scribble it down and hand it to her. She takes it and holds it out in front of her, almost like it's a lit match. "Think about it, over break. And if you want to move in at the start of the semester, the room is yours."

I can hear my mom talking with Leah, so I let Paige go. She looks at me a few times while she gathers her things, and once again before she walks out the main door.

"And who was that?" my mom asks. She's using her nosey-mother tone.

"A potential renter."

"Uh huh . . . " She lets her response linger for a while, her eyes scanning me, looking for me to give something more away.

"Stop it. She's nice, and she's in need of a new place to live. She said she'd call during the holidays if she decides," I say.

"I see," my mom answers, a tight smile holding in everything she's dying to say.

"Stop it!" I roll my eyes at her and pull my apron over my head.

"I didn't say anything," she practically sings.

"You don't have to. You never have to. You have that *mom* look. It's so damned annoying," I say, feeling Leah wrap her arms around my leg from behind.

"Damned," Leah repeats.

"Awww, okay. Hey Leah? That's one of those daddy words. And daddy shouldn't say it, okay?" I say, bending down to meet her eye-to-eye. I pull her hands into mine, and we swing them back and forth.

"Damn, damn, damn," she giggles. Oh my god, is this my kid!

"Let's go, Leah. Time for pre-school," my mom says, grabbing her granddaughter's hand. Mom makes a face at me as she passes, her eyebrows raised excitedly. She's still hung up over Paige.

"Stop it," I mouth, making her laugh. I watch them leave, Leah's hair swinging side-to-side, slapping at the base of her neck. I wish Bethany could have seen this. She would have loved our little girl's hair.

"You want to slice the meat or prep the deli foods today, Houston?" Sheila asks, her hand already on the slicer. I smile because she's already made the decision for me.

"I'll get the side dishes," I say, and I move to the back. While I pass, I notice an orange notebook on the floor under the table where Paige was sitting. I pick it up and flip through a few pages, realizing it's her biology notes. The ink is purple, and her handwriting is perfect—not loopy or bubbly, but more like a traditional cursive, thin letters and straight lines. It doesn't seem like her. But then again, it does.

I walk out front to see if I can still see her along the sidewalk, but she's already gone. I'm sure she needs this for her final, and I half consider jogging down the roadway until I get to the walkway that leads to the sorority houses. But the lot is starting to fill up; there are a few regulars who I know can be difficult, so I turn back and join Sheila behind the counter, dropping the notebook on my school bag, hoping to reunite it with Paige soon.

The day drags, but I was able to squeeze out a little early and Chuck still offered to pay me for the hour. I'm moving my bag up higher on my shoulder when I feel my phone buzz. It's Casey.

CASEY: *Dude. Lunch. Now.*
ME: *I ate. Go ahead.*
CASEY: *You suck. I wanted to eat one of your sandwiches.*
ME: *I'm sure Sheila will make you one.*
CASEY: *U not there?*
ME: *Got off at 1.*
CASEY: *So...2nd lunch?*
ME: *Go feed your face. I've got some things.*
CASEY: *You always have things.*

I do always have things. What I should be doing is reviewing my history notes for my final exam tomorrow. But instead, I'm walking up the steps of the Delta House, an orange notebook in my hand. I feel like Prince Charming, but a really nerdy one—no glass slipper, just a laundry list of bones, intestinal mapping, and the phases of cellular division.

"Can I help you?" There's one girl sitting out on the porch, her feet curled up in her lap along with a heavy book. She has a pencil stuffed in a twist of hair piled up on her head.

"Yeah, uh...I'm looking for someone. Paige Owens?" Her eyes turn to slits quickly, and there's a flash of a menacing smile on her face. It's strange.

"She isn't here," she says.

I can't explain why exactly, but I don't believe her.

"Do you want me to tell her something?" she asks, closing her book and dropping it in the seat next to her. She stands and pulls her hair down, letting dark waves from the twist fall over her shoulders. She's trying to distract me. This is getting stranger.

64

"Just a notebook. She left it...somewhere," I leave that vague, suddenly not wanting to tell this chick how I know Paige—why I know Paige—where I saw Paige. "Anyhow, I think she needs it to study," I say, taking a step back as she approaches.

"You can leave it with me," she says.

Yeah, that's not happening.

"No, it's okay. I have to talk to her about something too," I say, making quick note of the disappointment on her face. Mission failed.

"Oh, well, I'm not sure when she'll be back. Maybe try later on today," she says, walking back to her seat, as if she's suddenly lost interest.

"I'll wait," I say, sitting on a wood bench at the other end of the porch. The girl freezes when I do. It takes her a few seconds to move again, and when she finally gets back to her seat, she smiles at me in a way that says I just ruined her day.

"Suit yourself," she says, one last attempt to make me leave.

I pull out my phone and check my text messages while I wait.

CASEY: *Sheila's sandwich was better than yours.*
CASEY: *No, it wasn't really. I said that to make you feel bad.*
CASEY: *Next time just make me one and leave it in the fridge.*
ME: *You just don't like paying for them.*
CASEY: *This is true.*
ME: *I'm going to start charging you.*
CASEY: *We're no longer friends.*
ME: *I knew you wanted me for my meat.*
CASEY: *That's what she said.*
CASEY: *Dude, where are you? I just stopped by your house?*
ME: *I have things.*
CASEY: *There's more to this. To be continued.*

I don't write back. Instead, I flip through the pages of the notebook while I wait, peering up every few seconds to check the status on the girl at the other end of the porch. When she seems lost again in her own studying, I slip the pencil out from the spiral part of the notebook and draw a few doodles in the margins of the first few pages.

Once I reach the middle pages, I start to draw arrows at a few of her graphs, making commentary on her diagrams.

"What is this supposed to be?" I write next to a penciled sketch that I think is a cell. I draw legs, a tail, and a pig nose on another, and add a few more artistic additions to the page until I've basically left her with an elementary sketch of various farm animals.

I spare one more glance to the girl, waiting for her to look up at me. When she doesn't, I write one more note to Paige.

Your own room, bathroom, regular meals, and someone who may or may not leave random works of art for you when you least expect it. Just...think about it, okay? You would actually be helping us out.

I pause for a few more seconds before finishing my note, adding in my phone number so she can call me. Now she has it twice. I read the note back to myself, each time thinking I sound more desperate, my attempt at humor becoming less and less humorous. By the fifth read, I poise the pencil's eraser over my phone number and get ready to erase.

"What are you doing here?" As if she just announced the end of time for my SATs, I put the pencil down, folding it in the pages of the notebook. I push my phone back in my pocket and stand, my feet squaring with Paige's as she steps out from the main door of the house. She looks so pissed at first, but then she glances over her shoulder at the girl I was just speaking to. This girl is way too invested in our conversation.

"Biology notes. Thought you might want them," I say, holding up the notebook with one hand, handing it to her, and glancing over her shoulder noticeably so she knows this conversation—it isn't private.

"Oh," she says, sucking in her bottom lip, smile tight. She got my message. "Thanks."

An awkward pause develops over the next several seconds, and it feels a lot like torture—no, it's actual torture—long seconds that tick by slowly, like the way everything feels when I'm sick with the flu and drugged on Nyquil. Paige is looking at me, but not quite in the eye, thankful I brought her notebook back, and perhaps also glad I gave her the option of moving into our house. She's also staring at me like she can't match up my roles as both *deli guy* and *dad*.

And then there are these little flits of moments in between where she's looking at me in a different way, like maybe she's looking at me and liking what she sees. Now that I've had that thought play out in my head though, in a full sentence, I feel pretty stupid.

"Yeah, so...I'm just gonna...go," I say, pointing over my shoulder, pushing my hands into my pockets and backing down the steps. I should turn around, but now I've walked backward for a good six or seven strides, and I know I'm at the stairs; I'm going to gamble I won't trip and fall on my ass in front of her. I could turn around completely, but I'm also keeping an eye on that other girl, the one very much interested in Paige.

Once I clear the steps, I spin around and pick up my speed, pulling my phone out to text Casey back:

ME: *Nothing more to anything. I'm all done. Just had to deal with some personal shit.*

It's sort of a lie, and Casey's been my best friend for years; he knows I have mountains of personal shit to deal with—I'm usually buried by it.

CASEY: *Whatever. I'm coming over for dinner later.*
ME: *See you at 5.*

When he doesn't write back, I figure he must have gotten busy. I move to put my phone in my back pocket, but stop when it buzzes one last time. I'm expecting a note from him, something snarky written back. But instead, the number is unknown. The small portion of the message I see tells me who it is.

Clearly you are not majoring in art. And your farm animals messed up my graph. Not cool.

I smile, and I smile big, and I feel stupid walking down the street with the growing grin on my face. But I can't help it; I love that she wrote back.

Damn. I'm actually glad she wrote back. I type a quick response.

ME: *Actually, I am an art major. That's a major style movement, and I can't believe you don't recognize it.*
PAIGE: *Yes, stick figures. Very expressive.*
ME: *Clearly you haven't been exposed to enough stick figures.*
PAIGE: *I've met you, haven't I?*
ME: *Ouch.*

I keep staring at the phone, waiting for her to write more, but almost a minute passes without hearing back from her. I'm close to our neighborhood by the time she writes back.

PAIGE: *Thanks.*

At that rate, she spent about eleven seconds on each letter she typed. I wonder how many messages she started and finished before settling on that one simple word.

ME: *You're welcome.*

I try to keep it simple back, but before I step inside my house—into my world of layers upon layers of responsibility, I add a little more.

ME: *And just think about it. I think you'd be happy here.*

There are no more messages from Paige for the rest of the night, and even though I keep looking, through dinner, through

Leah's lessons, through her bedtime preparation, through conversations with Casey where I pretend I'm not looking at anything at all, I know she's not writing back tonight.

But I have a feeling she will...eventually. And I smile about it.

Chapter 5

Paige

I think you'd be happy here.

I've read that last text from Houston maybe once an hour for the last twenty-four hours. I open it every time I get that feeling in my stomach saying I should run—abandon this plan and this version of college life. But then the other part of my brain kicks in and tells me to be stubborn because being a Delta, being *this* girl—is what I've always wanted.

This is what I wanted...

Funny how when I imagined this in high school, I wasn't sitting alone in my room, staring at my packed bags and wishing for time to speed up so I could return home faster.

I was going to take a shower, freshen up before I could finally call a cab to take me to the airport, but I had a feeling something was...*off.* I'm meticulous. It drives my sister nuts, which is weird, because I probably get this trait from my father, and Cass is so much more like our father. This one trait seems to be the one thing I got from him that she didn't.

When I grabbed my basket from under my sink, I noticed the bottles were out of order. Honestly, if someone took the time to put them back as they found them—I may have never noticed. But they didn't, whoever *they* are; and I did notice. I unscrewed the cap on my conditioner first, pouring a little over my fingertips, rubbing them together and sniffing. Everything there seemed normal, so I did the same with the shampoo. I thought I was being crazy until I felt the tingle on my palm.

It's been exactly thirty minutes since I've done the test on the small strip of hair I clipped from the back of my head, and the longer I wait, the more washed out that color becomes—the gold dissolving and whiteness taking over. The chemical smell is faint; whoever did this—they knew what they were doing.

Ashley walks by my room quickly while I'm cleaning off the small strip I've bound together, dipping it in a cup of cold water and holding it to the light just to confirm it's different.

"Hey, come in here," I say, not bothering to look at her as she passes. She'll either stop, or she won't. I half expect both.

"Oh...you're still here," she says; those words hit me in so many ways.

"Uh huh," I say, now flattening the strip of hair on a paper towel at my desk, folding it over to dry it well. I hold it up again against my own hair, noticing the massive difference in shades. Even though I'm not really focusing on Ashley's face in the background, I see her swallow. With a slow blink, I change my focus, reopening my eyes on her. I have found one of *they.*

"Bleach...or something else?" I ask. Ashley takes in a quick breath, preparing to lie.

"What?" she asks, exaggerating her pinched brow.

Looking to the side, I let out a sigh. She's never going to own up to her part, let alone throw Chandra under the bus with her. "Never mind," I say, tossing the hair back on my desk and turning my attention to my bags and belongings.

Ashley lingers for a few seconds, but finally lets her balance fall back toward the hall. Her coyness pisses me off. I can't help but cast one more line to see if I can catch her.

"Hey," I say, and she pauses. I walk toward her with my small basket of hair products, holding it out to her. Her eyes grow a little wider, and she sucks her bottom lip in. "My flight leaves soon, and I'm not packing these. It's expensive product...if you wanna use the rest."

Her eyes flash to mine, and for the first fraction of a second, there is panic. But frostiness takes over. "I think we both know I don't want any of that," she says, tapping her finger over the bottles. Her lip curls into a smirk, a sign she's telling me without telling me—giving me a warning, and also letting me know whose side she's on.

I breathe in deeply, filling my chest, my lips pushed together tightly, and my eyes never once leaving hers. Her newfound power and confidence trying to stand against mine. "No, Ashley. I suppose you're right," I say, letting my lips slide into a smirk. "You don't want any of this."

Her pupils give her away. I know as tough as she's being in front of me, she's scared shitless of choosing wrong. I don't like her enough to tell her it's too late, she better cling to Chandra with all she's got. Once you burn me, you don't get back in. That's how *my* circle works.

She slides her hand along the edge of my desk as she turns to leave, pulling the knob of my door behind her, and shutting me off from the world on the other side. I don't let my smile slip until I hear the door click. But when it does, I allow myself to feel the rejection.

My fingers work on their own accord, scrolling through my messages, landing on Houston's, and hitting VOICE DIAL before I'm able to really think it through. By about the fifth ring, I'm aware of what I'm doing, and I'm feeling foolish—readying my arm to pull my phone away from my head so I can hang up before leaving a really desperate message.

"Hey—" Houston answers, his voice sounding a little out of breath.

"Hi, sorry," I say, not really sure why I feel the need to apologize. I was ready for his voicemail, for hanging up. Now I feel pitiful. "I didn't think you'd pick up."

"Paige? Can I call you back in just a few minutes? I'm sort of in the middle...just...I'll call you right back, okay?" His voice is partly muffled while he juggles his phone and whatever else.

"Yeah, sure. I'm leaving soon, so if you get a chance..." I say, before he talks over my words.

"Great. Thanks. Call you back," he says, ending the call barely after his last word.

I stare at my phone in my hands. The time stamp reads 27 SECONDS. I sit on the edge of my bed and let my eyes wander to the towel at my desk and the science experiment from moments before. I can't stay here. *They* will never stop making it clear they don't want me here. When Houston calls back, I'll tell him I'd like the room, and I'll move my things. I'll come back early from holiday break to do it. And I'll find a way to talk to my parents about it—to make it okay. Then I'll fix my relationship with my sister.

I'll find my way. I always do.

These thoughts circle in my head for the next three hours until finally I can call for the cab to take me to the airport. When I hang up, I scroll back to those twenty-seven seconds from the morning and delete the record of the call. Then, I roll my bags down the hall, down the stairs, and out the door of the Delta House.

Houston

"Dude, it smells like vomit in here," Casey says, his arm folded across his nose as he steps into the kitchen with a small bag of groceries.

"She just threw up again. Sorry, I haven't had a chance to really get the smell from that last round out of the house yet. I think maybe I'm immune to it," I say, rinsing out the yellow bucket that I threw up in when I was a kid and have now passed along to my daughter. What a gift.

"So you just, what...like...hose that shit out?" His voice is still muffled in his sleeve.

"Yeah. Didn't you throw up when you were a kid, man? Is this so foreign to you?" I ask, wiping down the inside with a dry paper towel, and setting the bucket on the floor, then unhooking the plastic bag from Casey's thumb.

"My mom wouldn't let us leave the bathroom until we were done spewing," he says, letting his arm fall away, but only for a second while he speaks. I chuckle and roll my eyes.

"I guess I don't like the idea of making her sleep on the bathroom tile," I say, pulling out a packet of soda crackers, removing two, and placing them on a napkin.

"So what is it, like the flu or something?" Casey asks as he follows me back up the steps, bucket and crackers in my hands.

"I think so. She's been at it since two this morning. I had to call in to work, which sucks ass," I whisper, not wanting Leah to hear as we get closer to her room.

"Nah man, you're looking at this wrong. You got a sick day without being sick. When she's napping, you should totally hit the Xbox," he says, finally letting his arm drop. Casey's gotten used to it too.

"All I see is six less hours of pay I'm going to get this week," I say as I lean into Leah's door to slide it open.

"Un-co Casey!" Leah says, coughing when she screams Casey's name, her voice hoarse from being sick.

"Take it easy, kiddo. Don't overdo it," he says, reaching out his hand and ruffling Leah's hair, which is wild and juts in a million directions. We didn't really do the *brushing* thing today.

Her face bunches when I set the napkin on her lap. "I don't like those," she whispers, her voice lacking the enthusiasm it had when she greeted my friend.

"I know. But here's the deal," I say, sitting down on the bed next to her, rolling up my sleeve and resting my forearm on her forehead, feeling for a fever. We've been lucky so far, and she's still cool now. "If you can eat two of these and not throw up for..." I look at my watch, trying to think of a safe, but arbitrary time, "thirty minutes..." Leah looks up at me, her bottom lips sucked into her mouth so far that her chin is white. "I'll let you try a sugar cookie next."

Leah grabs a cracker fast, stuffing the entire thing in her mouth at once.

"Slowly. Eat them slowly. Remember...they have to stay *in the tummy*," I say, standing as she moves on to the second cracker, this time taking nibbles, her eyes wide on me with hope. She'll get a cookie anyway, because that face does me in. But I'm exhausted, so this throwing up thing needs to stop too.

"I'll come check on you in thirty minutes, okay? Watch some of your show," I say, pressing START on the iPad, propping it on her night table and backing out of the room, but not before leaving the bucket by her bedside along with about a million prayers that she doesn't need it any more.

"So...does that mean you have cookies?" Casey asks. I stare at him. "What? I'm just saying if you have cookies, then...maybe...I can have one?"

"Do you have food of your own? I mean, like...could you even survive without me?" I say, moving back to the stairs.

"I have food, douchebag," he says, paused at the top of the steps. "I just like yours better."

I take a few steps, then something halts me. I don't know why suddenly the empty room to the right catches my attention, especially since I've walked by it at least forty times since Leah woke me up before the sun was up, and another twenty since Paige called hours ago, but it hits me now.

"Shit!" I grit through my teeth, rushing down the stairs to the charging station next to our refrigerator. My phone isn't even on. It was so dead when I got off the phone with her the first time, I plugged it in and turned it off, thinking I'd give it a good charge and call her back when Leah was napping. Only Leah never napped, and I never called. "Goddamn it!"

It takes my phone *way too* long to power up, but it finally does. I sort through my missed calls and text messages. Nothing from Paige, just an update from my mom that she's only putting in a half-day at her job at the church and will be home to take over Leah in an hour.

I move to the call log and redial Paige, something I promised to do...*shit!*...five hours ago now! The phone rings twice before going right to voicemail. I hang up and dial again, only to get the same result.

"Fuuuuuuuuuck," I groan, tossing the phone into the middle of the counter. I flip open the lid on the plastic container and pull out a cookie. When Casey's eyebrows light up, I hand him one too.

With his mouth full, and sugar coating his lips, he finally talks. "Gonna fill me in on that little dramatic display right there?" he asks, taking another bite and leaning into the table.

"I was supposed to call someone back about renting out the room, but I forgot. Kinda got into the whole vomit-bucket routine and lost track of time," I say, leaning my head back against one of the cabinets and shutting my eyes. When I open them, Casey's reaching back into the cookie tub. He arches a brow and shrugs when I catch him, then closes the lid and takes another bite, getting comfortable on one of our kitchen stools.

Casey's staring at me while he chews, his mouth doing that annoying thing he's always done where he waits on the verge of laughter. He used to look at me like that across the room in grade school until I finally broke out into laughter. I'd always get in trouble, and that fuck nut would turn around and pretend he was doing homework. I reach across the counter and put my palm on his forehead, pushing him off balance from the stool.

"Quit looking at me like that. It's annoying," I say.

"Like what?" he says, still *almost* laughing.

"Like...like a creepy asshole," I say.

"This is about that girl you want to move in, huh?" he says, finally letting one chuckle out—one big, loud, punctuated chuckle.

I take the rest of his cookie from his hand. "It's about me blowing an easy three hundred a month we really could use right now. That's what this is about," I say, throwing the rest of his cookie away. I know it's a waste, but dickhead doesn't deserve one of Mom's cookies right now.

"First off, dude? What the fuck?" he says, actually pulling the cookie out of the trash and inspecting it before deciding it's still good and eating the rest whole. "And second, you could rent that room in a day if you put a listing up—so don't give me that shit."

I look at him, processing what he said. I don't respond, because he might be a little bit right, and that only pisses me off more. I run my hand over my chin and look to my phone, pulling it back in my hand and scrolling to Paige's number.

"You're right," he's already grinning. "But it's not about *the girl*. It's about the fact that I don't like being an asshole. I made an offer to her, and then kind of blew her off. I just don't want her to think I'm a dick. That's all."

I dial her number, ignoring the penetrating stare of my friend. I don't care what he thinks, and I don't care if he's a little bit right. Even though, yeah...there's a part of me that sort of likes the idea of Paige living here, because she's a hot girl who I find interesting—but mostly I like the idea of a friendly, non-threatening girl who I don't mind being near Leah or alone with my mom. The fact that she needs a place to go—badly from what I could tell—is also sort of important.

Her phone goes to voicemail again quickly. I turn away from Casey so I can concentrate. "Hey, Paige..." I pause. Shit, I don't really know what to say next. And Casey is listening. And now I've left about five seconds of silence on the phone. "Sorry, I...got distracted with something. Not earlier, I mean right now, when I just stopped talking. Well, now and earlier. That's why I didn't call back. Leah's sick. That's what I meant. Anyhow, I'm sorry I had to hang up so fast. Did you want to talk about the room? It's still yours...if you want it. Just let me know. So...yeah. Call me. Oh, this is Houston."

Fucking weak. My cheeks hurt from a fifth-grade brand of embarrassment, and it only gets worse when I turn around and Casey has his thumb and pinky finger stretched out like a phone. "So, like, totally call me, okay?" he says, mocking me.

"Shut up and eat another cookie," I say. He wastes no time, pulling out one more and biting nearly half away. I hear Leah clapping upstairs, and I know that means she's feeling better. It's only been about ten minutes, but I guess throwing up a cookie is a lot more fun than throwing up Saltines and Sprite. I pull a cookie out for her, putting it on a plate, then pour a small glass of soda, and start to walk back up the stairs.

"Oh, this is Houston by the way," Casey says through a full mouth, laughing before he can get the entire insulting sentence out. I don't even acknowledge him. I know he's just warming up, and I'll have plenty of opportunities to say something to his face when I'm done with Leah.

Paige

Dad picked me up from the airport. That was good. I'm sure Mom has worked herself up trying to figure out why I wanted to come home early, dreaming up theories and worst-case scenarios. She does this with Cass more than me, probably because she worries over my sister's health. Getting carried away is kind of her thing.

I had a few hours at home alone when Dad dropped me off. He headed back into the office, probably dealing with the assault case for my sister. I welcomed the alone time. Here, in my room, where I could erase the last six months and pretend I was still me—the girl I was before everything got so fucked up and twisted.

I haven't been good at staying in touch with my friends from high school. Most of them stayed in California. I was going to stay in California...until I sacrificed everything for Cass. I think I blamed her for a while. Maybe I still do. But I know ultimately I made the choice to go to Oklahoma; I made all of the choices that got me where I am now.

Looking at my phone, I hover over Lexi's number. She and I were best friends in high school, and she went to Long Beach for college. I know she's in town. I text her.

Just got back for the holidays. Would love to see you! Call me and let's hang out! XO

The feeling she's not going to call sinks into my chest quickly, and I instantly regret messaging her. When I toss it on my bed, my phone buzzes with a message. I grab it with hope, but it isn't a text message. It's a voicemail. I flip to the missed calls, and see there's three from Houston. I'm not sure why I didn't hear it ring, or maybe I'm just now getting the message from the time my phone was on *airplane mode*. Either way, I'm glad I didn't pick up. I may be starting to waver on my decision to move in with him.

His message is short, and sort of...weird. He sounds flustered, which only adds to my own anxiety. By the time my mom gets home, I have a raging headache and my neck is stiff from scrunching my shoulders up to my head with stress. I'm still happy to see her; her hug feels like a soft blanket, making me feel safe—if only for a moment.

"How was your flight?" she asks, letting go, standing back, and holding me by both arms, like she's taking an inventory to make sure I didn't come back with broken parts. *I did, just nothing she can see.*

"Good, no turbulence," I say. My mom smiles. She hates turbulence. Add that to her long list of things she freaked out about when Cass and I told her we were both going to Oklahoma.

"Oh, thank god," she says, hooking her bags on the rack by the door and kicking her shoes from her feet. My mom always brings home samples of things from the store. She has this grand idea of working on new display items and jewelry at night, but never really does any of it—she just takes the bags back and forth. Cass and I used to pull a few of the beads out at night, when she was asleep, to make things for our friends. Right now, the familiarity of her routine is comforting.

"We were thinking of going to dinner tonight—maybe to the pier, since your sister doesn't like seafood as much as we do. What do you think?" she asks, and I start to answer with a smile when my phone chimes in the distance.

"Dinner sounds great," I say over my shoulder, moving to my room to check my phone. There's a part of me that both hopes and dreads another message from Houston. When I see it's just a return from Lexi, I'm equally conflicted—disappointment...meet relief.

OMG you are such a rescue. Please. Mall. Now. Parents making me crazy. Pick you up in five?

I laugh lightly as I read her words. As much as things have changed, nothing has changed. Lexi's parents are the kind of couple that should have divorced a decade ago, only they're stubborn and don't want to be labeled failures. Instead, they hang on and fight and exist in an awful marriage. Lexi used to spend the night at our house a lot. Whenever I went to her house, her parents would make these little remarks to one another, passive-aggressive things since they didn't want to fight in front of company. I kind of think the childish picking at one another was worse, though.

I write her back.

Give me 10 mins. Mom just got home. But I can go. Excited to see you!

For a minute, I feel normal. I change quickly, putting on my skinny jeans and my favorite tight, black sweater so I can wear my new boots. I didn't bring them to campus with me the first time. I wasn't sure how cold the weather would be, or what snow would be like there. But now that I've lived there, I think I can wear these without much trouble.

My mom's smile falls a little when she sees me, and I feel bad leaving so quickly. But I need a dose of a real friend—a friend from before. There are some things that my girlfriends can do that my parents can't.

"I'm sorry. I won't be long. And I'll be home for dinner. It was Lexi; she needs to *escape*," I say, pulling my purse over my shoulder and moving close enough to my mom to grab a hold of her arm and swing it. She squeezes me in return and smiles easily again.

"Okay, I understand. But make sure you save some time for your dad and me, okay?" she says.

"I promise," I say, crossing my heart and leaning in to kiss her on the cheek. Truth is, my mom is really my only other friend right now.

True to form, Lexi shows up right at ten minutes. I skip down the driveway to her car. She's still driving the red Camaro she got for her sixteenth birthday, and the top is down. I pull the hair tie from my wrist and fasten my hair by my neck. Hopefully it will survive Lexi's driving.

The ride to the mall is spent catching up. Lexi joined a sorority at Long Beach, and she's also gotten involved with a few clubs on campus. She was always into things like student council and the social committees in high school, so nothing she says is a surprise. She has a boyfriend—some guy named Curtis. She met him at the first sorority mixer. I start to tell her about Carson, about how I met a guy too, but then I stop short, remembering everything my life is in Oklahoma. It's not something I want to brag about, so instead, I lie.

"I haven't really met anyone," I say, shrugging. But for some reason, at that very moment, all I can think about is Houston.

"Well, you will. College is amazing, isn't it?" she says, turning the car sharply to the right, fitting into a spot I'm fairly sure isn't really a spot.

"It's pretty great," I respond, keeping my face from her while I exit the car. I can feign happiness in my words, but I don't think I'm up for making happy faces.

We spend the first hour trying out new makeup samples. I sprayed my wrists with my favorite Chanel, but stopped there. I don't like tainting the good scent with a bunch of crappy ones—I won't even smell something I'm not sure I'm going to like. I have a feeling my parents bought me the new set for Christmas, so I buy a few new lip colors, but nothing else.

The afternoon is easy—like old times. And when we're trying on boots at our favorite shoe store, I realize I'm actually smiling—from joy.

"I wish I would have stayed in California," I let slip out. My eyes fall down to my hands working on a zipper for a knee-high pair of gray leather boots.

"You're a good sister," Lexi says, touching her hand to my arm. I wasn't shy about telling everyone why I was going to Oklahoma. Paige, the martyr—giving up her dreams for her sister's. Six months ago, having Lexi stroke my arm because she feels bad for me and is impressed with this sacrifice I'm making...that would have been enough. That would have satisfied me. Today, I don't feel worthy.

"So, do I get to meet this Curtis guy?" I ask, changing the subject. There's a flash of something in her face; I can't tell for sure, but I think...I think it has to do with me.

"He lives in San Diego. I'm not even sure if I'll see him over the break," she says, her focus back to the box of black strappy heels she's repackaging. I hold her gaze, willing her to look at me from the periphery, but she doesn't budge. She's avoiding me, because she knows I can tell when she's lying.

"Right," I say, taking in a deep breath and exhaling slowly while I let my teeth saw at the inside of my bottom lip. Six months ago, I wouldn't even hesitate. I'd call her out right in front of me—ask her what she's hiding. But now...I'm a little tired of sleuthing and finding out the ugly things really going on in people's heads. I decide to let Lexi off the hook, and we step out from the store into the main area of the mall. The closer we get to the next store, the more I dismiss the feeling from moments before.

And then we run into more familiar faces. Courtney and Steph, the other half of our regular crew—the four of us inseparable only months before. Now, they look at me with what I can only describe as contempt, shifting their attention to Lexi, dismissing me with short waves of hello.

I'm standing on the outside of their very small circle, smiling and pretending they're engaging me as they discuss some party happening in the Valley, plans for New Year's, the state of Lexi's parents' ever-crumbling marriage, and then one of them makes an error.

"You should totally bring Curtis to the party, since he's staying with you," Steph says, only realizing she messed up when the silence practically chokes the other two.

I've heard when people leave the earth's atmosphere, there's a thin layer of space and time where they're both inside and out—that small moment where they have a chance to stay or to abandon their world behind them. I'm in that moment now. I could continue to pretend—go home and never text or call Lexi

82

again, letting my curiosity over why everyone is awkward and dismissive toward me eat away from the inside until there was nothing recognizable left. Or, I could find that last scrap of me that's truly *me* and open my mouth. Either way, I'd be burning bridges, but by standing up for myself, at least I'd be going out with one hell of a fire.

"Yes, Lexi," I say, twisting my head to face my now former-friend with a snap, catching her by surprise. She shouldn't be surprised; she has no idea how weak I've become. This version of me—this is the only one she knows. "Bring Curtis. You were just saying how I should meet him soon."

There's no mistaking the expression on my face, the blaze in my eyes, and the word *bitch* that I'm holding back behind my newly-glossed and red lips. Lexi knows it. She's caught, but she's not going to cause a scene. She shakes her head with a polite smile and agrees with me.

Courtney makes an excuse to leave, and Steph hugs Lexi from the side, practically pushing her in front of me to shield herself, afraid I might want some form of affectionate farewell too. *Relax, Steph. I don't want to hug you either. If I did, I'd likely choke you.*

Lexi walks a few paces in front of me, watching our *friends* fade into the crowd and eventually another boutique. She stops, knowing her time is up. When she turns to face me, I don't give her a chance to feed me a line.

"Tell me what that was all about. Tell me the truth—because you know I will see your lies. Tell me here, in public, right now, because I don't care if you're uncomfortable. I don't want you to get to put off *whatever the hell* you can't seem to pull out of your throat any longer," I say, my voice syrupy-sweet as I keep the smile on my mouth for the benefit of the crowded mall around us.

Lexi's posture slumps, her eyes terrified.

"Spill it," I say, my fingers tingling like they want to hit something. I've never hit anything, well...not hard anyhow. But right now...I want to punch someone.

"We all know," she says finally, and the way she relaxes, the breath leaving her chest in a whoosh, it feels like those words should be enough. Somehow, I'm supposed to know what it is *they know,* and the weight of that makes me even more agitated. Because I don't know shit. And if it's something I don't know, then it's either about my sister or...

"We saw it..." she says, her eyebrows raised as she leans forward to me to whisper. "Your...*porn.*"

You have to be fucking kidding me!

"My...I'm sorry. Did you say...*porn?*" I'm actually laughing with nerves and fury as I speak.

Lexi tugs on my arm, moving us to a small cluster of seats in the middle of the mall, pushing me down into a chair nestled right next to the one she takes. I'm kind of pissed that she's manhandling me, but I'm also freaking numb as hell, so I go along with it.

"I don't think it's online, but Paige...what were you thinking?" She honestly believes I'm in porn.

"Ah...ha..." I start to laugh, looking around to see who's watching us. Nobody cares, and no one has turned their heads once. Porn. The one girl—not related to me—who has known me longest, thinks I'm an adult-film star.

"This is serious, Paige," she says, her brow pinched, her face in *intervention* mode. I hate the way she keeps saying my name for emphasis. She looks ridiculous. This whole thing...it's ridiculous.

"Lexi," I say her name back with a little bite, and she flinches. "I am not, let me repeat, *am not* in a porno film.

"I saw it Paige," she says, leaning her head to one side and affecting pity. I hold her stare for a few long seconds, the crowd behind her blurring out as women rush by with bags and high schoolers ditching class for the day swear and push one another. And then I realize...I *remember.*

"Oh. My. God!" I say in a short and panicked voice, standing and looking around. Still...nobody notices me. I sit back down and let my face fall into my hands.

Rush week was hell, and Chandra made us do a lot of embarrassing things. One of them was strip for the Sigma guys, and she filmed it. It was sort of innocent, and we only went down to our bra and panties—but Chandra filmed it. And last month, with Carson, he might have filmed...*something else*. And fuck!

"Who showed you this? Where was it? How did they show you? Who gave it to them..." I watch her shake her head as she tries to sort through my barrage of questions.

"Steph goes to UCLA, and she lives on Tabitha Snyder's floor. I guess Tab knows your sister and some chick on Cass's soccer team is her cousin or something? Cass didn't show her. I don't think Cass even knows, if that's what you're worried about, but that other girl had the video and emailed it to her. She told her it was *going around.*"

I stand before Lexi's done talking, and she stands with me, pulling her purse close to her body like somehow now that she's told me the sordid secret going around about me, we're in danger. *Look out! Muggers coming out of the woodwork because there's a stupid fucking rumor floating around about me.*

I feel her hand reach for the back of my shirt, and I shrug her off.

"Paige? Why? Did you need money or something? I mean, how much money can you really make from something like that?" I note the way she's looking at me while she talks. I think there's a part of her concern that is genuine. But she's also made it clear she'd cut me loose in a heartbeat to save her own reputation—even if it meant letting me fall down a cliff.

"No, Lexi. I didn't get money for it," I say, my answer clipped on purpose. She's waiting with her mouth ajar for me to fill her in more. Maybe she's waiting for the big protest, for my explanation—which I actually do have. I probably should defend myself, but I just don't feel like it. I don't think Lexi deserves it, and I don't think it would do any good.

I turn and leave Lexi behind, calling my mom to come pick me up at a restaurant a block away. When she comes, her face painted with that same worried expression I've seen too much of today, I snap at her and tell her Lexi ditched me to go smoke pot and she should just be happy that her daughter doesn't do shit like that.

Tabitha went to our high school, and she played on the team there with Cass. She's also Chandra's cousin—and like Chandra, Tabitha never really cared for my sister. So I'm sure she was happy to help spread a lie about me, and I'm sure Chandra told her it would hurt Cass.

When we get back to the house, I do a frenzied search online for myself, for the video. Nothing comes up, but now I know it might. The threat is real. I search through Tabitha's Facebook posts—glad she's too stupid to keep her page private. When I see pictures of her and Chandra, I feel my blood boil. Without waiting, I pull my phone into my hand and type a message to Houston.

Got your message. Yes. I'll take the room.

Chapter 6

Houston

Sounds good.

I wrote that to Paige a week ago, and then nothing. I should probably find out when she's coming back to campus, when she'll be here, when I should start her lease. Lease! I need to send her paperwork for that, too. Not that I don't trust her, but my mom insists on lease papers ever since we had a freshman guy leave in the middle of the night two years ago—owing us six hundred bucks.

I need you to sign a lease...

I look at my text and delete it before sending. That sounds cold. I don't want to sound cold, but I don't want to sound...I don't know...flirty? That's why I haven't written anything since. If she's really moving in, then things need to stay a certain way. But I also don't want her to think I'm just her landlord now. But I guess that's really all I am.

Hey. When you have a sec, I need to get some lease papers to you. Email?

I hit SEND and quit worrying about it, returning to my empty shopping cart and the list my mom pulled together of things to get for Christmas. I missed the visit to Santa this year, so Mom took notes. It seems Leah is into Barbie now. Last year, she was all about trucks and things with wheels. I understand that stuff. Barbie, though—that was more of a Bethany thing. She would have loved this shopping list.

I'm standing in the aisle labeled BARBIE ACCESSORIES when my phone buzzes with a call. It's Paige, and I'm a little surprised she's calling instead of just texting back.

"Hey, what's up?" I answer, tucking the phone in the crook of my neck while I read some package of various Barbie shoes and purses. They're all made of plastic, and the entire thing costs forty bucks. Seems like a rip-off.

"You needed lease info. Remember?" I smirk when she speaks, the irony that I'm looking at college-girl Barbie, and talking to one on the phone, strikes me as funny.

"Right. I kinda thought I could just email it to you?" I ask, picking up a pink car, wondering if maybe I can get away with something like this instead. "Hey...would Barbie rather have a bunch of plastic boots or a Corvette?"

"What?" Paige sounds confused, and irritated. Her phone is breaking up, and I can tell she's out somewhere doing something. Whatever, she called me.

"I'm shopping for Leah, and she wants Barbie stuff. But it all looks kind of, I don't know...lame," I put the car back when I realize the doors don't even open.

"Right, anyhow..." she says. "So can you just fill it out with me over the phone? I can sign when I get there. I don't really have a scanner or whatever here. I'm at my parents' house."

"Sure, yeah. I guess. I'll call you later and go through the questions. It's all pretty simple," I say.

"Great," she says. I wait for her to hang up, but when I realize she hasn't, I feel kind of oddly glad. "So...that's a *no* on the Corvette?"

Paige huffs into the phone, and it makes me laugh. "Is there a horse?" she asks.

"No, it's not those little pony things. Just Barbie," I say, my eyes glazing over at the row of dolls. They all look exactly the same, just different dresses. It's weird.

"Uhm, I know that. I meant Barbie's horse. Barbie has a horse. Is there one of those?" She's insistent.

"I don't know. Hang on," I say, kneeling and scanning down the row of pink and yellow and purple things, until I finally come across a horse and carriage. "Yeah! There is one!"

"That's what you get," she says.

"Just this? You sure? I shouldn't back it up with like," I pick up another accessory pack, "*Barbie's Mission to Mars* set or *Barbie Loves Dogs* vet set?" This marketing is amazing. Does this shit really work?

"If you want. But the horse will be it. That's the best gift she'll get. Trust me on this," she says, and I look at the other things in my hands and decide to believe her, putting them all back and tossing the horse and carriage set in the basket and moving on to clothes.

"Awesome, thanks. You just saved me an hour and probably a hundred bucks," I say.

"Well, that's the toy I always wanted, so..." Her voice trails off, but I hang on. Something about what she says makes me happy and sad at the same time. The silence lasts for a few seconds, and then she shakes it off. "All right, so call me when you want to get that info...for the lease."

"Yeah, okay," I say, wondering if I should say more. It doesn't matter though, because Paige hangs up first.

After another thirty minutes at the store, I manage to find princess pajamas, some frilly hair things to go along with the horse, and a wand—Leah wanted a wand. It's not much, but my mom always makes a few things to go along with the stuff we put under the tree for Leah. She's turning five soon, so we can still kind of get away with small stuff.

I sneak the bag inside quickly, managing to get upstairs without Leah noticing me. I surprise her when I come back down and put my hands over her eyes at the kitchen table.

"Boo!" I say, and she jumps, but immediately giggles.

"Where were you?" she asks. I flip my eyes to my mom with a smile.

"I had work," I say, winking.

"No you didn't. You're not wearing your shirt," she says. Damn my girl is smart.

"True. It was a special workday. I just had to help with something, so I didn't have to stay long," I lie.

"Oh," she says, turning her attention back to the small cheese crackers on a plate in front of her.

"One day, you're not going to get off so easily," my mom whispers in my ear as she pats my back and leaves the kitchen. I lean against the counter and watch my daughter pick up each cracker and inspect it before eating it. She's so curious about everything. She's so much like her mom.

I need to prep her for someone new moving in. We've had five roommates since we decided to start renting out the spare room, and each time it takes Leah about two weeks to finally sleep at night. Change makes her nervous. Even though she was barely a month old when her mom died, I think there's a part of her that always thinks about it. The slightest changes to her routine seem to send her anxiety up.

I pull up a chair to talk to her about it, reaching over and grabbing one of her crackers and stuffing it in my mouth.

"Heyyyyy," she says through a laugh that turns into a cough. "You didn't ask."

"May I please have a cracker?" I say with a full mouth. Leah giggles and nods *yes*.

"So I need to talk to you about something," I say, walking my fingers over to her plate again to steal another cracker. She stands her own fingers up and walks them over to me, ready to face off. I grab her hand instead and pull it to my mouth with a gobbling noise, then I kiss her tiny knuckles. "We're going to have a new roommate. You'll like her; it's a girl this time."

I'm hoping that she'll do better with a girl, that somehow it will be less threatening.

"Okay," she says, sucking her bottom lip in. She pushes her plate a few inches away, sliding it slowly. I can tell she's already getting stressed.

"Her name is Paige," I say, suddenly struck with an idea. Paige might hate me for this, but... "and guess what?"

"What?" Leah whispers.

"She looks just like Barbie."

Leah's eyes widen a little, and her smile slowly pushes into her cheeks making a small dimple on either side.

"Really?" she asks.

"Really," I say. No, not *really*. But she's pretty close.

"Okay," Leah says, reaching over to the table and pulling her plate close again.

I stand and push my chair in, but before I leave, I reach at her plate and snatch one more cracker, stuffing it in my mouth fast. Leah turns to look at me with her cheeks puffed and her hands on her hips, but she can't keep the look up for long, giving way to laughter in seconds.

I head upstairs and push the door closed, locking it behind me so I can pull the bag of things I bought today out from under my bed. I let my mom do the wrapping for obvious reasons. If these things are supposed to be from Santa, then the wrapping probably shouldn't be done with painter's tape and staples.

I slip the horse out from the bag and prop it on my knees. It has pink hair, and it comes with a brush it claims is "made of stars." The eyes are purple, and everything about this toy reminds me of Paige.

Leah is going to love it.

Paige

Cass and I managed to shop together last night, on Christmas Eve. It's been our thing for years. Our dad started it, always waiting until the last minute to buy something for our mom. He used to take us along when we were little. We'd binge on treats at the department stores and my dad would bribe us to keep going with hot cocoa. He hated the crowds, but we loved it.

By the time we started high school, Dad would just give us money and drop us off to get everything. He was happy not to have to do it. When we both got our licenses, we started driving ourselves. I was worried that this year would be the first time we skipped. But yesterday afternoon, Cass came into my room and asked me what time we should leave.

We've talked. It started when I picked her up from the airport. That car ride back to the house was so quiet and strange. It actually hurt to be close to her. *That's probably guilt I felt.* Whatever it was, it all boiled to the surface, and I let everything out when we got home. I admitted I used to want to hate her. I did. There were so many times when I thought it would be easier to have a sister I didn't love—one I didn't want to defend. I stopped short of telling her I sometimes wondered what it would have been like if we weren't twins. Not if she weren't born at all, just if she were born later...or earlier.

That conversation—it wasn't good. But it was honest. It was a start. And we've talked more. Not much, but a little. And never about anything very important. She doesn't talk about the assault, and I don't talk about Chandra. There's so much she doesn't know, but right now things between her and me are...well, they are what they are.

I got a text from Carson last night. He wished me a Merry Christmas. I'm pretty sure he was drunk. It was a picture of him out with his brother at some bar, their shirts off, and beers in their hands. He said he missed me, whatever that means. He misses me. Right. That's why he shares private videos of me with my enemies. You know...to get over *missing me* so fucking much.

I glance one more time at the picture he sent. His abs are nice, so at least there's that. I slide through a few more texts, and I'm back to the short string of messages between Houston and me. Somehow, I hit his contact button, and my phone dials him. *Maybe there's a part of me that meant to call.*

By the time it's ringing, it's too late to hang up, so I let it go. On the fifth ring, I'm looking at my phone screen, ready to hang up. I'll blame a purse dial if he sees this. I'm about to bail when he answers.

"Hey! Happy Christmas!" His immediate answer, his overly holly-jolly voice—it makes me smile at first, but I catch myself, force my lips back to serious.

"Hey, I'm sorry. I hope I'm not interrupting family time," I say, looking at the clock. It's almost six here, so that makes it almost eight in Oklahoma. I didn't need to talk to him now; this could have waited until tomorrow. Or the next day. I don't know why I called now really.

"No, it's good. Leah just went to bed, and my mom is still at my aunt's house—we do a big Christmas thing over there...lasts all day," he says.

We spent the day here, exchanging gifts we already knew we got one another. Cass made me a bracelet, something she said she made months ago—back when she *wanted* to make me things. I gave her a gift card to her favorite Pilates place. I bought it three days ago. I'm kind of envious over Houston's Christmas.

"I thought if you had a second we could take care of that lease thing. Is now okay?" I ask.

"Uh...now?" he says, and I can hear him laugh a little under his breath. "Sure...uhm, give me a second. I kind of don't have anything out. But, I can log on to my computer. Just..."

My cheeks are hot and my chest feels tight. I think maybe I'm embarrassed. It's Christmas, and I'm calling him to take care of *lease* paperwork. I'm calling him because I'm lonely. Because my sister's boyfriend is coming to stay with us in a few days, and she has someone who loves her—*really* loves her.

I have Houston—my knight and shining landlord.

"I'm sorry. I guess it's Christmas. I just like to take care of things. We can do this later this week," I start to backtrack, but he interrupts.

"No, no. Here, I got it. Hang on, let me sit down," he says. I hear his door close behind him, and I wonder where he is. Is he in his room? In his bed? I bet he wears one of those old-man pajama sets, the flannel kind with a matching shirt and pants.

"Current address? Did you hear me?" He must have asked once before, when I was mentally making him less attractive.

"Oh, right. I guess...do you want the Delta address?" I ask.

"Your parents' address is fine. It's just so my mom is comfortable. Really, whatever works," he says.

We go through a short list of questions, filling out my address, various income things, which all point back to my parents. After about ten minutes of me talking, and Houston typing, we're done.

Done. I can go back to flipping through celebrity magazines in the living room with my mom, spending Christmas trying to chip away at the ice I've formed between my sister and me.

"Did she like her horse?" My question takes him a little off guard. There really wasn't a segue. I just didn't want to hang up yet. Even *not* talking to Houston is better than *not* talking to nobody.

"The horse?" he asks, but quickly following my question. "Oh! Yeah! You were so right on with that. She's sleeping with it."

"Good," I say, and I let myself smile, a little proud. I'm like a Christmas elf.

There's a long silence that settles in again, and I start to get that sinking sensation in my stomach. I'm intruding, and he's just being polite. Me calling—*on Christmas!*—this weird conversation, it's going to make it weird when I move in.

"I told her you were coming to live with us. And there's something you should know," he says, finally filling the void. I'm a little thrown by what he says. He already has a daughter, and his wife...she's...*gone.* I'm not sure what else there could possibly be.

"I maybe sort of, kind of, told her that you...well..." I hear him laugh a little under his breath.

"Jesus! I what?" I say loudly.

"I kind of told her you were Barbie," he says, letting his laugh take over and spill through the phone.

"Nice," I say and on instinct lean over the edge of my bed to look into the mirror anchored to the back of my door, I run my fingers through my hair, letting the curls fall from my hand one at a time. *Barbie.*

"I'm sorry," he's still laughing, but less. "I wanted her to be comfortable with you. New people make her nervous."

"But she met me. At the store," I say, standing now and twisting to the side. I'm posing—like *Barbie*—with my right hand to the side, fingers stuck together but my thumb out.

"Yeah, I know. But she might not remember, and she gets a little freaked out..."

"It's okay," I interrupt. I don't want him to feel bad. Now that I'm over the shock, it's actually sweet that he wants to make his daughter comfortable with me. "I guess I do kind of look like Barbie."

"Nah, not really. I just panicked," he says.

A silence settles in again, but this time it feels different, and it makes me smile.

"So...Paige..." I can hear him relax, and there's something extra in the tone of his voice that makes me bite my lip. My door is still open, so I get up to close it, feeling suddenly protective over this conversation.

"So...Houston," I mimic his inflection, and he chuckles— that raspy tired laugh I remember from our late-night studying. It's probably not good that I remember that sound. And it's *definitely* not good that I'm chewing my fingernail. It's not good because I'm pretty sure we're flirting.

"How was your Christmas?" His question is so warm, so genuine; it makes my eyes sting. I've been holding on so hard— trying to fight off things hitting me from all directions—this simple question from Houston has me floored. *How was my Christmas?*

"It was..." I pause, letting a tear slide down my cheek, but only halfway before I stop it. "It was incredibly uneventful," I laugh through my cry, mostly so Houston doesn't sense my sadness.

"Mine too," he says.

"Oh I don't know. All day at Aunt..." I wait for him to fill in her name.

"Jody's," he says.

"Right, Aunt Jody's. I bet you spent the day eating homemade things and playing some games and singing around the piano." I'm basically imagining his Christmas as every single one of my favorite holiday movies.

"Something like that," he confirms. "How about you? Why was yours so, what did you call it? *Uneventful.*"

"We had sushi," I say. There really isn't a need to elaborate; that kind of says it all. My entire winter break has been a series of nothing-days and blank-evenings. My dad worked most of the time; he's been wrapping up my sister's assault charge. We exchanged gifts this morning, mostly items we all could have easily bought for ourselves, and then we went our separate directions. It's too bad I don't like reading more. I could have filled my lonely hours with that today.

"Sushi's...*good,*" Houston says, and I hear him fighting against his laughter, finally losing the war. "I'm sorry, I can't lie. Sushi...for Christmas? I'm sorry, Paige. That's pretty uneventful."

"Yep," I say.

"Well, if you're living here while there's some holiday, *any* holiday, I promise you one thing—it won't be uneventful," he says. I shut my eyes and imagine what his house must look like, picturing it filled with plates of cookies, holly, and candles. That comfortable lull drapes over our conversation again, and I let myself crawl into bed and pull my blanket up to my chin. I'm strangely more at ease talking with Houston than I am talking with my sister and parents.

Perhaps too relaxed, as I let myself ask Houston one of the millions of deeply personal questions that have been pecking away inside my head since I met his daughter.

"What happened...to Leah's mom?" The calm in our silence from before gets icier as my question lingers, Houston's breath heavy enough to be heard through the phone. "I'm sorry. Too...that's probably too personal."

"No, it's okay. It's something I talk about. We don't really keep secrets or hide things in my family," he says. Maybe I'm jaded, but my mind immediately throws up a dozen flares ready to call him on that bullshit statement. It's not possible for a family to be *that* honest. Everyone has secrets.

"That's novel," I say, not really masking my cynicism.

"I guess," he says, with a sharp laugh. "But...it's sort of sad that you think that. I don't *blame* you. Most people do. I guess I mean it's sad that most people think being honest is strange. I just feel like even the ugliest truth feels a whole lot better than carrying around the weight of lies."

His argument resonates with me, and even though my instincts are still to reject it, I tuck what he said in the background, on top of that pile in my head of reasons-I-should-respect-Houston.

"In that case, I'd like to hear your story...Leah's story," I say, giving in to my natural tendency to charge forward and question, to test his *open-and-honest* policy.

"Bethany moved here her sophomore year," he begins, and I don't know why, but hearing her name hurts inside, as if her name instantly makes her more real to me, even though I never met her. "Her parents got divorced, and she wanted to stay with her mom, and since she had family here—"

"Aunt Jody," I fill in the blank.

"Ha, yes. Aunt Jody, and about a dozen other people," he chuckles. There's a longer pause as he breathes again, almost as if he's gathering breath to save himself from suffocating through the rest of his memories. "Bethany was pretty much the hottest girl ever to step foot in our school. She had this long dark hair, and a body..."

"Uhm okay, you can skip the locker-room talk. I'm a girl, so not really interested in hearing about her body," I say, not wanting to get the details on Bethany's ass and tits.

"Haha, right...well, I *noticed* her...pretty fast, almost the minute she finished registering for school. I saw her through the office windows, and waited in the hallway until she exited with her school map and a schedule in her hand," he says.

"And let me guess, you guided her to her class...and asked her to the prom, and the rest is history," I say, not really sure why I'm rushing him, or why I'm jealous. I'm jealous; *mother fuck.*

"Uh, no. I walked up to her, and before I could get a single word out, she held up her hand and said 'Not interested,'" he says. Now I regret dismissing Bethany so quickly; I actually feel kind of proud of her.

"Romantic," I tease.

"Indeed," he says. "But I kept trying. I walked up to her every time I saw her, and every single time, she shot me down. When her mom dropped her off in the morning and I saw her outside, I'd ask. When I happened to be behind her in line at lunch, I'd ask. In biology—*every single day*—I'd ask. She always said *no*. I was relentless!" He almost seems proud of his portfolio of rejections. It's so odd.

"Why not give up?" I ask.

"Because Bethany was the one," he says. I can't help it, and I laugh harshly. That whole concept of *the one*—it's preposterous. And *the one*, when you're what? Sixteen? Uhm, no. Just...no.

"I know it sounds crazy. And really...at the time, I wasn't thinking she was *the one*. I just knew there was this really hot chick at school that I couldn't stop thinking about, and the fact that she didn't want me was killing me," he says. "And then one day, she said *yes.*"

"Just out of the blue, just like that?" I respond, suddenly hooked on this melodrama from Houston's past.

"Just like that," he says, practically holding his breath before letting out another laugh. "Okay, so maybe she had a flat tire in the school parking lot, and no one was around to help...and maybe I said I would if she agreed to dinner."

"So you extorted her into dating you," I say, sitting up again in my bed, and smiling. I've been smiling through most of this conversation, and it strikes me that I haven't smiled much since I've been home.

"Wow, that sure makes me sound like a creep," he says.

"If the shoe fits..." I tease.

"Anyhow..." he shrugs off my remark, but his voice is a little more guarded when he continues, and I feel badly that I took things too far. But he's still sharing, so I admonish myself in my head and vow to be good for the rest of his story. "I had these big plans. I was going to take her to this big fancy restaurant on the top floor of the Marley building downtown. You know...one of those places that has waiters standing behind you the entire time, waiting for you to need *anything.* Only the day I went to pick her up, my shitty-ass car blew up."

"What, like a battery or something?" I ask.

"No, I mean it literally blew up. Something caught fire in the engine, and the thing was smoking in my parents' driveway," he says, chuckling at the memory.

"What'd you do?" I ask, now totally invested in how this ends.

"Like any respectable sixteen-year-old, I got on my bike with a backpack filled with lame-ass picnic food and rode to her house," he says. "She was dressed in this really nice outfit, and here I was in Dockers and a shirt that I sweat up on my way to her house. It was a truly pathetic display."

"It sounds sweet," I say, surprising myself when I hear my voice speak. That...*that* was meant for my thoughts. Houston remains quiet for a few seconds, and I lie back down, rolling my face into my pillow, wishing like hell I had the power to reverse time.

"Thanks," he says finally, his voice soft. "She...Bethany...she thought it was pretty sweet too. We sat in her front yard, eating crackers and cheese and weird Hostess snacks, and then...she kissed me."

My smile fades when he says this part, but I force it back on my mouth. I don't know why; no one can see me. But I shouldn't be upset hearing about Houston kissing his late...*wife?* This...it shouldn't upset me, so that smile—it's staying on my damn face, even if I have to hold it there with my fingers.

"So, when did Leah happen?" I ask, getting to the part I really want to know.

"About six months later," he says. "We started dating near the end of sophomore year. Junior year I was on the football team. We were pretty good, and every Friday, we'd have these huge parties. There was a lot of drinking, and other...*stuff.*"

"So you and Bethany...did some of that other...*stuff?*" I say it like him, amused that he can't just say *we had unprotected sex and whoops!*

"Yeah, pretty much. I mean, we were always really careful, but I was coming off a huge win, and Beth and I were doing shots, and we were at my friend Casey's house. It was late, and we just got caught up in it," he says. "About three weeks later, Bethany started throwing up. She tried to keep it from me for the first week, I think because she was afraid to find out for sure. But I could tell something was up. She was really emotional, and she'd get so pissed at me, out of nowhere. She finally got sick in front of me, and she just broke down and started crying. I knew the second she looked at me."

I'm rapt now. This scenario scared the hell out of me in high school. It's why I was always in charge, why I was careful about who I gave it up to—why I always have condoms in my purse. The thought of something going *wrong* and me ending up pregnant with Carson's baby runs through my mind, albeit briefly, and my stomach sours fast.

"Was there ever talk of...of maybe...*not* having Leah?" I ask, biting my lip, hoping I asked that delicately enough. The longer Houston takes to respond, the worse I feel for asking. I'm about to take it back, to tell him it's none of my business, when he breaks in.

"There was," he says finally. He doesn't elaborate, and his tone—it's flat and emotionless and broken, as if the fact that he ever had that thought at all kills him. After long seconds, I hear him let out a heavy sigh, the kind weighed down by a past made up of nothing but life-altering, complicated decisions. That single admission shows that Houston wasn't kidding when he said he believed in honesty. That right there—that was honest. And I think it might have been a little painful for him to say aloud, too.

"How did you lose Bethany?" I ask, after rehearsing this question several different ways in my own mind. It's not like me to be sensitive, but I feel maybe Houston deserves it.

"Drunk driver," he says. This time his words come fast, and there's an edge, an angry edge. I've gotten the sense that Houston's wife has been gone for a while, but the way he sounds right now...his voice reacting as if it happened yesterday. I think of all the times Carson drove home from parties drunk. And I

100

think of the times I let him drive me home that way too. I'm struck with a sudden sense of fortune.

"Leah was a month old, and Beth and I had just gotten married. Getting married—having a *real* family—that was something important to her. Her dad pretty much disowned her when he found out she was pregnant—not that he'd been much of a part of her life in the first place," he says, his anger still obvious. He slowly lets it go as he continues, as his setting shifts to his world, away from Bethany's. "We were living with my parents. My mom and dad were supportive, and my mom always wanted more kids, so I think in some weird way, she loved having a full house. I don't even think she minded helping with Leah those first few weeks."

I let Houston continue without interjecting. He'll tell me what he's comfortable with me knowing. I nestle deep into my covers, pressing the phone tightly to my ear so no one else could ever hear his story. Every word he speaks feels intensely private.

"Beth was smart. I know what you're thinking...*smart girls don't get knocked up.* But Beth...she was *crazy* smart. She was on her way to being our valedictorian, and she had tons of scholarship offers. She had one night with me where we both...we didn't think, but just acted, in a moment of weakness, and she got pregnant...but that doesn't mean she wasn't smart."

I open my mouth a few times, before I finally find the right words to respond. "I would never think otherwise. We've all made mistakes," I say, and Houston interrupts.

"Leah wasn't a mistake," he says quickly, his voice still kind, but his intention direct and maybe also a bit of a warning.

"Right...right," I whisper. "I only meant I wouldn't assume something about Beth." My heart is starting to beat faster, and my forehead is damp; I'm feeling my nerves, and I think it's because somehow I've gotten to a place where I care what Houston thinks of me.

Mother-fuck!

I swallow hard and close my eyes, regrouping and breathing in deeply through my nose. "How did you find out?" I ask, wanting him to finish his story, needing to know how this sad-beautiful tale ends.

"Leah was sleeping. She had just started taking naps on a schedule, and it was the middle of the afternoon on a Sunday. My mom and I stayed at the house while Beth and my dad ran to the store. When they were gone for an hour, we started to get worried. I was just grabbing my keys and stepping through the front door when the officer was walking up our driveway..."

His words trail, and his breath catches. I can't see him, but I know he's crying. He's doing his best not to make a sound, but I can hear those small nuances, the way he swallows, the movement of his hand over his face, the rustling sound in the phone as he moves. "The guy veered over two lanes and hit them head on. Everyone died on impact," he says all at once, as if he had one breath left to get those words out. I know that's it— that's where the story ends for Houston.

The silence that follows is long, and there's no way to break it. I mouth *I'm sorry* a few times without making sound, imagining it each time, and knowing that me saying sorry isn't what Houston wants to hear. He doesn't want to hear anything. He doesn't need condolences, and he doesn't ask for them. I asked him a personal question, and he gave me an honest answer—just as he promised.

I hate myself for asking him to tell me. I hate that I had to know. And I regret agreeing to live with him now. Because when I move in, all I'm going to be doing is looking for ghosts, wondering what Houston and his mother see in rooms that are just going to be nothing more than rooms to me.

But I'm also grateful for him—maybe even a little more grateful now that I know. And I also don't want to let him go. I think maybe...maybe I sort of like him. And I don't want to like him, because Houston is *definitely* not according to plan.

"Thank you for telling me," I finally decide on saying. It's the only thing that seems...*safe.*

"Thank you for being interested," he says, his words just as careful as my own, and followed by more silence.

"Merry Christmas, Houston," I say, my heartbeat finally back as it belongs.

"Merry Christmas, Paige," he returns, and for the first time all day, I feel the sentiment of this holiday in my heart. "Call me…if you need anything."

He hangs up first, and I linger, my eyes entranced on a small stitch of fabric on my blanket. The sun set only an hour ago, but I think maybe I should end my day now, shut my eyes, and protect my ears from hearing anything more. Tomorrow I'll go back to being the girl in a makeshift porn, with an arrogant, self-centered ex-boyfriend who misses her when he's drunk and sends her pictures of his body parts. Tonight, I will enjoy knowing that nice guys do exist. I'll let myself smile because I'm the kind of girl who nice guys trust enough to share their secrets with. And maybe I'll indulge in the fact that I have a crush—a crush on a guy whom I, under *no* circumstances really want to be with—but a crush all the same.

And it feels pretty damn good.

Chapter 7

Houston

I'm honest. I didn't lie when I told Paige that. But...I also haven't told anyone about Beth, about that night, about much really. My life is simple, and the people in it are small in number. There's Leah, my mom, Casey, Chuck, and Sheila—that's my immediate family. So the need to *share*—doesn't come up often. I guess I'm glad I still can, but ever since...I've felt a little bit like I've somehow pulled that pain closer, dug it up from the grave and dusted it off so I could feel it again.

The only thing that's made it go away again has been talking to Paige. I called her the next night, as soon as I got home from work and once Leah was bathed and fed. I had no reason to call her, other than...I wanted to. I shouldn't want to, and my head kept screaming to me what a bad idea it was. Paige and I live on different planets, and she is nothing like the girls I date. When I date. Not that I *ever* date. Which is also the point—I don't date. There have been the occasional late nights at the bar with Casey...resulting in me being at some girl's apartment or dorm room, usually by his prodding and with the fuel of alcohol. Then there's the eventual awful conversation the next morning where I leave early, so I can go back to my *real* life full of responsibilities. I never talk about being a dad, because it doesn't matter. Sober, I'm no longer interested in whoever's bed I wound up in. Instead, I just deliver the overplayed *it's not you, it's me* speech that has gotten me slapped and thrown out, sometimes both. Usually both.

Always deserved.

But Paige got the story. She got the story first. She got the story without me even having the thought of *something else.* No, that's not true. I've thought about it. I'm a man and she's gorgeous. But the thoughts have been fantasies, almost jokes I tell myself. Nothing I plan to act on—*ever!* Yet she asked me about Beth, and I told her everything. I *wanted* to tell her everything. It was like I couldn't help myself.

I was prepared never to call again, just to wait for her to show up for the beginning of the semester, to make our relationship business only. But there I was, dialing. Then she answered, and she started talking the second I called. I started listening, and there was this weird give and take. It was as if this was what we did. That conversation, it was far less heavy. We talked about music, about food, about those stupid things you talk about when you're flirting with a girl at summer camp and you want to kiss her. Damn, I was thinking about kissing her, too.

I did it again the next day. And the next. And each time, I think more about kissing her. I look forward to talking to her, to making her laugh. I want to hear the sound of her laugh. We've fallen into a comfortable routine—making plans every night to talk the next. And she texts me during the day. Sometimes, she asks me questions, about things that I know nothing about—like shoes, or is it better to fly into Oklahoma in the evening.

The last time we talked, it was about her sister, Cass. She's sick. She has multiple sclerosis, and she's been having an episode. Paige gets weird when she talks about her sister. She's worried about her; I can tell. But she won't go on about her long, and she dismisses things. I guess for a while, Cass was having trouble walking, but Paige said it wasn't a big deal. I could tell she didn't mean that, but when I started to question, she grew short with me and ended our call a few seconds after.

We haven't talked for two days now, and I've missed her. But maybe it's better that she doesn't call, better that *I* don't call. I want to get along with her. It's good for Leah if we're friendly.

But she's still a tenant—my roommate. I need to keep the line there, and even though it hasn't moved, I've been more aware of it. I shouldn't be *aware* of anything when it comes to Paige. I should just know when her rent check comes in.

School starts next week, and I know Paige is flying in later today. She at least sent me a text about that. I've already got Casey prepped to help me move her things. I have a feeling Paige comes with *a lot* of things. Just like Barbie, she has...accessories.

The store has been busy this week, with the students returning. A lot of people are stocking up on things like beer, bread, and peanut butter—pretty much the college-diet staples. The beer thing stresses Sheila out. Freshmen buy more beer than anyone, but they are also the ones not allowed. Sheila cards everyone, and I know most of those IDs are fake, but she gets overwhelmed, pulling her glasses down her nose and trying to match up the photos to the faces. I took over that duty today, and so far, I've been called a *dickhead* and a *pussy* for telling two guys to beat it.

"Hey...sandwich guy," his voice fills the store before he even makes it to the counter. Paige's ex-boyfriend is an asshole. She hasn't talked about him once, so I'm assuming that's done. It better be. I think I'll kick her out if it's not.

"Hey, asshole," I say. I'm feeling brave, and now that I stand here, a little more prepared, I realize we're the same height. I'm pretty sure I could take him if he threw a punch at me while I was looking.

He spits—on the floor of the grocery store—and looks back up at me, his six-pack of beer in his hand. I shake my head and grab the mop rag from behind the register and round the counter. Holding his gaze, I drop the rag on the area he just spit and wipe it around with my foot. I don't pick it up again, instead kicking it into the corner behind the register, next to the trash.

"Dude, this place has bad service," he says. "I've been standing here for almost five minutes now."

"Oh that's because you spit on the floor like a fucking douchebag so I plan on ignoring you now," I say, internally noting he's only been waiting for thirty seconds, at the most. Lying douchebag.

He shoves his beer forward with his fingers, as if somehow moving it closer is going to inspire me to do something about it. I lean back, pulling out the magazine Sheila has stashed under the register, and I flip through a few pages. It's one of those chick magazines, about diet and organizing your life. It only takes a few seconds for him to reach over the counter and grab it from my hands, tossing it to the side.

"What's your fucking problem, bro?" he asks, tossing a twenty down on top of the beer.

I look at it, then to him, then back to the money. Placing my finger on the bill, I slowly slide it toward me, lifting it with two fingers and holding it up between us.

"What's this for?" I ask. I catch Sheila watching us beyond his shoulder. She's shaking her head, but she's not worried. She knows I can take him too. And she's sick of being pushed around. I'm sick of watching her be pushed around.

"Listen, jack-off! Just ring up the beer, and I'll get out of here," he says.

I fold the bill into quarters and hand it back to him, letting it linger in my hand waiting for him to take it.

"I'm afraid I can't do that, *bro*," I say, and I hear Sheila snicker behind him. When he turns to look at her, she busies herself quickly, pretending to straighten the deli display. Chuck is now peering out of his office. He's...*less* amused.

Carson—I think that's his name—pulls the bill from my hand, crinkles it and tosses it against my chest. I let it fall to the ground.

"Keep the change," he says, picking up the beer and tucking it under his arm. I pick up his money quickly and round the counter, confronting him—chest to chest. I grab the beer before he has time to react, shoving his crumpled money back at him.

"You're not of age. And I *know* you're not. I read the football roster, and you're a sophomore—a *true* sophomore. That makes you...twenty at the most?

"Dude, fuck you! Give me my beer," he says, reaching for it. I tug it away, toying with him. I can actually see his face growing red. I step back behind the counter and drop his beer in a cart to restock later. I turned my back for a fraction of a second, and in that time, he's raced around the counter and has the collar of my shirt in his hand. The sensation of him yanking me backward chokes me a little. I see Chuck step out from his office with a bat in his hand. No way am I letting this guy kick my ass again.

I push hard, using my legs to shove him until his back is flat against the rack of firewood and propane—the lock digging into his shoulder blade. He works his arms around to grab more of my shirt, but I'm so full of adrenaline now, it's going to take a hell of a lot more than that to get me off him.

"I don't know what your deal is, but you need to leave this store...right now!" I seethe. "If I *ever* hear you are in here—that you're trying to get away with your shitty-ass fake ID, or that you're being a disrespectful asshole—I will find where you live, wake your ass up in the middle of the night, and drag you into the middle of the street to make sure your pleas for help echo for all of those nobodies that give a shit."

My face is close to his. I sniff once, and lean my head to the side to crack my neck. The more I stare at his smug face, the more I wonder about how he treated Paige. I wonder if he ever hit her...or if he just treated her like shit with his words. Neither is acceptable, but if he touched her—hurt her *physically*—I will kill him now, without any more reason.

"Whatever, dude," he says finally, pushing out from my arms, his muscles relaxing their hold on me. As he walks away, I keep my muscles flexed; I've learned he fights dirty. He'd turn around and clock me when I wasn't expecting it. I watch him walk all the way out the door, down the sidewalk, and around the building.

"Houston," Chuck says, his voice carrying a sense of scolding. Chuck doesn't like problems. Part of owning a business in a college town is dealing with young tempers. I just became one.

"Sorry, Chuck," I say, looking down at the dirty rag crumpled on the floor and the wheels of the cart with ten bucks of beer inside. "That guy pushes my buttons, and I sort of let it get to me." *He gets to me, and I'm tired of letting him get to me. I'm tired of not acting like a twenty-one-year-old.*

I stare up into Chuck's eyes, silently apologizing, but showing him how tired I am of everything. He walks over and looks at the rag, bends down, picks it up and drops it in the basket. He leans his head toward the cart. "Go on and put that back, then throw the rag in the washer. Maybe this is a good time for your break, yeah?" he says, patting me twice on the shoulder.

"Yeah...maybe," I say, pulling my clothing straight, turning my collar and re-tucking my shirt.

I get to the back of the store, my heart still pounding from almost getting punched in the face, when my phone chirps. I pull it from my pocket, my nostrils flaring with my heavy breath as I sit against the stack of cardboard bundled along the wall.

I need your help with something. It's stupid. But it's important.

Paige needs my help. I notice those words first, and my heart kicks into action. I'm standing and reading again when I get the rest of the message—what she needs is *stupid.* She needs me, and I jumped. That's...that's probably not good.

I text her back.

Okay, I'm your guy for stupid, important things. Whatcha need?

It takes her a while to write, and eventually I get back to work, now restocking shelves and cleaning the aisles. Seems Chuck thinks I should stay away from people for the rest of the day. I'm just finishing the last aisle when Paige finally messages me.

I need you to meet me at my sister's dorm. Hayden. And bring help.

I start to write back, but I have too many questions. I give up on the last aisle and pull my apron and badge off, rolling them as I walk into Chuck's office. I stuff them in my cubby and pull out my keys and hat. As I turn to leave, I catch Chuck's attention on me, his feet on his desk and the bat still in his hands. He's trying to be intimidating. He's in his sixties, but the man has several tattoos from his years in the Navy. I've only heard the stories behind a few of them, but the one's I've heard have all ended with a guy with a broken arm, nose, or face at the end.

Deciding it's better to just own up to my outburst, I wipe my hand dry along my pants and walk over to where he's sitting and reach out my hand. He pats the bat in his hand a few times before finally resting it on his desk and leaning forward to grab my hand. We shake once.

"Sorry, sir. Won't happen again," I say, looking down as I slide my hat on. Old man or not, I still don't want to make eye contact and deal with facing his disappointment. That shit sucks.

"Sounds good," he says, returning to his resting position, picking the bat up again.

Once I'm in my car, I dial Paige, and she answers quickly.

"You didn't have to call," she says. I smile at her greeting, and then I laugh over the fact that *this* is what I've missed for two days.

"And hello to you. Yes, I had a fine day, thank you for asking," I tease.

"Oh, don't be an asshole. I'm at the airport, about to get on a plane. What do you want?" she asks.

"Uh, you need *me*...remember?" I say. She's being a little meaner than usual.

"Oh," she says, and I can tell she also means *sorry*. "Hang on," she says. I hear someone speaking over the loudspeaker at the airport, and the voice grows quieter until I can barely hear it. "Okay, I'm in the ladies room."

"Sexy," I say, knowing it will piss her off.

"Gross! This is not sexy, Houston. We pee here; that's all," she says.

"Well, maybe that's all *you've* done," I tease. I should probably get to the point, but I haven't talked to her for a few days, and the last time she was pissed at me. Joking with her is kind of fun.

"Right, like *you've* had sex in an airport," she says, her voice so sure. She has that *I-know-I'm-right* tone. I'm going to shock her.

"*I've* had sex lots of places...Paige," I say, and there is no mistaking my innuendo. There's a long quiet between us. That...saying that...to her...it felt strange to do. That was me— completely obliterating the line I thought was so important this morning. Mentally, I draw it right back in place, and check myself to make sure I don't let *that* voice slip out again. It also felt kind of good, which is an even bigger reason to draw that line again— this time in permanent marker.

"What do you need, Paige?" I ask, wincing that I've set her off, made her uncomfortable, or...I don't know...that I'm now some creep.

She takes her time answering, and I can tell she's affected by what I said. "I told you in the text," she says, clearing her throat, trying to regain her place as the dominant one. It makes me smile.

"You told me to meet you at Hayden Hall. But...when? What am I doing? And you said bring help?" I don't want to tell her, but I don't really have help to bring. I'll call Casey—if I *have* to—and maybe his roommate can come. But that's all I've got...unless she wants a church secretary and a four-year-old to show up to this thing.

"We land at about four, if you can be there then. And I'll explain more. Just...just be ready to move things. *Lot's* of things," she says. "Oh, that's us. I gotta go. See you soon! Miss you!"

And just like that, Paige is back on top.

Miss you? Miss you. She...*misses*...me.

Line gone.

Again.

Paige

Shit!

That just slipped out. *Miss you.* I said, "Miss you." I don't think I've ever missed anyone. Maybe my old life. My high school life—the one that was simple and didn't require planning or plotting or moving in with a dude I met at the grocery store. I fucking *miss you?* What the hell.

That last sentence is all I think about the entire flight back to Oklahoma. I've been pretending to read a magazine, not wanting to talk to Cass because it's her fault I called Houston in the first place. She has a scheme cooked up to prank her boyfriend and his brother, and that's what I need his help with. I'm helping her—Houston is helping me. Cass's fault.

We get to the dorm, exchanging a few words about her plan, what she needs me to do, but now that we're back here, I can't help but let thoughts of Chandra creep back in too. I'm moving tomorrow morning. If I had my way, I'd move everything tonight—before more people are there.

Before Chandra is there.

I wonder if my things have been destroyed or sold? I would have sold her things. In fact, that's a good idea. If I'm ever in a position, I'm putting her things up on Craigslist—*with her phone number!*

I let these thoughts of revenge amuse me for the elevator ride upstairs, but then reality slams right back into my face. Rowe, my old roommate, is jumping up and down. I smile, not a fake smile, but a real one—genuine—because Rowe...she's actually always been good to me. Even when I wasn't so good to her when we lived together. In a way, I'm kind of glad to have this chance to help her with something, no matter how unimportant it is. Maybe she and I can somehow start over too.

"Okay, so here are their keys," Rowe says, handing me a ring with hers and another set with a Playboy cover attached to it. I hold the keys up and dangle them in front of my sister.

"These are your boyfriend's keys," I deadpan to Cass. Her boyfriend, Ty, is one of those over-the-top guys. I didn't trust him at first. He's in a wheelchair, but you don't even notice because his personality is enormous—*arrogant*. His arrogance grew on me; maybe I recognize it in myself. Either way, watching him with Cass at my parents' house when she was suffering last week sold me in his favor.

"Apparently, she was Miss April 2009, and that makes her special," Cass rolls her eyes.

"I see," I say, holding the laminated cover photo in front of me. It makes me think about the video floating around of me, and I wonder if maybe I'll make someone's key ring some day. *Jesus, I hope not!*

"Are you sure you're good with this?" Cass asks as she pushes the elevator button.

"I can handle this," I say as I pull my jacket from my arms and drop it on top of our suitcase. We came right here, which is good, because my things don't really have a place to go until Houston shows up anyhow. I kick off my Jimmy Choos too, which for some reason, makes Rowe and Cass laugh.

"What? I'm not lifting in those!" I motion down to my prized shoes, the ones I scored on after-Christmas clearance back home. I've wanted Jimmy Choos for years!

Rowe and Cass only giggle more. I blow my hair out of my face and retie the band around my ponytail, trying to ignore them. My back is still to the elevator when it opens, so I don't notice Houston step off, or the two guys he's brought with him. Suddenly, though, I'm in his arms. He's squeezing me tightly, lifting me from the ground, and spinning me.

He's...*he's happy to see me!* Probably because I told him I missed him. And I did. But...not in the *spin me around like a ballerina in love* kind of way. His arms, though—they do feel...*nice.*

"Okay, you can put me down now," I say, purposely not looking up at him. I direct my gaze right to my shoes on the floor. I pick them up as soon as he sets me down, tucking them in my suitcase so they don't get damaged, or stolen.

"Sorry," Houston says, and his mouth is grimacing. His friends are both looking at him trying not to laugh. "So," he breathes out, clapping his hands together once. Back to business. No more *whatever that was.*

"Hey, I'm Casey. And you must be the hot new roommate," says one of the guys standing behind Houston. He reaches past him, his build nowhere near as broad or muscular, but he's tall, and I immediately size him up to make sure he can lift things.

"Hot new roommate, meet Casey, my dumb-ass friend," Houston says as we shake hands. I can tell he's annoyed that his friend called me hot, and in a way gave away the fact that Houston probably called me hot, too. I've been called hot before, though. This isn't special. There are lots of other things about me, things that only someone who really understood me would point out. Hot isn't one of them.

"Dumb-ass Casey, nice to meet you," I say, for Houston's benefit. He seems happy when I take the dig at his friend. His smile dimples his cheek, and I...I notice.

"I'm Eli," the other guy says. This guy's bigger, strong like Houston. His face is half covered in a beard, and he's wearing a shirt with a beard on it.

"Eli, nice to meet you. Clever shirt," I say. He smiles and says *thanks,* even though I wasn't really complimenting him. I glance at Houston, and he's holding in a laugh. When our eyes meet, we both break a little and have to turn away. I need Eli to move a shitload of furniture, so I can't go offending him right from the start.

"So what are we doing here, Paige?" Houston asks, leaning against one of the hallway walls. He's wearing a white T-shirt that hugs his body more than most of the things I've seen him in, and when he crosses his arms, I notice that there's a tattoo on his right arm. I don't have to ask to know it's for her.

"Follow me," I say, walking down the hall toward my old room. The smell of paint is still strong, and when I open the door and see the horrible brown color that my sister's boyfriend and his brother Nate have painted on the walls, I understand why my sister is doing this now. Rowe only sent pictures—and honestly, in the photos, it didn't seem so bad. But seeing it live—*in person?* The brown paint looks more like a stain, a gigantic stain that drips all around the room. I have to give Ty credit—it's pretty funny, and it's far away from the pink we painted his room a few months ago.

"Dude, the paint stinks," Eli says as he steps into the room and around me. Houston and Casey are still behind me, surveying the space.

"Okay, so here's the deal. About three months ago, me, my sister, and our other roommate painted Ty and Nate's room," I start.

"Who are Ty and Nate?" Casey asks, now covering his own nose with his sleeve. Babies. The paint smell isn't *that* bad.

"Keep up. Ty's my sister's boyfriend, and Nate's his brother. He's dating Rowe, my other old roommate. They have this stupid prank war. And now I have this to deal with," I say, turning in a slow circle with my hand outstretched to take it all in. Their room honestly looks like one of those dens from the seventies. All it needs is orange shag carpet.

"So, we're painting it back? That's easy," Eli says, rolling up his sleeves. Bless his little heart; he's eager to get started.

"Not exactly. We're moving their stuff down the hall, and putting the boys' stuff...in here," I say, stepping over to my sister's bed. I start folding her blankets into my arms, and when I turn around, all three guys are staring at me, their mouths parted, their foreheads showing their confusion. "Just start grabbing crap and help me. We have two hours."

Amazingly, they don't protest, after an hour and a half of sweating and lifting more than I think I ever have, we have successfully relocated everyone's belongings. I lock up both rooms, and direct the boys downstairs. We stop at the mailbox area, and I sweet-talk the very shy guy working the front desk into putting both sets of keys in Cass's mailbox. By the time I turn around, Eli and Casey have left. It's just Houston, me, and my giant suitcase and travel bag—and a landfill-sized feeling of *awkward.*

Houston pushes his hands in his pockets. His jeans are dark; they're the kind I would think a guy would wear going out to a club, not when moving furniture around a chick's dorm room. I kind of think he dressed up, a little, for me. He's staring down at his feet, and I watch as his mouth opens and closes twice, each time with a breath, about to speak. Finally, he just settles on smiling and looking up at me.

"I guess I'll see you in the morning?" I say, looping my hand through the strap to pull my bag along behind me. My things are heavy, and going to the Delta House is really the last thing I want to do. But I'm not asking Houston for any more favors.

"Here, let me," he says, reading my mind. He grabs the heaviest bag, pulling the strap over his shoulder. I take the opportunity to study his tattoo when he does—it's a cross, with the letters M and B. I'm guessing the *M* is for his father's name, because I'm sure I know who the B is.

"Thanks," I say, pulling my roller bag behind us. We step through the main doors and out to the walkway. It's a good ten-minute walk from here to the Delta House, so when Houston turns toward the parking lot, I sigh with relief. I'm glad he brought his car—no matter how shitty and old it is.

Houston puts my things in the trunk, then opens my door for me. I'm prepared for the seatbelt this time. What I'm not prepared for is the familiar smell of being in a small space that is permeated with Houston—his cologne—I don't know what it is, but I like it.

I...like it.

Shit.

We drive the two blocks to the Delta House, the radio filling the awkward void for two minutes. Houston pulls up to the curb, and I sigh, relieved I don't see anyone else's car parked along the road. Chandra has a white Acura. Her license plate says W1N3R. She tells everyone it's the only combination left she could get for *winner.* But I don't know, it reads *whiner* in my head. I keep searching for the whiner car, not satisfied that I don't see it. She could still be here.

116

"Hey, you wanna just stay tonight?" Houston's question bursts through the silence, and it makes me start to sweat instantly. He's leaning to the side in his seat, his head resting on the back, his hair a little disheveled from the move. He's adorable. I can't deny that. And yeah, I want to stay, because I don't want to be *here!* But if I stay with you, it's going to look like I want to *stay with you,* when in reality I just want to hide, and you're giving me shelter.

No matter how adorable you are.

"It's...it's okay. It's just one night. But if you can, maybe you can help me move in the morning? I'm kind of done with this place," I admit. I haven't told Houston why I'm leaving, but when we talked over break, I did let it slip that some of the girls I counted on as friends turned out to be ruthless bitches.

"Are you sure? I don't mind. And Leah is excited about having a sister. Oh, yeah...by the way, she says you're going to be blood sisters," he says, the right side of his lip lifting, doing that dimple thing. I'm not sure what's making my heartbeat race—the look on his face or the thought of Leah liking me.

For a few long seconds, I stare at him and consider his offer. My night can take two paths, one in a place I hate, and the other in a place I...

"I'll be fine, really. See you at eight?" I make my voice sound definitive so he doesn't try again. If he asks me once more, I'll go with him. And for some reason, I feel like going with him now will make me notice those other things about him more. And Houston is a whole different life—one that I don't want.

He meets me behind the car, and when I reach for my bag, our hands touch. He doesn't move, and my fingers clutch around his on the bag's handle. It's a touch that's somewhere between a standoff and fire.

"I can get it," I say, my voice sounding a little bossier than I mean. "Really, thank you, but..."

"Paige," he says, his head doing that tilt thing, and...yeah...there's the dimple. "I'd be a real asshole to just drop you off and not help you carry your things. Just let me not be an asshole, okay?"

I let my muscles relax and smile as I let go of my grip over his hand. When he turns, I flex my fingers, trying to rid them of the feel of his hand in mine. It wasn't even a handholding kind of touch. But still.

Once I open the door, I drop my bag and reach for the one Houston's holding, pulling it inside with me. When he steps toward me, wanting to enter, I place my palm on his chest. I can't have him come in here with me. That will make me look desperate. And maybe there's a part of me that wants to keep my Houston-world pure, untainted from *this place.*

"I appreciate it, but there are some people here I just want to deal with and move on. I can't put it off," I say, glancing up at him. He's close enough he has to look down to see into my eyes, and the moment our gaze locks my heart starts to pick up its rhythm again. He looks like he wants to argue with me, like he has more to say, and we stare at each other for what feels like minutes, even though I'm sure it's only a second or two. It's long enough for me to imagine his hand coming up to lift my chin, and the moment I do that, I shake my head and take a step away.

"I'll see you in the morning," I say, waiting as he holds a few fingers up for a polite wave. He turns and walks down the front steps back to his car. I close the door when he opens his, not wanting him to see me watch him leave. But I want to watch him leave. I settle for listening to his engine start and fade instead.

The warmth from being near him evaporates as soon as I turn around and face the dark emptiness of the sorority house. Only a handful of the girls are back, but the ones who are—they hate me.

And I hate them.

I drag my bags up the steps, letting them scratch and scuff along the way. What do I care? Once I get to my room, I take a deep breath and push my key in, knowing my key—it's a farce. There isn't anything that can keep *everyone* out. My bed is packed up, the blankets and pillows all stacked in the center. The clothes I left behind in the drawers and closet are all piled in a basket at the foot of the bed. And the makeup and perfume I decided not to bring—it's gone, most of it cracked and spilled in the metal trashcan at the edge of my vanity. I'm not surprised, but this act—it's still a slap in my face.

There's a note in the middle of my mirror, and I hesitate to read it. Reading it gives it power. I walk past it and sit at the edge of my bed to survey the details, wondering what else they've done that I'm not seeing. My saved belongings are protected in my bags by the door. I hear someone down the hall giggle, and I hear a door close. The Delta House is old—historic. And the hardware sounds as such. I used to hate the noises—the creaking and the pops. But I adore them now—the way they expose the rats.

Standing, I walk to my mirror and pull the purple sticky note from the glass.

We gave you a head start.

I crumple the paper and throw it in the trash bin along with my cosmetics. I turn back to the bed and slide the pile of pillows and blankets to the floor, pulling one comforter out of the pile to sleep on, and another to sleep under. I bundle my hair in a bun and slip into a pair of sweatpants and my sister's old soccer T-shirt. She gave it to me when I needed something to work out in over the break, and I kept it. It's nothing like I normally wear—plain, red, with a giant logo on the front and her number on the back. There's a hole at the bottom, and I loop my thumb through it to stretch the shirt out so I can take my reflection in. At a quick glance, I look like Cass in this.

With one more check on my lock, I pull my bags closer to my bed. If anyone tries to fuck with me tonight, I'm going to hear them. And maybe, wearing Cass's shirt will give me Cass's strength. I slip my phone from my purse, and set the alarm. Then, I shoot one last text to Houston:

Make it 7.

I keep the phone clutched in my hand, and when it buzzes minutes later, I smile, knowing it's from him. I tilt it just enough to read his response:

OK

It's short, and there's no pretense to it. It's what I want. But yet, I'm also disappointed that there isn't more to his message, that he isn't asking me if I want him to come back, if I haven't changed my mind about staying tonight. I laugh silently to myself at how unfair I'm being.

It's almost midnight.

Seven hours.

I can handle one night.

I let my eyes drift shut, and soon my ears take in only the gentle hum of the heater. It lulls me to near sleep, and I start to forget why my arms are flexed and my fingers are gripping my phone so hard. And then I hear the creak down the hall and I remember.

One night. But not a minute more.

Chapter 8

Houston

I showed up at seven, and Paige was already packed and waiting for me. She doesn't strike me as the wake-up-early kind of girl. She's been yawning most of the morning while we load things into my car and then out of my car, upstairs, and to her new room.

"Why don't you rest for a while? I'm off today, and was just planning on taking Leah to the park. You can get settled in your room—maybe take a nap?" I suggest.

Paige flops on her new bed, bouncing on it a few times, testing the softness. I can tell she's disappointed, but she's biting her lip, looking off to the side, like she's searching for a way to show she's grateful.

"It's a really crappy mattress, I know," I say for her.

"No, it's okay. I'll get a mattress pad or something…" she says, standing and pushing down on it a few times. That mattress is probably two decades old. I'd switch mine with hers, but I'm pretty sure mine is even worse. The only one with a good mattress in this house is Leah, and hers is built for a child.

Paige paces around the room, pulling out a few drawers and flipping the light on in her closet, getting familiar with her new surroundings. I was sort of surprised when her sister and that girl Rowe weren't there to help us move her things this morning. I know she said their relationship was strained, but I also thought they were working on it. When I asked her about her sister, she flinched, and then begged me not to tell anyone she was living here. I get it; she's hiding. But I also feel like she's embarrassed to be here.

"All right, well, we'll be back early this afternoon. My mom is making dinner—you know, to welcome you? Hope that's okay..." I'm holding her doorknob, my body halfway in and out of her room. I don't want to leave.

"That's nice of her," she says, her eyes coming up to mine, but retreating. She's standing in the middle of her room, her fingers fidgeting in front of her body, and her teeth chewing at her lip so much I think she may actually bite through her own skin.

"You're welcome to join us—Leah and me—if you want..."

"Yes," she interjects. Her enthusiasm makes me smile, but I hide it with my hand. I don't know why I like that she's uncomfortable, but I do.

"Okay, we'll leave in an hour. Leah takes a while to wake up and get ready," I say, pulling her door closed behind me.

"I can relate," she says just before the door shuts.

Leah finishes her pancakes, using her sleeve to wipe the syrup from her mouth. My mom hates it when she does that, but she learned it from me, so I feel like I don't have the right to correct her. If you want sugar on your arm kid, have at it!

I pull her plate from the table and rinse it quickly at the sink, setting it in a rack to wash better later. We don't have a dishwasher. There's a spot for one, but we have a mini-fridge, filled with my mom's jams and jellies, stuffed in there instead. She sells them at the store, too.

When I turn back to the open kitchen, Leah is standing near the foot of the steps—her fingers fidgeting just as Paige's were an hour ago—her lips tight and her breath held while she stretches up on her toes to see the top of the steps. She's waiting for Paige, and she's nervous.

"Whatcha doing there, sport?" I ask, pulling her jacket from the small rack by the door. I hold the sleeves out for her, and she stuffs her arms inside the purple unicorn coat, leaving them stretched out to either side so I can zip it up. I kneel down in front of her and she pushes one hand on top of my head so she can see over me.

"Is she up there?" she whispers. I smile as I look down at her shoes, stopping to fix the Velcro straps.

"She'll be right down. She's coming to the park with us," I say. Leah pushes on my head with both hands now, forcing my hair in my eyes. I reach around and lift her in my arms, picking her up in the air so she can see to the top of the steps more easily.

"Is she coming now?" she asks.

"Soon," I say, blowing hard on her neck, my lips to her skin so it makes a noise. She bends into me and giggles.

I set her down and walk to the living room to grab my own jacket and shoes. I lean against the sofa to put my shoes on and watch as Leah remains in the same spot, her hands back to wringing in front of her, her neck craning to see. Her eyes light up the second I hear the creaking sound of Paige's door, and Leah flashes her eyes to me, frozen. She's not sure if she should stand there or run. I step over to her so she doesn't feel nervous, and she folds into my side, hiding her face on my leg, then peering out with her cheek firm against me.

I don't look at Paige until she's almost completely down the steps, but Leah, she watches the entire time, her eyes widening, and her smile growing. When I look up, I see why.

I'm pretty sure she's done this on purpose. Paige is wearing a pink dress with matching shoes, and her hair is a perfect glow around her face. She's holding a pink purse in her hands, and the closer she gets to Leah, the bigger my daughter's smile becomes.

"Hey, Leah. I'm Paige. We met once, at your dad's work?" she says, kneeling down so she can look Leah in the eyes.

"I remember," Leah says, her voice soft. She's swaying side-to-side, her teeth pinning her lips in a forever kind of smile.

"Can I come to the park with you today?" Paige asks, peering up at me for approval. I give her a thumbs up.

"Yes," Leah says, her swaying picking up speed. I hold my hand against her side to calm her. She's excited.

I urge Leah toward the door, and Paige and I follow. Leah runs ahead, climbing into the backseat of my car and buckling herself quickly in her booster seat. Paige waits for me while I lock the front door, and I catch a glimpse of pink as she twists behind me. I think she wants me to notice her, to say something. I laugh once under my breath when I catch her hand on her purse as I turn. The woman even painted her nails pink.

"Thanks," I say, nodding my head toward her. "You have just replaced Santa Claus on the hierarchy of cool people in Leah's life."

Paige beams, satisfied; she pulls the edge of her dress out a little, bending her knees in a curtsy. "What girl doesn't want to be Barbie?" she smiles. I notice her soft lips—they are perfect, too. Her lips—that's something I shouldn't notice. Those aren't part of the costume. Those are just...*her.* And I've been looking at them for too long; I look down quickly and begin patting my pockets.

"Damn, keys..." I say, and a second later I feel Paige tug on my thumb, where the key ring is linked. Yeah, that was lame. I shrug, signaling that I'm a dumb-ass, then I let her walk to the car in front of me, so I can watch without her catching me. I'm starting to think Leah isn't the one who needs to get used to our new roommate—I am.

We get to the park in minutes, and Leah warms up to Paige almost immediately, pulling her to the swings to push her, then dragging her to the slides to watch her race up and down. When she tries to talk Paige into helping her fill water cups to dump in the sand, Paige waves her hand in front of her face and says she's getting a little warm and tired, and Leah lets her off the hook. She joins me on the bench while Leah runs from the drinking fountain to the sand and back again.

"Hey, thanks for being her playmate today. That's usually my gig, but she seemed pretty emphatic about you doing it today," I say, glancing at her as she sits next to me. She lifts her arms and pulls her hair into a pile on top of her head, exposing her neck—I look at that too.

She turns her head to the side to face me, and I adjust quickly, meeting her eyes. *No, Paige...I wasn't looking at your neck, or thinking about kissing it.*

"I was going to walk through campus later, find my classes. What time is your mom making dinner? I don't want to be late," she says.

"We usually eat early, probably around five thirty," I say.

"That should work," she says, looking forward, picking up her hair again, and I watch. Her fingers move slowly through her hair, wrapping strands around knuckles. It's such a simple movement, but damn—it's kind of sexy.

"Stop it!" a voice yells. A voice. A voice! Leah's voice! I get to my feet, out of my trance fast, and I storm into the sand, but Paige is already ahead of me, her pink shoes kicked off in the grass. I slow my step as Paige has her hand around a little boy's wrist, a full cup of water in his hand, which is hovering above Leah.

"Owwww, Mommy!" the boy is yelling, twisting his neck over his shoulder. I walk toward Leah and give her my hand to help her up, letting Paige take over the role of bad cop. Another woman rushes to the sand and grabs Paige's arm, jerking it away from the boy.

"Get your hands off my kid!" the woman practically spits at Paige. Paige doesn't flinch, instead taking a step toward the woman, leaning in close, her hands on her hip.

"You should teach your kid how to treat girls. This little creep was going to pour water all over her. He was teasing her; I saw the whole thing!" Paige is seething. I feel Leah clutch my leg and I look down at her, worried she's scared. She's smiling. She's watching Paige stand up to someone, and she's grinning ear-to-ear.

"I should have you arrested!" the woman yells as Paige is turning to walk away. She flips around quickly, stopping at the edge of the sand where she bends down to pick up her shoes, then spins with them dangling from one hand.

"Yeah, well I should have punched you in the nose. So touché," she says, turning back to me. Her lips are in a hard, straight line, and she passes Leah and me, walking straight to the car. We follow, and Leah skips ahead, climbing in the back seat to reach around from behind to hug Paige. I pause at the front of the car to watch, noting the initial surprise on Paige's face at the feel of tiny hands around her neck. That shock slides into a proud grin, and she brings her hand up to squeeze Leah's, patting it once. When she looks up at me, she drops the smile quickly, then looks down at her lap.

Don't worry, Paige. I didn't see a thing.

We're about halfway back to the house, the only sound a commercial playing on the radio, and some haphazard humming coming from Leah in the back seat, when Paige finally talks. "I hate bullies," she says, her eyes staring straight out the front window.

"Me too," I say, keeping my gaze on her while we wait at the red light. She never turns to look at me, and she never looks nervous that I'm staring at her. I know she can feel my eyes on her; I catch hers moving to take me in once or twice from the side. But she lets me look, and she doesn't elaborate on her statement. I don't ask, but I wonder who was the bully in her life—and maybe, was it her?

Paige

"We're all going to Sally's for dinner. I thought maybe you'd like to come?" Cass asks. I wasn't going to answer her call, but I'm walking to campus, and I have to pass the row of frat houses. There are always people hanging outside, and I'd rather be busy on the phone than run into someone I know.

"Oh, uhm…thanks," I say, kind of surprised that my sister is asking. I had a feeling that the progress we made at home would stop once we got to school. Maybe she just wants to thank me for helping her prank the guys. "I would love to, but I can't. I have…plans…" I fade my words at the end, suddenly worried I've said too much. Cass doesn't know where I'm living. She doesn't know much of anything about me right now. "Delta thing," I add quickly, straightening my posture as I lie through the phone, as if she could see me.

"Oh, okay. Maybe…maybe later this week?" she asks. I feel bad.

"For sure," I say, looking to my right at a group of guys sitting on one of the front porches. They watch me walk by, and I hear one of them say something to the others; I'm pretty sure one of the words was *ass*. I step a little longer, but I also let my hips move a little more.

I'm not sticking around, boys, but you're welcome to watch.

Cass says goodbye, and I push my phone in my purse, glad that I was able to stretch my conversation with my sister long enough to make it to campus. I pull the folded campus map from my front purse-pocket, noting the buildings I've highlighted. I walk to the first two, relieved when I realize how close they are to each other. They're different from the buildings I went to last semester, but they're all familiar. I hate feeling lost. I move to the last one, my Friday lab class, the farthest one from where I'm living now. At least the class is in the late morning, so I won't have to walk through campus at night.

Satisfied that I can find my way Monday, I begin my trip back to Houston's house…*my* house. I'm nearing the library when I see Houston sitting on one of the concrete blocks outside the main doors. I stop immediately. I'm not sure why I stop, but I do, because he's here, and I have a feeling he's here waiting for me. That's not okay. I don't want him here waiting for me.

I pull out my phone and fire off a text.

What are you doing here?

I wait and watch as he pulls his phone out of his pocket, then gets to his feet, looking in all directions until he spots me. His shoulders slump, and he pulls his phone up in both hands in front of him, his fingers working while he walks slowly in my direction. Oh no, buddy. You stay put!

Something came up, I didn't want you to go home and see the house empty, or freak out or...can we just talk in 15 seconds?

I'm reading his words and taking slow steps backward when I hear his voice.

"Paranoid much?" he asks.

"Stalker much?" I say back. He smirks, then pushes his phone back into his pocket.

"My mom called. She has to work late. Church is having a carnival. Leah found out, so she wanted to go. I just dropped her off with my mom, but I didn't want you to think we abandoned you, so..." he says, holding his hands out as if he just performed some amazing magic trick and appeared here in a puff of smoke.

"So, you came to rescue me," I say through pursed lips.

"Uh...yeah, I guess," he says.

"I don't need rescuing," I fire back, pulling my purse over my body. My shoulder hurts, and I'm tired of carrying it. I want to go home.

"No rescues. Got it," he says, taking a deep breath. We start to walk back in the direction of his place, and I rewind what just happened in my head. I may have overreacted a little.

"Sorry," I say, under my breath. "I'm a little...*stressed, maybe?*"

I'm not stressed. I'm angry, and I'm sad, and I'm confused. I'm a lot of things, but none of them are really very happy. I glance to where Houston is walking next to me, his thumbs in his pockets. He's wearing the same jeans he wore last night.

"Don't you own other pants?" I ask through a laugh.

He stretches his hands out, leaving his thumbs in his pockets, and I move my eyes up to his quickly, not wanting to stare at his hips, his zipper, his...crotch.

"My closet can't compete with yours," he says, his eyes narrowing on me.

My pace relaxes, and we continue to walk slowly through the main part of campus, the more steps we take, the more relaxed I become, and the more ridiculous I feel about snapping at him in the first place.

128

"I'm sorry I yelled at you," I say finally, glancing up at him. His eyes are soft, and the way he looks down at me is different from the way the guys on the porch looked at me. Those guys liked what they saw, but Houston, he actually *sees* me.

"It's okay. You're...*stressed*," he says, making quote marks with his fingers in the air around the word. I laugh at my own expense, but not in agreement. "You maybe want to tell me a little more about it?"

I think about his offer, and I actually consider it. Those two weeks that I spent talking to Houston on the phone—me in California, him in Oklahoma—were nice. They were more than nice, they were the first time I've actually talked to a guy and had him listen. There wasn't some pretense about parties or getting laid. He asked me questions, and I answered. He listened. The more I consider his offer, the stronger this feeling is that's washing over me—it's a comfort level, and maybe something else.

When I part my lips to speak, I peer up, and his eyes are intent on me, his focus is there, and it feels nice. "I caught one of the Delta girls..." I start to say, but am interrupted by deep moaning sounds coming from behind us.

We both look over our shoulders. The frat guys who watched me walk by before are now following us. They're several feet back, and when we look at them, they turn their focus to the side. Houston thinks nothing of it, turning around and looking back at me. "You caught someone doing what?" he asks. I barely hear him because I'm still looking over my shoulder. Now that Houston isn't looking, they aren't pretending any longer, their eyes on me again.

The one in the middle, the largest of the three, moans again, making the other two laugh. The heavier guy on the right covers his mouth, saying something that only makes them all laugh harder. I glare at them, and even though I can barely make out the shapes of their eyes, I can tell they're glaring back, mocking me. I face our direction again, doing my best to shake them off.

"I'm sorry, where was I?" I say, knowing exactly where I was. The comfort from before is gone now, though.

"*Mmmmmmmmmm*, oh yeah. Oh yeah, baby. Like that," a voice says behind me. My body shivers, and my fingertips and toes feel numb, the blood retreating, leaving me feeling helpless—weak.

"Ah! Ah! Ah!" I hear again. They're making sex noises, and I know why. My entire body is flushed, my head is furious, and my heart is dead. They've seen it—they've seen *it*! Which means it's out there, somewhere, where people are able to see it.

My mind is racing, my heart is thumping, and my back is sweating—even though it's only fifty degrees outside. I need to solve this. Houston—he can't know! I'm about to come up with an excuse, to lie to him and just tell him to ignore those guys...when he stops me, his hand hard on my arm as he turns me to face him. He doesn't ask me a question, but only looks at me, his eyes penetrating mine, searching deep inside me for a truth to understand what this scenario is all about. My strength fades, if only for a second, and I lose my breath, my body shaking twice as I gasp. The sting in my eyes is instant, and I know they're on the verge of crying, so I squeeze them shut, which only makes a tear fall down my cheek. Steadying myself, I take a deep breath, then reopen my eyes to look at Houston.

"I'm fine," I say, my voice once again strong, my bluff good. He holds his hand in place on my arm, his eyes still boring through me, his mouth in a firm line and his jaw flexing as he considers everything—what he saw, what he heard, what I said, and the way I look now. *I'm fine, Houston. I'm fine. I'm fine. I'm fine. I don't need rescuing!*

"Like hell you are," he grits, and he leaves me, charging the few steps behind us toward the trio of guys who are suddenly speechless. Within seconds, Houston's fist slams into the face of the one in the middle, and his friends take wide steps back, not wanting to be the next one getting Houston's attention.

Houston doesn't say anything as he pummels the guy, his knuckles ricocheting off the side of his head until he drops to his knees unable to hold his balance any longer. Houston reaches down to grab the collar of the guy's shirt, lifting him back to a stand, and stares him down, his lips moving to say something. I can't hear him, but I see the fear in the faces of the others. I know Houston must have said something threatening. With one thrust of his arm, he pushes him off balance again, then flexes his hand at the one now bleeding from punches and walks back to me.

"Let's go," he says, and I pick up my steps to keep up.

We walk in silence until we're close to home. The blood on his knuckles is leaving a trail of drops on the sidewalk, and when he reaches into his pocket for his keys not thinking, he winces.

"Fuck," he says under his breath, reaching around with his other arm instead, protecting his hurt hand.

"Yeah, well that's what you get," I say, shaking my head, folding my arms and waiting for him to unlock the door for me, reminding me that I still need a key of my own.

Houston stops abruptly, leaning away from the door and letting the screen slam to a close. "Excuse me?" he asks.

"When you go all Neanderthal for no reason, then I'm not going to feel bad for you when you're hurt," I say, glancing at his eyes, then back down at the lock on the door. I jerk my head toward it, willing him to hurry up.

"You're kidding me, right?" he says, staring at me and waiting for my response. I shrug my shoulders, lifting my brow once.

No, I'm not kidding Houston. I. Don't. Need. Rescuing.

"Un-fucking believable," he mutters, finally unlocking the door. If only he just did that in the first place. I step inside quickly, and I hear the door slam behind us. I don't stop, instead continuing to the steps, hearing the sound of his keys being tossed on the table.

"Are you for real with this shit?" he asks as I reach the top step. I steady myself, my hand on the banister, and I turn to face him.

"If you could leave the lease paperwork on the table for me, along with a key, I'll sign it in the morning and leave your rent check," I say, before turning and walking into my room. With the door closed, I drop my purse to the ground and move to my hard-as-a-board bed, sitting down, then falling to my back. I close my eyes, bringing my palms to my face, and in the quiet of the house, I hear the sounds of moans taunting me from my imagination.

Chapter 9

Houston

My knuckles are already showing the bruise. I haven't hit someone that hard in a long time. The fights I'd had with Carson, Paige's ex *whatever he was*, weren't as intense as what happened yesterday walking Paige home. When I heard that guy taunting her—making those sounds, being disrespectful—something entirely different came over me, and when I swung at his face, I swung hard.

It felt good. Though I felt a little...embarrassed, I guess? When Paige called me out on it, I didn't see that coming. Not that I thought it through much before I turned and went all ape-fist. But I did sort of expect her to be grateful. At least a *thank you*. Certainly not the cold-ass shoulder I ended up with.

I thought about just leaving when we got home, going to the carnival—saying *fuck it*. But I didn't want to leave her alone. Not that she came out of her room a single time. I finally gave up on waiting her out when Leah and my mom came home.

Paige must have left for class early this morning, because as promised, she left a check along with the signed lease agreement in the middle of the counter, a sticky note on the check that read I DON'T KNOW YOUR STUPID LAST NAME, SO FILL IT IN FOR ME. I'm glad I found this before my mom. I don't think she'd quite appreciate Paige's bite, not like I do.

God, why do I?

I wrote in our *stupid* last name, then added a note to the bottom of her sticky and left it on her bedroom door.

ORR. MY STUPID LAST NAME'S ORR. PRACTICE WRITING IT ON THE THANK YOU NOTE I DESERVE FOR DECKING THAT ASSHOLE.

I went back and pulled it off her door a few minutes ago though, because I don't want my mom seeing that, either. Maybe I don't want Paige to read it. Writing it was enough. I felt better—for a minute. I tore it into small pieces and put it in the trash when I got back downstairs, deciding to be an adult and just tell her my last name instead of passing notes like grade school.

"Morning, sweetheart! Leah up and ready?" My mom startles me from my daydream at the kitchen table. Joyce *Orr* is a morning person. She's really an every-time person—cheer and glee and...cheer...seeps from her pores, hitting people in all directions, no matter how much they *aren't* morning people.

"Oh...uh, yeah. She's getting dressed. Wanted to pick her own outfit this morning," I say, eyebrows high. My mom reflects my expression—both of us wondering what she'll come ambling down the stairs in.

Leah spends her day at the church daycare with my mom. I'm fortunate that we're able to make this work. I'm lucky my mom is able to help. There are days where I'm not sure how I've survived without Beth.

Beth was excited about being a mom. It's really the reason we ultimately decided to keep Leah. Beth—she wanted that little girl with all her heart. She only had her for a month, but it was long enough for my daughter to look just like her, to act like her. It's almost like a soul left Beth's body the day that car sliced through her and found a home in Leah's heart, sharing space— mother and daughter welded together. It used to hurt looking at her, especially when she got older, a toddler with a personality and mannerisms. All I saw was Beth. But over the last year, I've realized how lucky I am to have this small piece of her with me every day. Now, I sneak her door open at night, casting a light across her face from the hallway, just so I can remember and find peace.

Leah's footsteps literally tap along the wood at the top of the steps, and it piques both my mom and my interests; we move into her view, only to see Leah taking the steps one at a time, sitting, tucking her pink skirt around her legs to help her slide down each step more easily. She's in pink—every pink thing she owns. And she's wearing a pair of my mother's pink high heels on her feet, rolled up socks stuffed in the back, poorly, to try to keep them on her feet.

She's trying to look like Paige. I recognize it immediately. My mom arches a brow at me, almost like a warning. She has only spoken to Paige in passing, but I think she sees Leah's fantasy being played out too. And I think it concerns her.

"Baby girl, I don't think you're quite ready for my shoes," my mom says, meeting her halfway down the steps. Leah's head falls, and I see the disappointment all over her face.

"But your outfit looks really nice," I say, just wanting to see her smile again.

Leah bites her lip and holds on to the banister, trying to stand in my mom's shoes to show me everything she has on. She twists from side to side, letting the pink material around her knees sway. "Do you think *she* would like it?" she asks, bottom lip fully sucked in her mouth.

She wants to *be* like Paige. I'm not sure if that's a good thing. But the moment I have that thought, I regret it, and I feel guilty for even thinking it—almost like Paige must hear my thoughts from wherever she is. I feel bad because I know it would hurt her feelings. And I feel bad because...I'm wrong. Why wouldn't it be a good thing to be like Paige? The way Paige stood up to those kids, the way she's trying to fix things with her sister—those things...they're part of the kind of the person I want Leah to be.

"I think she'd love it. You can show her when she gets home from school tonight," I say, Leah's mouth returning to the smile she was wearing when she first tried to walk down the steps.

"What if we go with the sandals today, though—for safety?" my mom asks, holding her hand out for Leah's foot. She takes each shoe off, rolling the socks in her hands. Leah nods a concession, and my mom walks her back upstairs to find her shoes, but she glances at me over her shoulder, that same concerned line of her lips.

When they come back downstairs, I pick Leah up, propping her at my side, and kissing her cheeks, marveling at her ability to remind me of others—it's strange looking at her and seeing Beth *and* Paige.

After she and my mom leave, I pack my bag for class, and take off for my shift at the store. My classes are all late in the afternoon this semester. I'm only taking two, because one is an intense programming section, the other...Spanish. And even taking two is going to make my work schedule a challenge. There won't be time to stop by the house often—no time to run into Paige.

When I get to the store, I help Chuck unload a few boxes in the back from the late-night deliveries, and he notices when I protect my hand.

"That from the other day?" he asks, remembering my run-in with Carson. Maybe not one of my finest moments, but damn, it felt good to put that guy in his place.

"No, this...was a different incident," I say, turning, because I don't want to look him in the eye. This would have been a good time to lie. But I'm so bad at lying, I couldn't think of anything quickly enough.

"Is this becoming a pattern, Houston?" he asks from behind me as we walk through the storage racks. I don't like the idea of Chuck thinking I'm a problem. I also don't like him parenting me. He's done it, on occasion—given me fatherly advice. I think he does it because he knows mine isn't around to give it. But I don't want to hear it from someone else. I'd rather go without.

"No, sir," I say. "This time there was a girl who was being harassed. I'd hope *that* asshole's pattern is broken, so no need for mine." I let my eyes go to his for a second, just so he sees how serious I am. He nods, and pats me on the back once as he heads inside.

"Chivalry is always okay in my book," he says.

I smile thinking of how he treats Sheila. I catch them sometimes, in those small moments. The way she'll let her hand run along his arm, squeezing his hand. Or the way he spins her in his arms to the music humming throughout the store—just to dance with her for no reason at all. It's a far cry from the way my grandpa used to call my grandmother "useless" and "dumb" in front of others, or the way he used to tell my mom she would have gotten married sooner, or could have had a better husband, if she weren't so fat. My mom never talks about it—the emotional abuse—but I know it's left scars on her. I knew it was wrong when I was a kid, I only wish I were brave enough when my grandparents were alive to tell my grandpa how wrong he was—about *everything.*

"Dude, burrito me!" Casey yells as he walks in through the side door. Chuck yells at him for coming in through the employee entrance, and Casey grabs the badge from my shirt, pinning it to himself. "That better?" he teases. Chuck grumbles something and heads into his office. I smack my hand across my friend's chest, knocking the wind from him a little.

"Why do you have to be like that to him?" I say, holding my hand out for my badge.

"He doesn't like me. I don't know why?" Casey says, handing it to me.

"Yeah, I wonder," I mutter. I move to my usual duties, getting the deli ready, then spend a few minutes on my friend's breakfast. I'm rolling the tortilla when he notices my hand.

"What happened to your knuckles, bro?" he asks. I roll my hand over, and wiggle my fingers, buying myself time. Still unable to come up with a good lie, I opt for nothing instead, and shrug as I finish his burrito.

When Casey takes it from me, he holds my gaze for a second, quirking a brow up in suspicion. "That's bullshit," he points at me, then takes a bite of his food. "And you'll tell me eventually."

Maybe I will. Or maybe there's nothing to tell, because on my short drive here, I decided that finding any reason not to run into Paige at the house—not to be alone with her—was a good move. I'm thinking about her too much, and Leah's only been with her for a day and she's already attached. There's no stopping that, but I need to remember the arrangement. Paige lives with us, and she and Leah can be friends. And while I'm attracted to her, doing anything about it would open a Pandora's box.

"So, hey," Casey says, walking around to the other side of the counter to stand next to me. I make a face at him, but he shrugs me off with a *whatever*. Chuck hates it when he does this too; I look over to his office. The door's closed, so I indulge my friend, hoping he'll hurry up with whatever he's all excited to show me on his phone.

"The real reason I came this morning," he says, and I laugh, folding up the paper from his burrito and tossing it in the trash. "Dude, yeah. The burrito was good. And that's *usually* the reason. But Eli got this from a friend last night at some party and I *had* to show you. I'm...I'm not going to tell you, because I can't wait to see your face when you realize."

He starts playing some video, and the moaning sounds are loud. I slap his hand away and look back over to Chuck's office, the door still closed. "Case, what the fuck?" I say, as he's fumbling with his phone, pushing buttons on the side to mute it.

"Sorry, I had it up loud last time. Come on dude, I turned it down. Just watch. Trust me!" he says, holding the phone out again.

I stare at him for a few seconds before I realize this is a battle I'm not going to win, and the only way through this is to watch this damn video. I take the phone back from him and push the play icon. The quality isn't great, and the picture is pretty grainy. I can tell it's two people having sex on some crappy dorm-room bed, and it looks like the entire thing was filmed from a laptop, the view of some chick's bare back and a dude's hairy legs. I watch for about fifteen seconds, getting the drift, not really seeing what the big deal is—college porn happens at

McConnell all the time. I think there are even a few guys in the broadcast school who use the equipment lab for a side business.

"Dude, I get it—a porn. Whatever," I say, handing the phone back, but Casey pushes it to me again.

"Just. Watch," he says, the bend in his lips painting a sinister smirk that hits me the wrong way. I look back at the screen a second later, and then holy fucking hell!

"Wait a minute! Is that..." I say, pulling the screen closer to my face, pausing it and taking the full frame in. It's only from her side—*so far*—but there's no disputing that's Paige on the screen. Those are her eyes. Her lips. Her hair. Her breasts. There isn't much left to discover.

"Where did you get this?" I ask, dragging the video forward and rewinding a few times, wanting to get an idea of the full extent of what this is—*what she's done.*

"Right? I knew that would get you! Pretty fuckin' hot, right?" Casey says, leaning over to look with me. I shut the phone off and clutch it in my hands, feeling my chest constrict and my throat burn with anger.

"Where. Did. You. Get this?" I ask through gritted teeth. Casey's brow pinches and he pauses before parting his lips to speak. He waits another breath, examining me.

"I told you, Eli got it from some dude at a party," he says.

I shut my eyes, more pieces of Paige's puzzle pulling together—the guys harassing her, the sounds they were making, her running away. What the hell did she do? I shove Casey's phone in my pocket, and go back to my work, this time working a little faster, with a little more force to every movement. I can't tell if I'm mad *for* Paige or *at* her.

"Dickhead, give me my phone," he says, and I point my finger at him, my lips a hard line, trying to hold back saying things I'd regret.

"I'll give it back to you later," I say.

"What, wanna go home and watch it? I can just text it to you, ya know," he says, and I point at him again, this time pushing my finger into his chest hard enough to make his breath falter.

"What I want is to find out exactly what the hell this is, if Paige knows about it, and if there are...I don't know...*more*?" I stop working again, pulling my gloves from my hands and tossing them on the counter, flipping the lids of the various food cases closed and finally leaning back against the opposite counter as I push my fingers deep into my temples. "Fuck, man? What if Leah sees this shit? What the hell is this?"

The evil grin that was on Casey's face a minute ago is now replaced with wide eyes and understanding. Yeah, Leah, asshole!

"Dude, how is she ever going to see this?" he says, laughing nervously and pointing to my pocket where his phone is still buried.

"I don't know, man. I...I don't know," I say, running my hand through my hair once. "But...if she does...shit! Case, she barely knows her and already she thinks Paige is her best friend. She dressed like her today—put on heels and everything."

"I'm sorry man," Casey says quietly. I think he regrets letting me know. I regret knowing. But a surprise would have been worse. This...this was a surprise. But at least finding out this way, I feel like maybe I can do some damage control? All I know is—I need to talk to Paige before I jump to any conclusions.

"Let me just have your phone for the afternoon. I don't want to be sending this thing around places. Not until I know exactly what it is, okay?" I say. I feel the burn of the bruise on my hand as I ask, and I'm reminded of my brawl in her honor. I feel a little foolish about it now. And I also feel really fucking sad.

Paige

It doesn't matter how many people have seen it. Now that I know it's out there—*it's really out there*—I'm expecting everyone to know. In my head, this low-grade video of me is a blockbuster. I walk back from my morning classes quickly, still hearing those guys from last night in my head.

Nobody is around. But I imagine them there anyway. The sounds in my head carry me all the way through the front door of Houston's house—*my* house. It feels so temporary, not at all like home. Not that the Delta House ever felt like home, I suppose. The only place that ever really felt like home—other than my *real* home—was the tiny dorm space I shared with my sister and Rowe for a month.

I never should have left.

All I want is to run upstairs and hide, to search for myself more on the Internet, just like I did all night instead of sleeping. Maybe I'll sleep. Maybe, if I shut my eyes here, in this house, I won't hear them taunting me.

"We need to talk," Houston says, stepping out of his room across the hall from me. He startles me, and my bag slips from my shoulder, dropping at my feet and spilling my books on the floor. I kneel down to pick them up, but Houston beats me, collecting my biology and algebra books in his hands then reaching for my bag. His hand covers mine, and I know I'm trembling and he can feel it.

"Just...just give them to me," I say, not looking at him, jerking the bag away and reaching for my books. I glance up and his brow is pinched. I know he thinks I'm trembling because of him. But I'm not. I'm nervous lately because of everyone. And I fucking hate it.

"Look, this is awkward, and I was ready to confront you about this about an hour ago, but then I came home and have been waiting, and now I'm not really as mad as I was before, maybe just confused. Just...just tell me the truth. I need to know." He's rambling, but he lets just enough escape, his words giving me faint clues that point me in the right direction. My chest constricts, and breathing...it gets harder. "Is this...you?"

When he hands the phone to me, a video displayed on the screen, paused in a close-up of my face, I feel everything inside of me ignite and then die all at once. Even with the rumors, I still hadn't seen it for myself. I could pretend it wasn't real then, pretend that it was all just words being passed around, without any visual proof.

What Houston is handing me now, though—that begs to differ. What he's handing me is real. It's also a nightmare, a walking, digital nightmare, wrapped up and sent to me with the hope of taking me out of the equation.

I pull the phone into my palms, stepping back a few strides until my back hits the wall. I need that wall there, to support me. I hover my finger over the screen, bringing myself to tap once. I hear the sounds—like the evil echoes that have been replaying in my head since last night—and I stop it instantly. My eyes close.

"Paige?" Houston's voice oozes disappointment. I won't look at him.

"Houston," I respond, my eyes flickering open, but remaining focused on my feet, as well as on the phone in my hands. My voice comes out even. I'm working hard to make it so. My heart is beating wildly, hurting me from the inside. I think I may be sick.

"No, you don't get to do that," he says, his indignation growing, stirring my emotions, making everything that hurts inside me right now feel messier.

"Get to do what? Be angry? Because...ha!" I laugh once, the sound coming out in a punctuated puff of air, louder than I anticipated, and I glance at Leah's door. It's open, as is Houston's mom's. We're alone, which means I can be as loud as I want. Like hell am I going to be the one wrong here.

"Paige!" he says in a loud whisper, his hands flying to his forehead, pushing through his damned perfect hair, his eyes wide. "How could you do something like this?"

"You think...I'm...I'm sorry...you think I *purposely* did this?" I laugh again.

"I don't know what to think. All I know is those guys the other night; that was about this, wasn't it? And I...goddamnit Paige, I defended you against them. But they were..." his voice grows weak before he finishes that sentence, so I step in and finish it for him.

"They were what, Houston? They were...*right*? Is that what you meant to say?" I push off from the wall, my hands folded in front of me. I turn and kick my bag of books into my room, so I can close the door on him as soon as I want to and not have to come back out for anything.

142

"Well they weren't exactly wrong, Paige," he sighs, his hand rubbing at his neck. I want to punch him. The longer he looks at me, like that—like I did something wrong—the more blood pumps through my arms and fingers and neck and legs. Every limb, every muscle feels strong. Houston is twice my size, but with the energy I feel right now, I'm confidant I would kill him if I tried.

"Watch it," I seethe, pointing a finger at him, my eyes narrowing. To think there were times when I actually let myself indulge in the thought of kissing him—of crossing the line with him, of making an exception and breaking my rules about dating boys who can only get me somewhere. "You don't get to judge me," I say, my voice picking up strength with every word, every sentence. "And that video...this video?" I hold the phone up. He reaches for it, but I shake my head *no*, pushing the phone into the back pocket of my jeans. "Uh, no. I'm taking this copy, and you can have the phone back when I've erased it."

"It's not my phone," he grumbles.

"Well then, you shouldn't care how long I keep it," I say, folding my arms again over my chest. I can feel the steady drumming against my skin, my heartbeat now in a cadence, a pissed-off, ready-to-slay-someone cadence. "This video is out there to hurt me. I didn't make it. At least not knowingly. And the fact that you ever thought I would...means I was *way wrong* about the kind of guy I thought you were."

"What, the kind of guy who wants to make sure he didn't move a porn star in with his four-year-old daughter? That guy's not good enough for you?" he laughs. His arms are outstretched, and now his arrogance is fueling me. I take one more step backward in the direction of my room—I'm a foot away from closing the door on him and locking him out. My mouth is watering, and my lips are tingling. This sensation, it's not the kind you get when you want to be kissed. It's the kind you get when you want to say something hurtful. The urge is familiar, and I'm not very good at controlling it.

We stare at one another, both of us breathing hard and even, like a bull and a fighter in the ring. Then Houston waves a blanket of red, and my instincts take over.

"How could you be so careless, Paige? So...so stupid?" he asks, his eyes smaller, his gaze locked with my own, his head shaking in disgrace.

"Says the single dad who knocked up his high-school girlfriend."

My words fall out, all at once. They were purposeful. They were meant as an attack. They were meant as a defense. They were meant to destroy, to puncture his heart, and make it bleed—to wreck him where he's most vulnerable. Houston's eyes never leave mine, and the shift within them is subtle, yet intense all the same. The green color grows darker, and the hurt washes over everything else.

"Houston..." I start, my eyes falling closed, my heart no longer beating. The guilt stronger than anything I've ever felt.

"Don't, Paige. Don't try to make that better. You can't," he says, holding a hand up as he walks away. I stand still, watching as his hand reaches his door. He never turns to face me, but he pauses, leaning his head against the wood. "Just slide the phone under my door whenever you're done."

I nod in response, even though he can't see me. My voice, so strong seconds before, fails me now.

"Oh, and *Orr*," he turns his knob, pushes the door open, and slowly steps inside, his body facing mine again. He looks up from the ground, and the disappointment I thought I saw on his face earlier is nothing compared to the look he's wearing now. "My last name's Orr. So is Leah's."

His door shuts, and I stand there frozen, looking at the ghost of where he was for a full minute before I'm able to retreat back to my own space, shutting my door as well. The tingling is gone, my control lost. But that rush I usually get from being strong, from standing up to someone—it never comes. The only thing I feel is sad.

It takes me an hour to find the courage to watch the video—yet another to let myself *really* watch it. By the evening hours, I'm finally capable of thought and reason, and I realize—the girl in this video, she isn't always me.

The things I thought might be in there—they're there. There's the strip tease at the frat house, and a few close-ups of me in my bra. There's also a heavy make-out scene with Carson, where my shirt gets stripped away. But then some things get really strange. My hair doesn't look right, and there's a noticeable mismatch where my head meets my neck. I can't prove it for certain, but I think maybe this video has been edited. I don't remember any of it—which I know doesn't say much, and would never stand up in a court of law—but the more I watch, the more sure I am.

Hours after my fight with Houston, I step out into the hall. The room to his door is open now, and I know I heard him come and go at least once tonight. I heard Leah, too. She asked if I was home, and Houston said I was busy.

I slow as I reach the entrance to his room, and my body starts to flush when I see him lying on his side on his bed, headphones pressed into his ears. He's tapping a pen on a pad of paper, and I notice his Spanish book to the side. I smirk at the memory, but lose it the second I remember why I'm here, and the awful thing I said to him.

I consider leaving unnoticed, but before I can, he looks up—his expression void of feeling, his green eyes cold. He used to look at me like I was beautiful, not every time, but many times. Right now I'm a stranger.

He pulls his headphones from his ears, but doesn't speak.

"I'm done...with the phone," I say, reaching around the corner of his wall and sliding it on his desk. He watches my movement then brings his eyes back to mine. "I...I watched it," I say, feeling the rolling sensation in my stomach as I struggle for the courage to keep talking. "Houston...it isn't me. The girl in that video...most of it...it's fake."

He stands as I stutter through my words, and with every step closer to me he comes, the stronger I begin to feel. Relief is such a powerful emotion. I begin explaining what I saw, how I think the video was made, and I'm about to ask him for help, when he reaches for the edge of his door and closes it—shutting me out—my feet curling the inch or so required to move out of his way.

I've been stunned so few times in my life: when my sister was diagnosed with MS, and when she was assaulted—and I'm stunned now. And I'm embarrassed. I think maybe also a little heartbroken. The tears come faster than I can stop them, falling harder as I wipe them away. I turn to retreat back to my room, wishing for this moment to be a dream, but it's anything but.

"You okay?" a tiny voice whispers. I bite my bottom lip, knowing my eyes are red and watering. I try not to look at her head on, but Leah steps out from her room, toward me.

"Yeah, I'm okay," I whisper, forcing a smile where it doesn't belong. "Just a bad dream. I'm sorry, Leah. I didn't mean to wake you."

"I was up," she says. "I wanted to say goodnight."

She slides close to me, her socks rolled around her ankles, the toes pulled out, flopping at the ends of her feet like a clown's shoes. When her fingers reach my waist, she grabs onto me, and squeezes, pressing her cheek into my hip before turning to face it, kissing it. My eyes lose their strength, and another tear rolls down my cheek, coming to rest at the edge of my chin.

"Goodnight," I say, my lip quivering. I tuck it in my teeth so I can hold it at bay.

"He's good with bad dreams. I always go to him, too," she says over her shoulder, smiling one more time before getting lost in the darkness of her room.

I turn quickly, shutting off my light and closing my door. I crawl under my covers without even changing, pulling the blankets up around my face, muffling my cry. Houston may be good with bad dreams, but I come bearing nightmares. I also come with regret. I don't know whether I'm angry with him...or I miss him. I think maybe it's both. Admitting that to myself hurts most of all.

Chapter 10

Houston

I have to stop this thing with Paige. It was innocent flirting—safe. And then all of a sudden it wasn't. There was a time, maybe even only a day ago, when it felt a lot like falling. And that scares me. Then there are other times, like last night, where I hate her. She found the center of my insecurities, and was willing to push them—open up wounds and actually speak the words I worry everyone thinks...the words sometimes I think and am ashamed of—*I had a kid instead of a life.*

Maybe it's her honesty I dislike. I'm honest. Or I try to be. But Paige—fuck, she's honest. She calls out my insecurities. And I think she wants answers when she does.

That scares me too.

Maybe I don't really hate her at all. Maybe it's all just mixed together in this mess I started—I shouldn't have ever started.

Would I have forgotten about her if she never moved in?

She was so angry, so...so...cruel when she spoke. I could have handled anything but the one place she went. I've endured a lot of judgment for being a young dad. When we found out and broke the news to Beth's family, the names I was called for "ruining our young lives" were vile. And truthfully, Paige didn't label me directly—she only held up a mirror, reflecting the words I said to her.

I think that's what has my head all twisted the most. She was only repeating my words, and she didn't even truly say them. Especially that one word—*stupid*. I called her stupid for an error in judgment.

What a hypocrite.

I felt bad the moment the last letter left my breath. I wanted to catch the sound, to grab it and swallow it so it never hit her ears.

But it was too late.

She heard it, and swung right back. In that tiny second in between, before she spoke, I felt like the man I never wanted to be. I was being like my grandfather. And I thought of how ashamed my own dad would have been. Before I could apologize though, before I could make it right, Paige attacked Leah's very existence—and my anger and hurt washed any regret away, like the tide.

In an instant, I felt justified, and spent the day sure I would ask Paige to leave. Then she walked in my room and told me it wasn't her in the video. She didn't walk in to apologize—to take back what she said about Beth or Leah—she went right to herself, the only thing she worries about. My heart was going to explode in my chest from the rush of rage, and I bit my tongue, not wanting to add any more layers onto our tangled conversations.

I got up, and simply shut the door.

Justified.

All the way until this very moment, when—per usual with my life—a four-year-old puts things into perspective.

"Why was Paige crying?" she asks, mouth full of Cheerios, milk dripping down her chin. She's talking to me at the breakfast table, and I'm pretending not to hear her or register her. I'm playing dumb. My mom slides out a chair and sits between us.

"Paige was crying?" my mom asks. Great—she's engaging. We're only moments away from someone blurting out that Paige was crying because I was an asshole. Doesn't matter— sometimes being an asshole is warranted.

It was justified.

"Yeah, she was by daddy's door. I heard her so I went to check on her in the hallway. She said it was a bad dream. But daddy will make it better; I told her he would." My eyes close as Leah speaks. I catch enough of her face to see my daughter smiling at me proudly. *I'll make it better.* No, baby girl—I'll make it worse. I turn away enough so my mom can't see my face, bringing my focus back down to the pad of notes next to my bowl of cereal. Like I'm really studying.

"Well that's good...that he made it better," my mom says. I hear the tone. I feel her stare, so I look up and smile and shrug. She doesn't ask anything more, but I know she will—the second Leah goes up stairs to change. When she does, I brace myself for the look I know will show up on my mom's face. She'll glance at me, and everything will unravel. It's why I could never get away with lies when I was a kid.

Joyce Orr is a magician.

The look comes, and I let my head fall forward. "I'm not sure what happened," I say. It's really the truth. I have a bunch of facts—Paige is in a sordid video floating around online. She says it isn't her. I believe her. But I'm still mad at her anyway. It isn't fair. I don't care. I called her stupid. She told me Leah was a mistake. And now I want her to move out.

I also want her to stay.

And I want to fix things for her.

And I want her to say she's sorry.

And I'm sorry.

I don't say any of that, though. I just shrug and keep my head down, waiting for my mom to work her magic. Then there's a knock at our front door.

"I got it," I say, leaping from my chair. If it's someone selling something, I think I'll invite him inside. I'll watch a demo, let him spill shit on our carpet and try to mop it up. Anything—whatever it takes to make the other crap in my head disappear.

When I swing the door open, I'm hit with recognition. It only takes a second or two for me to place it, and when I see the guy in a wheelchair behind the blonde—who looks like he could kick my ass—my hunch is confirmed.

"Oh...wow. I did NOT see this coming," says the girl I *know* is Cass. We haven't officially met. "You are the last person I thought was on the other side of this door."

"I'm sorry...can I help you?" I ask, like I don't know she's looking for Paige. Did Paige tell her to come here?

"I know she's not here right now. Mind if I come in and wait?" Cass asks, pushing right by me through the door. Leah's eyes flash, and I can tell she's nervous.

"It's okay. This is Paige's sister," I say, wanting to allay her fears, maybe stave some of her innocent young questions. Leah smiles when I explain, and goes right back to finishing her cereal, looking up to make sure our guests are watching. The sun revolves around Paige in Leah's mind.

"Come on in," I say, waving the guy I am pretty sure is Cass's boyfriend in so I can close the door. He has some trouble with the stoop, but with a rock of his wheels he clears it without my help. My mom scoots a chair out of the way and looks to me when our guests are turned around. I smile with tight lips because I have no clue what this visit is all about.

"Oh, are those Cheerios?" the guy asks, leaning low toward Leah. She smirks at him and starts to nod and giggle. She pushes the box closer to him, and he pours a handful to start munching along with her.

"She's...living here," Cass says, looking around our simple kitchen. I get the look on her face. Paige doesn't *go* here. My god how she doesn't *go* here.

"For a few days," I say, my attention consumed with the guy who's now in a Cheerio crunch-off with Leah. He glances up at me and pours the rest of the cereal in his mouth from his palm, dusting it off on his jeans before reaching for my hand.

"I'm Ty. Sorry to barge in. Cass followed her sister here yesterday, like a stalker," Ty says, sending a wry smile in his girlfriend's direction.

"Like I had a choice," she says back, her tone defensive.

"Yeah, good point. Asking her would have been, like...*way* complicated," he says, earning a scowl from her next. I like this guy.

"I'm sure you know this, or…maybe you don't. Hard to say what you know, or what's really going on, but…anyhow…Paige and I don't talk much," Cass says. I nod in agreement, for some reason not wanting Paige's family drama to play out for my mom. She'll ask later; she has a lot to ask me about later. But maybe by then I'll come up with a way to protect Paige and her story. Of course, I also want her to move out. I still want that…right?

"So…you and Paige, like…" Ty whispers in a growly voice, leaning toward me. His eyebrows raise, and I glance from him to Leah then back again.

"No, dude. Not like that. We're…friends," I say, finding it hard to pick the right word, settling on friends. Cass glares at me when I speak, and I don't know if it's because I chose the wrong word, or because she doesn't believe it.

"Mind if I wait here for her?" Cass asks. I take a deep breath, mentally debating, weighing the pros and cons, when the door swings open and Paige takes the decision out of my hands.

Her mouth is open, and I can tell by the look on her face that she's gained strength since last night—she came home with the intention of standing up to me, but thankfully she took in the entire room before speaking. Now she's simply rolling her eyes, closing the door, and walking over to hook her purse and backpack on the last open chair.

"What are you doing here?" she sighs to her sister.

"What am *I* doing here? Paige—you're supposed to be in the Delta House!" Cass leans forward, speaking loudly. Leah is watching the entire thing like my grandmother used to watch soap operas. My mom notices and ushers her upstairs to get ready for the day.

"Yeah, well that plan fell through. Houston is giving me a place to crash, while I figure some things out," Paige says, like it's no big deal. It shouldn't be a big deal, but then there's this video—which I'm pretty sure has something to do with some of the girls at the sorority house, and I'm almost positive Cass knows none of this. I decide to keep my mouth shut, instead opting to clean up the table. I'm listening while rinsing dishes when I feel Ty move closer to me.

"Hey, I'm sorry we barged in, man. Really—totally against this idea, but when Cass gets something in her head..." he says, and I chuckle.

"They're twins. She gets shit in her head too, so I've learned," I say, and there's a certain fondness that settles in my chest thinking about Paige and all of her pain-in-the-assness. I hate that fondness.

Ty laughs at my observation, then moves to the table and brings the rest of the items over to help me clean up. Paige and Cass have moved into a weird yelling-whisper mode now, with hand gestures, and lots of *tsking* sounds and eye-rolls.

"So, how'd you two meet?" Ty asks, clearly accustomed to this type of situation between the two sisters.

"I work at a grocery store. I made her a sandwich, and the rest is history," I say, smirking. It's simple, but it's true. I looked forward to her coming in when I knew she would, and sometimes, when she'd just stop in for her own things—not for the sorority—I'd have a little flash of a fantasy that she came in to see me.

Fuck, I'm in trouble. I'm pretty sure Ty knows too, because he's grinning, his face a lot like my friend Casey's when he's right and I'm wrong—which doesn't happen *often*.

"We're going out tonight—happy hour at Sally's. You should come. Maybe you can get *that* one there, to hang out with her sister. They need to do more of that," he says. My smile comes without my permission, but I stifle it quickly.

I can't go out. I spend my nights at home, with my daughter snoring on the other side of the hall...ready in case the bad dream comes, or worse, the one where she sees her mother's ghost. But I nod indifferently, making him believe I might show up.

When I look back, Cass and Paige are standing. They're not hugging, but they're laughing. It's like they both want to touch each other, show how much that bond is there, but there's something awkward about it. I think Cass forgives Paige more than she realizes; she's just waiting for Paige to make the first move.

Cass shakes my hand, and I notice how strong her grip is—I'm frankly not sure whose was stronger, hers or Ty's. I shut the door behind them and ready myself to forgive Paige, to forget about everything from twelve hours ago.

"I can't believe you told her I was here!" she launches into me. I actually laugh, because I'm a little dumbfounded. "And you—"

She takes a step closer to me, her finger actually touching my chest. This entire scene is getting more ridiculous by the minute. "You are *not* going to Sally's tonight. You don't need to be my sister's friend, because *this*?" she says, waving her hand emphatically between the both of us. "This is a nothing thing! There isn't an *us* for her to get to know—so just forget about whatever bond you're thinking about making, okay?"

I stand silent, a little stunned; she loads her purse and backpack over her shoulders. Finally, when she does hit the stairs, I speak.

"Are you crazy? I mean...like, should I be concerned that you're actually crazy? Because *that*...whatever you just did there?" I mimic her wave between us. "That was kinda crazy."

She points her finger at me, and her body is actually shaking a little. "Your ass stays home tonight," she says. I salute her when she turns around, and when I hear her door slam shut, I can't help but laugh, hard.

My mom comes down just as I'm getting ready to head to class for the day, and I can tell that questions are still begging to be cleared off her chest. But Leah's here, so I let my daughter throw me a block on this one. And then I get an idea.

"Hey, are you home tonight? Book club or anything?" I ask, my mom's eyes squinting as she nods.

"I'm home," she says, her glance sideways and suspicious.

"Would you mind if I go out, for just a few hours, after bedtime? Paige is trying to mend some bridges with her sister, and I get the sense she kind of wants my support," I lie. I just lied to my mom, and I swear to god she knows. My lips are twitching, and I'm about to ruin it with a smile, when my mom agrees.

"I'll be home," she says, moving beyond me and gathering her lunch together with Leah's for their day at the church. "You should go out more, you know? I can help with things. And it's good for you. Maybe...maybe wear something *nice.*"

I wince when her innuendo hits my ear. As many questions as my mom has, she also likes the idea of a girl catching my interest. Which must mean there's something about Paige that's okay with my mom.

"Thanks," I say, leaving before we get into any more detail. I plan on looking good. But I'm not going because I'm full of hope—I'm going because Paige is going to be ticked as hell when I show up.

Which...gives me goddamned hope.

Paige

If there is one thing I've always liked about Cass's boyfriend, it's his willingness to help me get drunk when I need to. There's a very loose ID policy at Sally's, and when Ty orders up rounds, the questions never seem to come. He's twenty-two—and he's in a wheelchair. If he wants a pitcher for the table, nobody's arguing with him. Wrong as it is, it's still a fact. And I'm cashing in on it tonight.

I need to be drunk to have this conversation with Cass.

"So let me understand this better—Chandra basically kicked you out of the house?" Cass is shouting, and I can't help but look around the crowded bar, sure someone heard her. I hate that I've become so paranoid.

"Yes," I say, taking a big gulp from my mug, emptying it, and filling it more. Not drunk enough. Nowhere near drunk enough. "No," I continue, waving down a cute guy walking by. He has four shots in his hand; I take one from him, then stand to kiss him on the cheek. It works, and he lets me drink another. "Yes, no, sort of," I say, waving the guy away so I can get back to my sister.

"Sorry," Cass shrugs at him over my shoulder. I turn around and the guy is still standing there—I stand up and kiss him one more time, a little sexier, but still on the cheek. Who knows, I may need him for more shots later tonight. It seems to make him happy, because he walks backward toward the bar and keeps his eyes on me. Like there's a shot in hell of that going anywhere.

"Yeah, I'm way confused," Cass says, shaking her head. She's feeling her buzz; I'm jealous. "I thought you and Chandra were like..." she holds up her fingers, crossing them, and makes a clicking sound. "You know...tight."

"We were never *tight*, Cass. Not really," I say.

"Fuck that. You were tight enough to tell her my personal shit," she bites. She's been trying really hard to forgive me, but sometimes—it just comes out. I wish she wouldn't *try* all the time. If I'm pissed at someone, I let it all come out. And then when I'm done, that's when I go back to being nice to them. Wishy-washy isn't me. I'm hot or I'm cold. Lukewarm is stupid.

I grimace at my sister, and take another drink.

"Anyway..." I say, knowing if Cass knew *everything* she'd drop the wronged act and start kissing my ass. "I saw some...things, and despite what you think, I'm not really happy about how she treats you, and I stood up to her. In my own sort of way," I say. Part of me wants to just pull out my phone, show her the pictures of Chandra passed out, the drugs, tell her about the blackmail—I take another drink instead.

"Okay, okay..." she slurs. I could always hold my shit better than her. "But *why* are you living with that guy? I mean, you could have just come back to our room."

I don't answer, instead, swishing my last gulp of beer around my mouth without making eye contact. At the time, going back to live with Cass felt impossible. But now that I'm where I am—living with Houston—I think the impossible with Cass may have been smarter. Harder, perhaps, but definitely smarter.

"I have to pee," I say, leaving my sister without an answer.

Sally's happy hour during the middle of the week is...interesting. The college crowd is usually a mix of freshmen that look nothing like their fake IDs, and grad students more than ready to help freshmen girls get drunk. Add onto that the really creepy old guys who are waiting to give a girl a ride home, and it's a bad mix. I may be drunk, but I'll never be *that* drunk.

The line for the women's bathroom is wrapping down the hallway and out the back door. By the time I get to the end, I'm actually near the trash bins where a guy is peeing in the alley. I cover my nose with my long sleeve and retrace my path back inside. The men's room door is closed. No line. There's never a fucking line here.

I look around, then duck inside. There's only one stall, but I've been in worse bathrooms, especially at the beach. I'm careful not to touch anything, washing my hands and grabbing a fistful of towels to turn off the faucet and open and close the door as I leave the restroom.

"I saw that," he says, scaring me so badly I swing at him, punching him in the gut.

"Fuck, who does that?" I say, holding my other hand on my heart. It's beating wildly. My head is spinning, and it takes me a second to regain my bearings. Part of it's the shots, but most of it is the adrenaline from having the shit scared out of me. Houston is bent in half, coughing.

"Punches the guy they're living with? I know...who does that?" he grunts, still a little out of breath.

"I hit you hard," I say, now noticing the tightness in my knuckles. I'm not sure I've ever actually punched someone. I flex my fingers in and out, and they tingle.

He brings his gaze up, his hand flat against the wall next to me, and for a second his eyes pause on mine.

"Yeah...you did," he says.

A few more seconds pass of him looking at me—me looking at him, and things begin to feel weird. Good. I can't feel good being this close to him. And his breath is tickling my face. And it smells...good. *He* smells good. I need to get back to my table. I'm about to dodge beneath his arm, when his lip curves up on one side.

His hand is still next to me, his fingers rapping once along the wall. I clear my throat and adjust my posture. Houston's head falls forward and he pushes back, stepping in the opposite direction, clearing room for my escape.

Thank god!

I make it most of the way back to the table I'm sharing with my sister, when I notice Houston is only a step or two behind me. Spinning fast, I lose my balance, and he catches me by my elbows, his grip on my arms steady—fast. His hands are strong, and I get caught up looking at them, at his arms. Shaking my head, I shirk his grip.

"I'm fine!" I yell, causing a few people sitting at tables near us to turn and look at me. I stretch my arms out in a *WTF* stance, and they all turn around, back to their own conversations. "You!" I point at him. I'm expecting him to be shocked, to start in with his defensive mode, but instead he smirks again—that same cocked-lip smile that had me feeling dizzy in the hallway by the bathroom. "You were not invited. I *disinvited* you!"

"Yeah, I'm pretty sure I don't work that way. You know, taking orders from you?" Houston says, folding his arms, the black shirt he's wearing stretching tight along his chest. And then I see his arms, and I get lost again. Until he dips his head lower, catching my gaze, and snapping me out of this stupid puppy-crush I seem to suddenly have on his hot arms.

Shit. He has hot arms.

I'm drunk; that's all. I'm just a little buzzed, and I'm feeling it.

"Dude, you made it. We have a pitcher, come on over," Ty says, pushing past us toward the table we've taken over in the corner of Sally's. He begins to pour a beer for Houston, but stops short of full when Houston holds his hand up.

"Thanks, man. But I'm sticking with water tonight. I've got...some things," he says, and I laugh under my breath. He has things, like a kid. His head twists fast to look at me, and his eyebrow cocks.

"Sure, whatever man," Ty says, taking the glass he poured and sliding it over to his brother Nate, who's just stepping up to our table.

"Awe, for me?" Nate says, winking at his brother and taking a drink from the mug.

"Yeah, well I spit in that one," Ty says. Nate swishes his sip around in his mouth and swallows.

"I figured. Thought it tasted weird," Nate says, shrugging and taking another drink. Even though Ty is in a wheelchair and four years older, he and his brother look so much alike.

"Hey, this is Houston. Houston, this is my brother, Nate," Ty says, and Houston reaches his hand across the table, shaking Nate's.

"Nice to meet you," Nate says, looking toward his brother and slapping him on the chest. "Oh, and hey, I meant to tell you—scouts are coming Friday. As in Astros, Marlins, Cardinals, and Nats."

"Scouts?" Houston asks, waving a waitress over and requesting a water. She looks at him with a smile. I take one step closer, leaning my arms on the table next to his, so our arms are touching. *That's right, bitch—those arms you're smiling about are touching mine.* What the hell is wrong with me?

"Nate plays ball for McConnell," Ty says.

"I'm the catcher," Nate shrugs.

"Uh, he bats in the four slot, and he came in with a four-twenty average," Ty says. I have no idea what any of that means, but it seems to impress Houston.

"Nice! So...scouts. Congrats, man," Houston says. A silence falls over the table for a few minutes while everyone looks around the bar. Cass has pulled Rowe out to the dance floor, leaving me here—with this.

"So, how do you know Ty?" Nate asks. I catch the smirk on Ty's face, and I shoot him a warning glance not to fuck with me.

"He's Paige's new roommate," Ty says, a tiny hint of that smug arrogance he wears all the fucking time in his tone. He's loving teasing me. I've been hard on Ty; when he started dating my sister, I didn't trust him—and I told him as much. I trust him a smidge more now, and I was starting to like him. But if he's going to be a dick about me moving out of Delta, I'll move him right back into the "asshole" box.

"Roommate?" Nate asks, glancing at me sideways, then looking back at Houston, who isn't helping the cause at all. He's standing there, arms folded, looking all...hot. Have his arms always been that big?

"Yeah, whatever. Deltas were bitches, and I needed out, and he needed a roommate. It's temporary. So drop it," I say, pulling Nate's half-gone beer into my own hands and downing the rest. I smack the mug down on the table and huff, then turn to face Houston's chest.

"If you're going to be here, at least dance with me," I say, tugging on the taut fabric of his shirt, ushering him out to the dance floor. The song playing isn't really a slow song, but it's too slow to dance apart, so Houston holds out a hand like he wants to *dance*-dance. I stare at it like he's holding a dead cricket.

"You're the one who dragged me out here," he sighs. I look up at him, his smile soft, and his eyes tired. "You know what? Forget it. I'm going back to the table..."

"No," I interrupt, catching his hand before he has a chance to put it in his pocket. I run my fingers up the back of his hands, up his arms—*oh my god those arms*—until both of my hands meet around his neck. I feel Houston's hands nervously search for my hips, and when he lets them rest at the small of my back, I let out the air I've been holding since I ran into him in the hallway. After a few awkward turns of dancing like eighth-graders, I grow more comfortable, finally resting my head against his chest, and when his chin lays on top, completely cradling me to his body, I close my eyes.

Everything right now feels so nice. It feels *more* than nice, and I admit that to myself. It's so different from the chaos and the constant chase of guys for the wrong reasons. This feels simple—the longer the song lasts, the more perfect everything feels.

For two full songs, we dance in silence—the only movement the small twitches and repositioning of our hands, until I feel him slide one up my back, following the line of my spine under my hair until his fingers are at my neck. My lips part as my eyes open.

"Temporary," Houston says, and even though he said a word, all I hear is the way the sound reverberates around his chest, like a deep echo that somehow scratches my every itch. He's not whispering, yet he's talking only to me.

"I'm sorry...what's temporary?" I respond finally, not bothering to pull my ear from his body, not wanting to let my face feel any second of air parting from its very comfortable home along his chest. I am definitely drunk. But even sober, I'm pretty sure I would have a hard time leaving this place. Right. Here.

"When Ty introduced me to his brother and said you and I were...roommates," he says, and I register more words this time. Still not all of them, but enough. "You said it was...temporary."

"Mmmm, yeah...I did," I breathe, my eyes no longer able to open, my voice coming out in an amusing hum. I like the way I sound right now. But Houston sounds sad. Why is he sad?

"Is it because...of the video, and the fight we had?" he asks. Video? Oh, yeah...there's a video. And he wasn't happy about it. He didn't believe me when I told him it wasn't me in the video, at least I don't think he did. My feet aren't moving anymore. I don't think we're swaying, but the floor feels like it's moving.

"Paige? Do you want to move out?" he asks.

"No," I say quickly, reaching my arms around his body and squeezing myself to him tighter. I don't want to move at all. I just want to sleep, standing up, against his chest.

"Then why say *temporary*?" he asks. His hand moves slowly upward until his fingers find my head and begin stroking my hair.

"Because I like you, Houston," I exhale, letting the smile sit comfortably on my lips, nestling in for more of his warmth. "I like you. I don't wanna like you. But I do."

His hand moves faster all of a sudden, and his arms swoop under my legs, and then all I remember is blackness.

Chapter 11

Houston

Her room is dark. I've been waiting for a light to come on, for a sign of something to shine through the small inch of space underneath her door. I've been up all morning. I've been up all night.

She never got sick, but I have a feeling Paige is going to have a wicked hangover today. I'm also pretty sure she's not going to remember a word she said. And that's probably a good thing.

I won't mention it either. Doesn't mean I didn't like hearing it, that I don't like *knowing* it—how she feels. I like it a lot. But last night was like being in a time out—like summer camp, where stupid things you do *don't* count. I went to camp when I was twelve and kissed a girl three years older than me. It was camp. Free pass for her to do something she never would anywhere else in a million years. I benefited. That's what Paige got last night. She got lit, and her mouth said some things I know she would never let slip out otherwise. She likes me, and she doesn't want to. That last part...it's the reason I'll keep my mouth shut, pretend it didn't happen. That and whenever I think about the idea of being something more I also think of the never-ending list of reasons why it's a bad idea, why it would end badly.

I think of Leah.

161

But I like knowing it all the same.

Mom took Leah to work with her already, and she grilled me a little at breakfast.

"That girl seems to have a lot of drama," she said this morning. All I could do was shrug because yeah, she does. I didn't want to add on to my mom's conclusion—or defend Paige. Whatever move I made would have brought my mom down a new path of questioning, one I wasn't ready for. So I kept my mouth shut. But the entire time, I kept thinking about how Paige said she likes me and wishes she didn't. It stings and feels awesome at the same time.

Life is such a tease.

I have about ten minutes before I need to leave for class when Paige's door opens, her body backlit by the small lamp in her room. Her hair is matted to the side of her face, and her makeup is in all of the wrong places.

"Ugh. Why are you here?" she asks, holding a hand up to block my line of sight, like I'm a cameraman.

"I live here," I chuckle, getting to my feet from the spot I've been sitting in the hallway outside my door. "How you feeling?"

I know how she's feeling—like shit. It's confirmed when she bunches her lips and sends me a sour expression like she wants to be sick.

"Don't let me mix beer and shots ever again," she says, rubbing her fingers into her temples. *Again.* As in, I'll be there the next time she does that. It catches my attention, and I dwell on it while she's saying something else.

"I said..." she's shouting now, so I turn my attention back to her. "Would you drive me to class today? I don't think I can walk without it killing me. I'll be ready in a few minutes."

I laugh again, because I've seen her routine a few times now, and I think the fastest she's ever gotten out of the house is forty minutes. "I'm pretty sure you're being dramatic—it won't *kill* you. But...I leave in ten, so if you're ready then, sure," I say, stepping into my room. I hear the shower on the other side of my wall. Pausing, I stand next to it, thinking how we're only a foot apart right now.

I like you. I don't wanna like you. But I do.

I smirk and step out from my room, dropping my bag at the edge of the steps. Standing outside the bathroom door, I let my head fall forward onto it, and I listen to the water; I hear the shower curtain slide and listen for the change in the pattern of the spray when I know it's hitting her body.

I like you. I don't wanna like you. But I do.

I have been repeating her words in my own head since I heard them. I've been saying them like a mantra because of that part of me that doesn't want her to like me either. Because if she likes me, then maybe how I feel is okay too, and maybe acting on it is okay, and then shit gets real. *What does that even mean? Shit gets real?* Shit gets hard—that's what it means. Real hard. I have to make time for someone else; I have to have conversations with Leah; I have to take a leap of faith and risk that my world will fall apart again. That's what that means.

"I like you too, Paige," I whisper. "And fuck if I don't want to. But I do."

I take a few seconds to jog in place, stretching my neck from side to side like I'm about to step into a fight. Maybe I am. But fuck it, shit got real a long time ago. What do I have to lose now?

"I'm not looking, I swear," I say, keeping my eyes at the floor as I barge into the bathroom. I cannot believe I'm doing this.

"Out!" she yells from behind the shower curtain. "Not even funny. Not even clever. Out, you fuck stick, out!"

Her anger makes me laugh, and *fuck stick? Really?*

"I have to brush my teeth. We're pushing it close on time. I'll be fast, and I'll keep my face forward. I swear," I say.

I've already brushed my teeth, but she doesn't know that. I turn on the water and load up my brush. I hear the curtain slide behind me, and I know she's looking at me. I don't have to turn around or look into the reflection to know what her face looks like—her brow is furrowed and her lips are tight, and she's making sure I'm keeping my promise. Don't worry Paige; I won't look. But I know you want me to.

I'm spitting into the sink and reaching for the towel by feeling, careful not to glance up, when I hear the water switch off and the curtain slide open. There's no towel near her or the tub; I know it because I see them hanging on the rack several steps away. She's cheating.

I notice her shape move into my periphery to my right, and I glance briefly to catch her hand reach for the towel. When I see her back is to me, I go ahead and look long enough to take a mental picture. Her hair is soaking wet and dripping a line down her perfectly sun-kissed skin, a trail of water I let my eyes follow down her shoulder blades, to the small of her back, to an ass that is so perfect I wish I were the kind of asshole who would reach out and smack it at a time like this. I just hold my breath and memorize it instead. I turn back to the sink, lay my towel down, and move to leave.

"You looked," she says, and I pause with my hand on the doorknob, the curves of her body now ingrained in my memory. I smile.

"Yeah, I did," I say, before stepping into the hallway and shutting the door behind me.

Paige is true to her word, and she's dressed and ready to leave within five minutes, her wet hair twisted and tucked into a McConnell hat. She meets me at the bottom of the stairs, and I expect her to be blushing. The fact that she isn't is somehow sexier. I'm playing with fire, but I think I'll be okay getting a little burned.

"Hey, so . . . I have to confess something," I say as we step through the door. I pull out my keys to lock up, and when I turn, she's already marched to the car, not waiting for me, or caring what I have to confess it seems. I can't help but laugh quietly.

I open the back door to drop my bag in the back seat, but before shutting it, I unzip the laptop pouch and slide her computer out, bringing it into the front seat with me.

"I borrowed your laptop last night," I say, holding it out for her to take. She stares at it, her face questioning why I have it in the first place. It's heavy, so after a few seconds I rest it on her lap, my fingers grazing the tops of her thighs as I pull my hand away. She looks at me fast, almost offended, but I avert my eyes. "Relax, it's just a laptop."

I stare forward long enough to feel her scowl at me from the side; I turn to face out my window, not wanting her to see my smirk.

We drive in silence for a block or two, and she finally slides her laptop into her own bag, slowly pulling the zipper. Letting myself glance in her direction, I see the worry lines on her forehead as she keeps her gaze on her bag, which she's now hugging in her lap. She knows I took it to watch the video.

"You said it wasn't you...the other night," I speak carefully, not saying the word *video* or even admitting out loud that I watched it. She already knows, but keeping the conversation less direct might make her more willing to talk about it. Especially after I shut her out the first time she tried.

"You...watched it?" she asks. "The whole thing..."

I nod.

We pull into my lot. I don't like to spend money on parking fees since I live close, so we're still a bit of a haul away from the main part of campus. Sometimes when I'm running late, though, even getting this much closer saves me precious seconds in my carefully-timed life.

"I saw it the first time, on Casey's phone," I say, glancing at her. She's frozen in her seat, her normal fire gone.

"Oh," she says, her eyes lost out the front window at the row of cars parked in front of us.

"You're right," I say, expecting her to smile. Expecting...something. Instead, she inhales slowly before turning to face me. "It isn't you—at least, not in the bad parts. That's not...you."

I didn't make a copy; not one I saved. But I did run her video through editing software so I could look at sections frame by frame. Whoever did this was sloppy.

She lets her head fall against the headrest, her eyes focused just beyond me at first, then moving to mine. She shrugs. "I know. But what good does that do me?"

I sigh heavily, but I don't have an answer for her.

"Is this why you left Delta? Why you had to move out?" I ask.

"It's...part of it," she says. Everything about her looks defeated. I'm sure the alcohol is partly to blame for dragging her down this morning. But this sadness...it's more than that.

"Cass doesn't know?" I ask, and her eyes flit back up to mine for a second. She shakes her head *no*.

"I won't tell her," I say.

"Thanks," she says, a smile there for me, if only for a second.

"Maybe no one else will see it," I say, trying to give her hope.

"You saw it," she says, the tears welling in her eyes. She takes a sharp breath, and in a second, they're dry. I know she's hurt, but I also know it's more important to her to act this way— to be strong.

We both step out of the car, bags slung over our shoulders. I watch her transformation, the way she shuffles her posture, tucks the few drying strands of hair under her hat, and touches up the lipstick in the corners of her mouth. Nobody would ever guess how broken she is inside. When she turns to face me, she smiles as if nothing's wrong. It's the same expression she wore the first time we met, when she slid an order ticket over the counter to me at the store.

"Don't look at me like I'm pathetic," she says, her lips forming a tight line, the slightest curl masking her hurt. She's a politician. "I'm not, and I don't need you to feel sorry for me."

I nod once, and she turns to walk away. After a few steps, she twists and takes a few steps backward. "Oh, and Ty sent me a text. He wants you to come play poker with him and a few of the guys tonight—early, at like six. You should go. Ty...he's a good guy. You'd like him. I'll hang out with Leah."

She's still looking at me, slowly walking away, waiting for my approval. This is a test; I can tell. She wants to know if I trust her to stay home with Leah. Will I put my heart in her hands?

166

"Sounds good," I say, careful to keep the pounding of nerves in my stomach away from my expression. "Text me his info."

She smiles again, and this time, it's different. It's not painted on, or pretend. It's real. And I put it there. Because I trust her. Because I believe her. And she might not think there's anything she can do about the video, but I'm not giving up quite so easily.

I finished my coding for class in record time, and I got to work an hour early. It was an inventory day, and because I started early, Chuck was fine with me leaving a little early too. I wanted to be home before my mom, in time to prep Leah. I didn't want my mom stepping in, taking over. I wanted Paige to have this chance to prove she could do this.

I want her to succeed.

My mom gave me the face she's famous for, laced with warnings to be careful and be guarded in trusting Leah in the care of just anyone. Dating is one thing, but getting Leah attached to someone is something else entirely. I get it. But she still left and went to her bunko game-night. I think it helped that she's only down the road. I think knowing that helped Paige a little, too.

Paige looked nervous. Leah looked excited. The second I told my daughter that Paige would be babysitting her tonight, she proceeded to pull out every single game in her closet— digging into the depths to find the ones she hasn't played with in months. She's showing off. That's part of showing off when you're a kid—you don't have much of your own, but you've got toys. And Leah pulled them all out and put them on display.

I could sense the nerves in Paige's voice when I told her I wouldn't be late. And I saw the relief when I held up my phone and told her to call if she needed anything. But she hasn't called. Not once.

We've gone through two hours of Texas Hold 'em, and I've lost forty bucks to Nate, the king of poker faces. I'm down to my final chips, and as much fun as I've had being a regular guy for once, I'm sort of itching to get home.

"One more hand, and I think I'm out, guys. Sorry, this is late for me," I say, realizing mid-sentence how strange that probably sounds. They don't know about Leah, and I feel like maybe I should talk to Paige before I let them in on it. Ty met her, but as far as he knows, she's my baby sister.

"Dude, it's like, what...nine? Nine-thirty?" Ty says, shuffling, then dealing out another round of cards. There are five of us here; Nate brought two of the guys from his team.

"Yeah, but I work crazy hours, so my clock's sort of messed up," I say, glancing at my hand and trying to hide two poker faces now. I have a pair of jacks. I also have more than just a messed-up work schedule. This table doesn't need to know either.

"I feel ya. I guess that's why you can live with Paige. I bet you hardly see her," Ty says, looking up at me as he takes a long sip from his beer. He's studying me, waiting for my tell.

"I guess so," I say, moving my attention back to my cards. They're still two jacks, just like they were when I first got them dealt to me. I'm staring at the heart and the club, pretending to be thinking about odds and possibilities, but I'm really wondering if Ty's still watching me, waiting for me to break about Paige. I risk it and look back up, and his eyes are waiting for me. Everyone else is into their own hands, but Ty's got me figured out. He smiles, then slowly chuckles to himself. This has nothing to do with poker, and everything to do with what he's just figured out—Paige is mine. More accurately, I'm hers.

"All right, Texas," Ty says to me. "Bet's to you."

I glance at my cards again, a move that's only for show, then lay them face down and sit back with my hands behind my neck, chewing at the inside of my cheek, looking at the cards on the table.

"I'm all in," I say, pushing my stack, which isn't much, to the center of the table.

Ty's eyes are waiting for me when I look up, and he raises a brow, glances at his own cards, and tosses them on the table.

"I'm out," he says, sitting back and folding his arms.

"I don't know, I think dude's bluffin'. I call," Nate says.

"Get ready to lose your shirt, bro. This dude's the real deal," Ty says, laughing to himself as he moves away from the table and pushes into a small kitchen area. I think the apartment belongs to one of the other guys—who follows Ty's lead and folds. The other one has most of the chips on the table, so he tosses in the few it takes to see my bet through.

With every flip of the cards, nothing comes up, and even though I can't bet, the others raise their own. I'm probably screwed; when I make eye contact with Ty, I realize I'm probably screwed in more ways than one. I'm ruined because I'm falling for a girl who's a tremendous pain in the ass. That's where Ty thinks the line is—little does he know that the baggage I drag over that line makes things a whole hell of a lot more complicated.

But I'm all in, falling for her anyway. There's no taking that bet back now.

With the last cards tipped on the table, I flip mine over first, expecting to watch my final chips get swept away.

"You're kidding me—a pair of jacks? You went *all in* with a pair of jacks?" Nate says, rubbing his face and leaning back in his chair, tipping it so the front legs lift from the floor.

"Go big or go home," I say.

"Hell yeah, bro," Ty says, reaching his beer over the table to tap it into mine. I drank two beers tonight, slowly, over two hours. I wanted to be able to drive if I had to, but I also didn't want to seem like a pansy-ass in front of Ty. I'm pretty sure he's the kind of guy who can really give someone shit when he feels like it. "Take your chips."

I look down when he says that and realize I bluffed my way into winning my money back. I didn't mean to. When I went all in, I felt pretty good about the jacks. Didn't think they'd be all I needed.

"Thanks, boys. It's been a pleasure," I say, cashing out and putting the forty bucks back in my wallet.

"Yeah, yeah," Nate says, sweeping the cards into a pile and shuffling as I head to the door.

"Oh hey, and Houston...Nate's game with the scouts is next week. Cass is coming, and I think she'd like it if Paige came. Just...if you can help that out a little," Ty says. We exchange an understanding stare.

"Yeah, I'll work on it," I say.

"Good. Thanks. Oh, and just a tip...that bluffing shit—" he pauses, holding the door open as I step outside onto the pavement, "it won't work with her. She'll see right through it all—trust me. Just give it to her straight. Ya know, if you wanna get anywhere."

I hold up my hand with my keys, eyes wide, and nod. I don't think I can really bluff Ty either. I won't pretend to.

The trip in my car is silent. I don't even bother with the radio; I'm too consumed with *her*. I pulled my phone out at the first stoplight, wanting to send Paige a text that I was on my way, but then I wasn't sure what to type. I turned the lights out before I drove into the driveway. I know it's barely ten at night, but they both might be asleep.

I can see the light from Leah's room spilling into the hallway upstairs, so I slip my shoes from my feet and glide up as quietly as I can. She usually stays awake waiting for me on late work nights. She says she just likes to say goodnight, but I kind of think she worries I won't come home at all.

"But what about the princess?" I hear Leah ask. I'm about to step into her room when I pause, not wanting to interrupt. I turn the corner so my back is flush against the wall outside her door.

"Right. The princess," Paige says. She's quiet for a few seconds, and I can hear the pages of the book turning. Leah loves princesses—anything in a big dress with hair and glitter. "How does this story usually go?"

"The mean witch locks Delilah up in the tower, and then the prince gets his friends together so they can save her, but when he gets there, the tower is scary, so all his friends leave, and he has to fight the witch and her dragon alone. He kills them, and then saves the princess and they run away and get married."

Leah is out of breath when she finishes retelling Paige the entire princess book. I smile at her voice, doing my best not to

170

laugh at her enthusiasm over a story she's heard no less than a hundred times.

Then Paige begins to talk, and my chest grows heavy.

"I'd like to tell you a different version, if that's okay," she says.

"What's a *version*?" Leah asks. I cover my mouth with my knuckle, smiling against it.

"It's sort of like, *hmmmm*...it's kind of a different way the story could go. You know how you get up in the morning and decide what you're going to wear? And maybe if you wear a dress, that means you can't do cartwheels or swing on the swings. But what if you wore shorts instead?"

"I'd swing," Leah says excitedly, then whispers, "sometimes I swing in the dress. Grandma yells that I'm showing my underwear."

She giggles and Paige laughs with her.

"Right, but most of the time, what you decide in the morning might mean you do different things later. Well what would happen if Delilah decided not to wait for the prince?" Paige asks.

"Oh no!" Leah's genuinely worried by this. I'm...fascinated. I slide down slowly so I'm sitting against the wall now, my legs bent up under my arms, careful not to be seen. I don't want to distract either of them.

"Well maybe...*oh no*. Or...maybe what Delilah decides—when the evil witch locks her up—is that she's tired of being pushed around," Paige says. I lay my face flat against my hands, so desperate for her version now.

"Delilah is scared at first. She's never really been good at fighting. Her dad always led the army. And her mom only decorates for balls and picks flowers in the garden and things like that. So Delilah spends the first night alone, in the dark room, locked away in the tower, hoping someone will save her. But when she wakes up the next morning, she realizes that nothing bad happened to her. The dark was scary, but nothing happened. She's okay. So she finds a slender piece of wood along the floor and uses it to pick the lock."

"Oh no!" Leah says, but Paige stops her from worrying.

"Just wait," Paige says. "She picks the lock, and nobody is near by. So she decides to explore the stairway, to see how high it goes, how deep it is, and if there is a way to get outside. When she hears someone coming, she runs back to her small room and locks the door, tucking the tiny wood pick into the braid of her hair."

"Every day, she explores a little farther, finding new doors, trying new hallways. And then finally...she finds a tunnel."

"There's a tunnel?" Leah asks.

"Oh yes. There's a tunnel. But you only find it if you're brave enough to look. Delilah was brave, so she found it. She was also getting stronger, because every night, when she would explore, she would run, and have to pull herself up high on walls, crawl through tight spaces, and lift heavy things. When she found the tunnel, she decided she needed to escape the next night, well after midnight, when she knew the guards would be sleepy. But what she didn't know, was that the prince was coming to save her at the very same time."

"He was?" Leah asks.

"Yes, he was. When the moon was at its highest, Delilah picked her lock and made her way to her tunnel, crawling through the narrow damp passageway until she felt the cold air from outside hit her cheeks. She kept her body low to the ground, crawling on her belly under fence after fence, through mud, through a thick forest of trees, all the way to the dangerous guard gates and the wall of fire. She'd practiced the timing, and she knew she could get across it if she was careful counting the seconds in-between flames. But when the time was ready for her to run and make her escape, she heard shouting and fighting."

"Did someone catch her?" Leah asks.

"No. They caught...*the prince!*" Paige says, and I hear Leah gasp. "Delilah was only one leap away from her freedom, but when she saw the prince was in trouble, she couldn't leave him."

"What did she do?" Leah asks.

"She ran through the darkness to the drawbridge. The prince was being tied with rope to the back of a horse, to be led into the witch's tower for punishment. She looked everywhere for something she could use, something that would help her defeat the guards. There were so many of them, but only one of her. And then she noticed a large barrel of oil. The guards used the oil to keep their torches lit.

"Delilah had grown strong enough, she was able to push the barrel over, spreading the slick liquid all over the bridge in their path. She waited, hidden underneath one of the bridge's trusses, holding herself with her tiring arms, until she heard the horses begin to walk above her. Careful not to make any sound, she crawled around the bridge's edge, doing her best to not be seen. The mud that covered her body kept her disguised. Then, she reached into her hair, and pulled out the tiny wood stick, sharp on one end, and she poked the leg of one of the horses.

"The horse leapt up on his back legs, and began jerking wildly, scaring every other horse, which caused many of the guards to lose their balance and drop their torches into the oil. The oil caught fire—igniting the bridge in fiery flames, which frightened the horses even more. They all took off in various directions, including the horse that the prince was still tied to. That horse is the only one Delilah cared about. She followed it, deep into the forest, but didn't make a sound or let the prince know she was near until she was sure they were far enough away from the others."

"What happened then?" Leah asks.

"When Delilah felt it was safe, she spoke softly. 'It's me, don't be frightened,' she said to the prince. He looked around for her in the darkness, and when he saw her, he was so happy. She ran to him, untied him, and hugged him tight, so happy he was safe. He told her that he was trying to rescue her, and she laughed, climbing onto the horse behind him so they could both ride away for their escape. Then, she told him that she wasn't the kind of girl who needed rescuing, but she's glad she could save him. And they lived happily ever after."

Leah's quiet. So is Paige. I'm pretty sure she's the princess in the story, and I kind of think Leah knows it too. After a few seconds, I hear her light click *off*, so I stand, still keeping my back to the wall, my body out of sight.

"Paige?" Leah says.

"Yes, Leah," she responds.

"I like that version," Leah says.

I can hear Paige's steps moving closer to the door, closer to me, and it's beginning to get harder to breathe.

"Me, too, Leah. Me, too," she says, stepping through the door and closing it behind her.

She sees me quickly, jumping a little, but not making a sound.

"Sorry, I didn't mean to scare you," I say, my hands flat on the wall behind me. I'm a little stunned from...*that*. My heart is pounding in my stomach. "I didn't want to interrupt your story. I think she liked it."

"I think she did too," Paige says, folding her arms over her body. She's dressed in a long cotton shirt with a large heart on the front, her arms guarding it tightly with all her might. I'm struck by the irony. "How was your night with the guys?" she asks.

"I had a good time. Thanks for making me go," I say, my voice low, not wanting to stir Leah. Not wanting to disturb our space—to ruin our *alone*. "You're right. Ty's a pretty good guy."

"He is," she sighs, her eyes lingering on mine. Even in the darkness, I can see the mix of blue and specks of green. She's prettier this way, her hair long and messy, hanging over her shoulders, draping to her breasts. Her face is a blank canvas, the makeup gone, nothing to take away from her eyes and her mouth. My eyes can't seem to leave her lips. They're nervous. She's nervous. She's...beautiful.

And I'm all in.

"I like you, Paige," I say, watching intently as her eyes show her tell—flashing wider for a brief second, before she flits them away, looking down at her feet, at her arms that are hugging her body, her heart, tighter. "I like you. I don't wanna like you...but I do."

174

Her eyes find mine quickly. The recognition is there. She remembers. I heard. We both feel. And now things are messy...messier.

"I can't," she says.

"I know," I say, my voice more broken than I expected. The rawness makes her smile fade when she hears me.

"I want to," she says, her eyes locked on mine now. She's no longer breathing, and her lips are quivering.

"I know," I say, taking my breaths for her.

Neither of us is moving. Why can't I move? Why isn't she moving?

The longer I stand here and stare at her, the more impossible it feels to leave—to ever leave. This strong goddess who doesn't need anyone to save her, but damn does she need someone to believe in her.

Her breath catches, just when she realizes she hasn't tasted air for nearly a minute, and her lips part in a way that makes them that much more beautiful. I take deliberate steps across the hallway, but I move slowly enough she won't flinch. She can't run—I can't let her run. If she runs, I will chase her. I will have to convince her. I will beg her.

It will get messy.

When my toes touch hers, I finally let my eyes move from her mouth to her eyes. She's wearing her warrior face; her lids lowered slightly to dare me—to show me how strong she is, to prove she's not the one giving me permission. But she isn't running. She isn't yelling. She isn't protesting. She's scared.

Fuck, I'm scared. I get scared. And my life is scary. I don't come into anything alone. I'm a package.

But she isn't running.

I'm slow with my hand, and when she sees my fingers near her cheek, her breath hitches again.

"I like you, Paige," I repeat, my voice a whisper, my lips close to her ear. I barely remember how to do this, how to do any of this, but every movement, every word with her right now feels so natural. "I don't want to. You don't want me to. But I do. And so do you. And we can keep fighting, and you can walk away from things, and you can yell at me when nothing makes sense, and you don't have anyone else to blame. I'm okay with that. I'll be that guy. Even though part of me doesn't want to. That part is fucking terrified. But the rest of me..."

I step back again, my hand fully on her cheek now, her weight resting on me, her eyes closed, lips still trembling.

"The rest of me just wants to kiss you," I say, closing the inches quickly until my lips touch hers, surprise hers, claim hers and quell her fears all in one action. Her protest is short, and soon her hands find my shoulders and then my back and she pulls me into her. My hands are holding her face, and we both walk backward until her back is against my door.

I reach with one hand, frantic to find it—desperate to open the damn door. Panicked that if I break this contact she'll stop, that she'll slap me...that she'll go back to not wanting to...*anything*. When I get the door open, we both fall inside, but our lips never part, our grip remains tight on one another. Reaching with one hand, I close the door behind us gently, not wanting to make any sound that could possibly get us caught.

This cannot be interrupted. It's still too new, too at risk for being the only time I get to feel this. Goddamn does she taste like the most expensive drink I've ever had. Scooping her into my arms, I pull her even closer to me, until my legs hit the bed. I don't want her to think anything other than this kiss is enough. I've thought about more. Fuck, I think about *more* twenty-three of my twenty-four hours, dreaming when I'm sleeping, daydreaming when I'm awake. But this kiss—it's enough right now.

Her mouth breaks from mine long enough for her to breathe, and our foreheads fall together, my hands still cupping her face, memorizing every curve and contour of her cheeks, chin, mouth. Her eyes finally open to mine, and her hands move from my back to the sides of my face, her fingertips reaching into my hair. Her bottom lip is caught in her teeth, and just when I think I see worry—maybe even regret—flash in her features, her lip curves up into a smile.

176

"I might like you a lot," I say, and she giggles, her breath soft and sweet.

She places one hand flat against my chest, putting pressure on me, urging me to sit. I do as she says, but I keep my eyes on hers just in case she changes her mind, my hands holding hers, relishing the feel of her fingertips, the softness of her skin. She crawls onto my lap, straddling me with one leg on either side until she's completely wrapped herself around my waist, and simply the feel of the weight of her, of holding her...*like this*, awakens my most basic male instincts. My eyes close, and I growl a deep moan into her neck, my hands finding her ass, fingers teasing the line of her lace panties, and pulling her closer to me until her lips are again only a beat away from touching mine.

I watch her eyes for permission, dragging my hands around her body, up her thigh, to her hips and sides until my thumbs feel the perfect curve of her breasts. I leave her eyes, only for a few seconds, because her body has been invading my thoughts for too long for me not to see how it reacts when I touch her. I let my fingers linger at her ribs, my thumbs caressing the roundness, sliding cautiously until my thumbs run over the hardness of her nipples. As they do, her legs clutch onto me, and her body rolls into mine, pressing into me so hard I know there is no way she doesn't feel everything I'm feeling. There are no more secrets. I want her—every single piece.

"You feel...I'm sorry, but you feel fucking fantastic," I say, my breathing heavy and the pressure of everything in my pants truly the only thing I can focus on. She laughs again, the breathy kind, almost like panting. Fuck, I think she's panting.

"I don't know what Ty told you, or what you've heard about me, but I need to take this slow, Houston. I want you, but this is...it's just...you're so much," she says, her head resting on mine, her hands against my face. My fingers are digging into her sides, fighting against the animal urge.

I laugh at her words. "I've been called big, but too much?" I joke, and she shoves me to my back, her hands on my chest, her hair cascading down her face, her center pressing even harder on mine. Oh my god slow is going to kill me.

"That's not what I meant," she says, her smile almost bashful. Beautiful.

I reach up and sweep her hair behind her, running my thumb over her cheek. "I know. I know what you meant. And honestly, if all I ever got to do again was kiss you, I'd be fine with that," I say, letting my hand trace her shoulder and then stop again at her ribs before moving slowly up her unbelievably perfect breasts.

"That's a lie," I say, letting my thumbs tease across her nipples once more. "Kissing is good for now, but I'm pretty sure if all I ever got to do was kiss you I'd die."

She laughs at my confession, but lets it fade into this sexy, sinister smile as her hands run up my arms until her fingers intertwine with mine against her breasts, squeezing them and pulling at her skin. I let her guide my hands lower to her legs, running them up her thighs, pushing the edge of her night shirt up higher until now I can see the pink lace of her underwear, the shirt that once draped to her knees now bunched around her waist. She moves my hands back around her, until I'm gripping her ass again hard, her body moving against mine in a purposeful sway, and she lets her head fall back, her hair falling in waves along her shoulders, her lips parting as she moans.

She moves her head back to face me, leaning forward, her hands running along my chest and down my arms, purposefully, and then she stops as her mouth hovers above mine. "I'm pretty sure it would kill me too, but for tonight, that's the line," she says, waiting for me to accept.

I do. Of course I do. And I grab her head and kiss her hard and roll her on her back underneath me and relish the next hour that she lets me have her lips, taste her neck, and let my hands roam, but never too far. She's the one to pull away. I let her be the one to say when this moment is over, because I will forgo sleep.

She doesn't say anything. She doesn't say this was a mistake, and she doesn't look sad. She looks worried. But underneath, she's also hungry. And I know she'll be back, and I know that the kissing line will move a little farther. I also know that I love gambling, and I'm pretty sure I'm addicted.

And my poker face is just fine.

Chapter 12

Paige

Is this what falling for someone is supposed to feel like? I wake up every morning—after sneaking away late at night, tiptoeing from Houston's room back to mine—feeling...alive. When I'm with him, there is no video, no pitiful freshman year, no former Delta-sisters, or blackmail drug-photos locked away in my phone and computer. No drama. There's just Houston, and me—and kissing. Lots and lots of kissing.

What's strange is how he always holds that line. Maybe, in a way, I've been testing him these last few nights, to see if his hands would roam a little more, if he'd pressure me. He doesn't. I think maybe this is also what a gentleman is like.

I see why Beth loved him.

When I look at myself, I don't see a person trying to pretend to be anything other than who I am. With Houston, I'm me—I'm my flaws and my good stuff all at once. And he seems to want both parts. Being with him isn't exhausting. There is no worry—other than the fear that Leah will catch me during one of my late-night trips, or that his mother will ask about us.

I worry about that a lot. But when we're kissing, I worry about it *less.*

Maybe it's just the sneaking around I enjoy. Houston and I share this secret, and it's distracting—*unbelievably distracting.* I've had moments this week where I start to think he's in a place different from me with this thing we're doing. Sometimes I think he might be taking us too seriously, and the next I think that he's not taking us seriously enough. Truth is, I'm not sure what place *I'm* in with this thing we're doing. All I know is that when his hands are on me, I feel safe. I don't feel the need to pretend everything's okay. Everything just...is.

I hate that I ever let a guy touch me just because I was afraid of losing him. My sister was like that, and I persecuted her for it. Turns out I wasn't so different.

With Houston, it's more than the kissing, than the touching—than the thought of him crossing that line and the tease of temptation. Houston looks at me as if I'm more than some hot score. He doesn't slap my ass then want me out of his way as soon as he's done. He wants to talk. He wants to listen. We don't have many secrets left. In fact, I don't think he has any. All I have are those photos on my phone, the ones that started this all. I don't bring them up...because I'm not sure they make me any better than Chandra now. She leaked a video. I leaked some photos. Of course, mine were real. I haven't thought about them for days. It seems the world's forgotten about them, too. Turns out—money *can* stop the Internet.

Houston left early this morning, leaving me alone to get ready for class and to eat breakfast downstairs with his mom and Leah. Thank god for Leah; she fills the silence with constant questions about the story I told her the other night and with her plans for the next time we play. She's maybe the most precious little girl I've ever met. But...I don't want to be her mother.

Which, of course, means this thing with Houston, it can't...

"Leah, you need to get your shoes on so we can make it to the church in time for the puppet lady," Joyce says, her voice coming out in a singsong way that makes Leah obey. I bet she raised Houston with that same voice, and I bet it's why he's so attentive and willing to listen.

"Thank you," I say to Joyce as she pulls my plate from the table and moves it to the sink. She's fed me almost every meal that I've had since I've been here. I was thinking about it last night, and I should really try to contribute more. I have points on my meal plan I can use for things.

"It's nice having you here," she says, her smile lingering a little longer than it should. It feels like she's working the muscles to make sure it stays in place. I don't get the impression that she doesn't like me, but there's something underneath—I can tell.

"I want to help out, maybe shop for some groceries when I can? Is there anything that I can get? I could go later today," I say.

Her smile gets tighter, and I'm expecting her to speak long before she finally does. "Get whatever you would like. We're fine with what we have," she says, turning from me so I can't see her face. I get the sense those words are talking about more than the food in the pantry.

"All right, well thank you, again," I say, my voice weaker. I'm gathering my backpack and things when I hear Leah skipping down the stairs, so I pause at the back door to make sure I say goodbye to her for the day. Before I fully turn, I feel her arms around me, her face nuzzled into my side, and she kisses my hip.

"Have a good day," she says.

"Oh...thank you. You too," I say, a little stunned by her affection. I glance back up at Joyce—her worried smile still the same. I understand it a little more.

Leah.

This isn't about me and Houston—her concern is about me...and Leah.

I leave without voicing any of the nonverbal conversations Joyce and I just had. Houston's mother is warm and wonderful. Much of her reminds me of my mom, only far less flighty. Joyce is strong, and she's very much the glue that holds this house together. I respect that. She and I are more similar than she knows—we're both protectors. Which means as welcome as she makes me feel, she also prefers me to leave everything exactly as I found it. And maybe a week ago, I would have.

Before I let him in that little bit more.

Before he believed me.

Before my heart latched on to the feeling it gets when he comes home, when I see him, when he calls.

182

Oh my god, somehow I've turned into one of those girls, the kinds who have crushes! I've been hot for guys. I've chased guys, flirted, won them over, made them mine. I'm like a conqueror when it comes to making boys obey. But Houston is like...he's like an invasion! I like him more than I'm ready to admit. Maybe I just admitted to it. *Damn it*—that thought is in there now. I admit it. If I had a girlfriend left to talk to, she probably wouldn't be able to shut me up about Houston. There's one benefit to being shunned—no witnesses for my descent into happily-ever-afters and fairytales.

My lab class is biology, and the lecture room is very clinical. Clinical—yes, I need the white board, the sterile metal chairs. Nothing in that room looks like hearts and flowers. If only the lecture promised to be interesting enough to distract me. I've only been to a few this semester, but so far, the lessons feel like everything I already learned in high school. It makes me wonder what my parents are paying for, and why I can't just move into studying what I want to be doing. I take the long route to class whenever I can, just so I can pass the architecture and design building. I love watching the students in the design lab work with colors and textiles. As I pass by today, they're working with mood boards on giant monitors, which makes the building look even more like a real interior-design shop—just like the ones on the same street as my mom's bead store in Burbank. I've already been promised internships there for the summer.

I wouldn't mind spending the summer here either.

That thought comes out of nowhere. Staying here—in Oklahoma? That's never even been a consideration for me. Like...ever. This thought. It's Houston's fault. I will forever keep it to myself. I'll probably just go home, stick to the plan, so no harm. No need to ever let that thought pop into my head again.

Butterflies.

Fairytales.

Motherfuck!

As I step into the lecture room, my pocket vibrates with my phone, and I pull it out quickly to take the call—glad to have something extract me from that weird fantasy of staying here, of a more permanent here. Of...here...with Houston.

Leah, Leah, Leah. I repeat her name in my head before answering my phone. That's the only word that grounds me. Leah's all about reality—*big time* reality.

"Me and Rowe want pizza. Lunch. Ditch the class," Cass says the second I answer. I look up at the clock, and it's not quite yet ten. My lab goes until one—it was either this class or a night one, and I hate the idea of school ruining my evening. Of course, when I made my schedule, I had planned on being at parties on Friday nights or out with the girls.

Plans change.

Somehow, my first year at college was revolving around school and studies, and less on social things.

"It's still breakfast time. My palate is not ready for that," I say moving to an aisle seat near the middle. I've learned the routine—about a half an hour of lecture then we move to the lab for the day's project. The stupid sterile, metal chairs snag my clothes when I walk through the rows. Aisle seats are the only way to go.

"You and your uppity, snooty-ass palate. Palates don't have anything to do with pizza. Boo, I'm super hungry, and I can't wait until one. I went six miles this morning," Cass whines, accentuating each word just to irritate me.

"That voice? That's never going to work on me, just FYI. Look, wait until twelve thirty or so, and I can meet you. I'll be done by then with whatever lame thing we're doing in here today," I say.

"Fine," Cass huffs. "But you're eating pizza then. None of that salad and rabbit food crap you pull."

"Whatever," I say, clicking my phone to silent and slipping it in the side of my bag. I turn to face the seat and my legs come square with another set, and when I look up I realize they belong to a pair of khaki pants and a plain button-down, tucked in to perfection—the bearded chin trimmed neatly as if to mimic the perfect lines of the horn-rimmed glasses that sit above. It's the professor.

"Glad to know that my *lame* plans for the day aren't going to interfere with whatever that was," he says, circling his finger in the air, pointing to the pocket I stuffed my phone in. I'm not a big fan of being made an example of—clearly.

"No, they shouldn't," I say, lips tight as I take my seat and pull out my notebook and pen.

"Shouldn't what?" he asks. Heads are turning now. He picked the wrong example to make.

"Your tired, decade-old lesson plans for class shouldn't interfere with my lunch plans," I respond. He remains in his place for a few seconds, brow lowered—then chuckles to himself and raps his knuckles on my desktop as he continues his path to the front of the class. A few girls sitting a row in front of me are still turned my direction. I don't look up again, only raising my finger and twirling it so they know the show is over and they can face the front again.

The professor begins speaking and writing notes, most of which I recognize—from high school a year ago—about the various parts of the spine. The few times we make eye contact, there's a silent acknowledgement of our brief interaction. *Yes, young lady, I know this lesson is lame. But you'll pass this class easily, and still others will fail.*

My phone chirps again, the vibration triggering against my leg. I pull the phone up from the bag to my lap, glancing at the screen to see a text from Houston.

Nate invited us to his tournament this weekend. Cass wants you to go. I was supposed to tell you that a few days ago, but I got...distracted.

Biting my lip to hide the smile Houston puts on my face, I glance back up to the front of the class, the professor now engrossed in his own voice, the entire row in front of me staring at him with expressions of blankness—which match the notes they've written on their many empty computer screens. He's right; a lot of these people are still going to fail.

I write back to Houston.

Ok. We'll go.

I hit SEND and get a response from him almost immediately.

What are we doing here, Paige? What is this thing between us?

I liked his first question better. Yes, I'll go to a baseball tournament with you. That's an easy answer. The second question, unless he is expecting me to respond with *we're texting, that's what we're doing,* which I very much doubt, is the kind riddled with expectations and pitfalls. That question is full-blown butterflies and fairytales. And I just kicked that shit out of my head. Okay, so maybe it was five minutes ago, but I kicked that shit out all the same.

Leah, Leah, Leah.

My finger is hovering over the response area when another message from him sneaks in.

Shit. That was not one of those SEND texts. That was supposed to be pretend.

Too late, Houston. It's out there now.

Guess I can't really take that back though, huh?

I write back quickly, because at least this part I can answer.

No.

Thank god he doesn't text again. I check about a kajillion more times anyhow, because *fucking butterflies and fairytales!* But my answer is always the only thing left to see.

No.

That's the only word I see. No, no, no, no, no! I close my eyes, morphing it into *Leah, Leah, Leah, Leah, Leah.*

The class begins to shuffle notes and students are getting to their feet, which means it's time to switch rooms and move to the lab. For added measure, I pair myself with the girl who usually sits up front and asks lots of questions. She's one of those thorough students, and even though I don't need her help for my grade, I do need her to stretch out this dissection assignment. I also need to see my sister—and her friend Rowe—for lunch, to talk about boy problems, which makes me want to throw up. Not because I don't like talking about guys, and plotting and gossip. I just don't like talking about feelings. I'm actually a little grateful Rowe will be there. She won't pry like Cass. She'll let me pretend things are hypothetical. I wonder if I can find a way to get my sister to leave? Probably not.

I stretch my lab project to the very end, and by one, Cass is texting me, demanding my drink order for the pizza place at the other end of campus. She's also sent a picture of the greasiest pizza I've ever seen. I type that I'm on my way and have no intention of eating that insult for food.

Good, because it's already halfway gone. Oh, and Houston's here ;-)

As unappetizing as the pizza was to me, it's the second part of her text that has my stomach in knots. It's going to be pretty hard to talk about him when he's actually there. Not to mention, he's only there because of his stupid text fuck up.

With every step closer I take to the restaurant, the less I want to be there. I can see my sister's smile through the window; she's laughing at something Houston said. He's funny; of course she's laughing. And Rowe is gazing between the two of them. Bonding is happening inside—they're bonding. Houston is being charming, and my sister is going to like him, and she's going to *want* there to be a *me* and him.

There is a *me* and him. But I also think maybe it only works if we keep it a secret. Otherwise, it becomes a me and him and a whole lot of other people.

"So lots of cold showers, huh?" Cass says through laughter as I step up to the booth. *What the fuck? Cold showers?*

"You wouldn't believe how many," Houston says, startling when I drop myself into the booth next to him. His leg slides toward mine a second later. I kick it.

"Who's taking cold showers?" I ask, lips pursed, my face ready to accuse Houston of sharing too much.

"Houston is," Cass says, pulling off a piece of crust and eating it like a carrot. My face feels hot, and Houston suddenly looks guilty.

"And he'll be taking more," I say, my lips pursed. I glance up to the counter to wave the waitress over, and when I glance back, Houston's eyes are wider.

"You're planning on taking even longer showers to drain the hot water tank?" he says, the words coming out slowly, his eyes signaling mine that I got that wrong—so fucking wrong.

"I am," I say curtly, turning to the waitress and keeping up my persona. Frankly, it's not unlike me to be a bitch just because I heard someone complaining about me. "Diet Coke, with a slice of lime, please."

"She's high maintenance," Cass says, her mouth still full with her crust bite. "But I think you'll find she grows on you."

I smile into my lap and glance to the side at Cass, who winks. It's been a while since she's said something nice about me. It feels good.

"What do you study, Houston?" Rowe asks from the corner seat. Rowe always sits in a corner, her back to the wall. There was a shooting at her high school a couple years ago, and some of her friends didn't survive. She's only talked to me about it once. It strikes me how much she and Houston have in common.

"I'm in the Computer Science program. I'm a geek," he shrugs.

"Oh, well that's good," Cass laughs, winking at me again. It doesn't feel good this time. "My sister only falls for meathead athletes. You should be safe."

I can't stop the instant sour face I make at her statement, but I catch it quickly, before she notices. Not before Rowe, though.

"There's nothing wrong with meatheads," Rowe says through nervous laughter. She doesn't like confrontation, and I think she might be changing the subject for me.

"Oh, no...I didn't mean Nate," Cass continues, putting her hand on Houston's arm as she shifts her body to face him more. My eyes lock on that small touch, and I know the sour face is back. When I look at Rowe, she's looking at me still. *Double shit.* "You see, Paige had a thing for Nate when school first started, but he was into Rowe. It was a little awkward, because we were all living together then. But turns out Nate wasn't really her type anyway, wouldn't you say Paige?"

I nod in agreement, reluctantly, my stomach sick. I'm too worried about where this conversation is going to be insulted by it.

"And what's her type?" Houston asks. I kick him again under the table, and I don't care that both Cass and Rowe see it.

"Well..." Cass smirks.

"Be nice," I point at her, relieved when the waitress drops my drink off at the table. At least I can busy myself with the straw.

"Paige needs someone who has a spotlight," Cass starts. I feel Houston shift, and I keep my eyes at my drink. I should argue with her, be offended or defend myself. But the old me, the girl I was before, wouldn't. She'd agree. "Paige has always been a leader. Ever since grade school. I think maybe it started when the principal let her cut the ribbon to unveil the new playground equipment. Do you remember that?"

I nod, the face I show on the outside a little proud, my inside face nothing but worried about where this is going—and what Houston will think of me the more he learns.

Leah, Leah, Leah.

"Paige got to be the first one to go down the slide, and after that, it became known as *her* slide. She didn't name it, the other kids did. They wanted her in charge," Cass says. I know she's sharing this because she's trying to show how proud she is of me. But I also sound like a diva. "It's always been like that—the kids at school looking to Paige to see what to do next. And if she decided a guy was the *it* guy, he became the *it* guy. And then he was hers. And every girl always wanted him. Even when she was done. Because Paige Owen's exes were still better than any other guy in school."

"So we're talking like quarterback, homecoming king stuff, huh?" Houston chuckles. He's amused by these stories about me. I fear he won't be for long.

"Yeah, pretty much," Cass says, chewing with her mouth open. All I feel is embarrassed. "She's never dated a computer geek, unless of course he was on his way to being a tycoon."

Maybe it's her laugh that follows that makes me react. It's not any different from her normal laugh, but for some reason—at this moment—it strikes me like a cackle. It's harsh, and I feel small.

"So as you can see, I'm super shallow," I butt in before Cass says anything more. I speak through a tight smile, my heart sad to hear how my sister sees me. This is how everyone sees me. And they all think I'm fine with it.

"Paige, that's not what I meant..." Cass says quickly. The laughing has stopped.

I step out from the booth with my purse in my hand and my backpack looped over my shoulder. "I know," I say, smile still tight. Always. Tight. Everything always perfect. "Stories about me just sort of come out that way, though."

The table falls silent. I just made things uncomfortable. I'm not sure what she was expecting. That I'd laugh along with her? Or maybe that I'd tease back. That's all this was—teasing. I guess I've outgrown being in the mood for it. Or maybe it's the fact that Houston was here for it. Maybe...maybe I'm worried about the butterflies and fairytales.

"I've got a lot of homework, so I'm going to head back," I say over my shoulder. "Cass, you can buy my drink."

I pick up my pace as soon as I exit the building, disappointed in myself—in the person I am, the person I was, and the person who just let that all play out inside the restaurant. My phone chirps, so I pull it from my pocket. It's Cass.

That all came out wrong. I'm so sorry.

I don't respond. I know she was just telling stories, trying to be funny, but fuck if it didn't hurt.

I'm rounding the corner, ready to walk down the fraternity row when I stop in my tracks. The sidewalks are busy, and for a second, I swear I see Carson walking with Chandra. When I focus, though, I realize it isn't them.

"Hey," I hear Houston's familiar voice, his hand brushing against mine. I push my hand into the pocket of my jacket so he can't touch it again.

"Sorry, I didn't mean to just bail like that," I say, still unable to meet his eyes.

"I get it," he says, his eyes going to my hand, the one I put away. I don't want to be touched right now. And why would he want to? "I, uh...I'm an only child. So sorry if I'm a little off-base here, but was that what they call sibling rivalry?"

A breathy laugh escapes me.

"Something like that," I say, my gaze quickly falling to my feet. I can't seem to shake feeling small.

"You know," he says, kicking one of his feet into mine. My hand twitches, wanting to be touched, too. It's betraying me. "Just because computer geeks weren't your thing before...doesn't mean they aren't now. I have a way of converting people, just sayin'."

I laugh again, this time a little harder, and finally I let myself look at him. His eyes are so kind. He's so kind. And he sees me so differently.

"Yes, you are the Mr. November of the Computer-Geek Calendar," I joke. Houston quirks an eyebrow and strikes a ridiculous GQ pose. Any girl on this campus would turn their head when he walked by. In fact, they do—they do all the time. I hate them when they do. As much as he's nice-guy, computer geek on the inside, his outside is pretty damned opposite. He's a paradox. Before I can react, he puts a hand on each of my hips, squaring me to him. My heart halts, and I start to look around to see who's noticing.

"What do you care?" he asks, bending lower, bringing his line of vision to mine. I keep trying to look around him—worried our secret is going to be uncovered, when he brings his hand to my chin, pulling my face to look at his. "What do you care who sees us? Who cares if I'm not some beefcake quarterback or if you..."

He stops before he says it and I step away.

"If I'm the girl in that video?" I finish, my chest burning.

"That's...not what I was going to say," he says, stepping closer. I take one more away.

"Yes it is," I argue. I hate that I argue. I always argue.

His hand reaches for my arm, sliding down to my hand, pulling it loose from my pocket until his fingers find mine. God, they fit together so well. They shouldn't, but they do.

"No, Paige. It's not," he says, his voice stern. "What I was going to say is what do you care if you have to carry the spotlight all on your own, no guy to do it for you?"

I freeze at his words, my tongue literally feeling numb.

"Look, I am never going to be the guy doing a keg stand at some party. I'm not a Sigma Theta Kappa whatever. I'm probably not going to be a CEO, because frankly, I don't want to work that hard. And I'm never going to throw a touchdown pass, unless it's to my daughter—who, by the way, I believe has every right to catch one. I'm just a guy with a kid trying to figure out things as they come, trying to hang on to my youth where there's a little bit left. I'm trying to figure *you* out, because I have to. I'd like to date you, Paige. And it's weird, because now we're roommates. And it's weird because I have a kid. And it's probably weirder for you than it is for me, but who cares anyway? I like you, and that's what this all is to me—it's me liking you and being perfectly fine with being the guy in the background, beyond *your* spotlight.

192

That's what I got out of that story your sister shared. I heard that you're a leader, that you're the one people gravitate to—people adore you! How have you forgotten that? I want to see that girl, more of that girl—the girl who rules the playground. This place needs her."

I love the way he looks at me. I don't think I breathed once while he spoke; I didn't want to make a sound, do anything to make him stop. As much as the attention hurts, it also soothes. He's so right. Where did that girl go? And since when did she need some guy with a title to define her?

Squeezing his fingers tightly, I reach up on my toes and brush my lips against his, my hand resting on his face.

"That was a pretty good speech, huh?" he says, his lip quirked up on one side in a half smile.

"It was okay," I joke, shrugging and turning to walk down the main road back to Houston's house, his hand still linked with mine.

"You're just playing tough," he says, with a sniffle. "That speech was bad-assery."

"Oh...my god," I roll my eyes. His playful arrogance is adorable. But yes, it was...*bad-assery. Bad-assery at it's finest.*

We continue to make jokes all the way home. Making jokes is easier than being serious—it's something we both have in common. This morning, I had myself convinced that Houston and I were a fling, something that would stay secret until I moved out for the summer, moved on. But we're not a fling. And the closer we get to his house, the more aware I am of the fact that he's ready to tell his mom about us, to talk to Leah about us, to be a real *us*. That feels fast and intimidating, but I still want it.

I do...want it?

Leah, Leah, Leah. That word still feels heavy as it drums in my head.

What I'm sure of is that I want to be that girl in his speech. That's partly why when he opens the back door and leads me into the kitchen, I don't fight to loosen his hold of my hand. I let him hold it, and when his mother sees it, I ignore the flash in her eyes and the heat of her stare.

"Houston?" she asks, her voice not really upset, but more concerned...cautious.

Leah, Leah, Leah.

Houston scratches the back of his neck, then lifts our linked hands in the air, looking at them, looking at me beyond them, his nervous smile falling into place. His dimple. His eyes sparkle. Did I ever really stand a chance?

"I know," he sighs, letting our hands fall together back to our sides. I keep my eyes on him, waiting for him to speak. *Please don't apologize; please don't say you're sorry for us.*

"Is this a...new thing?" Joyce asks, gesturing her coffee cup toward our hands. Houston lifts them again, smiling again.

"This part," he says, shaking our linked hands between us, "is a new thing, yes. But the idea of this part...it's been there for a while."

His eyes skirt to me as he smiles, sweet and bashful. He looks like a teenaged boy, caught—in trouble. I can't help but compare my thoughts to what it must have been like when he and Beth came to Joyce and his father—telling them about the baby. I squeeze his hand in acknowledgement and encouragement.

"Have you talked to Leah?" Joyce asks. I know this is her concern, and she glances at me, giving me the same look she did this morning.

"No, but I will," he says, every word, so sure. There's a small blip in my chest that feels like nerves; I ignore it. The chant of Leah's name is softer now.

Joyce looks between the two of us, then slides from her chair and stands, passing by us without any expression at all. With her back to us while she rinses her cup off in the sink, she speaks. "Leah's upstairs, coloring Paige a picture," she says.

I swallow.

"It's just...dating. We're only...dating," I hear my voice and wonder why it's making a sound. Houston looks at me curiously, maybe a little hurt and offended. I nod at him, my eyes widening, telling him *I'm sorry. I'm nervous. I panicked.*

194

"Cee Cee's coming over for dinner, so maybe you two can hold off your...*dating*...until tomorrow?" Joyce says, her back still to us. I let my eyes fall shut, embarrassed that I'm not as brave as Houston.

His grip loosens, but he still hooks his pinky around mine. "Probably smart, in case Leah has questions," he says. He doesn't look worried at all. In fact, his face is nothing but calmness, like one of those soldiers standing guard outside the palace in London. Inside, I'm still working to keep my fingers on the holes in the dam that is every fear I have over what this all means. I like Houston. I like him a lot. But telling Leah—making this a thing that's not just a secret is so very big. I haven't even worked out what to tell Cass in my head. I might be okay with us waiting more than a day. He though...he seems ready to roll.

When Joyce finally turns, she doesn't speak, but her expression says volumes. This isn't how she saw this step going for Houston, but she's never going to tell him not to take it. I let go of Houston's hand completely, nodding toward the stairs, toward Leah's room, partly as an excuse. He smiles, and leads me up the stairs. With every step we take, I realize I let go of his hand because I'm afraid it's my last chance—to let go.

"Hey, are you really okay...with waiting? We should probably talk about it before we talk to Leah," he whispers, his hand brushing into mine, tempting me to grab hold again. Something holds me back.

"Yeah, we should get on the same page...with what to say," I smile. He leans in to kiss my neck quickly, and I keep my breathing in check, careful not to show how terrified I am of this step. He moves to his door, and I let the air slowly escape my lungs, quietly, so he can't hear the breath I've been holding.

I'm that girl—the strong one. People follow me.

"Dinner won't last long. It never does with Cee Cee," he says, pausing at his door. "She's..." his lips twist on one side, his eyes gazing down at the floor before coming back to mine, a touch of sadness suddenly added to them. "She's Beth's half sister, but she's nothing like Beth at all. She's not even really family—honestly. She wanted to know Leah, though. And Leah gets a trust from Beth's dad when she turns twenty-one. That's the only reason we do this, because Cee Cee likes to visit with Leah. And Leah seems to love her. She comes over once every few months."

"Oh," I say, feeling sicker now that Beth's memory has entered into this equation. I feel selfish for wanting Houston, and I feel guilty for wanting to keep him my secret. "Sure, I understand. If it's family, I could just...you know...go hang out with Cass or something? She's already texted me because she feels bad about today."

"No, please stay...I mean, I think my mom would love you to stay," he pauses, looking downstairs. He bites his lip, holding in a chuckle. "I mean, I know it doesn't *seem* like she wants you to stay. But she does. She's just...we're...dating. Just dating, apparently," he says, holding both hands up, playing offended by my little display downstairs.

"I'm sorry. I freaked out. That's going to happen. If we could just...call this dating?" I say, my fingers finding my scalp, ruffling my hair, scratching at my head that suddenly feels full, hot, and itchy. This is overwhelming.

"Sure, Paige," Houston says, stepping to me again. He puts one hand behind my head, steadying it and cradling me to him. He kisses my forehead, his lips brushing against my skin. "We're dating."

His eyes stay on mine as he backs away. He gets my fear. I so don't understand his lack of fear. Maybe things are less scary on his side. He already has the kid. I'm eighteen. Those three years between us—sometimes they feel massive.

I back into my room, and when I close the door, the enormity of the last hour hits me. It seems a decision was made. Maybe I made it. Maybe it was made for me. I'm excited about it. I'm terrified. I both want to cry and laugh at the same time.

I've gone mad.

I realize suddenly I haven't spoken to my mom in more than a week. And at some point, I'm probably going to have to share where I'm living with her. Unless I move out. Would dating be more appropriate if I moved out?

I consider texting Cass. There's so much to catch her up on. I know Cass won't tell my parents. My sister keeps secrets. Yet one more thing she's better at than I am. But I'm the leader.

I'm the leader.

I decide instead to keep my worries to myself. For the next hour, I freshen up, changing into a white-lace dress and cowboy boots. I touch up the ends of my hair, spraying curls into place. I opt for the pink lipstick, a subtle shade for me—different from the bold red I usually go with. This color says youth. But it also says strong.

The longer I look at my reflection, the more I remember how I used to feel in high school and before. That girl is still in there. There's a knock at the door downstairs, and I listen to Leah sprint down the steps. I hear the formal voice Joyce uses with their guest—and it makes me smile, because now hearing her talk to someone else, I realize how informal she is with me.

Houston's door is still closed when I step from mine, so I head downstairs before him, a tiny part of me also a little jealous that Leah is hugging another girl about my age, excited by someone other than me.

Leah, Leah, Leah.

And then the visitor stands tall, her jet-black hair clearing her face, the shiny red of her lips like a bullet, aiming for my artery. She aims to shoot me dead. And she did not come here tonight to visit Leah.

She did not come here for Leah at all.

Chandra came here to see me.

Chapter 13

Houston

I know we said we'd wait to be more public about...things, but then she put on cowboy boots. And a white lace dress? There's symbolism in that—something about virginity, and *NOT* virginity. Her legs make me bite my knuckles. I bite them every time she walks by. She's walking by...a lot.

She's being...weird. Flirty maybe?

Or maybe not. Maybe it's just nerves.

She keeps moving around the living room and kitchen. It's like she can't get settled. She's like a damn feral cat. She doesn't seem to know where to stand, or where to be. Damn, I think that's my fault. I shouldn't have made revealing that there's an *us* such a big deal, shouldn't have let my mom make it a big deal.

But it is...a big deal.

Of all days for Cee Cee to show up—I've been in a room with her maybe five times in my life. The first time I met her was when Leah was born. She was the only one from the other side of the family—from Beth's dad's side—to show up. Martin Campbell's name means oil around here. He's a bigger deal in Texas, his name on buildings and rigs off the coast. I remember the first time Beth told me who her father was. She was sitting in the passenger seat of my shitty-ass car, coming home from a football game, and one of her father's trucks drove by, with the silver and black CAMPBELL logo on the side.

"Fuck you!" she screamed as it passed. She didn't talk the rest of the way home, and when she got out of the car, she slammed the door. I waited in her driveway for two hours until she came back out, shutting herself inside the car with me again. She proceeded to tell me the saddest story I'd ever heard—at least until our own story happened. Her dad had a mistress, and another daughter, and then one day, he decided to pick them instead.

As much as they share a father, they're nothing alike. Martin Campbell passed all of his traits down to Cee Cee—harsh, abrasive, entitled; the litany of unflattering yet confidence-boosting attributes goes on. Bethany was always completely her mom—generous, cautious, and fragile. I've never met Cee Cee's mom, so I can only guess she sways more on the Martin Campbell way of living.

Beth's dad—Cee Cee's dad—has never met Leah. I offered, a few days after she was born. My dad was my world, and I felt like it was important. I kind of thought maybe, if he just saw this beautiful little girl, he'd get it, that his heart would soften a little. He told me, in not so many words, that he wasn't interested in meeting "some bastard granddaughter" of his. *What irony that his bastard daughter was now standing in my house.* A few days later, paperwork showed up at the door for our signature. He wasn't interested in knowing her, but by god he would buy her. The trust paperwork was pretty straight forward, bestowing her with nearly half a million dollars when she turns twenty-one. Bethany wanted to say *no*, but I'm not a fool. I know Martin Campbell's money means a good life for our daughter. That money means more than college—it means she gets to be whoever she wants. I talked Beth into signing. And I can handle seeing Cee Cee once or twice a year to make sure it comes to her.

That's my penance. Cee Cee shows up because—as much as she's Beth's opposite, I think maybe she also always wanted to have a real sister. And maybe having a relationship with Leah is her way of remembering Beth. Or maybe, she just feels guilty for not knowing her enough.

"So someone has a birthday coming up," Cee Cee says, putting on this high-pitched little kid voice. It's annoying, and a little belittling. An annual visit, I remind myself—I can survive this hour.

"Her birthday's not until July," my mom corrects. She barely tolerates the visits. I don't think my mom thinks the money is worth it. I don't think it's her choice though. And Leah isn't old enough to be able to choose.

"I know that," Cee Cee says, rolling her eyes, but letting them glow bright again when she kneels down in front of Leah. She winks at my daughter, then hands her a small gift bag. "I was just looking for an excuse to spoil you."

Leah's grin is the only reason I wave my mother off. Paige has disappeared into the kitchen, behind the counter. I wasn't down here when Cee Cee came in, but Paige told me they made their acquaintance with one another. I hope Cee Cee wasn't rude to her. Maybe that's why Paige has gotten weird.

Weirder.

"An iPod!" Leah screams, clutching the electronic device in her hand and bouncing around in circles. It's too much, a gift my daughter has no need for. I glance at my mom and her look reflects mine, but we don't do anything about it. It's not like we can take it away.

"And guess what?" Cee Cee asks, urging Leah to repeat.

"What?" she says, her gift pressed in her hands against her chest, her skirt swaying against her nervously excited legs.

"It plays videos!" Cee Cee says. More jumping. More swaying.

"Like movies?" Leah asks.

"Uh huh!" Cee Cee says.

"Can I watch one? Daddy, can I watch one now? Can I, please?"

I look to my mom for help; she waves a tattered potholder at me, dismissing herself into the kitchen, behind Paige, busying herself with the pre-bought lasagna she put in the oven earlier. My mother didn't put much effort into this visit, and she has no interest in helping *wow* Leah with Cee Cee's non-birthday gift.

"Oh, princess. I'll need to set it up, but maybe later, okay?" I say. I'm buying myself time. My dad used this same line with me for dozens of toys that he didn't feel like assembling—and I hated having to wait every time he did. That's where Leah's at right now, her chin dented with the dimple from her frown. If only I could tell her what this gift feels like to me and her grandma...like a bribe. I just don't want to give it any more attention than I have to.

"Maybe your new friend knows how to find one," I hear Cee Cee say, her voice lower; low enough that I don't think I was suppose to hear that part.

"Paige? Can you help me get a video on my iPod?" Leah asks, holding her device in her hand, moving closer to Paige.

Leah stops in front of her, her hands holding it up, and Paige takes the pink, metal device in her own hand, a strange smile playing out on her face. It doesn't look happy, but just the opposite. Leah continues to ask, begging in her persistent way at Paige's waist, but Paige remains silent, her eyes fixed on the iPod.

The discomfort of the silence breaks my mom first, who disrupts it with the clatter of a heavy pan on the counter and the announcement that dinner's ready. I move into the kitchen to help, but I give a look to Cee Cee first, and I can't help but note the way she seems to be obsessed with Paige, and the way Paige is refusing to look at her.

"Time for dinner. Go wash up," I say to Leah.

"But what about my iPod?" she asks. I don't like that she's taken with it so quickly. Mostly, because I didn't give it to her, and I don't like that I feel that way either.

"Later," I say, nodding her toward the sink. I'm shorter with her than I mean to be, and her frown comes back.

I hate Cee Cee.

We all gather around the table, and I notice Paige stalling, taking her seat last, laughing silently to herself and shaking her head when the seat at the end is the last one open, the one next to Cee Cee.

My mom wastes no time, scooping helpings of food onto everyone's plate, wanting to get through this ransom dinner we're beholden to. The last time we had Cee Cee for a visit, it was Leah's actual birthday, and Cee Cee showed up drunk. My mom asked her to leave, but she said she had a right to see her niece—unless we'd like her to call her daddy and tell him we kicked her out. I'm surprised my mom agreed to this dinner when Cee Cee called. I wasn't here for that call though, so maybe she didn't.

For several minutes, the table is filled with only the sounds of Leah's humming and forks scratching at the surfaces of our plates. Despite all the noise, I seem to be the only one actually eating—everyone else opting to push their food around in pretense. I shrug and lean forward, scooping another helping onto my plate. No sense in wasting what's a pretty decent frozen lasagna.

"You seem so familiar," Cee Cee says finally, holding her fork out, pointing at Paige.

Paige sets hers down carefully, taking time with her napkin against her lips, not that she's eaten a single bite. She places it next to her plate then pushes back from the table slightly, giving her legs enough room to cross underneath. She turns her body to the right—her head cocked so the curls in her hair slide down her shoulder.

"Wow," she says, her lips wrapping around the smallness of that word, making it sound so much bigger than the three letters it is. "You're really going to take this thing far, aren't you?"

Not that anyone was actually eating before, but nobody is chewing now. Even Leah has stopped humming.

"Am I missing something?" I ask after a few painful and long seconds of silence as we all watch the showdown at the dinner table. I feel stupid that I'm still smiling. Clearly, by the tone in Paige's voice, I shouldn't be smiling. Whatever this is—isn't something funny. But it's damn sure uncomfortable.

"Oh sweetie. You've always been the one in control of how far this thing goes," Cee Cee says. I watch as both women level one another with similar looks. It's pretty obvious they know each other. And it's pretty obvious they hate each other. The only part I'm missing is *why*.

"I have, haven't I?" Paige says, her eyes never leaving Cee Cee's face. I glance at Leah, and my mom is a step ahead of me, leading her from the table, distracting her with her new iPod and accompanying her into the other room. I'm left in here, on the set of the *Bold and the Beautiful*.

"Okay, I'm going to need the full story on this one," I say, folding my hands on the table. I may as well be invisible, because Paige is standing now, walking to the door. She pulls it open, pressing her back against it, her eyes giving Cee Cee a challenge.

"You're going to get a call from the Herald Tribune. You're going to tell them you were wrong. Understand?" Cee Cee says, standing, moving closer to Paige until each of them flanks one side of the open door.

"Yeah, so I'm pretty sure I'm not. What happens in that scenario?" Paige asks, and even though there's a certain swagger to her defiance, I can also see she's nervous, her fingers rubbing anxiously on the doorknob behind her back.

Cee Cee smirks, letting out one of those breathy laughs I thought chicks only did in teen movies. Is that what scoffing sounds like?

"Thanks for dinner, Houston. You might want to do better background checks on your renters, though. Just sayin'," she says, leaving without even acknowledging Leah in the next room.

She wasn't here for Leah.

She never really is.

"Paige?" I ask.

Her head falls to the side along the door, her gaze on my daughter at first, then finally sliding to me. As long as I've known her, she's never looked nervous—she's never looked scared. She's wearing both right now.

Paige

That was unfair. That was so fucking, unbelievably, horribly unfair.

Houston is waiting for an answer. His mom is just over his shoulder, distracting a beautiful, innocent little girl, but her eyes are on me, too—waiting. I don't know what to do.

"Paige?" This is the second time he's said my name like a question.

"I'm sorry, Houston, but I can't stay here any more," I say. I shuffle past him up the stairs and close my door, careful not to slam it. I don't want it to look like I'm throwing a tantrum, but that's exactly what I'm doing. I'm so rattled—thrown by her level of *crazy*. I don't know who told her I was here, but she knew. That...all of that...tonight? It was all orchestrated for me, for her to *get* at me. I hate that I let her get to me. Chandra might actually be dangerous, and right now—I need my sister. I need to call her. We're broken, but we're still stronger together.

I knew he'd follow. There's a soft knock at my door, and when his eyes ask if he can enter, I nod for him to come in.

"Mom took Leah to the park. We have...some time," he says, wanting me to know I can feel comfortable being honest. It's not the people in the house, though, it's this mental game I've been roped into.

"I don't know...ha—" I stop, a look of surprise on my face because I literally don't know what word to say next. I shrug, then move to my bed and sit on it, looking around at my few sparse things. It should be easy to move out; I've barely made this room my own.

"Just tell me. Whatever it is, whatever *that* was. Just tell me, I won't judge you...I promise," he says.

I'm the girl who rules the playground.

I let my lungs take in as much air as they'll hold. My mom always says that a deep breath is like a giant reset button for the body. I've been breathing a lot lately, and somehow I keep waking up to the same shit.

He doesn't make me talk until I'm ready. And we spend almost fifteen minutes in silence—me trying to open my mouth to make words, then just as quickly shutting it again and putting my hands to my head, trying to figure this out.

My lips are parted, and I feel Houston's hand slide over mine, his touch trying to give me strength, when my phone begins buzzing on the bed next to me. The number reads *UNKNOWN.*

I pick it up and hold it in my hand, not sure if I'm going to answer or not. Then Houston moves his hand to my wrist, relaxing my grip and taking my phone from me.

"Hello?" he answers.

My eyes lock open staring at his mouth.

"Hold on, let me see if she's here," he says, bringing the phone down to his lap, cupping it.

"Are you here?" he whispers.

I look to the phone in his hand.

You're going to get a call from the Herald Tribune.

I nod *yes,* and Houston hands my phone to me, careful with the exchange, like we're passing a bomb. He has no idea that we are.

"Be that girl," he whispers. "I swear to god I'll still think she's beautiful."

My lips twitch into a smile from his words. He's ridiculous. Lovely and ridiculous.

"This is Paige," I say. Long, deep breath. I straighten my posture, rolling my shoulders back. I look the part—confident and strong—on the outside.

"Yes, hi...Paige Owens, correct?" The voice on the other end of the line is an older woman.

"That would be me," I say, every muscle in my body growing tighter waiting for her to get to her point.

"Great, thank you. I'm Roberta Flynn, and I'm the managing editor here at the Herald Tribune. A couple months ago, one of our reporters received an email with some pictures that pretty clearly show a woman named Chandra Campbell in a room with a large amount of illegal drugs. Is this sounding...familiar?"

Familiar? It's on repeat in my goddamned memory—those pictures...in my hand, on the phone pressed to my face.

"Yes, it does," I respond.

"I'm going to be frank," Roberta continues. "We don't do gossip here. And my gut instinct was to dismiss these photos and not get involved. But one of our reporters has been working on a story for years involving the Campbell family. When we got a call from their lawyer—pretty much threatening to sue every single person who works here for reporting these photos—we were a little *less* inclined to dismiss them."

"Okay?" I say, in a question. I'm still not certain how this affects me, but I'm also not anxious to get to that part.

"I know you took these photos, Paige," she says, like a punch in my stomach—so much for sending something anonymously. "I need you to go on the record. We will protect your name, as best we can, as an *inside source.* But we're at a point with the other stories...we have to have everything nailed down and buttoned up. If we open this, we have to be ready to fight."

I heard her question. Houston didn't. He's still holding my other hand, his thumb rubbing softly over my knuckles. His thumb feels so nice. Why can't I just sit here and feel his thumb? Why do I have to go on the record? Why am I even in a situation where I have to think about records? For a brief second, I think about how easy it would be to do what Chandra asked—*tell her I was wrong.* But I wasn't wrong. And as much as I jumped into this for the wrong reasons—for revenge—I still feel like I'm the good guy in this one.

"I'll still think you're hot," Houston whispers, one eyebrow raised. He's being playful, and I'm pretty sure he's clueless to how serious this all is. He might think this is just Greek-system politics, but it's not.

"You won't use my name?" I repeat. Houston's cheek dimples with his smile.

"Not unless they take us to court and a judge tells us we have to," Roberta answers. I think for a few long seconds—not so much about the name—but about the ways Chandra and her family will attack my credibility the second this story goes live. It doesn't really matter that the Herald protects my name; the Campbells will be sure everyone knows *who* this unnamed source is and just how *not credible* I am. I move my eyes to Houston's, looking for courage. He already knows the girl in the video isn't me, but the rest of the world won't. How much do I care?

"Paige, this story goes today or it doesn't go at all," Roberta says, as if any more pressure is necessary.

I'm the girl everyone looks up to.

I close my eyes, and allow myself one more deep breath. The air is cool, and my lungs grow full; I relish the feeling, because I don't think they will feel that way again for a while.

"I'll go on the record," I say. "I saw it. The drugs, her—I saw it all."

Houston's smile slips away.

"Thank you, Paige. What you're doing—it's very brave," she says, her voice sounding through a tin can. I feel dizzy, so I lay back. Houston stays sitting, he doesn't join me.

"If you say so," I say, hanging up. I let my hand fall to the side, the phone sliding out of my grip. His thumb has stopped. Why has his thumb stopped?

"How do you know Cee Cee?" he asks finally, his back is still to me. He hasn't let go of my hand, but that feeling—the one that was a little like love? That's gone from his grip. I think he's worried about the trouble I've brought into this house.

"You know her real name is Chandra, right?" I say, and he shrugs.

"Her family always called her Cee Cee," he says. "Honestly, I know very little about her. Her and Beth—they had this weird connection. They were so different, and sometimes I was sure Beth hated her. But sometimes she would act like she didn't. She'd call; they'd talk. I think Cee Cee leaned on Beth. When she came to see Leah when she was born, Beth cried—and I could never tell if her tears were happy or sad that Cee Cee had come."

It grows quiet while I wait to see if he has more to say. When he doesn't, I begin to let him know everything else I have left—nothing more to hide.

"She goes to McConnell. Did you know that?" I say.

"Business major, or something. Her dad's name is on a building, so I just assumed. I don't go out of my way to see her. Kind of the opposite, really," he shrugs, turning his body to face me more.

"She's the Delta president. She's also on the soccer team. And my sister's better than her." I lift myself to my elbows, looking at him so our eyes meet, and I smirk. "Chandra *hates* that."

His smile comes again, not as full as before, but it's back. Houston isn't disappointed in me. He's disappointed in Chandra, and maybe a little disappointed with the fact that he lets her near his daughter.

"She used some things I told her in confidence...well...all right, maybe not in confidence, but...you know..." His brow is pinching. "I didn't think she was that mean."

Houston chuckles. "I don't know her well, but I know she's mean," he laughs.

"Right, well, you get the award for being a better judge of character. Good for you," I say. I start to feel guilty that I'm snapping at him, but he picks my hand up again, his thumb stroking the knuckles, so I don't apologize. "I told her things about Cass, and she used them to spread rumors and hurt my sister."

Houston nods in understanding. "So when you saw her..." he leads me.

"Naked in a bedroom passed out and nearly OD'd?" I give it to him straight, and his eyes flash as he winces. "Yeah, I snapped some photos. It was a party. I was a little buzzed, but not *that* buzzed. I knew what I was doing. I sent them. To. Everybody."

"And the video?" he asks.

"I have no proof, but..." I don't need to finish it; Houston has it all put together.

"And that phone call...that was the paper?" he asks.

"Story goes live this afternoon," I say, my eyes losing focus, the edges getting bright. I lie back down and close them, the anxiety of everything overwhelming me.

I feel the weight of his body slide next to me, his finger sweeping my hair behind my ear as I turn into him. When I open my eyes again, he's looking at that hair, watching his hand move slowly. I watch him watch me for minutes, neither of us talking. For a small window, everything feels...okay.

"So, there's this park," he says, his hand still stroking, his eyes still on everything but mine, his smile full of sympathy. "It has a slide. And I mean, like, a REALLY big slide. I think it needs a queen. And...it's been *years* since I've taken a girl on a picnic."

His hand stops. His eyes drift to mine, and stop. As much as Beth isn't here, she's very much *here* right now. I'm both melting and terrified at once, and when I finally look into his eyes, I feel myself fall into the green layers that grow dark around the edges and are golden in the middle. I swim in them. I drown.

"Are you asking me on a date?" I bite my lower lip. Within hours, I'm going to be the porn star who threw stones at the millionaire's daughter because she was jealous. I might as well let myself get wooed a little before everything becomes cheap and sensational.

"Yeah, Paige. Like I said earlier...I'd like to *date* you," he says.

"Good, because I didn't eat a damn thing at dinner," I say, putting on a pushy voice. I can't hold it, though, and I let myself laugh. There's also a little sadness that escapes with the sound. It's one of those desperate laughs, and Houston can tell. He sweeps me into his arms and rolls until I'm on top of him, holding my hair from my face so he can kiss me. I look for any sign of doubt in his lips, but it isn't there. He literally. Knows. Everything. And he's still kissing me.

"You still think I'm hot?" I tease. His hand slaps my ass hard at my question, and I squeal a little as he squeezes, his fingers mostly on bare skin where my dress has ridden up enough to leave me exposed.

"You have no fucking idea," he says against my mouth.

"How committed are you to this picnic thing?" I tease, not really tease. His hand—it's on my bare ass.

"I'm not committed to the picnic at all, but my mom gave me half an hour of alone time in the house, and I'm pretty sure the non-picnic thoughts I'm having are going to take a lot longer than that," he says, pressing his forehead into mine, his eyes shut tight, his smile enormous and embarrassed.

"Okay," I say, mine closed too. "But just so you know, that line I was holding at kissing..."

"Mmmmmmmm?" he questions.

"It's moved," I grin, letting my eyes blink open to see his fully staring back at me now. I lean back against him, my palms pressed to his chest, and his hands grip my wrists—tightly.

"We're home!" Joyce is using the sing-song voice, like an alarm sounding, so we know that whatever intense conversation we're having needs to lighten up now that Leah's here. She probably thinks we're still talking about *Cee Cee*. But the longer I lie here, against him, the less I give a shit about Cee Cee and what she can do to me.

Do your worst, Cee Cee. Playground Paige is back, and she's a little pissed you've made her take this dumb-ass detour through your shadow.

Chapter 14

Houston

I let Paige leave her room before me. It took me a good ten minutes to get things back...well, in place. I'd like to blame the boots and the dress, but I've been with a few women over the last year with boots and dresses and bodies almost as good as hers, and they've never made me want to do the things to them that were running through my head when Paige looked down at me.

It definitely wasn't her boots and dress. It's just her.

My mom is watching me scurry around the kitchen. I look like a maniac. I think I might look like an asshole too. She hasn't directly asked what the story is—just if we had an okay talk, if Paige is okay. I want to fill her in, maybe warn her a little. I think she'd like Paige more—trust her more—if she knew just how much she despises Cee Cee. But then that's the thing—I'm caught in that weird place where Cee Cee is *who she is* and can call her dad and tell him I haven't been keeping up my end of the bargain and all he has to do is *snap* and Leah's money is gone.

My mom would be fine with losing it, cutting the few strings he holds, never letting Cee Cee into our house again. But I'm not okay with my daughter not getting what's hers.

And I don't want to think about any of that right now because boots and dresses and Paige's ass in my hands is all I can fucking think about!

"Where's the damn picnic basket?" My voice comes out in a yell as I slam the last two cupboard doors closed. My mother is laughing at me. "What?"

"You. What in the world has you so wound? And why do you need the picnic basket?" she asks, finally standing from the stool where she's been watching me for the last twenty minutes, amused. It's almost ten at night, and Leah's been in bed for more than an hour.

"I just...need it," I say. I sound like a teenager.

"Relax," she says, pushing my arms down to my side, pulling them away from my neck that I'm rubbing obsessively. I might be a little stressed.

She reaches below the sink, moving a bucket out of the way, and slides out an orange, plastic cooler. It's not a basket. It's not even close to a basket.

"Is this all we've got?" I ask.

"Honey, this is all we ever had," she laughs.

"No...we had a basket. I swear we did," I say, looking where she just looked. There's only cleaning supplies left.

"You must remember it differently. Things seem better when you're younger," she says, and I flash to that night with Beth, then look at the cooler. It feels familiar.

"It's fine," I say, opening the cooler and rinsing out the debris that's collected in it.

"Are we taking a trip?" she asks, sliding back on her stool. It's like her perch, where she can look down at me—it's how she sees when I'm lying, I swear.

"No. I'm taking Paige on a picnic," I say, rushing through the pantry, grabbing bread for sandwiches, looking for anything else. I drop the bag of bread on the ground and two slices slide out. Swearing under my breath, I pick them up and toss them in the trash. The only pieces left are the heels—who makes sandwiches out of heels? I toss the bag on the counter and look back to the pantry, for crackers or anything else. My mom's hand slides on mine as I'm fumbling the peanut-butter jar, halting me. I look up at her.

"Let me," she smiles. "You go put something nice on."

212

I stare at her with a blank face, trying to read her, wondering what her motive is, but she just pats my hand twice and starts spreading peanut butter on the last good piece of bread, cutting crust and blowing crumbs into the sink.

"Thank you," I say, looking down at my shirt that...damn, does have a stain on it. I run up the stairs and toss out whatever's clean in my bottom drawer, pulling together a dark pair of jeans and the black sweater I wore the last time I went on a date. Everything looks new—like I just went out and bought it, like I'm trying too hard. I am trying hard!

I'm staring at my reflection, second-guessing myself, when Paige's door opens. She pauses across from me, her light still on behind her. It's the same dress, same boots—I'm sure she's done something to her hair, or maybe it's just the jacket slung over her arm. Whatever she's spent the last two hours doing, she's somehow *more* beautiful, yet exactly the same.

"I like the sweater," she says, her lip tucked in her teeth.

Good. Settled. Sweater and jeans it is.

"You ready?" I ask, giving her my arm at the steps. I guide her down, and just the simple squeeze of her arm linked through mine is enough to remind me how she felt two hours earlier. My mom is no longer downstairs, just the packed cooler, a rolled up blanket, and an extra jacket—which catches Paige's eye.

"Did your mom leave this?" she asks.

"I might have gotten a little...help," I say. Paige swallows, and her face flushes for some reason.

"I didn't think your mom really cared for me," she says as her eyes drift back to the blanket, her finger running along the fringe on the edge.

"Why would you think that?" I ask, pulling her chin to me, her gaze following a fraction behind.

Paige shrugs, and looks down to her feet.

"My mom is just a little protective. And I haven't really...well I don't...date?" My words come out unsure, maybe embarrassed. The last time I dated someone my mom knew about, I was in high school—and *that* resulted in Leah.

"Look," I say, pulling her hand into mine, running my fingers through hers. God, I love the way they look together. "My mom wouldn't let you live here if she didn't like you. You saw how she was tonight, playing hostess to Cee Cee...or *Chandra*. My mom hates her, and I don't think she's very subtle about it. And you have to understand...she and Leah have been the only women in my life for about five years—at least, that she knows of."

"And I don't need to know about any others either," Paige interrupts, pulling the blanket into her other arm and flashing me what I now recognize as her jealous smile, her cheeks blushing. She's given me that smile before, and I love that she has. She's actually jealous that I've dated—both sweet and ridiculous at the same time. I lift the cooler and carry it in both arms out the door, Paige following behind me. We both walk to the car silently, and the nervous sensation of everything makes me smile like a schoolboy about to meet up with the popular girl in the tree house for a first kiss. Only we've already kissed. Which, of course, makes me about a million times more freaked out. I take the blanket from Paige, and tuck it in the back seat along with the cooler, opening the door for her and waiting while she climbs in so I can watch her skirt slide up her leg. I'm not even discreet about it.

"Damn," I say when it does. She looks at her leg then up to me, and smiles, leaving her skirt in place—just where I like it. I pull the collar of my sweater up into my teeth and bite as I close the door. She giggles, probably because she thinks I'm playing, but with the rush she just sent through me with one glimpse of her bare skin, I may have just chewed a hole through the threads of my shirt.

I climb into my side, and in my overzealous hurry to get to the park—I squeal the tires while backing out of the driveway.

"Sorry," I say through gritted teeth. I need to calm down. I glance at her, and I can see she's smiling at me, at how nervous I am. At least I can make her smile.

We drive through campus and then out of town about fifteen miles until we get to a small forest preserve area. They

214

rent boats here. I should bring her back again during the day. But tonight wasn't really about boats. The lot is empty—which is what I had hoped for—but suddenly, now that I'm putting the car in park, and the dim lights are all that's illuminating the walkway to the playground and the hill of grass, the fact that we are completely alone has my sweater choking me, and my body burning up. That was the plan, though. Stars, romance, privacy—I need to remember how to do this. Did I ever really know how to do this?

When I unbuckle my seatbelt, I glance at Paige, and notice her fingers are obsessively rubbing the rough edges along her seatbelt, her teeth clamped down on her lip, her eyes not blinking as she gazes out the window. She's nervous too.

I get out of the car and walk around to her side, but I take the route around the back so I can jump in the air a few times, jog my legs, and stretch my neck. I'm searching for courage.

"What was that?" she asks.

Shit. I never thought she'd open her own damn door.

"Oh, I was..." For a moment, I consider lying, saying I'm cold. But it's balmy out tonight. "That's a really pretty dress." I decide to go with honesty, or at least the icing on my honest cake. I couldn't very well say I've spent fifteen miles imagining my hand running up the leg you flashed me back in the driveway.

"Thank you, Houston," she smiles, and I swear she's blushing again. I could spend the entire night complimenting her. But I can do that at home. Tonight, I need to find my inner Romeo.

"So, where's this slide?" she asks, her hand on her hip. She thinks I made the slide up—which I totally would have, if I had to, just to get her to come. But the truth is, this park happens to be Leah's favorite, and the slide is actually pretty fantastic.

"Right this way, Miss Owens," I say, giving her my arm, leaving the picnic supplies in the back seat and taking her jacket in my other hand, anxious to see this new spark in her eyes. She looks down as she steps into me, our arms crossing, goosebumps coming to the surface on her skin. How is it possible that *this* girl is affected by *me*?

We walk through the picnic tables and ramadas along the winding path until we get to a large wood-chipped area filled with swings and jungle gyms.

"You weren't kidding. This must be Leah's favorite place in the world," Paige says, looking around at the various metal and wooden play structures. I love that she's thinking of Leah right now.

"It is," I say, watching her face as she takes it all in. "She might get a little upset, though, when she finds out you've taken over her slide," I say, tilting my head to the left, encouraging her to turn around. She looks up to the start of the winding slide, a series of red and blue tubes that link and wind together for five turns. It's almost impossible to make it all the way down without having to scoot yourself through the last turn. Leah's secret is a running start—and she slides on her belly. Something tells me that's not Paige's style.

"How do you even get up there?" she asks, a light in her eyes as she looks up. I was worried she would think this was silly, but she's actually excited by the challenge. That girl, the one she talks about, the one she's been searching for—she is so close to the surface I can taste it.

"You climb," I say, leading the way, hoping like hell she's following. I don't turn around to check, instead, setting her jacket on the ground by the entrance and grabbing a bar and starting my ascent up the three platforms to the start of the slide. I catch a glimpse of her behind me somewhere in the middle of my climb, and I start to take the steps and bars faster, looping my body over and under each obstacle.

"Houston Orr you are not going down that slide first. Not if you brought me here," she shouts. It's funny how competitive she is over this all of a sudden, and it's adorable, too. She said my entire name, and it was like she's known me for years—the syllables so comfortable falling from her lips.

"You are going to have to earn it, woman," I tease, pulling and climbing. It's dark near the top, so I slow down a little to make sure I'm gripping the right bars. Paige doesn't break at all, and she gains on me, her hands at my feet for the last few steps. I get to the bridge before her, and I can hear her heavy boots pounding on the wobbling wood and metal, so I stop and lift my body up with my arms on both railings, then bring my feet down with force to really make the bridge shake. It trips Paige up, and it also pisses her off.

"You were *that* kid on the playground, weren't you? Oh, that's it," she says, standing facing me on the opposite side of the bridge. In two swift motions, she reaches for each foot and pulls her boots from her feet, tossing them over the side into the woodchips below. I watch them fall into the darkness.

"You better remember where you threw those, 'cause I'm not helping your ass find them," I joke.

"You better start running, because my twin's fast as hell, and I got some of those genes," she says, darting in my direction, holding the skirt of her dress in her hand. As dark as it is out, the smile on her face is unmistakable. It's also incredibly distracting, and before I can get my feet moving, she's equal with me, pushing and shoving against me as we work our way up the last few steps to the top of the slide.

"Houston, don't you dare!" she shouts through the most beautiful fit of laughter. My arms are on the bars to swing my feet down the slide, and her hands are fighting to loosen my grip. This stupid game, this small moment, has brought more happiness than I can remember in years.

Without letting her pass, I spin quickly so my back is against the tunnel entry to the slide. My hands find her cheeks, and I bring her mouth to mine without giving either of us a chance to think, to breathe. I kiss her two stories up, under a perfectly clear Oklahoma sky, on a slide made for those who think kissing is gross. It's the best kiss of my life. Her lips are just as needy as mine, her hands finding my chest, gripping my sweater as she lifts to the tops of her bare toes to reach more of me.

The softness of her tongue sweeps against mine, making me moan against her mouth. My hands react, one cradling the back of her head while the other finds the small of her back, pulling her closer to me. Her hands do the same, fighting for something to grab, any part of me to touch. I want to stand up here forever, doing this. But then there's the thought of more than this, and *fuck...*

Needing air, I lean my forehead into hers, our lips coming apart as we both inhale as if waking up from being put under. This close, I can see all of her, the moonlight reflecting off the white lace of her dress, the cream of her skin almost glowing like an angel, her golden hair blowing loosely behind her in the breeze. I honestly never believed I would be so lucky to find someone who made me feel again, let alone who made me feel *more.*

"I used to steal your order tickets, and then I'd wait for you to show up. And when I knew you were coming, I'd get nervous," I confess, thinking back to the beginning of the year, to the time when she was just the pretty girl who came into the store. I shut my eyes when I catch her smiling. "I'm super lame. Ahhhh, I can't believe I told you that."

"I used to order sandwiches, then throw them away, because I don't eat sandwiches," she says. I crack open one eyelid to see the right side of her lip raise while her eyelashes flutter as she looks down at our feet. "Every time I did it, I told myself that I wouldn't do it again. But then I'd miss you..."

My hands cup her face, and I let my thumbs caress her cheeks, my eyes loving the way she looks when she's honest, when she's humbled.

"That's terribly wasteful," I joke. She lets out a breathy laugh as her palm slaps against my chest. I catch it and hold it there; I like how it feels, and I want her to feel my heart pick up with every second we stand here together. "Casey would be so mad at you. Don't ever let him know you did that; he lives for my sandwiches," I keep joking. She rolls her eyes, but pauses when they meet mine.

Beautiful.

I let my lungs fill, and she does the same. We just stand there and look at each other, two paths that missed their mark and somehow ended up connected. We both turn when we hear the sound of a train's whistle in the distance, I think both

218

worried that someone was coming into our sanctuary. We're not ready to give up being alone. I watch her for a few long seconds before she turns back to look at me, and I can tell she knows I'm watching. It's like I can see her think.

"Last one down buys lunch at Nate's game tomorrow," she says urgently, then in a flash, she pulls herself down into the darkness of the tunneled slide. I follow quickly, my ears filled with her laughter and the hissing sound of our bodies rubbing along the hard plastic of the winding slide. We're both pushing with our hands, and I laugh because there's literally no way for me to pass her. I don't even know why she's rushing. I'm rushing, because all I want in the world is to touch her again. I'm racing to it.

Her body slows near the end, and as I exit the tunnel, I push one final time, bringing my legs to a straddle around her body at the end of the slide, my arms quickly enveloping her and bringing her into me. She's still laughing, but when my hands find the bare tops of her thighs, she silences immediately, a sharp breath escaping her as her head falls back into my chest. In her race down the slide, her dress has risen up completely, the material pooled around her waist, and my hands couldn't help but find home on her skin.

"I'm...I'm sorry," I say, my touch frozen against her while we both sit, our bodies tangled on the flat landing of the slide, my mouth at her ear. I should probably move and let her get up. I'm not sure why I can't, but I. Just. Can't. Please, Paige—you're going to have to lead on this one.

Her chest rises and falls. My chest rises and falls. And soon we're in sync, a ragged rhythm that is making my hands feel tingling sensations, urges to claw their way up her body, to touch more than this. But I don't dare until she says so.

"Houston," she breathes. I shut my eyes and beg for her not to ask to go home. We'll just have a picnic. I'll leap out from my spot and give her my hand, help her with her dress. I'll find her damn boots in the dark, sift through wood chips for an hour, until the sun comes up if I have to, just please don't ask to go home, Paige.

She doesn't say anything more as the seconds keep ticking by. I keep mentally begging, until I feel her hair tickle my chin as it slips to the side, along her back, along the bareness of her neck. It's moving. She's moving. She's leaning her head to the side, her change in position long and subtle as her hand comes up to sweep the rest of her hair out of the way, her body leaning more into mine, her neck exposed.

I'm about to kiss her neck, and yeah, I've kissed her mouth, so this shouldn't be a big deal. But this feels like a *very* big deal. I'm Dracula, and she is letting me have her, giving me a taste, knowing I won't be able to stop. This is definitely submission. She's submitting, right? My lips barely brush that part of her neck that dips into her shoulder, even this slight touch makes me want to bite and taste her more. But I'm careful; I'm slow.

"Paige," I whisper, a mimic of how she said my name a minute before. She sighs when I speak, and I smile. I kiss more, letting the full weight of my mouth caress her skin. This time, she moans.

My hands act on their own, palms sliding up the tops of her legs until I reach the gathered material around the bend of her waist and grip it tightly, my mind consumed with the vision of what it would look like if I just ripped this damn dress off. I flex my fingers against her and feel the brush of her panties along the tips. The sensation makes my breath falter, so I return my focus to her neck, letting my tongue have its wish as I taste my way up her shoulder to her ear, tucking the delicate lobe between my teeth, letting my tongue run over the harsh metal and rock of her earring.

I'm content to stay here, to do this, for as long as she'll let me. Then I feel her hands slide down my arms and reach into my fingers, squeezing before the sharpness of her nails drags slowly back up my arms. She makes it to my biceps before she can't reach any farther; she lets her hands drift from my skin, bringing her arms over her head, reaching for me, my hair, my neck. The motion causes her body to arch, her legs shifting up and down, almost like she's trying to rid herself of her dress.

My hands obey—pulling up the gathered material while my mouth continues to memorize every contour of her neck. My knuckles brush along the lace top of her panties, against the smoothness of her waist, the length of her belly to her ribs until I feel the material of her bra against the tips of my fingers. I pause, waiting for those two voices to show up on either shoulder, for good and evil to battle it out and let me know what I'm supposed to do next. But Paige isn't waiting for either of them.

"Touch me," she whispers, her head falling to the side against my arm, her own arms linked around my neck, her body splayed in my lap, waiting for me. I let my hands continue their path, moving over the roundness of her breasts, dragging the material slowly, feeling every breath she takes while my hands are traveling over her.

Her dress is pulled to the top of her chest, the white lace of her bra drawing a perfect line against her milky skin. My thumbs run along the edge, tracing the line between good and the best kind of evil—from one side of each breast to the other. Paige arches into me again, silently begging my hands to move, and for the first time with this girl, I feel like I might hold a sliver of power.

"Touch you...here?" I ask, letting my thumbs run just inside the lace, not close enough to her nipples, which I know is where she wants my hands to go. If she arches any more, she will literally be doing a beck bend.

I feel her swallow, hear her breath falter as her lips part, but barely, and I let my thumbs trace the same path again, only this time moving closer to the peaks, touching more of her breast, my other fingers caressing the sides, teasing her more. Her body squirms against me and she leans her head even more to the side until her teeth find the fabric of my sweater and grab hold.

"Please," she whimpers.

I wouldn't be able to handle teasing her again either, so this time my thumbs sink completely into her lace bra, pulling the cups down and finding the hard peaks of her nipples desperate and waiting for me. The roughness of the pads of my thumbs run over each slowly, and Paige shifts her lower body, which makes me wish like hell I could shift mine too. I distract myself with my tongue against her neck, letting my teeth drag against her collar bone, but my eyes catch the sight of her naked breasts, her nipples hard and bare in the night air, out here where anyone could find us. Not that anyone would, but even the subtle threat makes all of this that much hotter.

My lips suck against her skin while my hands move around her breasts, finding the hard pebbles of her nipples again, and bringing them between my thumb and finger for a gentle pull, which only makes Paige writhe against me more.

Feeling brave, I let my right hand slide lower against her ribs, down her abdomen and against the wet lace of her panties, my fingers cupping her center and wishing they were inside. I run my hand over her again, and she lets her legs fall open to me, a nonverbal permission to dip my fingers beneath the material and touch her sensitive skin directly. Everything about her is warm and wet, and as I let my fingers run through her center, teasing and dipping inside her, I pull her into me so I can feel the weight of her body against my hardness.

"Please say you brought something," she says, her eyes peering up at me now, her head tilted and wanting, everything about her wanting.

"I did," I say, my voice coming out relieved and excited. Shit, I don't want her to think that's what my motive was all along. "I wasn't planning on...on *this*. Really, I swear to god there is food in the cooler. This was supposed to be a picnic." I'm babbling, but stop abruptly as she sits back on her knees in front of me, now facing me, her hands working to unbutton my jeans. I help her. Or I help until her hands find my hardness, then I fall back against the slide, the wind almost knocked out of me just from her touch.

"Houston..." she says, her hand stroking me once as she leans forward, her blond hair feathering against my chest as her other hand moves my sweater up so she can feel my bare skin. "The fact that you didn't plan this is precisely why I want it so bad. Like...now," she says, biting her lip. Her hand moves against me a few more times before she tugs my jeans lower. I feel her reach into the pocket of my jeans, and I lift my head to make eye contact with her, nodding that she's looking in the right place.

She finds the condom quickly, tearing it open with her teeth. As she reaches for me, my hands automatically go to hers to take over. I'm kind of paranoid about making sure I do this right, given my history, and thank god she doesn't make me explain it. She just lets me finish putting it on, then grabs my wrists when I'm done and guides my arms back over my head, holding me hostage.

I surrender.

The time it takes for her to crawl forward until she's straddling me is short yet torturous, but once she's there, she positions herself quickly, moving her panties out of the way just enough for me to find her entry—to slide into her and for her body to fall onto me.

"Holy fucking Christ," I say in one breath, my eyelids closing from being overcome with exactly how amazing this feels. I hear her breathe as she moves, and I'm able to will my eyes open just in time to see her close hers. I watch her move against me, lifting and falling as her hands leave my wrists and move to her dress, pulling it up and over her breasts—seeing them from this angle, they may in fact be the most perfect breasts I've ever seen.

I slide my hands up her thighs deliberately, stopping at her hips and letting my hands caress her ass, wanting to dig my fingers into her supple skin. I continue my path to her breasts and run my palms over her nipples again, watching her body convulse when I do. As much as her movement paralyzes me, mine seems to electrify her, each pass of my thumb over the hardness of her nipples coaxing her to let me sink even deeper into her.

She's lost in us, and it's the sexiest thing I've ever seen. Each movement against me forces her lips to part even more, until finally she relents and lets out a tiny cry with every rock of her hips. I know I won't last more than a few more thrusts, so I focus on her—on making her feel satisfied, on giving her a moment of absolute abandon and bliss. My hands on her hips, I slide them inward and let my thumbs move to her center, until I'm touching her where our bodies are already falling hard into pleasure. I stroke against her, pressing lightly against her and teasing until I feel her begin to clench. Her rocking becomes erratic, and when she's completely lost her rhythm I take over, letting my hands return to her hips, thrusting up into her two more times before following her over the edge.

"Jesus, Paige," I breathe, letting my body collapse into exhaustion under her, under the stars, in the middle of the outdoors. I wish for just a moment I were a teenager again so I could spend the next week bragging to Casey about what I just did. Instead, I'll keep this all to myself. I'm pretty good with that, too.

"Oh my god," she says, letting her body fall forward on top of mine. I bring my arms around her and hold her to me, stroking her hair down her back, loving the weight of her on me, loving...her.

"I fear the picnic is going to be a pretty big let down now. This night...it's kind of peaked," I say, leaning forward and kissing the top of her head. Her body shakes as she laughs against me.

"I don't know, I looked in there and saw some of that spray cheese and Ritz crackers," she says. I close my eyes and laugh again. I'm pretty sure she's right. I had that out on the counter, and I'm sure my mom threw it in.

"I fucking love spray cheese," I joke. Paige laughs against me again, her body relaxing into me. I let her lie there; let myself have this time—this pause in my life. I let myself touch her while she breathes against me. I made a joke because what I really fucking love is her. Not just because of this, or because of what we did, but because of the girl I get to see, the one who's strong, but scared.

And she is scared. She's scared of me. So I made a joke because if she runs now, it will absolutely break me.

224

Chapter 15

Paige

"So...Cee Cee...or...Chandra?" I ask, my stomach satisfied, surprisingly, with my combo of apple slices, crackers, and spray cheese. Mostly surprised about the spray cheese. Houston lies down, moving until his head is in my lap. I love looking at him like this. He looks like he's mine.

"She's loaded," he says, popping a full cracker in his mouth. He shouldn't eat lying down. If he chokes, I'm going to have to save him.

"Yeah, everyone knows that. Name...building...oil trucks...gas stations," I say, half distracted by the way his hair feels in between my fingers. I think about the times I've seen my sister do this with Ty, Rowe do this to Nate. I used to think it was so stupid—that they were so obsessed with a guy's hair. I never want to leave his hair alone.

"Right, yeah...but Leah's his granddaughter, so..." His eyes flit to mine for a second. He isn't proud of this, of wanting her to inherit money.

"I'd want my daughter to have everything she could, too," I say, feeling his chest relax as he exhales. I won't judge you, Houston. How could I?

"It's not really written, but it's sort of understood that Cee Cee gets to visit Leah whenever she wants if we don't want that trust to disappear before she's twenty-one," he says.

"No, that isn't right. Trusts don't work that way," I say, shaking my head. I have a trust, as does Cass. It's ours, and it's been funded ever since our grandmother set it up for us when we were in grade school. Granted, when I turn twenty-one, I get about ten grand. Something tells me Leah's number carries a few more zeroes.

"It's revocable," he says, pulling an apple from his chest and biting the end off of it, holding the other half up for me. I bite it and let my lips touch his fingers. I am breaking down all of the corny rules tonight.

"Who makes a trust revocable?" I ask.

"Someone who doesn't want to commit to a relationship, and who gets off on the idea of dangling carrots," he says. Chandra's father sounds a lot like Chandra.

"Bethany was okay with this arrangement?" I ask, and I can tell by the slight shift in his eyes—the wince that's barely there, but there—she wasn't all right with it. I can also tell that it's something that tortures him.

"Not really," he says, looking down at the few apples left on his chest. He picks them up and sets them to the side, brushing his sweater off before lifting himself so he's sitting in front of me, our knees touching.

"Sorry, I didn't mean to bring her up," I say as he looks down at his hands in his lap. He's playing with a blade of grass, one of those kinds that flower and blow in the wind, probably to go make more grass somewhere else.

"Don't be sorry. I don't regret a single thing, not even convincing Beth to go ahead with the trust," he says. I stare at his long dark lashes while he looks down. Even those are better than everyone else's.

"Do you miss her?" I ask. I've thought that question often over the last few days, and I'm not really brave enough to ask it now, my heart beating erratically, pounding as it tries to escape my body, ridding itself of the squeezing sensation that is bound to follow when he answers *yes.*

"Sometimes I ask myself what good missing her would do," he answers, not really the words I was expecting. His eyes come to mine for short meetings while he explains, gauging my reaction, making sure I don't think less of him for anything he says. "At first, yeah...I missed her. But I also think I mostly grieved her, and then I was scared to death wondering how I would be able to raise Leah on my own."

"Your mom is amazing," I say, acknowledging how much help she gives her son.

"My mom is a saint. I mean literally...a saint. Someone is carving a statue in her honor somewhere, I swear," he smiles, but it drifts back to a flat line when he continues. "Leah...she looks just like her. I think more than missing her, now I just sort of hate the things she missed—like seeing her daughter grow up to become the woman she was."

Houston leans back on his hands and tilts his head up to look at the stars. I follow his lead. A few wispy clouds have found the sky. It's incredible how dark it gets out here. In California, sometimes the sky is so bright, you can't really tell if there are clouds at night or not. Out here, though, there's no room for error—everything is clear.

"That's how I know it was really love, I guess," he says, his words bringing my head back to level, my eyes right to him. He's still lost in the stars. "When you want something for someone else more than you want them to be here for you—when you just wish they had more time, rather than more time with you. I'm pretty sure that's love."

My chest feels empty. I look back up before he looks to me; I don't want him to see the tears forming in my eyes. I can feel his eyes on me, but I won't give in. I'm not strong enough for this. I know his question is coming before he speaks.

"You ever feel that, Paige? Love?"

My eyes zero in on this one tiny star—it's smaller than most of the others surrounding it, but its light is wavering in and out. My dad once told me that's how you know when a star is dying.

"What you just described?" I question. "I'm pretty sure no, Houston. I don't think I've ever felt that."

I breathe in deeply, preparing to say more, but then I change my mind, because anything else I said would just be sad. I've never been in love. I've never had a boy say he loved me. All I've done is chase and be chased. I've had lust. I've been infatuated. But that feeling he described? This is the closest I've come to that.

"The sun will be up soon," he says, his voice a welcomed interruption to the silence and my connection with the star above—the one that's dying. I lift my head to look at the horizon, but all I see are his eyes. I wonder how long they've been on me; I wonder what they saw.

"We should go," I say, drawing my legs in to stand. I've been covered in the jackets for the last two hours, my legs wrapped in the edges of the blanket we were lying on. When I stand and expose my skin to the air, the coolness makes me shiver.

"Here," Houston says, shaking the blanket off, losing the speckles of grass from the back side and wrapping me in it, his arm still around me. Maybe this feeling is close enough to the real thing. I slide my arms around his waist, keeping him close as we walk to the car.

Houston keeps our hands linked during the drive home, his fingers never resting, always weaving in and out, stroking the skin of the top of my hand, making the most out of every second we have to touch. I don't think Carson ever held my hand—not once. Unless he was dragging me somewhere. He doesn't let go until we pull in the driveway and he gets out of the car.

He's doing his best to be quiet, the sun just now peaking over the horizon. It's been that strange kind of twilight for an hour. I kind of like the way the light painted everything purple— it felt like we were in one of those stories where time stops. We're nearly to the door when the handle on his cooler breaks off, sending the plastic container bouncing down the walkway and into the grass.

"You are really bad at being sneaky," I whisper, laughing at him. He shrugs, then we both look up when his mom is standing at the back door, propping it open for us.

"We...uh...lost track of time?" he says, his lips working hard not to let out the laugh he's holding inside from getting caught.

"Yeah, yeah. Get inside," she says, waving us in. I can't make eye contact with her. As much as I'm eighteen, and Houston and I are adults—I'm embarrassed knowing that she probably knows why we're late.

"Leah up yet?" he asks, looking up the stairs.

"No, not yet. You caught a break. That early-riser of yours slept in for once on a Saturday," Joyce says, her hand on her hip, her coffee mug in the other. "What time is this baseball game you're going to?"

"It's not until two I think," Houston says, glancing at me, his lips curling, making that small dimple. We were less shy in the twilight.

"Okay, good. I'm working the church rummage sale until noon, then I'll be back. You can handle making breakfast," she says. Houston opens his mouth to talk behind her, his brow pinched, but he shuts it quickly.

"Sounds good," is all he says instead.

Joyce retreats upstairs to change, and Houston and I both collapse on the dining room chairs, our lack of sleep catching up with us.

"I was kind of thinking I'd take a nap. I forgot about her rummage-sale thing," he says, rubbing his tired eyes and yawning. It makes me yawn, too, but I know I'm not as tired as he is.

"How about I handle breakfast, and you shower and take a nap?" I suggest. His eyes lock on mine for a few seconds, his head falling to the side while he looks at me. His attention starts to make me uncomfortable. "What?" I finally ask, standing and moving to the kitchen to get out from his stare. I sort through a few cabinets until I find the pancake mix. I used to make pancakes for Cass and me all the time; I'm sure I can remember.

Before I turn around, I feel Houston's hands slide through my arms and around me, bringing me into him, his mouth hot on my neck, my knees instantly weak. "You're pretty phenomenal, you know," he says. My brow pinches as I look at my hands.

229

"I don't know about that," I say. He spins me to face him, his hands on my hips, his face close. He needs to shave. I also hope he doesn't. He leans in and kisses the tip of my nose then rests his head on mine, rolling from side to side.

"You used to know you were phenomenal. I could tell by the way you walked. I don't know who made you forget, but let me remind you," he says, tipping my chin up, his lips brushing against mine with his final words. "You are quite phenomenal." His kiss is the perfect punctuation mark, an exclamation point— the deepness of it as his mouth slowly works mine, his tongue invading my mouth, his fingers soft against my cheeks. I love that I have to look up to kiss him. And I love that he thinks I'm...I'm...phenomenal?

He pulls away, leaving me breathless, then steps back slowly, his grin growing with every inch he moves away. "Now get in there and make me breakfast, woman!" he says, winking. Without hesitation, I dip the spoon in the powder mix and fling it at Houston, dusting his black sweater with a stripe of white.

"No, no," I say. "We don't even make jokes like that."

He bites his lip through his smile and looks down at his soiled sweater, then shakes his head before looking back up to me. My lips are still pursed, though I'm mostly kidding. "See?" he says, his eyes starting at mine, then drawing a slow, affectionate line down the center of my body to the hand holding the spoon. "Phenomenal," he says, meeting my eyes one more time before turning to the stairs.

"What happened here?" his mom asks, meeting him at the bottom step as they pass. She's pulling at the center of his sweater. I turn around and begin pouring ingredients in my bowl.

"Houston said something sexist," I say, adding water and stirring.

"Oh, well then lucky she didn't hit you," she says, and I smile, hearing him chuckle. It's a stupid little thing, but I like that his mom is proud of me for it.

I feel Joyce's presence at the table behind me, and I can hear her sorting through some things in her purse. I know she needs to leave soon, so I'm hoping she will. As much as it felt good to have her be proud, it also feels uncomfortable having her watch me make pancakes. There's always this look in her eye, something unsure.

"Paige," she says. I stop stirring and shut my eyes for a moment. Uncertainty is about to be voiced, I think. I wipe my arm over my forehead as I turn, pretending to have splashed something on my face. I don't even know why I do that, other than I just need to be busy, to do something with my hands. I should have kept the bowl in them.

"Yeah?" I ask, just as I would if she were about to ask me to reach something on a shelf or pick up milk at the store. That's not what this is, though. I know it.

"I need to ask you to do something for me," she says. Milk? Shelf? Please? Anything, but...

"Sure, Joyce," I smile.

She takes a deep breath while she pulls her things back into her purse, her words paused, sitting right on the cusp while she straightens for her day. It only takes a few seconds, but the torture of the wait feels like forever. When her eyes meet mine, they level me a little, and I turn around to grab the bowl, then face her again, holding it in front of me, like it's a shield. I stir, my ears focusing on the rhythmic sound of my spoon. I wonder if she can tell how nervous I am right now? Her soft smile at me tells me she can.

"Paige, Houston has a really big heart, and his capacity to love is maybe one of the things I'm most proud of," she says. I keep stirring, my eyes on her, my focus on the tense muscle of my forearm. Stirring. I'm stirring.

"He's an amazing guy," I say. I had to say something. I don't know why that's what I chose, but there was nothing else ready to come out. *He's an amazing guy.* I sound so stupid. She smiles anyway; I'm pretty sure because she knows I'm still nervous around her. I've never really cared about winning someone over, but Joyce—I want her to like me.

"He is," she agrees, her expression warm. Thank you, Joyce, for taking pity on my nerves. "My son cares for you. He cares...a lot," she says. My forearm is cramping, so I switch hands. Stirring. "Paige, he will love you, and it will be…" she pauses, looking for the right word.

Amazing.

Beautiful.

A dream.

What I want.

"It will be devastating," she says. Devastating—such a destructive word. So wounded. There's nothing happy about devastating. I don't respond; I'm still caught up in trying to understand how her interpretation of her son's love for me could be so out of line with my own. "I need you to be sure, Paige. If you think there's a chance that you're not…that you're not ready…for *this*," she says, looking up the stairs, up to where Houston and Leah are both existing. Both breathing. Both—they are a *both*. "You need to let him go. And you need to let him go before it becomes…"

"Devastating," I whisper, my eyes on the smooth paste in my bowl. I'm no longer hungry.

"I'm sorry to be so direct about it. I almost didn't have this conversation, but I saw the way you both looked at each other, and I care for you, too, Paige. You're…" she stops when I interrupt.

"Phenomenal," I breathe out in a single laugh. Her brow pinches, but she smiles soon after.

"Well, yes. I do think highly of you. I'm not sure what your history is with Cee Cee, but the fact that you stand up to her is something I wish more people in this house would do. But unfortunately, being a part of our small circle requires so much more of you. I just want you to be sure you're ready. As much as I worry about Houston, I also want to make sure you're being fair to yourself," she says.

"What if I am?" I ask. I'm a little surprised to hear my inner voice break the air, and I'm a little afraid, too—like I'm on a balance beam over shark-infested waters. Joyce is still with me, though. And she doesn't look defensive, or ready to argue. She's only smiling. "What if...what if I *am* ready for this, to be in a relationship with your son?"

A blanket of silence falls over us. I can tell Joyce cares for me in the way she takes a long deep breath, her eyes almost smiling. She's hopeful. But she's also a mom, a grandmother—and, a widow. All of that makes her guarded against anything that might disrupt the careful routine that has to happen within this house.

"Then that would be wonderful, Paige. But..." her brow pinches as she sighs. "But you are young. And I know from watching Houston what it looks like when someone grows up way too fast. You may fall in love many times in your life, but if you fall this time, you take two people with you. And that makes changing your mind pretty hard."

We stare at one another for a few seconds. Neither of us is upset; there's a strange sense of mutual understanding instead, maybe even appreciation. I do appreciate her. As much as I wish like hell I didn't hear everything going on in her head right now, I knew I had to hear it. It mirrors a lot of the things going on in my own head. Joyce and I are a lot alike, it's just when she's blunt with her words, they come out a lot nicer.

"Thank you for hearing me out," she says, finally, pulling her purse to her shoulder. "Leah should be down soon. She likes it when you draw faces on the pancakes with the blueberries."

I nod as she leaves, and as soon as the door closes, I search for the blueberries, because that task is so much easier than the other one she laid out for me—the one that requires me to question my feelings and my heart.

Houston

We haven't talked about it, but I'm sure she's seen it too. I checked as soon as I woke up to see if the story about Chandra had posted. It had, and there were no less than fifty comments from readers at the bottom. They didn't use Paige's photos in the story. It wasn't a long piece; more of a breaking-news item really. There was a quote from the coach about her official dismissal from the soccer team, and a vague statement from the university on its position on drug usage within sororities and fraternities.

The pictures were out, though. I'm not sure if it was someone at the paper, or if, perhaps, the other people Paige sent them to felt brave enough to begin Tweeting and sharing the photos. By the time we left for the game, a simple search for Chandra Campbell anywhere pulled up dozens of copies of the same image.

Paige was right. This shot—it was indisputable. It's clearly her, and the things around her are pretty intense—pipes, crystals, and lots of powder.

In a rush, we left the house for Nate's game. Paige said she was anxious to see her sister. I'm assuming to talk to her about the story and the pictures. Nobody on the outside would ever know she's the inside source mentioned, but Cass might just be enough on the inside to know.

We're sitting in a section by ourselves when Ty and Cass come up behind us. As soon as Paige hears them, she removes her hand from mine, crossing her arms in front of herself, closing herself off. It's pretty clear we're not sharing *us* with Cass today—and that disappoints me. I tuck that feeling away, though, because there are other things on her mind, other major things she's dealing with, and as anxious as I am to shout my feelings for her from a rooftop, I know it can wait.

"Houston, my man," Ty says, slapping my back hard. "Come check out the good seats with me. I get special access."

I look to Paige, and she's staring in her lap at her phone, sifting through messages—not making eye contact. This is weird; this whole thing—feeling—is weird.

"Yeah, sure," I say, leaning into Paige. I notice she leans a little away, to the left, as I come closer. "I'm going to head over there with Ty. I'll be right back."

"Sure," she says, her eyes never moving up.

"Ooooookayyyy," I say with a sigh. I follow Ty down a ramp near the front to a group of seats by the dugout. His brother steps out and shakes both our hands.

"Hey, Houston. Thanks for coming. And thanks for bringing *that one,*" Nate chuckles, nodding in Paige's direction.

"Well, it was hard to get the rope around her, but she came willingly after that," I joke. They both look at me silently for a few seconds, then erupt into laughter.

"Dude, for a second I thought you might be serious," Ty says.

"I know; I mean Paige can be stubborn," Nate says, kicking the mud from his cleats against the brick wall between us.

I turn back to glance at her, watching her talk—yet very much *not talk*—to her sister and Rowe. "Yeah...she can be stubborn all right," I say, letting my eyes linger on her until she looks up and meets me in the middle. She's saying something with that expression—but fuck if I know what it is. Maybe she's just tired. I slept, and she never took a nap.

"So what's the plan?" Nate asks Ty, the rest of the team starting to gather behind him to stretch and throw.

"You said something about a barbecue. Where's that at?" Ty asks. I'm watching their conversation, only half involved.

"That apartment complex over on Center. Cash lives there along with a few football players," Nate says.

"Beer?" Ty asks.

"Always," Nate laughs.

"We're in. Houston, dinner's on me," Ty says, slapping my arm.

"Isn't it just a barbecue at someone's house?" I ask.

"Precisely. That's why it's on me," he laughs. I smile and nod, never committing or agreeing, but letting the conversation keep moving onto topics like Ty's work schedule and the series Nate has next week. If Paige goes, I'll be there...until I have to go home. I feel bad just leaving Leah with my mom, and I feel like I've done that—a lot—lately.

When the game starts, the conversation shifts to every play. Ty is his brother's biggest fan, and there isn't a move that happens on that field he doesn't have something to say about—even if Nate's not involved in the play. Everyone was right, though, when they said Nate was gifted. He's not really any bigger than the other guys, but there's something about the way he carries his bat to the plate that makes him intimidating.

He picked off two people at second. I used to go to a lot of McConnell games with my dad when I was young—at least one a week when I was ten and eleven, and I don't think I've ever seen a successful pickoff in person. Nate just made two, and he made them look easy.

Paige stays near her sister and Rowe. The few times I look back, I can tell they're talking. I'm not sure if she's telling them about the story in the paper, or if she's talking about us. I'm in the dark, and it's starting to suffocate me a little. By the time the game's over, I'm anxious to stand. I take the steps and stop near the end of the bleachers while Ty waits for Nate, and the three girls huddle together talking even more. After a few minutes, Paige glances up and sees I'm standing alone.

"Hang on," she says to Cass and Rowe, excusing herself to come talk to me. I think I might be a little offended.

"Hey," she says. It's a guilty *hey*, and now I feel like shit that she feels guilty.

"Hey," I say back. Lame.

"Cass wants me to go with them, to some barbecue or whatever," she says. She looks tired, and she looks beaten down. It's from waiting for the other shoe to drop; I can tell.

"Yeah, Ty mentioned something. We can go...if you want," I say, but while I'm talking I can read her face. She doesn't want me to go. What the fuck?

"I was thinking, it might be nice...to have a little time with my sister? I'm sorry. Is that..." she doesn't finish.

Is that rude? Well not when she puts it that way. But it feels rude, or wrong, or something that is definitely opposite of good. But it's her sister, and she just lent her reputation to help expose drug abuse in the Greek system—or so the story played out this morning. I guess I can cut her some slack on wanting to go somewhere without me. I might be being a little...fuck, am I clingy?

"Sure," I smile. "If you need a ride, or...or whatever." I hold up my phone.

She glances back at her sister and Rowe, and they're watching us closely. I know she's not going to kiss me in front of them, so I nod in understanding. *It's okay, Paige. For now, this is still okay.*

Ty pushes up next to me.

"Nate will be a few minutes, then we'll head over to Center," he says.

"Actually, I've gotta run. I'm sorry, but it's my mom…you know how that goes," I lie. I hate using my mother as a pawn—almost as much as I hate lying, but the longer I stand here, the more I really want to leave. Paige is walking away with the girls, and she glances back at me once, our eyes meeting, and from this distance I can read them more clearly. She's saying she's sorry. I have no idea what for. And it's making me sick as hell.

Paige

"Why do they only ever serve beer at these damn parties," I say, my red cup in my hand while I stand in line with Rowe and Cass.

"Because it's cheap," Cass says, stepping up to the Keg and filling hers.

"Cheap," I say. "Exactly."

I don't really like beer, but I'll drink it. I'll drink dish soap tonight if I have to just to numb the guilt and stress. I had every intention of telling Cass about the video, but the words won't come out. I've searched a few times on my phone, and there still doesn't seem to be anything about the source in any of the stories. Maybe…just maybe I'll skate by.

"Are you seriously not drinking?" I ask, looking to Rowe standing behind me. She doesn't have her cup in her hand, and I'm not giving her mine.

"Rowe doesn't hold her liquor well," Cass teases.

"She's right," Rowe shrugs. "It's fine. I'll take care of you two; make sure you get home. Make sure *you* don't go home with the wrong person."

She's joking, and her nervous laugh is waiting for me to join in. I smile, then turn to the tap and let my lips fall back to a flat line. No, Rowe—I plan on going home *to* someone. But now I'm all fucked up over that, too.

"I can't believe she's here," Cass says, gripping at my arm, making me spill a little of my drink.

"Bitch," I say. I used to tease her with that word all the time, but it's been a while. It doesn't feel right saying it like it once did. I grab a towel from the table and wipe the drips from my jeans, then turn to see who she's talking about. I know before I look. I think part of me knew she'd be here. That's why I wanted Houston to stay home.

"Is that her?" Rowe asks. Cass nods and whispers something in her ear. I glide to the back, hiding behind them both as we pass into the living room, dozens of bodies and a few sofas coming between Chandra and me.

"Paige, go ask her about it. Go see what's up," Cass says, pulling on my arm, trying to urge me to the front of our small group.

"Stop it," I say, shirking her grip. Her brow pinches in. "I don't like being manhandled," I say, not quite the *I never want to see her again* that I really want to say, but it seems to work and Cass lets it drop.

"So coach completely tossed her this time, huh?" Rowe asks Cass.

"Yeah, she was on probation during the investigation, but I think the athletic director made the final decision. Sometimes the bad press just isn't worth it. Not like women's soccer is a big draw or anything, but then people start looking into drug-use for other things—like football," she says.

I notice Chandra along with my former sorority sister Ashley move through the kitchen to an outside patio. As long as I can keep an eye on her, I think I might be okay. And I can call Houston if I need to leave.

"You should try to get back into Delta," Cass says, bringing my attention to her. I nod slowly, then sip my beer, always keeping my sight on the crowd that's growing in the small apartment.

"Maybe," I say. Or maybe not. Maybe I'm okay not being friends with a bunch of backstabbing bitches. I'm pretty sure Chandra isn't the rarity anymore. Most of those girls, they're clones, just waiting to step into her shoes and run things their way. I guess I was waiting for that, too. Now the idea of having to deal with girl drama sounds like a fucking nightmare.

"Maybe not," I say aloud, still looking—always watching. Cass's eyes meet mine for a second, and she smirks.

"Yeah, maybe you do your own thing. You know, they're taking nominations for campus council. You should run for vice president. I'd say president, but you have to be a senior," Cass says.

I smile and go right back to my beer, drinking the rest of it down. I feel that first one—thank god. I head to the keg, telling Cass I'll be right back, but I think about her words while I wait in line. The fact that she thinks I could win an election like that feels nice.

"So hot," I hear a voice whisper behind me. I glance over my shoulder, not fully looking, to see a guy standing close with his friend.

"I know, I mean...damn," his friend says. I smile, but keep my concentration on my glass and the line ahead. Cass always hates it when guys talk about her, or any woman. She says it's demeaning. But damn it feels nice to be noticed. It's always made me feel sexy, even if it's a chauvinist move, and I think tonight, I needed to feel a little sexy.

When I finish filling my cup, I flip my hair over my shoulder and turn to face my fans, my eyes hazed and my lips barely smiling, just enough to let them know I heard them. But I look just in time to see one of the guys making the motion of a blowjob, and the other one laughing. They see me catch them, and don't even try to hide what they were doing.

"Hey," the tallest one says, taking a step forward, getting close enough that I can smell exactly how many beers he's had tonight. He's taller than me, even in my heels, and when he looks down on me, I actually feel a little trapped. "You wanna head to one of the bedrooms and make a video?"

"Fuck off," I say, shoving past him.

Well that answers that question. By morning, the inside source should pretty much be uncovered and discredited—I will be done. Funny how short my fantasy about running for student government lasted. It survived a five-minute beer line before burning up in scandal-ridden flames.

I spot Cass's back in the crowd and am thankful for my sister's constant ponytail. I'm weaving through bodies, when I feel a guy run his hand over my ass, his finger hooking in the pocket of my jeans.

"Okay, what the fu—" I stop when I come eye to eye with Chandra.

"You never could resist letting a guy feel you up," she says.

There are a lot of words that run through my mind—none of them kind. I should use them. She deserves them. But I don't want to stoop to her level, to argue about shit that doesn't matter to anyone but her and me here, in front of people. So I don't say anything at all.

"Your little game—you and your *sister*? You'll never win. Our lawyers are already picking apart that story," she says. I notice the flex in her jaw while she waits for a response. She's pissed, but she's also nervous. Her lawyers aren't picking apart anything.

"My sister couldn't care less about you," I say, wanting to make it clear that Cass is no part of this war. She's only a casualty to our warfare, an innocent bystander that I somehow keep hurting.

"How about that boyfriend of yours? Is he here? Abandoning my niece so he can spend time with a slut like you?" The fact that she brings him up, and so quickly, strikes me. I don't answer her immediately, taking a step away, working my tongue in my cheek, considering her question.

"He's not my boyfriend," I say, and she rolls her eyes. I can tell by the way she swallows, though—by the way she keeps her gaze at the crowd of people near us—whatever she needs would be easier to get if Houston *were* my boyfriend.

Leah.

She's going to use Leah.

"In fact," I say, hooking her. She's looking at me again, waiting. I'm not giving her any weapons. I've gotten smarter than that. "He overheard me talking to the paper. He was pissed that I talked to them. Not because he cares about you, but he said Leah wouldn't want to see those rumors spread around about her aunt. He told me to move out."

She leaves her eyes on mine, waiting for me to crack. I won't though. I'm good at lying.

"Well that sucks for you, doesn't it?" she finally says. I chuckle, because her response is pathetic.

"Yeah, *Cee Cee*," I say, loving the way she winces when I use her family name. "Sucks for me."

I step away, leaving her alone in a crowd that eventually swallows her up and quits caring she's here. I didn't ask about how she's here, if she's out on bail, or if anyone ever brought her in for anything. It's not like she was completely caught with possession, and she's been dealing with the rumor of her drug abuse for months thanks to me. But things are getting harder for her. I like that they are. I can see she's feeling the pinch.

The closer I get to Cass and Rowe, the more I also realize that I've made a choice, just like Joyce wanted. I'm moving out—it's going to be ugly, because Houston is going to think it's because of him. And while it's really because of Leah, it's not because I'm afraid to love that little girl and be a part of her life. It's quite the opposite, really.

I'm leaving because Leah deserves that money. And as long as I stay in that house, Chandra will threaten to run to daddy—to make it all go away, because of me.

Stay or go. Either way, Joyce was right.

I. Am. Devastated.

Chapter 16

Paige

He waited up. I knew he would. I think that's why I stayed out until now. It's two in the morning. My feet can barely carry me. I stopped drinking around midnight, so now my head hurts. All I want in the world is to lie down.

But I can't. Because I have to walk into this house and tell the only guy whose ever made me feel cherished that I have to move out. I have to convince him that it's for the best, and that it's what I really want. I have to lie better than I've ever lied in my entire life.

I told Cass it was just too uncomfortable living here. I also told her I missed her and wanted to spend the rest of the year living together, like we were supposed to. Most of what I said was true. A lot of it wasn't though.

Truth is, I'm almost too comfortable living here. When I think of home, this is where I want to be. But not if it costs Leah a future paved with opportunity—not if it causes pain for Houston. I can't bring that on their house. Joyce wouldn't want me to.

"I was worried," he says, his voice groggy from the other side of the sofa as I push open the door. The lights are off. He's been waiting for me, in the dark.

"I'm sorry," I say. I pull out my phone to check if I missed any messages, but he didn't text. He's standing close to me when

I look up; just not close enough to touch. That's good. This will be easier if he doesn't touch me.

"I didn't text. I figured you wouldn't see it until now anyhow," he says, his grin that lopsided one he wears when he's unsure of himself. He used to wear it a lot for me, in the beginning.

"I'm moving out," I say. I practiced this all the way home. I took a cab, but made it drop me off a block away so I had time to talk to myself as I walked down the street. Every time I practiced, this was always the best plan—to say it, and to say it fast.

"Why are you doing this?" he asks, stepping closer. I step back once. He stops, and his eyes—oh god, they are so sad right now.

"Houston, I don't know what's going to happen, with the video. But I need to be able to focus on that, when the shit hits the fan," I say. I wish my head didn't hurt. I need to be on my game right now, and I'm not. My words are thin—this isn't enough. I'm not saying enough. Everything hurts.

My heart...it hurts.

"Let me help," he says. He always has an answer for every worry.

I close my eyes, but keep my hands up, guarding myself. I can't let him touch me. I'll never be able to leave if he touches me.

"That's sweet, Houston. But I think maybe we rushed into things a little. This...*living here*—it's going to distract me. And it's not your fault. " I'm just saying words, trying to string something brave together.

"I love you, Paige," he says. The sound of his voice reaches into my chest and squeezes, so hard I think I might fall if I tried to walk. Joyce's words play on repeat through my head, as does the flash of evil on Chandra's face. If I stay here, can I promise I feel the same? And is it worth his daughter losing everything?

"No," I shake my head. "You don't, Houston. We were both...caught up."

He rushes me when I'm weak, his hands finding my face, his thumbs stroking my cheek, his eyes penetrating mine. I'm locked in his hold, held hostage by his stare, and I need to pass this test. If I fail, he won't let me go—and then I'll ruin them all.

"Don't run, Paige. And don't lie—not to me. I love you, and you know I love you. You feel it. You feel it right here," he says, pressing my palm flat against my chest, his hand over mine, my heart beating through us both. "And you love me too."

"I don't," I say quickly. That's my plan. Say the words that hurt quickly.

"Bullshit," he says, his voice growing louder. He presses his lips to mine, his tongue working its way through my tight lips, which ultimately submit and betray me. His kiss feels amazing. It feels like home. And I have to stop it—now!

With a hard push, I break free from his hold and step away until my back is flush to the door I just walked through. Houston starts to step toward me again, but I hold up my hand.

"Don't, Houston. Please," I say. My voice is forceful, but my emotions are in check. I won't cry, even though everything inside me hurts and is begging to pound on his chest, to commit treason against all of those things I know I'm supposed to do. I can't stay here; I can't be with Houston just because I want to. That...it isn't enough. I promised Joyce I wouldn't string him along if I couldn't love him as much as he loves me.

I can't. And even if I could—the Campbells would find out, and take away Leah's trust.

"Say it," he says. He's crying now. As dark as it is, I don't need to see his eyes to know. I hear it—his voice is ragged, and desperate. "Say it, Paige. Say you don't love me. Make me believe it."

"I'm sorry, Houston. But I don't love you," I say. I don't cry. I don't break. My words are calm and even, despite the absolute hell I'm living inside. I may as well have stabbed him in the heart with my words. He takes a step back, his face flinching in shock, and I know that I've sold it. He believes me.

A full minute passes—time filled with nothing but the way Houston is looking at me right now. I stand in place, my arms folded across my body, my eyes open and on his. He leans back against the counter, stretching his arms to either side, his hands gripping the edge as he stares into me. He's waiting for me to break, for both of us to wake up, and for this not to be real.

That is never going to happen.

"Don't...do...this," he whispers. I don't answer. Standing here, looking at him. Not being able to go to him—to press my cheek against his chest and feel his arms wrap around me—it's torture.

More time passes. Minutes. All we're doing is standing here in the dark, breathing. But if feels like we're dying.

"I'll help you in the morning," he says finally, his voice showing some resolve to the heartbreak I've just pummeled him with. I remind myself how much worse it would have been if I stayed.

"You don't have to. Nate will help," I say. Houston looks to the side.

"I can't even help you move out," he says, a sad smile crawling into place as he shakes his head.

"It would be better if you didn't," I say. What I mean is it would be better for *me.*

"Leah is going to be..." he doesn't finish, and I'm glad he doesn't. That was the only part of my plan that I couldn't find a way to do quickly. Nothing with Leah could be fast.

"I'll leave something for her," I say, grasping a little now. I breathe slowly, trying to hide it from him. "I'll write her a letter. And I'll leave her a present."

He smiles once, his gaze still off to the side, but it fades quickly.

"Okay," he relents. I know there's a chance he won't give it to her. He may hate me by the time this night is over. That would be better than what I think he's feeling now.

I wish I could hate him. That would make this easier, too.

"I'll be out by the time you get home from work," I say, and he lets out a breath of a laugh. He still won't look at me, and that hurts the most.

"You can leave everything on the counter. You know, keys and stuff. And don't worry about the lease, or paying for this month," he says, his eyes coming to mine finally, but only for a second.

I wait as he pushes off from the counter, my arms squeezing my body tightly, anticipating his approach again. But he stops after a step or two, his hands finding a home in his pockets, his body exhausted, his heart—broken.

"As bad as this feels," he says, lifting his eyes up from the ground to mine in a slow drag that cuts me in half, "I wouldn't take it back. Not any of it. Not even this. For a minute there—I know you loved me. Even if you don't now...I know you did."

His eyes give me one last challenge. I hold strong, and after a few painful seconds, he turns and climbs the stairs, switching off the lights on his way and closing his door behind him. I'm left alone, in the dark—so much of right now feels like the way my life began in this house. Only this time, I let myself cry.

Houston

Her things are gone.

I knew they would be. I've learned never to doubt her. I left before she woke up. I brought my mom up to speed over breakfast, letting her know things didn't work out, that Paige was moving out. I think my mom could tell I wasn't in the mood to elaborate; she didn't ask questions. My mom promised to have Leah out of the house for the day, too.

Paige left a gift behind for my daughter. I read the letter. It was...perfect.

Miss Leah,

I had to move out because my sister was sad not living with me. You know how you said your dad was good at making your bad dreams go away? Well, I do that for my sister. And she does that for me. We really need each other. But I wanted to make sure

I left something behind for you, since you are the princess of the house. I hope you will enjoy what's in this box.
   Love,
   Paige

It's that *L* word that mesmerizes me. She wrote it here, so easily. I don't open the box. It wouldn't be right. Instead, I move the gift and letter to Leah's room, setting it all in the center of her bed.

My mom let her come to her book club night. There's another little girl at the house that's hosting; she's a year older. Leah will be so happy with a friend. I hope what's in the box will help her get over Paige not being here when she comes home.

I dump out the things in my backpack, knowing I have Spanish tomorrow. Things are just starting to get challenging in that class. I didn't even get to take advantage of Paige's tutoring. I have a feeling I won't make it through this second semester.

I sit at the table, the house completely quiet, and slide my things out in front of me. Paige's handwriting is on a few note cards I've saved from my first semester; I pull them into my lap, looking at her handwriting. The things I'm left with are pitiful. I stack the few small notecards and tuck them in a side pocket on my bag. I won't throw them away.

After about an hour of trying to study for my Spanish quiz, I give up. I am no more prepared than I was when I first cracked the book open. I pull out my phone, scroll through my contacts, and press to dial Casey.

"What up, fool?" he answers. I hear Eli in the background. It's a Sunday night—they're playing video games.

"Not much. Paige is moving out," I say, rubbing my eyes. They're so tired. I'm tired. I lay in bed last night and stared at my ceiling for five hours until I had an excuse to get up and leave the house.

"Dude, come over. We're playing Madden. Madden makes everything better," Casey says.

"I don't really feel like hanging out with you and Eli and playing video games, Case," I say, leaning back in my chair, propping a foot on the table.

"Cool, and bring us sandwiches," he says, hanging up.

I smirk because I know he heard me. I'll go even though I don't want to, and he knew I would. And I'll probably have a better time there than here. Casey is good like that.

After a quick pass through our kitchen, I decide I'll have to stop by work because we're out of everything. I catch a glimpse of the orange cooler, still sitting on the counter in the corner. I grab it on my way out the door. Stopping by the metal trashcan by the curb. I toss it in, then hop in my car to go to the store and make my best friend a sandwich.

By the time I get to Casey's, he and Eli have moved on from video games to watching one of those reality shows on MTV. I toss him his sandwich and put three more on the table in front of us. Casey looks up at me, holding up four fingers.

"I know what *you* like, but I wasn't sure what Eli liked. I made one of each," I say, letting my body flop into the yellow easy chair that I helped Casey move in when he found it on the side of the road. It's quite possibly the most disgusting chair in the world. It's also the most comfortable.

"Sweet," Casey says, leaning forward and picking up a second sandwich.

"Dude, I made one the way you like it," I say as he unwraps both sandwiches in his lap.

"Every sandwich you make is the way I like it. And I'm fucking hungry, yo. I'm eating two," he says, taking a bite of the roast beef first, then wiping the mustard from his mouth along his sleeve.

"You're a goddamned animal, and it's more like you're eating *for* two," I say. He laughs with his mouth full, the yellow mustard and lettuce dangling from his lips, then flips me off, and continues to munch on his sandwich.

"Thanks, Houston," Eli says, leaning forward and picking up the remaining two sandwiches. He opens one a little then looks up at me.

"That one's ham, the other one's turkey," I say.

"Cool," he says. He picks the ham. I grab the turkey from the table, but I don't unwrap it. I'm not even close to hungry. We're watching a guy on TV try to put out a fire on his pants. Casey finds it hysterical.

"Oh hey, since you're here. Can you see what's wrong with this?" he says, shoving a stack of magazines off his laptop, then lifting it and handing it to me. He gets mustard on it, but just wipes his finger over the top, then licks his finger clean.

"It's amazing you live with Eli, and not a girl," I say, wiping the top of his laptop clean with the bottom of my shirt. Casey is incredibly smart, but his social skills are a little lacking.

"Eli finds that offensive," Eli says, his mouth full now. I hold up a hand in apology. His attention goes back to the guy on fire, who is now sitting in a baby pool filled with water. How is this my life right now?

"What's going on with it?" I say, flipping it open and noticing the hundreds of windows that seem to have taken over his screen. "Ahhhh, nevermind. Virus."

"I think it's those porn sites," he says through his bite.

"You think?" I laugh. I switch modes and go to work on the back-end of his computer—glad I have something to distract me for the next thirty minutes.

By the time Eli and Casey are done with their food, I have his computer back to normal. I should really start charging him, considering the amount of money I've saved him.

"All set, man," I say, sliding his now-working computer over to him on the coffee table.

"Beautimus," he says.

I lean back in the dumpster chair and stretch my hands behind my head, pulling my neck forward. Eli clears away their trash before heading to the door, slipping on a pair of shoes without his socks. I don't get how people can do that. It just makes shoes smell.

"Later, brothuh. I'm heading to Holly's," he says, showing us both the peace sign and then grabbing his bike from the entryway and carrying it over his shoulder out the door.

"Holly?" I ask, when the door closes.

"Some chick that works at the coffee stand. He's been hanging out with her the last few weeks. She gives me free coffee. It's cool," Casey says, opening up a porn site on his laptop.

"Are you trying to see how fast you can get another virus?" I ask.

"Dude, that was only because I went to the questionable sites. This one's legit. It requires a credit card and everything," he says.

"You're shit when it comes to money," I laugh, leaning back again and shutting my eyes.

It's quiet for a few seconds; I lift my arms and peer to my right over to Casey. He's not looking at the computer any more. Instead, it's on the table, and he's staring at me with his arms crossed.

"Are you like this because Paige left?" he asks, finally.

"Like what?" I ask. He's irritating me. I don't even know why I came here.

"Like . . . an asshole. Like that," he says.

I grimace. "Whatever," I say, covering my eyes with my arms again.

"You really liked that chick, huh?" he says, standing and walking into his kitchen. He comes back with two beers, tossing me one. It's early enough, so I crack it open and take a big drink.

"Yeah. I really liked that chick," I say, my eyes letting the television fall in and out of focus. This show is really lame. "Why do you even watch this crap?"

"Because it's funny to see people hurt themselves. Now focus," Casey says, leaning forward, pushing his laptop closer to me.

"What is that?" I ask, as he pulls open a window for a dating website. I shut his laptop. "Don't be stupid." I wince, because it reminds me of the one time I called Paige stupid. I sink back into my chair and rub my eyes again.

"Okay, so do we want to look for someone *like* Paige? Or are we thinking we want to look for someone *nothing* like Paige?" he says. I pull my fingers away to make eye contact. He's being serious.

"Dude, stop it," I say.

"Oh I'm filling this out. And you're going on a date. I don't care if it's a rebound date," he says, typing. Shit...he's typing.

"Casey, I'm not going out with some girl I met on the Internet," I say.

"Why?" he asks. Still typing. He won't fucking stop typing.

"Because...the same reasons why Paige moved out—why I'm not *dating* Paige," I say.

"And those reasons are?" he asks.

Typing.

"Because I have Leah." I say. He doesn't even acknowledge I've talked. "Because I'm twenty-one. Paige was only eighteen. Not that her age matters, but no girl is going to look at my relationship résumé and think I'm a catch. That three-year difference looks like a decade, real fast."

"Yeah, dude...people with kids are all dead inside and shit. Not allowed to be attracted to hot girls, bad in bed," he deadpans.

"Okay, now fuck you," I respond. I finish my beer and put my feet up. I'm going to be here for a while. As irritating as Casey is right now, it's a hell of a lot better than being alone.

"You're an awesome catch," he says after a long period of silence. When I turn my head his direction, he's looking at me. I laugh at his absurdity. "No, man. I mean look—you're an excellent cook who can fix hard drives and hack into things."

"Yes, that's what I'm putting on my online dating profile," I roll my eyes.

"Oh, wait...you know what? Yes! I'm adding that," he says. He's typing again. I grab the throw pillow from the floor and wedge it behind my neck and shut my eyes, slipping in and out of a nap to the rain sounds of Casey's hunting and pecking on the keyboard.

I pull into the driveway at the same time as my mom and Leah. My daughter has had a day filled with play and fun. I hate that I'm about to ruin that. Maybe she'll take it okay.

My mom's eyes are locked on mine, trying to convey to me to play this one carefully. I'm not sure what options I really have, though, so I follow them both inside, carrying her Hello Kitty backpack filled with coloring books and crayons, hooking it on the back of a kitchen chair once we get inside.

"You know what Madison let me do?" Leah asks. She's excited to tell me something; I can tell by the way she's standing on her tippy toes, like she wants to get the words to me faster.

"No, what did she let you do?" I ask, scooping Leah up on my hip, and carrying her up the stairs. Maybe she'll be so distracted by this story to feel sad about the news I'm going to give her at the top.

"She let me ride her pony," Leah beams.

"Did she?" I ask. Great, now she's going to want a real pony.

"Uh huh! And I fed it a carrot. And then we watched it poop," she giggles. I laugh with her, not letting myself look at the closed door across the hall from me.

"Well that sounds like you had a pretty good day," I say.

Leah nods.

"I have to tell you something, and I want you to remember that today was a really good day. And...when I'm done, I want you to know that there's a present for you, okay?" Thank god Paige left a present.

"Present?" Leah says. Her front teeth are larger than the rest, and it makes her lisp her *S*'s. It's may be my favorite sound on earth. I've recorded her saying the seashell thing a dozen times.

"Yep," I smile. It takes work to hold it in place, because telling her Paige is gone is like going through it all over again—and it makes me so unbelievably sad.

"You know how Paige came to live with us because she really needed a place to go?" I start. She's smiling at me for now, and nodding. "Well, her sister needed her to come live with her again. And she needed her just as much as Paige needed us for a while."

She did need me. For a while. And I know she loved me somewhere in there.

"She's not here anymore?" Leah asks, her bright smile falling. She's looking at the closed door, her hand picking at the bottom of her dress.

"No, sweetie. But…" I walk her to her room, opening the door so she sees the gift on her bed. "She left something for you."

Leah looks up at me for permission to go to her gift. I tilt my head toward her bed, urging her on. She walks toward it tentatively, pulling the letter out from under the ribbon that I tucked back in there after reading it earlier today. She holds it up for me to read to her, so I do. She likes that Paige calls her a princess. I like it too. It was a nice touch.

When I'm done reading, she has a faint smile on her face, and she pulls carefully at the lid on the perfectly-square pink box, almost peeking inside, afraid to see it all too quickly. She catches a glimpse of something she recognizes, then pulls the lid away, tossing the few sheets of tissue paper out of her way too. What she holds up is a very tall, very pink, very expensive-looking high heel. They're the exact shoes Paige was wearing the first time she met Leah at the stairs. My daughter loved her then.

I think maybe I did too.

She reaches into the box for the other one, next working her fingers on her sandals, kicking them away and putting her feet inside Paige's shoes. Her feet swim in them, but she stands and slides forward a few feet along the carpet, scooting in a circle so she can face me. Her smile—it lights up the room.

It lights up the emptiness in my heart, too.

And again, I have Paige to thank for that.

Chapter 17

Paige

Thank god they switched rooms. This is the room I started in, and I didn't want to be somewhere totally new...again. Nate felt guilty having the bigger room, so he talked Ty into moving back. They've repainted everything white, too. Cass said the floor's resident assistant got in trouble for letting them paint in the first place.

I like the white. It's clean—like a fresh start.

It's been a week. I don't think time has ever moved so slowly. Every morning, my routine is the same. I wake up before Cass and Rowe. I shower. I dress. And then I spend an hour hiding out in the hallway surfing the Internet, obsessing over Twitter, looking for a sign of anything more than what's come out.

That one story is still the only one that comes up. I know Chandra left campus. Cass said she thinks she took a medical withdrawal. I suppose that looks better on a college transcript than a forced trip to rehab. I hate that she was allowed to take a medical withdrawal. I'd rather see FAILURE stamped on her files. I'm spiteful when it comes to her—and I'm okay with that.

My video hasn't seemed to spread any farther either. Most days, I look for that first. I care about me more than her. I'm okay with that, too.

You would think that I would grow less worried over becoming a viral hit the more time that passes, but I don't—I worry more. I feel like the longer it takes to leak to the world, the more bang it will have when it does. But it seems that I'm just not worth going viral. I wish I could have predicted this would happen before I had a very honest and frank discussion with my father on Monday. Houston never cashed my check for the first month's rent, which means money that was supposed to come out of my checking account never disappeared. My mom freaked out, so I lied.

I told her I moved from the sorority back to Cass, since they weren't happy about me moving out in the first place, and the transfer messed up my payment, so it would come out later. But my lies were getting confounded—too many to keep track. Eventually, my father put together that there were holes in my story—time that I couldn't account for, periods where it seemed like I was homeless. Rather than tell him I lived with a man, one who fathered a little girl in high school, I decided it was better to switch his focus to Chandra and the video.

My dad went on a cyber-bullying mission, wanting to file a formal complaint with the university for allowing such activity to happen. My mom—she just cried—disappointed that I would let myself be in a video "like that." No matter how many times I explained that it wasn't *really* me, she didn't understand. I guess parts were actually of me, so she might as well be disappointed.

I'm pretty disappointed in myself, too, really.

My indiscretions have taken the focus off my sister and her MS, which is maybe the only silver lining thus far. Cass has had to endure daily calls on her health from one of our parents ever since we stepped foot on this campus. When she relapsed over the holidays, those calls became twice-daily routines. But for the last week, every time one of them calls, they ask to talk to me. My father is itching to sue someone—I think it's part of being a lawyer; he craves litigation. As long as that video stays hidden, and my name stays out of the newspaper, though, I should be able to avoid having nightly legal debriefs with him.

"You're up early," Rowe says, cracking the door open and spotting me sitting in the hall. She startles me, and the coffee I picked up from the stand downstairs spills on my lap.

"Shit!" I say, setting the cup aside and wiping the drops onto the floor.

"Sorry," she says, recoiling a little. I scare her. I don't mean to. Intimidating her—that used to be a goal. But not anymore. It's a habit I need to break.

"It's fine," I say, keeping my eyes on my screen. I don't hide what I'm looking for. Rowe and Cass know about the video. I told them before I called Dad. I needed reinforcement. They don't know that I'm the Chandra-whistleblower, though, but at this point, I don't really care if they find that out either. I just feel like it might be better for my sister if she's in the dark. Cass had the most to gain from Chandra being gone.

Rowe slips out the door, shutting it quietly, then slides her back along the wall so she's sitting next to me. Her nearness makes me uneasy—mostly because I haven't been very good to her. She's the only one who seems to sense there's more to Houston than a casual friendship. She hasn't verbalized it, but I notice the looks she gives me. Rowe is very observant, and I hate that she senses this about me, but it makes me love her, too...just a little.

She's looking at my screen, watching me type in my name and scroll through news sites. I keep my eyes on what I'm doing, but I'm trying to think of something to say to her. That's the biggest problem—when I'm alone with her, I don't know what to say. We have nothing in common.

After a few minutes, she slides a pink heart on top of my keyboard. It's made of paper, and one side is a little larger than the other. I can tell she cut it out herself, and there's a handwritten note scribbled on one side. I put my finger on it and slide it into my lap, glancing at it but not really reading in front of her.

I turn to the side to make eye contact, the side of my mouth curling up for a faint smile.

"Thanks," I say softly.

"You're welcome," she says, just as quietly.

It's Friday. Valentine's Day. And Rowe and Cass have plans with Nate and Ty tonight. There was a pathetic invite thrown my way, to be the *fifth* wheel on their double date. Pity—it's come to pity. What's worse...I'm actually considering meeting them at the bar. The thought of trying to get a cute guy to buy me a drink sounds like a good challenge for my ego.

When I moved back in, nobody asked any questions. Ty only asked if he could still call Houston for poker. I told him that we were fine, still friends. I just didn't want to live with him any more.

Friends.

I miss my friend.

Rowe stands, her legs pausing next to me. I can tell she's looking at me, waiting for me to say something more. But per usual, I have nothing to say to her, so I take a long sip of my coffee, pretending it's hot; it's lukewarm at best. When she finally slips back inside our room, I let out my breath and look at the closed door between us.

My classes don't start for another two hours. When Cass wakes up, I'll move back inside, maybe change what I'm wearing. I think I deserve to dress pretty today.

Closing my laptop, I slide the lopsided paper heart on top, twisting it in a circle with my fingertip. I eventually give in, and turn it over to read Rowe's note to me:

No heart is perfect. But yours...yours is big.
- R

I wipe the tear before it falls, then fold my only Valentine in half and slip it into the small pocket of my wallet behind my driver's license.

My homework done for the week, I spend a little time sketching out drawings in my notebook. I've started drawing ideas for Leah's room. I know I'll never be able to do anything with these drawings—but it makes me feel good to pretend. The one I'm finishing now makes her room look like a castle.

She would love it.

My sister's alarm sounds, so I get to my feet and move back inside the room. She's out the door for running without much conversation, and I'm glad. I've had enough conversation for the day through the two sentences Rowe wrote on paper for me. Those words—they said a lot.

Rowe keeps her headphones on for the few minutes we're both in the room together; she doesn't say anything more than "bye" when she finally leaves for class. I pull out my yellow dress. It's vintage. And wearing it always makes me feel stronger. I think today might just call for a little throwback muscle.

My hair pinned up, I leave our room before the lunch hour, walking slowly to my first class, stopping at the grocery stand in the center of campus for a fruit salad. I've been eating from this stand for five days, because I'm a big chicken. I know if I go to the store, I'll see him. And if I don't see him, I know I'll feel sad that I didn't.

I'm already torturing myself in enough ways. At night, I go to the library and sit near the window. I pretend I'm studying, but really—I'm only waiting.

He never comes.

He's probably avoiding this place for the very reason I'm coming here.

Us.

I saw a group of Spanish students meet yesterday, and I was hopeful. It's his second semester, and Houston is really quite awful at the language. But they worked in a group for an hour, and he never came.

I'm sad every time he doesn't. And relieved.

A little pathetic.

My classes feel like a review, more than usual. Probably because I've done nothing but work ahead. I suppose my parents would be proud of my focus on academics. Of course, right now they're kind of busy being shamed by my porn stint—however fabricated—so...

When my last class lets out in the late afternoon, I pass the library and pause at the steps, letting my backpack fall to my feet so I can lean forward on the railway and scan the expanse of windows. It's the same every day. The same *people* every day. And it's never him.

I usually come back later, but it's Valentine's Day, and I have a date with nobody—wouldn't want to be late for that. I make my daily trip early. I won't stay long. An hour. Maybe less. But if I don't come, I'll feel like I've missed him. It doesn't matter that he was probably never here.

Slinging my bag over my arm, I throw my shoulders back and enter the library the same way I have the last four days— like I'm fine, like everything is fine. My heels are harsh on the concrete floors, and I notice a few girls look up from their books and scowling while I walk by. Lowering my eyes at them, I stare back, putting a little more force into each step.

Get over it; they're shoes—and they make noise when I walk. Fuck, I'll be on the carpet in a second.

I round the corner and move to the back, to the window desk I've now claimed as my own. As I come closer, I notice there's something on the desk. It's a book, and there's a sticky note on it. I stop and look behind me, then peer down an aisle to see if someone is around. The desk really isn't mine, but seriously, who would sit here on purpose if they didn't have some crazy-ass ulterior motive like I did?

Nobody is around, and after I wait for a few seconds, I decide it must just be a book someone forgot to reshelf. It's not like I need the desktop to study. I couldn't possibly review another note. So I pull the seat back, then push the book to the edge of the desk, stopping when the words on the Post-It note catch my attention.

Happy Valentine's Day, Princess.

I turn my head, my heart racing in my stomach. My throat is instantly dry. Leaving my bag at the foot of the desk, I pace up and down a few of the aisles in my lonely corner—again, my search coming up empty. I'm alone.

Nobody is here.

But he *was* here. Houston was here. The book he pulled is Grimm's Fairytales. It's one of the older copies from the lit section of the library. I flip through a few of the pages, noting the violent illustrations; the bleak look for every story—the way these fairytales were intended. Then, a spark of color in the middle catches my eye. It's another note, with a lot more writing on it, taped to the opening page of Rapunzel.

This is the only one I know of that has a tower. I'm pretty sure I didn't get this quite right, but you tell a better story than I do anyhow. Rapunzel...or let's call her Princess P...is locked away in her tower, waiting for her prince to save her.

Tired of waiting, she learns to fight on her own.

When the evil witch comes to give her dinner one night, the princess has become so ripped she throws the witch out the window. The witch lands on the prince, who is really too late in coming to her rescue at this point, and seeing him as such a failure has completely turned Princess P off anyhow.

Having worked out so hard—and taken so many natural-growth hormones, which of course the bluebirds flew to her through her window—Princess P finds her hair has now grown long enough to reach the ground outside her window. She conveniently finds scissors in her tower room, cuts her hair, and braids it into a kick-ass ladder, upon which she climbs down, stepping on the bodies of the witch and the failed prince as she passes.

The end.

Yeah, I'm pretty sure that's nothing like the version you told. But the point is I miss you, and no one should go without feeling loved on Valentine's Day; so consider this me loving you still. And if this isn't who I think it is, the person I've seen here, by the window, every night this week, then feel free to

*pretend this was meant for you, because now I feel really bad
telling you it's not.*
   Sincerely,
   The failed prince

I'm laughing. Out loud. There's no one near me that would
ever hear, so I let myself laugh, and maybe cry a little. I peel the
sticky notes from the book and fold them to go along with my
crooked heart in my wallet. I flip through a few more pages of
the book and chuckle at the real, very sad ending of Rapunzel,
which results in basically everyone's death, then put the book on
the return cart parked nearby along the wall.

Knowing there is no longer a reason for me to be here, I lift
my bag and leave the library, my heart pulled in two
directions—between selfish and selfless. For the first time, I
have something I can talk to Rowe about, and I really think she
might be the only one who will understand.

When I get back to our room, everyone is inside, so I look at
my phone to check the time. It's not quite five, and I know they
weren't planning on going out until late. But I am glad Rowe is
here now. Maybe she'll have some time to talk.

I walk in behind her, ready to tap her shoulder, but glance
at our small television, which seems to have everyone
completely captivated.

"What's going on?" I ask, letting my hand fall to my side.
Cass turns to me, her eyes wide and her lips caught in a shocked-
type of smile.

"They just arrested Martin Campbell," she says. My face
mimics the look of surprise on my sister's, but only because I
need something to mimic, something that won't show the
concern consuming me inside that this news...it's bad news for
Leah and Houston.

"Why?" I ask, turning my attention to the TV, trying to read
the information scrolling along the bottom so fast it feels like it's
on fast-forward.

"Something about paying off cops, hiding a homicide," Nate
says. I keep my eyes glued to the TV, catching the last few words

spoken before the story flips to something else—a fire at a warehouse in Oklahoma City.

"Manslaughter," Rowe says after, her voice lost in a trance for a moment.

"Huh?" Nate asks, turning to look at her.

She shakes her head after a second, like she's coming out of something in her past, and I realize she probably doesn't watch the news a lot, not since there was a shooting at her school.

"It was a vehicle accident, a family member driving under the influence. They killed someone. They said the case is maybe four years old. He covered it up," she says, her face showing genuine remorse for people she doesn't know.

My breath is gone.

"Fuck, I bet it was Chandra," Ty says, his remark so nonchalant.

It's like that moment when a sand artist is running his hands through grains and all of a sudden a picture reveals itself. Everyone else has moved on—already talking about where they want to go for dinner, before the bar. The television remote is tossed on Rowe's bed after someone shuts it off. Cass is laughing at something Ty said. And I'm on the outside, still stuck in the time bomb that just went off.

When they aren't looking, I leave the room, kicking off my shoes and carrying them in my hands so I can walk faster, walk to Houston's house. Because that picture—I see it now. And if he hasn't seen it yet, I want to protect him from it.

The sidewalks are empty, and the sun is setting, an orangey hue cast along the trees, homes, and cars. The color makes everything feel hotter, and my heartbeat makes everything feel more urgent. My feet are slapping the concrete, running until I'm close enough to see Houston's house.

There are two cars out front, undercover squad cars. I can tell. The undercover isn't very good. The door is closed, and the closer I get, the quieter everything seems. Maybe they've already talked. Or maybe they're just sitting down, Joyce bringing them coffee—Houston wondering what this visit could be about. Someone is in there delivering news. Someone is telling Houston and Joyce news that will open up a scar so big I'm not sure how the wound ever healed in the first place.

I'm not sure cuts that deep ever really do heal.

I don't know what to do out here. The pull I feel to go to the door, to invite myself inside, is so strong. My phone chirps with a message. It's from Cass, asking where I went.

Forgot something at the library. Just go on without me.

I'm good at lying.

Okay, we'll see you after dinner.

I stand two houses away, under a giant tree just starting to grow new buds for leaves, and wait. Every time I talk myself into taking a step closer to his house, I take one back. I'm about to give in to the other urge—the one to run—when the door opens, and a flash of pink bursts through the door. It's Leah, and she's holding a bottle full of bubbles. Houston's hand is on her back, guiding her to the front porch. My feet step closer, the pull of him now enough to win the war.

"Do not leave from the driveway, okay?" he's saying. His face is ghost white. He knows.

I walk faster; fast enough to catch his sightline, then let my pace slow almost completely. His eyes are empty when he looks at me.

"I'll stay out front with her," I say, the words sliding from my mouth in a panicked rush as I shuffle closer. His eyes fall to my hands, which are still clutching my shoes, then to my feet, which are bare and dirty from running here.

"I ran here," I say. His eyes remain on my feet, his jaw working, and his teeth chewing at the inside of his cheek. He stays perfectly still for several seconds, until his mouth falls open, letting out what's left of a strained breath. When he looks up again, everything behind his eyes is broken.

"Thank you," his voice barely makes a sound as he turns to walk inside, slowly shutting the door.

He never looks back.

For two hours, I wait in the driveway with Leah. We spend the first several minutes blowing bubbles, each taking turns, soap dripping down both of our arms. We do this until the soap runs out.

The next hour is spent on hopscotch, each of us taking turns jumping through a course of squares I draw on the driveway with a rock from her yard. She's giggling through each hop, and when she looks at me, I smile. I'm careful to make sure she's no longer looking when I let my happiness fade back into the worry consuming me.

She hops through another series, taking several small hops on her right leg to turn around at the end and come back toward me. When she reaches me, she collapses against my body, her arms wrapping around my legs, her small voice humming.

"What's that for?" I ask, allowing myself to hug her back, my hands patting her shoulders.

"I missed you," she says, breaking my heart for everything she doesn't know. "I'm so glad you came to visit me."

"I'll always come visit you," I say, the words falling out before I can really think about what they mean.

Before I can say anything more, the door opens. Two men and a woman with badges and boring, black jackets step through. Turning to shake Houston's hand, the last one hands him a card. I smile at them as they pass, my hand still on Leah's shoulder, her head still resting against my thigh. She's pulling at her lip, watching these strangers leave her house. I bet she was an infant when they were here the first time.

We all wait as the cars back onto the road, the messengers of nightmares and ghosts driving away. When they reach the end of the street, I look back to Houston. His eyes are dark—haunted—but they are waiting for me.

"Thank you," he says, the same words he uttered before he went inside, his voice just as lost.

"You're welcome," I say, rubbing once on Leah's back and gently urging her to move toward her father. She takes a few steps in his direction, then turns back to hug me once more before running inside, sliding under his arm as it props open the door.

"Houston, I..." My mouth hung open, I let out a short breath and close it again quickly.

"It's not your fault," he says, his eyes drifting back down to my bare feet. I follow his gaze, then step into his front yard to pick up my shoes. "Do you...you need a ride?" he asks.

"No, I'm okay," I say. All I want to do is hug him, to let him drive me home, or better yet, pass my dorm, and just keep driving. He should stay here, though. He's needed...here. "How's your mom?" I ask.

His eyes shut slowly, and he gives a small shake of his head, no words necessary.

The distance between us is mere steps, but neither of us is willing to take one. Now is not the time—with worlds waiting for each of us in opposite directions. After nearly a minute of standing under the hold of his gaze, something catches Houston's attention behind him, snapping us both out of our trance. When his body is turned to the inside of the house, I take a few steps backward down his driveway.

"I..." he starts as he turns to look at me again, his voice catching when he sees I've already begun to leave. "I'm sorry. I have to go inside." For a moment, there's a smile on his face. For a moment, there's peace. It leaves just as quickly as it comes, the light gone again from his eyes.

"I understand. Tell Joyce that I'm so sorry. Unless...unless that's not the right thing to say right now. I don't even know," I say. Sorry. I keep saying sorry, and he keeps thanking me. Those words seem too meager for this moment. We let them do the job though, too weak to try harder.

Holding a hand up, I back away, then turn so I can't see him close the door again. I can't watch that—not again. Especially not this time.

Houston

My mom hasn't moved from the chair she sat in when the detectives delivered the news. I can't ask her to. I'm not sure how I'm moving.

Leah runs down the stairs, skipping through the kitchen, her hands pitter-pattering on the countertop under the cabinet where the water glasses are. She does this sometimes—instead of asking, she drums her hands on something until someone helps her.

"Leah!" I snap. I catch myself, then look to my mom, who still hasn't moved. Leah's clueless about the last two hours. In many ways, she's clueless about the last four and a half years. "I'm sorry," I say to her, seeing her lips quiver, afraid she's in trouble. I force my mouth into a smile. Leah hasn't done anything wrong, and she doesn't need to feel what my mother and I are feeling right now. "You want water?" I ask, opening the cabinet.

"Uh huh," she nods. I pull one of the big cups down, the ones that have lids, and fill the glass up for her, securing the lid and straw on top.

"Why don't you take your drink upstairs, maybe get some of your things ready for bath time?" I suggest. I've never been more grateful for routine. If only this one didn't end at eight thirty.

Leah carries her giant cup with two hands, taking each step one at a time. It's rare that we let her take drinks to her room, so she's being extra cautious. She thinks this is special. That's all I want her to think about tonight.

Her door closes, and the sound echoes through the complete stillness of the house. I stand in the small space between the kitchen and the living room, looking at the back of my mother's head, listening to the regular ticking sound of the clock that still sits on our mantel. My father's clock; it still beats with life.

"I let her into my house," my mom seethes, finally breaking more than an hour of silence. I swallow and step into the room with her, looking down at her as I walk past the chair. Her eyes are fixed on the clock, too.

"We didn't know," I say, as if that makes anything we're feeling any better—any more or less justified.

My mom is lost on the clock, and as I watch her, I count the ticks in my head, reaching forty-seven before she finally blinks. I do it again, and the space between each shutter of her eyes grows a second or two every time. I can't dwell like this. If I do, I'll only get angrier. And I need my head clear; I need to consider the various paths I can choose—not for me, but for Leah.

"I'm going to go sit with Leah while she takes a bath," I say, standing and watching her eyes for a few seconds. She doesn't respond, so I leave the room and move upstairs.

"You want me to fill your bath? Maybe add some bubbles?" I ask at Leah's door. She's standing at the foot of her bed in Paige's shoes. She's been wearing them a lot around the house. She has to take them off when she walks, but she always puts them back on, even if it's only for a ride in the car. My mom's been bringing them to the church for her, too.

"Yes, please," Leah says about the bubbles.

I step into the bathroom and draw her bath, then when she comes in with her folded towel and pajamas, I move to the hallway and sit with my back against the opposite wall and try to focus on only the sounds of the song my daughter's making up as she goes.

"Mermaids swim and so do I. I'm a mermaid, yes I am," she's singing, no real pattern or tone for anything. Random words strung together about mermaids, because mermaids make her happy. It's so perfect. I let it draw a smile on my face, and close my eyes. Her sound works to drown everything else out for a few minutes, but eventually, the reality of what I now know shadows it.

When the doorbell rang this afternoon, my heart leapt. I was so sure I would open that door and find Paige there. I left the book for her early this morning, before I went to work. Detective Hornsby greeted me before I had a chance to register what I was really seeing. I hadn't seen him since the day he came to my door more than four years ago and told me both my wife and my father were dead.

I was seventeen. Married with my parents' consent, widowed by a careless act of selfish behavior.

My mom had just gotten home, and she was changing upstairs when I let the three officers into our house today. The second she saw them as she came down the stairs, her legs gave out, and she slipped four or five steps down. Her ankle swelled immediately, but that pain was nothing compared to the slashing sensation happening to her heart from seeing the familiar faces in our house. That pain only grew with their visit, with every minute they were here, and each piece of information they shared, until my mother couldn't listen any more.

Chandra Campbell, *Cee Cee* Campbell, was driving the car that killed Beth and my father. And Martin Campbell covered it up. The only reason it's out is because Detective Hornsby's partner, Detective Christo, was caught—nearly a million dollars in bribes hidden in accounts overseas. A tenacious reporter, the same one who took the tip from Paige, had been digging at the department for years.

The body of the driver, who supposedly died in the crash, was actually a homeless man found drunk in a downtown alley earlier that day. Detective Christo was told to take care of things—like he'd done for Chandra's other indiscretions—though those other things were usually tickets and stops for driving under the influence. Christo split his payoff with the two beat cops who responded to the call. They helped him bludgeon to death the homeless man, making his body appear to have been the one involved. They got rid of Chandra's car, paid off anyone they thought would talk, and made sure Chandra was delivered to her father in Texas, more than four hundred miles away from her crime.

Detective Hornsby was off that day. But he knew my father from church, and when he heard the news, he wanted to be the one to deliver it to my mother. He ruined our lives that day— Michael and Bethany Orr were dead. Every loose end was paid for and tied up before he had a chance to do anything but pity us and offer us a card with his name on it and a false condolence to call him if there was anything he could do.

An entire state away, the story was unraveling differently, though. Martin Campbell was learning that his daughter from one marriage had killed his daughter from another—and he spent thousands of dollars to make it all disappear. To ease his guilt, he threatened to disown Chandra, too, just as he'd always done with problems in his life—cut the ties that bind. But Chandra is so much like her father. She threatened to tell the truth, so he kept his mouth shut.

As evil as she is, Chandra is also capable of some human emotions—namely, guilt. That's why she visited. That's why she was drunk for Leah's birthday. And that's why Leah's trust fund will never go away. That money is there for insurance, should I ever start to question things. I bet if I did, that money would have doubled, and kept doubling until I shut my mouth.

Blood money.

Bethany was always right. That money—it's worthless.

And I don't want Leah to have any part of it any more.

Chapter 18

Houston

Tragedies come in two phases—the first one that shocks you, rocks your earth, murders your soul, and leaves you lifeless—all without warning. Then there's the second phase, the one that you see coming. This phase is full of process, full of justice—or failed justice—and it feels...endless.

Meetings with lawyers and police officials dictated the first two weeks after the arrest. Any moments in between were filled with hounding requests from the media. The only benefit of the media's constant calling, emailing, texting, and camping outside our house was that it distracted my mom from despair. Instead of walking through the house listlessly, barely sleeping, and hardly eating—which she did for two days—she became obsessed with fending off reporters. Our family hasn't been quoted in a single story, and our lawyer quickly corrected the few reports that did attempt to quote us.

We have a lawyer. This is something I'm pretty sure we can't afford. Unless he wins—in which case we'll be able to literally buy him and mount him on our wall.

That's the other thing, though. This process—a trial, more investigations, more visits from the media—could go on for *years.* That's what the lawyer-we-can't-afford told us. We don't pay him until the end, so I'm not really sure how this is a good deal for him.

The meetings, the calls, the feeling of urgency—that all went away. It left weeks ago. And for the last month, our lives have gone back to normal. It feels like life before we knew any better. Only we do know better, and there's this heavy weight that's constantly hovering because of that. As much as the day feels like any other day, it also always feels like the bottom of it all is about to drop out.

Leah hasn't asked any questions, but she senses something is different. I had to leave work early last week to pick her up from the daycare at my mom's church. She punched a boy. Apparently, he called her *babe*, and she did not like that. Part of me was thrilled. His parents were *less* thrilled, though, so Leah was sent home. My mom couldn't leave work, and I ended up missing a full day of class. It was Spanish; I'm failing it anyhow. I never got to take advantage of Paige's tutoring.

I miss the way her tongue could trill an *R*. Her tongue. Her.

I pass the library every day, even the days I don't *have* to come to campus. I come anyway. I always look, and sometimes she's there. Our eyes meet, and we wave. Not a big one, just small gestures with our hands, acknowledgements that we're looking at each other.

Really...we're looking *for* each other.

I'm always looking for her. I'm starting to wonder if that will ever stop.

Our last conversation was the one on my doorstep, when the truth came out and swallowed my mother and me whole. The fact that Paige came—that she showed up the minute she heard the news of Martin's arrest—meant so much. I'm not sure if she realizes it, but that act—it was so selfless. She wasn't there for any reason other than to make sure we were okay...to make sure we were breathing and surviving this news. She was there because part of her loves me, loves *us*. I think she realized it then, too, but it's been nothing but quiet between us ever since. We just can't seem to go back to that feeling, to talk about it. We both know it's there, but there's just too much of everything else in the way.

"Dude, sandwich me," Casey says, snapping me back from the thoughts I tend to drift to lately. I spend a lot of time replaying every visit from Cee Cee—every moment of finding out our family was cut in half. I try to recall the face of each person we talked to and the words on every paper we signed. We never questioned anything. But why would we? Who gets news like that and starts asking questions about crooked cops and missing homeless men? Instead, we grieved.

"You are aware that sandwich is not a verb, right?" I ask, slicing a hoagie roll and lathering both sides with mayonnaise. I've been back to work for two weeks. Chuck insisted I take some time. And though I probably would have been able to return after a week, I think it's good for my mom that I was home more often. She's back at the church now, too. Routine is the best kind of savior.

"Your sandwiches *are* verbs, man," Casey says, sliding up to sit on the counter, but quickly leaping down when Chuck walks out from the back room.

"Why are you here?" Chuck asks, not bothering to look at Casey.

"I'm applying for a job," Casey jokes. I think part of him loves how much Chuck can't stand him.

"Don't bother; you're fired," Chuck says, pulling together a stack of binders from under the weigh station and continuing on to his office, never once glancing at my friend.

"He'll love me one day. You just wait—Casey Coffield, employee of the month," he says, pulling one of the slices of pepperoni away from the bread and stuffing it in his mouth.

I laugh as I finish his sandwich, deciding to cut it in half and share it with him. It's late afternoon, and my stomach is growling. The campus is just coming off spring break, so we've been dead for the last several days. And the library—it's been empty.

I nod to Casey to follow me to a table in the break room. Chuck's office door is closed, so he won't notice. We both dive in and start eating as soon as we sit down.

"Dude, I'm telling you," Casey says through a full mouth. "You really should have gone to culinary school. You missed your calling."

I chuckle then take a bite of my own. Unlike Casey, I chew most of it before answering. "I'm pretty sure sandwiches don't qualify as culinary," I say.

"Says you," he mumbles.

We both concentrate on finishing our food for the next few minutes, an early afternoon Thunder game playing on the radio, filling our silence. Casey finishes first, crumpling up the paper for his sandwich then pushing away from the table, his hands folded behind his head while he watches me.

"So are you going to wear that?" he asks. I look down at my apron, my nametag, green store-shirt, and gray jeans with flour handprints on my legs.

"I'm at work, jack-ass. What else would I wear?" I ask, standing and picking up our trash, encouraging Casey to follow me out to the deli. Chuck will only be distracted for so long.

"Yeah, you're at work *now*, but I meant later," he says. Smart-ass is stamped all over his face.

"And what is later?" I ask, not sure I really want to know.

"You've got a date," he says, reaching across me to grab two more slices of pepperoni before moving to the other side of the counter.

"First, stop that—your hands are fucking disgusting. And two, I do not have a date," I say, very firm about both.

"I washed my hands," he says.

"When? Last year?" I laugh.

"Ha, ha, ha!" He exaggerates each word. "And you do have a date. Her name's..." He stops talking so he can pull a paper from his back pocket. He has to unfold it, which seems to take him for-fucking-ever! "Tracey. That's right!"

I snatch the paper from his hands and gaze at a badly-printed photo of a girl that looks like she's maybe my age. Her hair is blue, though I think maybe that's because Casey's printer is jacked. I look at the top of the page and catch the logo and name for the website, FindYourNextGreatLove.com.

"Oh hell no," I say, tossing the paper back to him. I am not going on a date with someone Casey needs to unfold to remember. I'm not going on a date with *anyone!*

"What? You don't think Tracey's pretty?" he asks, picking the paper up from the floor and looking at it closely. "She's a nursing student at McConnell. A junior who likes going to concerts, riding horses, and Thunder basketball. I mean come on…what's not to love?"

"Casey, what were you thinking?" I ask. I'm actually a little pissed off he set up a dating profile without telling me, unless…he wasn't joking that day at his house. "Wait…how many sites am I on?"

"Only this one," he says. He won't look at me.

"Case," I warn.

"Okay, and maybe one or two others," he admits. I push back to lean against the opposite counter, on instinct my hands pull at my hair. "You shouldn't touch your hair while you're working with food, man. Really…that's unsanitary."

"I'm about to punch you," I say, shaking my head.

"Nah…you love me," he chuckles. I really want to hit him. And right now—*no.* No, I don't love him.

"You need to fix this date thing, or whatever. Just go wherever I'm supposed to meet this…"

"Tracey," he fills in her name, a cocky grin spreading across his face.

I sigh. "Just go and tell her there was a mistake. Tell her there was a glitch or something. Or better yet…*you* date her."

"No can do," he says, pulling his backpack up from the place he slid it next to the counter, tucking his arms under both straps. "I have a date with Holly."

"I thought Eli was seeing Holly?" I ask, pinching the bridge of my nose. My head hurts now.

"He was. Turns out she wasn't giving me free coffee because I was his roommate though. She was hooking me up because she wants some of this," he says, shrugging at himself. I'm not even sure how you shrug at yourself.

"Wow," I say, mocking his confidence. Casey isn't a bad-looking dude. He has a style—one of those super-hip looks with tight jeans, Converse shoes, and old concert T-shirts from bands his parents liked. "Not cool to Eli, dude. Not cool."

"He doesn't care. She's got a lot of sisters, and I guess he met one that he likes better," Casey shrugs. What the fuck is wrong with dating today?

"Okay, well, before you go see Holly, stop in at wherever you said I'd be, and fix this," I say.

"Yeah, I'm sorry man," he says through twisted lips, pretending he really cares that he can't help me out of the mess he made. "I'm late as it is. She'll meet you at Sally's at six. I made it a dinner date, so that way...ya know...if it doesn't go well or whatever. Or...if it goes *really* well."

"You are such a dick," I say blankly.

"Nah. I'm not," he says. He believes it, and I want to punch him even more now. Unfortunately, or perhaps fortunately for him, he leaves, and I'm left with nothing other than a deep wrinkle between my eyes, sick stomach, closed throat, and complete and utter sense of dread. I look at my watch to see it's almost five. I get off in half an hour, and then I'll have thirty minutes to race home to change, explain this debacle to my mom, and meet some innocent girl at a burger joint, staying just long enough not to feel like a complete tool wagon, but not so long that it gives her any false impressions.

Then, I'll call Casey, find out where he is, and drive there so I can punch him.

Paige

I wonder if this is the new norm—Ty goes everywhere my sister goes. He came home with us for spring break. Granted, the California beaches are pretty great for spring break, but still. He's everywhere. As annoying as it is that he's everywhere, he and I have also started to bond a little. Not so much that I'm okay with the fact that he was in our dorm room at five thirty this morning, but enough that I don't want to stab him for waking me up early so he and Cass could go workout. I just want to make him suffer a little. No, that's a lie. I still want to stab him. But I'll feel bad about it.

"You're buying," I say, nudging Ty's shoulder as we all stuff into the dorm elevator.

"What? You're still mad I wrecked your beauty sleep, aren't you? What if I said you don't need it; that you're beautiful without it," Ty says, laying his southern accent on a little thicker than normal. I'm doing my best to sneer at him while Nate, Rowe, and Cass watch, but his fucking charming smile cracks my armor, and I eventually give in and smile back.

"I'd say thank you," I blush, but then point my finger at him. "But you're still buying my dinner."

"You're on," he says. "Salads are cheap!"

"Yeah, well tonight, I'm ordering lobster," I say. "I don't even know if they serve lobster at Sally's, but whatever's expensive, I'm getting it." Ty nods and winks at me, but he doesn't say *no* to any of my requests. I don't want to stab him anymore.

We can tell just by walking up to the parking lot that Sally's is packed. It's a fish fry. Fish fries in Oklahoma seem weird to me. I'm not sure where they get the fish from, but the smell is pretty much all-consuming. And it only vaguely smells like fish. My luck, of course, the fish-fry all-you-can-eat ticket is the most expensive thing on the menu, so it's what Ty orders for me before I can even ask. I add a glass of Pinot Gris onto my order just to be a bitch, but Ty high-fives me for being a good sport, so my comeback feels thwarted before it even has a chance at wings. And I'm pretty sure the Pinot was trucked in and came out of a box.

"Wow, I never thought I'd see the day my sister ate fried fish," Cass says, slinging her arm around me and pulling me over to one of the outdoor benches set up for tonight's big crowd. I feel like I should be in overalls. I would *rock* overalls.

"Oh, I'm not eating any of it. I'm going to let it sit in front of me to piss him off," I smirk.

"He'll just start picking off your plate; trust me," Cass says.

I laugh, and Cass nudges me when we get into our seat.

"You like him," she says. I know she's talking about Ty, but the universe is cruel and the second she makes her joke, Houston walks out of one of the side doors of the restaurant, carrying a tray of food—enough food for two.

My initial hope is that he's here with Leah. But then the fact that we're at a bar smacks me in the chest, and my heart starts to squeeze. Too much time has passed since Cass spoke, which only makes her follow my gaze to see what's distracting me. What's pulling me is the dark-haired guy with perfect arms across the room. "Ohhhhhh," she starts to tease. She stops as soon as she looks back at me and sees my eyes are down in my lap, my lips tight.

"I was talking about Ty," she says, coughing.

"I know," I smile, raising one side of my mouth. I pick up my plastic cup of wine and chuckle at the absurdity of it, then take a slow sip, begging myself to look in any direction but the one he's moving in.

But I'm weak.

And Houston stops three tables away from me, a very tall, very pretty brunette sitting across from him. She's in scrubs, which means she probably has a job, which means she also probably has her shit together. I hate that a little...*a lot.*

"I loves me a fish fry!" Ty says, pushing up to our table, Nate and Rowe carrying their own trays behind him.

He's loud and recognizable, which makes Houston look in our direction. Our eyes meet almost instantly, and for a second, it's just as it is every time we see each other through a crowd, through the windows of the library, across a street—we hold up a hand and acknowledge the other one exists, and then we continue being chicken shits and going about our pathetic lonely days.

I'm almost fine with that being how things go, until the laugh...and the hair-flip—then the girl with him says something she finds so unbelievably hilarious that she is compelled to grasp his arm with her hand.

I'm out of my seat before my brain has time to catch up to what I'm doing. I'm a fast thinker, though. At least when it comes to words coming out of my mouth. Somehow, I'll say just the right thing.

"Pa...Paige," he stutters. Great. He's stuttering. This is so cliché.

"Hey, Houston. So, this your hot date?" That's seriously what comes out of my ever-loving mouth. I bluff my way through, and pretend I'm chewing gum, when really I'm only gnawing at the inside of my cheek. I realize too late that I've started this act, so I need to keep it up. I'm standing here, forcing my lips into a smile, knowing I've lost most of my lip-gloss on my plastic wine cup, and I'm literally eating myself from the inside.

There's a moment where his mouth actually forms an *oh*, and I can't quite tell if it's an "oh fuck!" or an "oh, no." I'm not sure it matters. Either way, I don't give him much time.

"Hi, I'm Paige," I say, sliding onto the other end of the bench next to his...*date.*

"Hi, Paige. I'm Tracey. It's nice to meet you," she says. Her shake is firm. Shit, she's nice. And her teeth are really white. She has her hair pinned in the front in these really cute twists. I should try that with my hair. I hate that I'm noticing things about her hair—things I want to emulate. She can't be around long enough for that to happen...for her and I to be friends. She needs to go.

"So, what brings you two out for Fish-Fry Friday?" I ask. I'm not even really sure if that's what this is called. It is now.

"Oh, well...we sort of met..." she's looking to Houston for confirmation, or maybe out of courtesy. I can tell she doesn't want to rat him out. Houston is wincing, his eyes closed tightly, and eventually he pops one open, right when she finishes her sentence. "Online?"

Online. She says it like a question.

"Oh," I say, not really sure what to do with that answer. "Oh." I just said it again.

Houston's doing that thing he does when he puts his hand on his neck and squeezes. My best guess is he's trying to work his own head off his body so he doesn't feel the pressure of this very situation. It's maybe one of the cutest quirks he has, but right now I wish he'd just stop.

There are a few seconds that pass when I think Houston is about to talk, but eventually he shakes his head and covers his mouth. He's as lost for words as I am. The longer I'm here, the more strange being here feels, and we're all starting to focus on the country song being piped through the speakers; Tracey—*I think?*—even bothering to go as far as to bob her head in time to the music.

"Well, you guys have a good time," I say, no longer able to bring my eyes up to meet anyone's. I wave my fingers lightly at Tracey as I leave our shared bench. "Nice to meet you."

"You, too," she says, or at least I think that's what I hear behind the swishing of air rushing over my ears, my head suddenly light. I stumble when I get back to our table, and I know it's not because I've had a plastic cup of wine. Rowe catches me.

Everyone's picking at the baskets of food, but nobody is really saying anything. They're trying to be polite. I know they all probably understand more about me and Houston—and the fact that there's something *between* me and Houston—than they say out loud. I kind of love them for pretending, but right now, I wish we could all just call a time out so I could feel sad and angry and pissed and hurt in front of my friends.

My friends. *These are my friends.*

"I hate fish," Rowe says. Nate doesn't skip a beat and grabs her basket, placing it in front of him, and begins to eat her dinner along with his. Their distraction does its job, and the rest of us laugh.

Rowe scratches the tips of her fingers along my arm to get my attention, then nods toward the exit. I silently tell her it's okay, but she silently insists.

"I'm gonna head back with Paige. We'll see you guys in a bit," she says.

"Peace!" Ty says, now fully invested in his dinner. I slide my basket over to him, and he glances up at me, one eyebrow cocked.

"You paid for it anyway. Might as well eat it. You do *loves a fish fry,*" I say. He winks at me, and as I pass he slaps my ass.

"Uhm, not okay!" Cass shouts behind me, slapping his arm. I keep walking away with Rowe, and when I turn back one last time to glance at Ty, he winks again. Fucker grew on me.

Rowe manages to fill our short walk home with random facts she's recently learned about San Diego. Her parents just moved there, and spring break was her first time seeing their new house. I let her go on, and I feel kind of bad when the realization hits her as we walk into our dorm room that I was born and raised in California.

"Shit, I'm sorry. That was really lame. You pretty much know all of that stuff I just told you, huh?" she says, bunching her face. She's one of those rare girls who can make that face without looking awful.

"It's okay. You were telling more as therapy; I get it," I smile.

She nods then tosses her keys on her bed.

"I forget that you and Cass are sisters sometimes," she says. "You're so..."

"Different?" I fill in for her, opting for that word rather than the millions of others she could say about me, like bitchy, unfriendly, cold, distant.

"Yeah," she agrees. I smile. "It's weird that you're twins; that's all."

I kick my shoes from my feet and crawl up into my own bed, pulling my blanket around me, making a fort like Cass and I used to do when we were little. Rowe lies on her bed, her head flat along the edge as she blinks at me.

"Why don't you just tell him?" she says finally. "Tell him you miss him, or that you..."

She doesn't finish her thought, waiting for me to fill in the blank for her. I don't answer, instead only blinking back. I don't know how to get all of the things tangled between my head and my heart out of my mouth in a way she would ever be able to understand.

"Is it because of his daughter?" she asks.

I breathe in deeply and think about her words. When the news broke about Martin's arrest and Chandra's recklessness, Leah became a part of every sentence that included Houston. When Cass found out he was a father, her only reaction was "Wow." Nate and Ty commented on how young he was to have a kid, but they moved on quickly, too. Rowe never said a word. Nobody's breathed a word about the fact that he has a child since, and I'm not sure if it's because it's just not that big of a deal to them, or if it's because they're trying not to breathe a word about *anything* Houston-related around me.

"It's...complicated," I answer. Rowe sits up when I do, folding her hands in front of her and leaning forward, resting her arms on her knees.

"Complicated for you? Or for him?" she asks.

I pinch my brow, not really sure how to answer that, maybe a little defensive, too.

"Sorry, that sounded harsh. I only meant that Houston has a lot of things on his plate—daughter, trial, all that," she says.

"Exactly," I respond, my eyes big just at the thought of *all that.*

"His world seems complicated," she acknowledges, nodding at me, my head in sync with hers. "But he seems to want you in it."

Does he? There have been days since that last conversation in his driveway where we've seen each other, where I've thought about pressing his number on my phone, calling him, running to him, and I was so sure he'd run to me just as quickly. But then there he was tonight...on a *date.* And as much as I wanted to brand him with my name—rip him from that table and carry him home as my own, I also couldn't help but think of what Joyce said, about his capacity to love, and how much he deserves to have someone who can feel just as much loving him back.

"I'm not sure I know how to love him enough." I breathe the words, my gaze getting lost on Rowe's. For a girl who's great at lying, I'm pretty terrible at telling the truth—at least when it's about me. I don't like the way it feels—self-reflection.

"His daughter...Leah...she's..." I focus on Rowe's eyes now, and I can't help but smile, because they look a lot like Leah's, ovals that dip on either side, lashes that bat slowly and a warmth that feels innocent. "She's amazing," I say. It feels good to say she's amazing. That little girl *is* amazing.

"I'd like to meet her," Rowe smiles. I'd like them to meet, too. I'd like everyone to meet Leah.

"She's part of the reason I left," I admit, realizing how negative that sounds when Rowe's smile falls. "Not...not because of her, but for her. She has a trust that's controlled by Chandra's dad. And I..."

"You complicate things," Rowe says, completely understanding.

"Like I said...it's complicated," I sigh, letting the weight of my body fall deep into my pillow and mattress.

"That sounds a lot like love to me," Rowe says.

"I don't know," I respond, looking away, trying to find the words to explain the rest. "Maybe."

Rowe stands, crosses the small space between our beds, and crawls up to sit next to me. Her hand moves a layer of hair away from my face. Her gesture is so simple, but it brings a tear to my eye. I wipe it away before it has a chance to grow.

"I think you know," she says, leaning forward enough to catch my sightline, to bring my eyes back to hers. "You're a little scared because, *hello,* he has a kid!" she says, waving both hands by her face. I laugh, catching the second tear in my eye before it falls. "But...I think you know. Leah's amazing, because Houston's amazing, and he made her that way. And you...you love the whole package."

I do.

I love the whole package.

I love the way Leah smiles, and I love the way Houston makes her laugh.

I love the feel of her small hands around my waist and the tender touch of his hand on my cheek.

282

I love the way he looks at me when I say something kind to his daughter.

Houston and Leah are so far off the map of where I ever thought I'd go. They were never on a list—never a goal, never anything I thought I wanted. But I want to deserve them. And I love the girl I am when I'm part of *them*.

"I'm really happy you and Nate are together," I say finally, smiling at her as I sit up next to her. When Rowe and I first met, we competed for Nate. It was stupid. And even though it was only months ago, I feel like I'm years away from being the person I was then.

Rowe squeezes my hand against the mattress, then stands and walks to her desk, pulling out a few things and busying herself with schoolwork. She knows that my comment was really my way of saying *thank you*. And the fact that she doesn't expect me to say anything else makes me like her even more.

Chapter 19

Houston

Tracey understood. It didn't take long for her to piece everything together after Paige walked out of the bar. The only part I had to fill her in on was the fact that my boneheaded friend—the one whose door I've been pounding on for the last five minutes—was the one who filled out the online profile.

She said he sounded like a good friend, but I don't know...right now, I kind of think he's a dick hole.

"I'm not going to quit knocking, because I know you're in there. And it's after noon, so I know you are awake, and if you're *not* awake, then you're hung over, and the fact that I'm knocking is really irritating the shit out of you, and that REALLY fucking makes me happy!" I shout while pounding. Casey's neighbor is a chain-smoking older woman whose hair is constantly in curlers. I wave with my other hand because she's been watching me this entire time, and she finds my latest rant funny. She waves back, and I start to pound harder because I sort of feel like now there's a team of us out here to piss him off.

"Dude!" he shouts, flinging the door open. I lose my balance and fall inside a step or two. "I mean, come on! Have some respect!"

He's wearing a robe, and he looks ridiculous. It's red velvet, like he just rolled in from the Playboy Mansion. That, on top of what he just said, has me in a fit of laughter. I have to bend over to catch my breath.

"Fuck," he says, gripping his head with one hand. I had a feeling he was hung over. He slams his door shut behind me, wincing at the sound he made.

"Get dressed," I say. He slouches on his couch, both hands on his head now, his hair wild and in all directions. He looks like a poor-man's mad scientist.

"I am dressed," he grunts.

"In clothes you can go out in. Come on, I'm hungry, and you're buying me lunch. Then, we're going to talk about all of the damned dating websites you've got me on, and then we're going to take me off those sites," I say. I refuse to sit down, instead pacing back and forth in front of his ugly plaid sofa.

Casey rubs his head for a few more seconds, but eventually peels one hand away, still shielding his eyes from light, and cocks an eyebrow at me underneath. "How was Tracey?" he asks, mustering enough energy to wiggle his eyebrows.

I grab his jacket from the hook by the door and throw it at him. "Dude, I don't even care if you're dressed. Put your coat on; we're going out," I say, holding the door open and waiting for him to poke his arms through his jacket. He keeps the red robe on underneath, a layer of T-shirts and sweatpants on under that. He looks like a hobo.

Casey finally shuffles out the door, his feet stuffed in sandals, the toe part pinching through his socks. Eli walks up just as we're leaving, so I invite him along too, and tell him Casey's buying. My friend is too hung over to argue, so Eli shrugs and joins us.

I could drive him, but the fact that he's dressed like that, and I'm pissed at him, makes me opt to walk to Sally's instead. The tables outside are still set up from the big fish fry, and I grimace at the memory, only refueling my anger at Casey for putting me in this bind in the first place. I can't believe Paige was there...at that exact moment. I had planned on a half-hour dinner, tops, over which I would explain what happened. I wanted to buy Tracey dinner, because it's the least she deserved.

And I was relieved when I saw it was fish fry night, knowing there was no way Paige would be around for that.

No way.

Thank you, fucking upside-down land.

I lead Casey and Eli to a spot near the bar, and we grab a high top. There's a decent crowd here for mid-afternoon on a Saturday. A Thunder game is playing on all the TVs; it's near the end of the season, so play-offs are in sight. I'm half tempted to move our table so Casey can't see the game, but I don't want to be a dick to Eli.

His beard is gone, and I swear he had it yesterday.

"You shave?" I ask, rubbing my chin.

"Shit!" Eli says, grabbing his face in response. "No, why? Where'd my beard go?"

I hold his gaze for a few seconds, confused, until he starts laughing hard, slapping my shoulder with his big hand. "Of course I fucking shaved, douchebag," he says.

I laugh with him because he's right; that was a really obvious question. Casey scowls at me, though.

"What's up your ass?" I ask.

"How come he can fuck with you and everything's all well and good, but I go and get you a hot date, and it's all *oh, Casey, you asshole, I'm gonna make you miserable when you're hung over because you set me up with a smokin' chick,*" Casey says, feigning what I think is supposed to be *my* voice during the last half of his sentence.

My smile drops fast. I place my hands flat on the table and take a deep breath before leaning toward him, backing off a little when I smell just how much he still reeks of last night.

"Because Eli is funny," I say. "And you are, in fact, an asshole."

He glares at me for a few seconds, then lets his head fall into his hands, giving up.

"Give me your wallet," I say, knowing deep down Casey knows I'm right. Eventually, he reaches into his pocket and slaps his wallet on the table. I pull his credit card out and walk it up to the bar for our tab. I order us all burgers and a round of beers, then turn to head to our table so I can get back to lecturing and annoying Casey. That's when I see her.

And she sees me.

She's with Rowe and Cass, standing at the other end of the bar. Nobody is sitting, and I start to worry that they're only stopping by, on their way somewhere...gone.

My initial step is in their direction, because I'm overcome with the need to explain everything to her, to let her know exactly what she saw in here last night. But then her first step is to turn her back to me, so I bail on plan *A* and return to the boys at the table.

Meg is standing at the table talking to Casey; I think she's lecturing him a little for being hung over, which pleases me. Meg's been waiting tables here since I used to come in with my dad on Sundays to watch football. My mom hated when we skipped church, but my dad promised her we'd pray at halftime. We never did.

Seeing Meg gives me an idea. As I step up to the table, I hand her Casey's card, his eyes wide on it as he reaches for it. I smack his hand away.

"Hey, Meg. Can you do me a favor?" I ask.

"Sure, hun. Whatcha need?" she asks, pulling out her pen and tablet. Casey reaches for his card again, and this time she smacks his hand away. It makes me chuckle, because I know she's mad at him for looking like he does—like a walking bottle of whiskey.

"See those ladies over there?" I ask, pointing to Rowe, Cass, and Paige. Rowe is the only one who notices me, and she keeps talking right through my instruction to Meg; *hopefully she's not talking about me.*

"Sure do. Those are lovely girls. You sweet on one?" she asks, the mint from her gum barely covering the stale smell of smoke on her breath.

"Whatever they ordered, charge it to that card," I say. Casey's mouth opens, but shuts quickly when I challenge his look with one of my own. "And buy them a round on us, too."

"You got it," she says, tapping her pen twice in front of me on the table. "You'll be buyin' them Cokes, though, 'cause I know those girls aren't twenty-one. I'm not helping this troublemaker out any more than he's already helped himself out today." She smacks the back of Casey's head as she leaves, and he pushes the palms of his hands into his eyebrows.

"Fuck, why can't a man be hung over without catching shit from his friends," he mumbles.

"Because you blew my shot with the girl I love," I say before realizing it was out loud. I can feel Casey and Eli both staring at me, so I resist the urge to look in their direction. I keep the serious expression on my face and my eyes on the TV just over their shoulders long enough for them to decide not to give me shit about what I just said.

After about a minute, I feel like I might get away with it, so I glance at my bum of a best friend. He's still staring at me, and I'm mad at myself for not waiting him out longer. But he doesn't make a joke. And he actually looks like he feels genuinely bad.

"So, is that her?" Eli asks, pointing behind me, while taking a sip of his beer.

I turn around and Paige is steps away, her hand playing with the stem of a cherry floating near the top of her Coke. She's smiling, and my heart starts to beat a little faster with hope until she talks.

"You honestly think I'm going to let you buy me a drink the day after your date with hottie McScrub Pants?" she says. I'm not sure what to laugh at most at first—the name she just gave the poor girl Casey set me up with, or the fact that she's so jealous.

"For the record, I bought the drinks," Casey says, holding his glass up to toast her. She squints at him, then moves her eyes back to me.

"Why is your friend dressed like a pimp?" she asks. She pulls the cherry out of her Coke and eats it while she waits, and I get a little lost watching her tongue play with the stem.

"I don't know," I chuckle, just happy she's decided to keep her drink, she's not throwing it at me, and she's still standing here. I take a deep breath, and she takes a long sip through her straw, both of us locked in this small little window of fresh air and happiness. I don't hesitate to step through the opening.

"Casey bought your drinks, because *he's* the one who was supposed to be on the date with..." I stop, shaking my head at her.

"Hottie McScrub Pants," she fills in for me, still not convinced or ready to let me off the hook easily.

"Right. Or we could call her Tracey," I say.

"You can call her Tracey," she fires back. Okay, I still have work to do.

I smile at her with my lips tight, letting her have that one. She can have more, too. Whatever she wants. Just don't leave, Paige.

"Okay," I nod. "Point is, I didn't have a date," I start, and she interrupts again.

"Ah, not sure about that. I saw you. On one. A date, that is," she says. I sigh with frustration, but when I look at her, I notice the right side of her mouth tick up, her smirk playful in her eyes, too. She's messing with me.

"Fine, we'll call it a date," I say, and when I feel her try to cut me off again, I hold my hand up to stop her. "But not a date I made or knew about until minutes before I showed up to cancel. It was a date my very annoying friend..."

"*Best* friend," Casey butts in. I smack his head just like Meg did, sending him back to the land of headaches so I can finish talking to Paige.

"My best friend decided it was time for me to get back in the game, not realizing there was only one place I wanted to be, one girl I wanted to go on a date with, one person who I would even consider." I say these words to her, not caring if Casey and Eli are hearing them, and Paige works so hard to keep herself from giving anything away. But I know her tells. I see her breathing change. I notice her eyes react, and her lips tremble for just a second.

She takes another long sip through her straw, her lips slipping even more into a grin. I let mine go too.

"We're going to Nate's game later today. Scouts are going to be there; it's suppose to be a big deal," she says, her teeth chewing at the tip of her straw as her eyes flit to mine. "You should come."

"I'll be there," I say. I have to work, but I'll quit before I miss this game, this moment, this chance.

The smile on her face does me in.

Before she leaves, she glances to Eli, furrowing her brow. "Who's this guy?" she says, pointing to him.

Eli shakes his head. "I'm Eli. We met. I moved, like, a shitload of furniture from one room to another for you," he says.

"Oh, yeah. You had a beard, right?" she asks.

"I shaved," he says, sitting up, almost proud that his beard has been the focus for two conversations today.

"Yeah. You should grow it back," Paige says, completely deflating his ego. He slumps back down on his stool. "See ya at the game, Houston," she says, turning away and never glancing back at me, even as she catches up with her friends and leaves the restaurant.

Her hips sway, though, and I know that she's found her swagger. I'd take that any day over her making this—any of this—easy.

"Wow, man. Your girl-crush is a bitch," Eli says, taking another drink of his beer, looking at me over the rim. I think he's expecting me to hit him, which I might if he were Casey. Instead, I laugh, because yeah, she's an acquired taste. But she's also a flavor I'd gladly get drunk on.

"That's girl love, dude," I say. "Girl...*love.*"

Paige

When he finally pulls up, I breathe and relax my clenching hands, suddenly aware of exactly how scared I was he wouldn't show. I didn't realize how badly I wanted him here until I got to the stadium and didn't see him waiting. I sent Cass in without me, telling her Houston was running late. I pretended to know, but really I had no idea if he was coming or not. It was all just hope.

Hope and fairytales.

He's dressed nice, and I almost lean into him when he steps up the curb alongside me, but stop myself before crossing the line. Giving in would be so easy.

"Sorry I'm late," he says.

"It's okay. I got your ticket," I say, handing it to him, our hands barely touching. I still feel it. I feel it every time.

We make our way into the stands, finding my sister and Ty near the front on the first-base side, Rowe leaning over the wall, talking to Nate.

"So, scouts are here today, huh?" Houston asks. I smile and nod. Apparently, there are some big scouts here, and it's all really exciting, and I'm thrilled for Nate. But all I can think about—all I care about—is figuring out how to navigate these feelings I have crushing my chest and how to get his hand, which is swinging so close to mine, to give in, to reach over and touch me, to hold on and to shake away my fears.

Personally, I think Nate has it easy with the scouts.

"Hey, you made it," Cass says, walking up and hugging me. I know she really means *Houston* made it. I can also tell that we're what she and Ty are talking about when she moves back to sit next to him. Cass isn't very good at subtle, and she looks directly at us at least a dozen times while whispering. When Ty does the full lift and turn in his chair to look at us, it's confirmed.

"Hey man, you want to save me from all this girl-talk over here? They're determined to ruin baseball," Ty calls to Houston.

"He's just being a big baby," Cass adds.

My phone in my lap, I keep my eyes on my email messages, pretending not to be listening, hoping Houston stays right where he is. I see him shake his head *no*, and I suck in my bottom lip to camouflage the enormous grin that wants to take up all real estate on my face.

"Whatcha reading?" he asks, leaning into me. God, his body feels warm.

"Email," I say.

"You get email?" he asks.

"Uh...*yeah.* I employ several means of technology," I say, scrolling through old messages about the student government application I filed last week.

"Sorry, I just thought you were all text and emoticons and junk," he laughs.

"I was," I say, dropping my phone back in my purse, using the movement as an excuse to run my leg against his, my heart thrilled with every single accidental-on-purpose touch. "Campaign business."

I have to contain my smile again, and this time because I love the way Houston's looking at me after what I just said. The right side of his lip raised, his cheek slightly dimpled. Damn...I just made him proud.

"You did it," he says, half question, half statement.

"I did it," I say. "I filed to become university council secretary. The election is next month. I even made posters."

"Oh, I'm gonna need one of those," he jokes. "Paige Owens, on a poster, with the word *secretary*. That's..."

"You better not say that's funny, you asshole," I rib.

"Funny wasn't quite the word I was thinking," he says, eyebrows raised.

"Oh," I blush.

"I mean...fuck, man. Secretary. That's like...a seriously hot image," he continues.

"You know, it's not that kind of secretary," I say.

"Doesn't matter," he says. "'Cause now that's the kind that's in my head."

His eyes aren't really on me any more; instead, they're grazing down the length of my leg, and it's making me want to accidentally-on-purpose touch him again.

"How's Leah?" I ask, our conversation now feeling familiar and comfortable. I've been dying to ask about her, about everything that's happening, but I didn't want it to be the only thing between us. I wanted today to be more than therapy.

"She's good. Surprisingly," he says, biting his lip, his teeth sawing back-and-forth on it while he thinks. "Or maybe not

292

surprisingly. I don't know; that girl is a lot stronger than I think. I know she doesn't totally understand what's happening, but she gets some of it. She uh...she punched a boy recently."

"Well that's always good," I say.

Houston smiles.

"I thought you'd think so," he says. "He called her *babe.*"

"Sexist," I accuse.

"I think the kid just thought she was pretty," he shrugs.

"Then call her pretty. Don't call her *babe,*" I say, sitting up a little taller.

He watches me carefully, his lips in a tight smirk.

"What if I call you babe?" he asks after a few seconds.

"I'd punch you," I say.

Houston chuckles to himself, letting his gaze draw forward to the field, watching the players come out to begin throwing. When he doesn't notice, I punch him in the arm.

"Owwww, what the..." he says, rubbing the sore spot.

"Technically, you did call me babe...just then," I glower. I can only hold my tough-girl act up for a few seconds though, because he mocks me, and it makes me laugh. Our laughter fades after a minute, and eventually we're just looking at each other.

"I miss her," I admit.

"She punched a boy," he says. "I think it's fair to say she misses you too."

Our stares only grow deeper, but never uncomfortable. It's like I'm reacquainting myself with every nuance of his face, remembering things so I can revisit them later, so I can use those visions to find the strength to let myself fall.

Our small moment together is quickly interrupted by a familiar voice—a student reporter who has been calling me repeatedly for information on Chandra's photos. Apparently, he interns at the Herald and saw something in someone's notes. I'm pretty sure he's breaking some major ethics rules by pursuing me, but I don't have anything to lose over those photos now, so I haven't wanted to make a big deal of it with the paper. I'm just not sure talking with him would be a great move for my student-government campaign. So I've been dodging his calls and deleting emails instead. I can keep this up for a while.

When I glance over my shoulder, I notice he's talking with my sister. Houston is talking with Nate, who's stopped over by the first-base wall. I pull my phone back into my lap and lean to my right, wanting to hear what the reporter is asking Cass. When I hear him bring up Chandra, Cass dismisses it quickly, as if the entire thing—and Chandra—are no big deal. It makes me smile.

"Crazy how that whole Chandra thing blew up, huh? The way those pictures found their way online?" Ty says to me over a few rows of seats to the section I'm in. I glance up at him ready to bluff, but I can tell right away in his eyes that he knows, and that he's proud of me.

"Yeah..." I say, standing and straightening my shorts and blouse, pulling my purse onto my arm. "Definitely...*crazy.*" I lean forward and whisper to Houston that I'm getting a drink, then turn to take the steps slowly, not wanting to draw the attention of my reporter friend, or to look like I'm running. I'm not. I'm done running. But I'm also done making a scene.

I give Ty one more look over my shoulder, and he's still watching me, just as I expected, so I give in, and nod—just a little. He winks in return.

He and I...we're better when we're on the same side.

Houston

All I wanted was a do-over, a window, just one damn opening so I could figure out what the hell went wrong. But now that I've got my do-over, I sort of wish I could just pick up where we left off instead, because now I don't know what's next. Part of me wants to scoop her up into my lap and kiss her right here in front of everyone. Then, there's part of me that thinks she'll smack me in the face if I do.

"You look nervous," Rowe says, sliding into Paige's seat while she's gone. I smile at her, rubbing my neck while I turn to look to see where Paige is. When I don't see her anywhere, I turn back to Rowe with a heavy sigh.

"I might be. I mean, I am. Can you tell? Is it bad?" I wince. I swear to god I was more confident in my game when I was a teenager. Fatherhood has done a number on me.

Rowe laughs lightly as she twists to the side in her seat, pulling one knee in while she faces me.

"She's nervous too," she says. For some reason, this helps. This helps a shit-ton.

"Has she…mentioned…" I'm careful with my words to her. Paige has always been very private about us, and I don't want to mess things up by telling someone too much.

Rowe lets out another breathy laugh, nodding *yes* while she looks down in her lap. "I think we *all* sort of know you two have, had, are, was, were, are working on a thing," she says.

"That's one way to put it," I chuckle, relaxing lower into my seat. I wish I wore a hat today. If I did, I'd pull it down so I could hide.

"Paige and I talked…a little," she says. This has my attention, and I sit up again, leaning forward with my arms on my knees, wringing my hands, and cracking my knuckles. "She only left because of Leah's trust, you know. Or…you should know."

Trust? My brow bunches, and I'm sure I'm staring blankly at her trying to decipher why in the hell Paige would think she had anything to do with Leah's trust, when understanding washes over me. "Ahhhhhhh," I breathe, shutting my eyes. "She thought that Chandra would use her against us."

"She did," Rowe says. "I guess she ran into her at that party, and…"

"And that's when she came home to me, and said she had to leave," I finish. Rowe notices something over my shoulder, and I can tell by the face she's making that Paige is on her way back.

"Thank you," I mouth.

"No problem," she says, laughing as if I just said something funny. She leans forward as she stands and whispers, "I fix break-ups; it's my thing. Now turn around and smile."

I do as Rowe says, and am greeted by Paige stepping into the seat on the other side of me.

"I don't think I like you two getting all chummy," she says, handing me a giant pretzel wrapped in paper. "You looked hungry."

I shake my head while I take my twisted bread from her, picking a piece off and stuffing it into my mouth. "I wasn't," I say, while chewing. "But I'll eat it anyway."

"Well, I needed something to buy, so you're welcome," she says. All I can do is laugh because she's so cute, even when she's flippant and thoughtlessly thoughtful. I love her, and I don't care if she hits me. I'm telling her. Right. Fucking. Now.

My deep breath is loud, and she notices, her body growing a little rigid as if she can sense I have a speech coming. I wish she would just tell me what I was about to say, because right now, I haven't got a clue. But I'm going to say some words, and they're going to be honest, because that has always worked for me. Why change things up now.

"I have to go to work, and Paige, I've gotta leave in like five minutes, so please, just let me say this without interrupting," I start, and she's already blowing my request.

"You have to work?" She's seriously repeating me, and it's frustrating and funny all at the same time.

"Yeah, I have to work. So quit interrupting, so I can..."

"Then why'd you come?" she asks, and now she sounds sad, and all I want to do is let her interrupt like crazy for the next ten minutes before I have to leave. And then not leave. Then quit my job because making her happy is way better than my paycheck.

"I came to see you," I say, shoulders up, nothing else to give. "I was supposed to spend the day painting Leah's room, and I was supposed to fix some things around the house for my mom, but instead I had to hunt down my friend and make him fix the mess he made between us. Then...I ran into you, and you said to come to the game, so I came. I'll always come. I'll always pick you, Paige. Always...you."

For once in the last five minutes she seems speechless, her sadness starting to look a little bit more like hope. This...is my opening.

"I'm just going to put it out there, Paige," I say, holding my hand up, not even letting her say another word. "I've learned that life twists and turns on you, that unexpected shit falls in your lap, and sometimes it's a blessing and other times it's your worst nightmare. Through all of that, I've learned that wasting time missing out on the things that really matter is just that—a waste of time."

I take a deep breath before this next part, because last time, it didn't go so well. "I love you, Paige," I say, waiting for a blip, gauging her reaction, bracing myself. Her smile is still in place, cautious as it might feel—so I continue. "I'm not expecting you to move back in, or marry me, or become some super stepmom. I just want you to love me back, however you can, and let me hold your hand and talk to you at night. All I want is to kiss you and untangle your purse when that strappy thing gets stuck in your hair."

Her lips twist into a bigger smile, and she giggles when I tug on the purse strap that first got tangled in the trash can the night she tutored me. I love that purse strap, and I owe it a fucking hell of a lot.

"I want to be the guy that you tell your secrets to—who'll give it to you honest, and who won't care if you give it right back," I say, noticing that Rowe is hearing most of this a few rows away. I don't care, because now Rowe is right up there with the purse strap for things I need to thank for bringing me Paige.

"Just...do me a favor, Paige," I say her name and pull her hand into mine, the touch of it so amazing, her fingers shaking, but so damn soft. I breathe out once just from the feel of her. "Just...think about it, because I know what being all of that *with me* means. I know being some other guy's girlfriend doesn't come with that extra little caveat of all the other hats I have to wear—including the father one. But thing is, with anyone else, you'd just be their girlfriend, and with me...you're kind of my world."

I stand, letting her fingers fall away from mine slowly, and I tell her I love her one more time before letting her go. I walk away, and I'm taken back to my life more than five years ago, when I was just some cocky football jock who refused to let the pretty girl say *no*. I never thought anyone else would be worth all of that rejection, over and over, but this one...she's worth walking through fire.

And I know she might make me.

Chapter 20

Paige

It didn't take Rowe long to move back to the seat next to me. As soon as Houston turned the corner through the stadium gate, she was at my side. The look on my face must have been enough, because all she said was "Go."

I left the game without even saying goodbye to my sister. She'd understand. Fuck, they probably all heard his speech. And I told Rowe she could tell them anything she wanted. If I put this thing with Houston and me out there, then that makes it real—and it's *so* real. I'm ready for it to be real.

But before I tell him any of that, I need to make a few things right.

I rush back to our dorm and gather every last bucket of paint left in the closet from the time we painted the rooms pink. There's still a can of white from when they all had to repaint, so I take that too. I grab anything I can get my hands on, and I let myself into the boys' room to take all of their things too.

I have to stuff things into a blanket and throw it over my shoulder just to get it downstairs. I'll never be able to walk it all the way to Houston's house. I ask a girl with a piercing through her nose and eyebrow smoking out front if she has a car. She looks at me like I'm about to break out in a flash mob, checking over her shoulder for the rest of the joke. When she realizes I'm not kidding, she shrugs, stomps out the butt of her cigarette, and tells me "Sure."

We don't talk, other than me telling her "Thank you," when I get into the passenger side, and her telling me to pay her ten bucks for the gas it takes to drive point two miles. Rather than arguing, I decide it's a bargain, and flip a ten on the center console when I get out of the car.

Hitching a ride was easy compared to this next part. I drag my blanket full of supplies up Houston's driveway, bundling it all in my arms before I lean in to ring the doorbell. This move...it's strategic. I feel like a physical barrier between Joyce and me might somehow make me braver.

When she opens the door, I feel a little doubt, but I stand tall and breathe deeply, smiling anyhow. "Hi," I say, pushing to the back the tears I know she's cried since the last time I was here. There is no forgetting the warning she gave me though. That's why I'm here really, to prove my worth. When she lets me in, and even helps to tug my load of junk through the door, I feel like I might have led with the right foot forward.

"Paige, hi," she says, sounding genuinely happy to see me. "Houston's...he's working."

"I know," I say. "That's why I'm here. He said..."

I'm not sure how to explain everything. There's just so much. I unravel the blanket, letting the cans of paint roll out, the pillows unfurl, and the scraps of material and rollers and brushes fall loose.

"He wanted to fix up Leah's room, but he didn't quite get to it. I thought maybe I'd surprise him," I say, standing on one side of the blanket from her that's now stretched out like a do-it-yourself picnic between the two of us. When I glance up, I fully take her in for the first time. Her eyes are so tired as they graze over the supplies I've brought into the house.

"I'll do it all. I didn't want to make any work for you," I start, but she jumps in.

"I wanna help," she says, her lips in a soft line, the smile there when I look closely enough.

300

Taking one end of the blanket while I take the other, we both walk everything up the stairs, opening the door to Leah's room and surprising her. Leah's surrounded by stuffed animals, and when I glance to the small television on her night table, I see her favorite cartoon.

"Paige!" she squeals, running to me after taking a leap off of the end of her bed. Her force into me sends me back a step or two, but I hug her just as hard as she embraces me, bending down and kissing the top of her head. This is the first time I've ever kissed her. She feels like home.

I glance up at Joyce again, and her smile is growing.

"I hear you want a new room?" I ask. She runs back to her bed and stands on the end of it, bobbing on her toes, her tiny body teeming with nervous, excited energy.

"I do!" she says, clapping.

"Well, how about we make you one and get it all done before your dad comes home so we can surprise him?" I ask, my mind realizing the amount of work I've just signed up for. As creative as I am with my pencils, I've never really liked the *doing it* part of design. But I know I'll have to embrace it one day, and I can't think of a better way to start.

Without pause, we all jump in and begin removing things from her room, Joyce thoughtfully giving Leah directions to do small tasks that will keep her busy and invested without getting in our way. We work for two straight hours, painting her walls swirls of white and pink, and I spend another hour drawing a castle on the wall behind her bed with whatever paint is left. Exhausted, Joyce and I finally lean against either side of her doorframe admiring our work, watching as Leah spins in circles taking in her new surroundings.

"Do you love it?" I ask. I probably should have waited for her to say it on her own, but I'm just so anxious to know. She turns to me and grins—but then bites her lip. There's something more; I can tell.

"Tell me," I urge, hoping her request is something I can pull off.

"I was kind of hoping...that maybe I could live in the tower," she says.

I look to Joyce, a little breathless. Leah wants to live in my fairytale—the one I made up just for her—and it makes my heart feel happier than it has in months. That, combined with the puzzled look on Joyce's face, makes me laugh enough that my eyes water.

"She wants a tower," I say.

Joyce is shaking her head; I think maybe begging me to find a way to divert Leah. But I won't let her down. If she wants a tower, I'll find her one.

Sucking in my top lip, I look around at the few things left in the hall that we pulled out of her room. When I see the hula-hoop, I know I've found gold.

"I need some material. Lots and lots of it," I say to Joyce. She nods, then heads out into the hall, into the linen closet where she begins pulling down bags of old sheets and other things. I rush downstairs into the garage and search through a few bins I remembered Houston keeping in storage—finding a bundle of rope and a few hooks left over from the ones he hung up for my towels.

As I rush back up the stairs, I begin announcing I have it figured out, but quickly pause, noticing Joyce sitting on the floor, a pile of strips of material, all different colors, layered in her lap. Her eyes are glistening, and her lips are barely parted, her breath heavy.

"These were Beth's," she says in a giant exhale, looking at me finally, showing the pain and joy she's feeling all at once. "She wanted to make Leah a quilt. She'd spent the last month of her pregnancy just cutting these strips, and she had planned on making it for her for her first birthday. She...she never got to sew a stitch."

I collapse to the ground next to her, letting the hardware fall from my hands so my fingers can touch the soft pieces of material, hundreds of squares, weighing down Joyce's legs. I lift a stack and look to her. "May I?" I ask.

She nods.

I pull the strips into my lap and flip through them slowly, like a picture book in slow motion—showing nothing but lost hopes and dreams, plans never realized and heartbreak found.

"I think we should use them," I say. I feel Joyce look up at me quickly, and I'm scared to take in her expression—so I wait a beat before meeting her eyes.

She's smiling, though, her lips growing fuller with every nod of her head.

Together, we carry the material into Leah's room and begin knotting the strips together into a colorful rainbow of rope. Eventually, I let Joyce take over tying, and I begin wrapping the strips around the hoop, letting long pieces drape down every few inches, like a tent.

Once we have it completely wrapped, we slide Leah's bed out of the way and drag over the ladder, so I can stand high enough to bolt and tie the hoop to the ceiling. When we slide her bed back, Beth's material frames it perfectly, the quilt she never got to finish, instead becoming a tower of strength—a place where Leah can escape to hide...become strong.

"I love it," she says, this time her voice a whisper. It's as if somehow she knows that this new addition is more important than everything else. Perhaps one day Joyce will tell her. Or maybe Houston will. It's not my story or my place, but I'm honored to have been a part of rebuilding something for everyone in this house.

We leave Leah in her tower as she busies herself moving her animal friends around her bed, deciding who gets to be in the tower with her.

I follow Joyce downstairs, and when I let my legs hit the edge of the sofa, my body follows, every last drop of energy gone.

"I'll make you coffee," Joyce says, somehow still strong enough to be able to walk through the kitchen, to clean the counters, and put away dishes. I think maybe for Joyce, stopping is when things get bad—so she doesn't stop.

She brings me my cup, and leans against one of the arms of the sofa, never letting herself fully sit. Her gaze is lost on a clock on the mantle behind me. It's old, carved in wood, and beautiful.

"I love that piece," I say. Her eyes slide to meet mine slowly, and her faint smile comes to life.

"Thank you. My husband made it," she says. I turn to look at it again, noticing the hand-painted touches. It's really a work of art.

"He was very talented," I say.

We both sip from our cups, looking at the mantle for a few quiet seconds.

"So are you," she says. She isn't loud when she speaks, but for some reason, her words surprise me. Maybe it's *what* she says that surprises me. "You're very talented, Paige. What you did in there...that was special."

I nod, glancing at her then looking back at the clock, pretty sure I'm nothing compared to the man who made that. "Thank you," I whisper, blowing on the hot liquid in my hands.

"Houston is a lot like Michael," she says. She's speaking about her husband; I can tell by the reverent tone she's using, so I give her my full respect and set my cup down, turning to face her, my hands folded on my lap. "Michael was *the man of the house*," she laughs. "He was so busy. All the time, making sure everyone else was okay, that everything was running, that we were all clothed and fed and happy. When he was gone...Houston stepped right in and took over."

"But nobody has done that for Houston, Paige," she says, looking back at the clock again, taking a slow drink from her cup, swallowing slowly. When she looks back at me, her smile has finally found its way to feeling complete. "Nobody...until you."

I'm not sure how to respond; uncomfortable under the pressure her words put on me, but thrilled to hear them. I soak in the silence between us, under the beam of her smile for several seconds, until the sound of the door sliding open startles us both.

"Hey, Ma...I forgot to bring home chicken and milk, so I'll..." he stops as soon as he sees us both. We look ragged, our hair matted and our arms covered in dots of paint. I can barely move, but somehow I stand.

I bite my lip as I step closer to him.

"I'll pick some up tomorrow, honey. I'm heading up to bed. I'll see you tomorrow," Joyce says, leaning in to kiss him on the cheek, winking at me from the side when she does.

"It's seven-thirty," Houston says, shaking his head and looking between the two of us. "You're going to bed at seven-thirty?"

"Yep," Joyce says, flipping off the kitchen light and sliding her half-full mug on the counter. "And I'm not even finishing the dishes."

Good for you, Joyce.

Houston watches her climb the steps, then turns his focus back to me, the look on his face confused. "Why are you hanging out with my mother?" he asks, reaching forward with his hand, hesitantly. "And why is there a chunk of...*Pepto*?"

"It's paint," I correct.

"Right...paint. Why is there a bunch of pink paint in your hair?" he asks, touching it carefully, so cautious and afraid of pushing me too far. He's already pushed me over the edge, though.

I step into him, his breath catching when I do, and I hold his eyes while I move under his gaze, my fingers reaching forward to grasp the badge on his shirt. I smirk when I look at it, his name— *Houston*. God, I love his name. I might even love all of Texas now for giving it to him.

I pull his badge away, then run my finger over the dent it left on his shirt, an excuse to let my hand touch the hardness of his chest underneath. I peer up to see his hooded eyes staring down at me.

"Don't kid with me, Paige," he says, his voice barely a breath as he shakes his head, his eyes shutting as his head falls forward to rest on mine. I bite my lip and relish the nearness of my mouth to his, the heaviness of standing here in his arms, his height above and around me.

Tipping up my chin, I let my lips find his, brushing against him softly, both of our lips parting the instant they touch, our tongues taking cautious tastes of one another's mouths and skin.

He sucks in my top lip, holding it between his teeth for a second before slowly letting it slide loose, his head still against mine.

"Follow me," I say against his lips, each minor touch feeling like the weight of castles and mountains and kingdoms.

Hope and fairytales.

I tug on his shirt, leading him up the stairs, and we get to his daughter's room. I hold my finger to my lips, not wanting to disturb Leah, who I can hear humming and talking to her animals inside. I push the door open just enough for him to see, and I wait while he takes it all in. I know he recognizes the material when he swallows hard, and his eyes reflect the same expression as his mother's.

I'm not jealous over it. I envy it, maybe. But only because it's so special. I'm still glad that he has those memories, and that I'm someone who he and Joyce and Leah think is worthy of sharing them with.

"You did all this?" he asks, backing away and quietly closing her door.

I nod, then look to his mom's room. "I had a little help," I say.

"Paige…" he starts, but stops just as quickly. "I…I don't know what to say."

"You said a lot already," I whisper, letting my eyes fall closed so I can finish everything I came here for. "I love you," I breathe out, my body shaking with the words. Saying this feels so amazing and terrifying, and when his hands and lips don't find me right away, I start to cry—like a child in line for the scariest ride of her life.

I look at him expecting to see doubt, or disbelief, but instead, he looks just as happy and scared as I do.

"Say it again," he says.

"I love you," I repeat, my heart starting to feel the adrenaline from the words. "I love you. I love you. I love you."

I can't stop, and my smile gets bigger each time I let it out.

Houston steps into me, lifting me in his arms until I slide against him, our mouths finding each other, unable to stop smiling long enough to kiss as hard as I can tell we both want to.

"One more time," he chuckles, stepping me back one pace at a time toward his room.

"I love you," I laugh against him. Each time, it gets easier. When I feel his door close behind us, and his lips finally crash into mine, everything from before becomes a blur—*everything*. Every second, minute, day, month, and year—that was all just before. When I look at him again, his eyes so clear, so green and potent, like a dream, I can see what he sees. I close my eyes again, wanting to hold on to that part of me inside that's strong enough, the girl who wants to be his world.

The girl who *is* his world.

The girl who broke out of her own tower.

Epilogue

Paige

I'm not sure how it's just as hot moving out of Hayden Hall as it was moving in. I suppose that's what happens when you come full circle; you end where you began.

I came here ten months ago with a very concrete plan—I would be popular, part of the elite, dating the kind of guy that other girls envied me for. I got everything I wanted; yet nothing is quite like I thought it would be.

We're all working on our last boxes of things, a line of us marching down the hallway to the front curb of our dorm. Ty is leading us, Nate behind him, Rowe and Cass in the middle. Houston is locking up the room behind me, shutting the door on my first chapter of college—maybe the most important chapter of my life.

Houston is taking most of my things, along with Cass's, in his car to his house. He's storing things for us while we travel home for the summer. Our time home will be short—and I have a strange feeling that it might be our last, too.

For all of us.

Part of being on the school's executive board for council is arriving two weeks early to plan orientation for the next year's group of freshmen. I'll be staying with Houston when I come. I'll be moving in to an apartment nearby with Cass, Ty, and Rowe a few weeks later, though. I'm not ready to stay with Houston again full-time yet. The next time I move in for good with him, I don't want to have to feel the pain of moving out. So I'm going to take it slow.

Slow is good, so I've learned.

In the meantime, I'm happy to be a part of Cass and Ty moving in together. I think that's the only reason my parents didn't freak out like they could have—because they knew there would be four of us living together—Rowe and me around constantly to keep Ty and Cass from having too much time *alone.*

Not that Rowe will be around much, either.

She was too nervous to ask her parents about moving in with Nate next year. So instead, he hooked up with one of his teammates, Cash. Their apartment is only a building away. I'm not sure how that makes a difference, and I'm pretty sure her parents are aware of how much time she'll be spending with Nate, too, but if it makes her feel more innocent, whatever.

I'm actually excited to be her roommate. Maybe next year, I'll get things right.

Nate won't be eligible again for the draft until he's twenty-one, but he impressed a lot of people over the spring—especially a group of scouts from the Houston Astros who spent a lot of time in the McConnell coaching suites.

I like the idea of him ending up in Houston. But maybe I'm partial.

I'm carrying the last box, and when Houston takes it from me to place in the back of his trunk, I hesitate a little on letting go. He tilts his head to the side, catching my attention, and I shake my head and smile, finally letting him take over lifting my things.

"Sorry, I was lost a little there," I say.

He slides the box into the only space remaining, then closes his trunk before walking back up the curb to me.

"You? Lost? Never," he teases. I laugh with him, but stop when the words hit me differently.

"No, I was pretty lost," I say, my face more serious, his reflecting nothing but love for me. I reach my hand up to touch his cheek, catching the vision of my sister and my friends climbing into the airport shuttle behind him. When I look back into his eyes, the way he looks at me proudly makes my hesitation fade away. "I think I was worried for a moment there—that if I left right now, when I come back nothing will be the same," I admit.

He exhales, pulling me to his chest to hold me tight, and his lips fall to my head. "Paige, when you're gone, time for me...it stops," he says. I step away to look at him, so happy with this place I've ended up. "I waited years for you. Seven weeks? That's nothin'."

"Seven weeks," I repeat.

"Seven weeks," he smiles. I press my lips to his, standing on my toes, until I have to peel away and join the others in the shuttle. Houston follows me to the edge of the curb, and just as he's about to shut the door, he reaches into his back pocket and pulls out a rolled-up booklet of notebook paper, stapled together on one side.

"What's this?" I ask, taking it from him, noticing his handwriting and doodles on the front page.

"It's your story," he says. "I wrote it for you. It's cheesy as hell, and I'm pretty sure the things I tried to write in Spanish mean totally the wrong thing, but it's...I don't know...romantic, I guess? I thought it would be, but now I feel sort of lame."

"It's *very* romantic," I smile, clasping my story to my chest. "And we'll work on the Spanish."

"Damn right, we will," he winks. "I failed last semester."

"Love you," I say one last time, the door closing between us. We both hold up a hand and press it on either side of the glass, and I watch his skin slide over it as the van slowly pulls away.

Ty and Nate are making fun of me from the front seat, and Cass and Rowe are yelling at them for me from the back. I'm in the middle, where I ignore their noise, flipping through my rag-tag fairytale—the notebook fringe flaking away on the edges. I run my finger over the stick-figure girl with long blonde hair and the prince standing next to her, holding a sandwich, and I smile when I read his butchered Spanish confession of love near the end, an arrow in the margin pointing to the words, reading *"this means I love you."*

Yes, Houston.

Yes, it does.

THE END

Acknowledgements

This is harder to write than it normally is. This series was a special one for me. It was special thanks to the many readers who found Nate Preeter first, then championed him, and asked for more. It's special because of his brother, Tyson Preeter, who will remain one of my favorite characters I've ever written for his ability to overcome adversity and his smart-ass mouth. And it's special because of Paige—my strong-willed, albeit a little harsh, girl on a mission. It didn't hit me when I wrote THE END on Paige's story. It didn't even hit me through the edits and the final read. But now...

Now...it's hitting me.

Book 3 in the Falling series is done. One year at McConnell College is complete. And Paige, Cass, Rowe, Nate, Tyson and Houston will move on. To where...well, I sort of left that up to you. Maybe I left that up to me a little, too. And maybe there will come a day where I check in on them, where we all gather at McConnell for graduation or for Nate's big day. I don't know. All I know is I couldn't make it a final goodbye forever, even if that ends up being the case. I didn't want to close that door, because these characters—I am going to miss them. And I just feel a whole hell of a lot better knowing they're still there should I need to visit.

I have so very many people to thank here. First and foremost, to the unbelievable blogging and reading community who hoisted the Preeter brothers on their shoulders and literally paraded them around the world in social media, in book clubs, conversations and more. You have no idea how happy you have made mama Preeter (that's me, btw). I would be lost without my beta reading team (I really need to make you ladies shirts, I swear). Thank you: Jen, Debbie, Ashley, Bianca, Shelley and Brigitte. Tina Scott and Billi Joy Carson, you never flinch when I throw thousands of words your way for editing, and I'm forever grateful for your talents. And the mighty women at Wordsmith Publicity—Autumn and Andrea—the muscle you lend in making sure that spotlight shines this way is so appreciated. I love you ladies.

I cannot forget the team who helped make that spot-on perfect cover image come to life for The Girl I Was Before. Firstly, thank you models Kelsey and Orlando for making Paige and Houston come to life in an adorably perfect way. And thank you Glendale Community College for serving as the McConnell College campus for this photo shoot. And finally, photographer Mark Lipczynski—thanks for making this so special. I've always been a fan, and working with you has always been a highlight. This one was simply icing on the cake.

If you enjoyed this book, please consider leaving a review. Your reviews are often the only way small stories like this can be seen, and I for one know the power readers have. I'm so grateful for every post, mention, recommendation, book club, Tweet, pin and more that readers have given to my books. I hope to give you lots to talk about in the future.

Until next time, enjoy the fall, and avoid the #fussyfuss.

XO
Ginger

About the Author

Ginger Scott is an Amazon-bestselling author of eight young and new adult romances, including Waiting on the Sidelines, Going Long, Blindness, How We Deal With Gravity, This Is Falling, You and Everything After, The Girl I Was Before and Wild Reckless.

A sucker for a good romance, Ginger's other passion is sports, and she often blends the two in her stories. (She's also a sucker for a hot quarterback, catcher, pitcher, point guard...the list goes on.) Ginger has been writing and editing for newspapers, magazines and blogs for more than 15 years. She has told the stories of Olympians, politicians, actors, scientists, cowboys, criminals and towns. For more on her and her work, visit her website at http://www.littlemisswrite.com.

When she's not writing, the odds are high that she's somewhere near a baseball diamond, either watching her son field pop flies like Bryce Harper or cheering on her favorite baseball team, the Arizona Diamondbacks. Ginger lives in Arizona and is married to her college sweetheart whom she met at ASU (fork 'em, Devils).

Books By Ginger Scott

Waiting On The Sidelines
Going Long

This Is Falling
You And Everything After
The Girl I Was Before

Wild Reckless

Blindness

How We Deal With Gravity